He held and she had to let him hold. She needed him.

Which was crazy. Sh
made that vow as a t
fifth of her endless
She'd yelled it as her
explain why she had t

'It's okay!' she'd yelled. 'I don't need you. I don't need anyone.'

Her foster mother had cried, but Jo hadn't. She'd learned never to let herself close enough to cry.

But now she was close, whether she'd willed it or not. Her rescuer was holding her in a grip so strong she couldn't break it even if she tried. He must be feeling her shaking, she thought, and part of her was despising herself for weakness but most of her was just letting him hold.

He was big and warm and solid, and he wasn't letting her go. Her face was hard against his chest. She could feel the beating of his heart.

His hand was stroking her head, as he'd stroke an injured animal.

'Hey, there. You're safe.'

And before she could even suspect what he intended he'd straightened, reached down and lifted her into his arms.

He held on as she had to let him hold.
She needed him.

Which was crazy. She didn't need anyone. She'd made that vow as a ten-year-old, in the fourth or fifth of her endless succession of foster homes. She'd yelled it as her foster mother had tried to explain why she had to move on yet again.

'It's okay,' she'd yelled. 'I don't need you. I don't need anyone.'

Her foster mother had cried, but Jo hadn't. She'd learned never to let herself care enough to cry.

But now she was close. [illegible] [illegible] [illegible] [illegible] [illegible] [illegible] [illegible] she thought, and part of her was despising herself for weakness but most of her was just [illegible] into him.

He was big and warm and solid, and he wasn't letting her go. Her face was hard against his chest. She could feel the beating of his heart.

His hand was stroking her hair as he'd stroke an injured animal.

'Hey, there. You're safe.'

And before she could even suspect what he intended, he'd [illegible] [illegible], reached down, and lifted her into his arms.

HIS CINDERELLA HEIRESS

BY

MARION LENNOX

First Published in Great Britain 2016
By Mills & Boon, an imprint of HarperCollins*Publishers*
1 London Bridge Street, London, SE1 9GF

ISBN: 978-0-263-91999-8

23-0716

Our policy is to use papers that are natural, renewable and recyclable products and made from wood grown in sustainable forests. The logging and manufacturing processes conform to the legal environmental regulations of the country of origin.

Marion Lennox has written more than one hundred romances and is published in over a hundred countries and thirty languages. Her multiple awards include the prestigious US RITA® Award (twice), and the *RT Book Reviews* Career Achievement Award for 'a body of work which makes us laugh and teaches us about love'. Marion adores her family, her kayak, her dog and lying on the beach with a book someone else has written. Heaven!

To Mitzi. My shadow.

CHAPTER ONE

A WOMAN WAS stuck in his bog.

Actually, Finn Conaill wasn't sure if this land was part of the estate, but even if this wasn't the property of the new Lord of Glenconaill he could hardly ignore a woman stuck in mud to her thighs.

He pulled off the road, making sure the ground he steered onto was solid.

A motorbike was parked nearby and he assumed it belonged to the woman who was stuck. To the unwary, the bike was on ground that looked like a solid grass verge. She'd been lucky. The wheels had only sunk a couple of inches.

She'd not been so lucky herself. She was a hundred yards from the road, and she looked stuck fast.

'Stay still,' he called.

'Struggling makes me sink deeper.' Her voice sounded wobbly and tired.

'Then don't struggle.'

Of all the idiot tourists… She could have been here all night, he thought, as he picked his way carefully across to her. This road was a little used shortcut across one of County Galway's vast bogs. The land was a sweep of sodden grasses, dotted with steel-coloured washes of ice-cold water. In the distance he could see the faint outline of Castle Glenconaill, its vast stone walls seemingly merging into the mountains behind it. There'd been a few tough sheep on the road from the village, but here there was nothing.

There was therefore no one but Finn to help.

'Can you come faster?' she called and he could hear panic.

'Only if you want us both stuck. You're in no danger. I'm coming as fast as I can.'

Though he wouldn't mind coming faster. He'd told the housekeeper at the castle he'd arrive mid-afternoon and he was late already.

He spent considerable time away from his farm now, researching farming methods, investigating innovative ideas, so he had the staff to take care of the day-to-day farming. He'd been prepared to leave early this morning, with his manager more than ready to take over.

But then Maeve had arrived from Dublin, glamorous, in designer clothes and a low-slung sports car. She looked a million light years away from the woman who'd torn around the farm with him as a kid—who once upon a time he was sure he wanted to spend his life with. After a year apart—she'd asked for twelve months 'to discover myself before we marry'—what she'd told him this morning had only confirmed what he already knew. Their relationship was over, but she'd been in tears and he owed her enough to listen.

And then, on top of everything else, there'd been trouble lambing. He'd bottle-fed Sadie from birth, she was an integral part of a tiny flock of sheep he was starting to build, and he hadn't had the heart to leave until she was safely delivered.

Finally he'd tugged on clean trousers, a decent shirt and serviceable boots, and there was an end to his preparation for inheriting title and castle. If the castle didn't approve, he'd decided, it could find itself another lord.

And now he was about to get muddy, which wasn't very lordly either.

At least he knew enough of bogland to move slowly, and not get into trouble himself. He knew innocuous grassland often overlaid mud and running water. It could give way at any moment. The only way to tread safely was to look for rocks that were big enough to have withstood centuries of sodden land sucking them down.

After that initial panicked call, the woman was now silent and still, watching him come. The ground around her was a mire, churned. The bog wasn't so dangerous that it'd suck her down like quicksand, but it was thick and claggy so, once she'd sunk past her knees, to take one step after another back to dry land would have proved impossible.

He was concentrating on his feet and she was concentrating on watching him. Which he appreciated. He had no intention of ending up stuck too.

When he was six feet away he stopped. From here the ground was a churned mess. A man needed to think before going further.

'Thank you for coming,' she said.

He nodded, still assessing.

She sounded Australian, he thought, and she was young, or youngish, maybe in her mid to late twenties. Her body was lithe, neat and trim. She had short cropped, burnt-red curls. Wide green eyes were framed by long dark lashes. Her face was spattered with freckles and smeared with mud; eyeliner and mascara were smudged down her face. She had a couple of piercings in one ear and four in the other.

She was wearing full biker gear, black, black and black, and she was gazing up at him almost defiantly. Her thanks had seemed forced—like *I know I've been stupid but I defy you to tell me I am.*

His lips twitched a little. He could tell her anything he liked—she was in no position to argue.

'You decided to take a stroll?' he asked, taking time to assess the ground around her.

'I read about this place on the Internet.' Still he could hear the defiance. Plus the accent. With those drawn-out vowels, she had to be Australian. 'It said this district was famous for its quaking bogs but they weren't dangerous. I asked in the village and the guy I asked said the same. He said if you found a soft part, you could jump up and down and it bounced. So I did.'

His brows lifted. 'Until it gave way?'

'The Internet didn't say anything about sinking. Neither did the guy I asked.'

'I'd imagine whoever you asked assumed you'd be with someone. This place is safe enough if you're with a friend who can tug you out before you get stuck.'

'I was on my bike. He knew I was alone.'

'Then he'd be trying to be helpful.' Finn was looking at the churned-up mud around her, figuring how stuck she truly was. 'He wouldn't be wanting to disappoint you. Folk around here are like that.'

'Very helpful!' She glowered some more. 'Stupid bog.'

'It's a bit hard to sue a bog, though,' he said gently. 'Meanwhile, I'll fetch planks from the truck. There's no way I'll get you out otherwise. I've no wish to be joining you.'

'Thank you,' she said again, and once more it was as if the words were forced out of her. She was independent, he thought. And feisty. He could see anger and frustration—and also fury that she was dependent on his help.

She was also cold. He could hear it in the quaver in her voice, and by the shudders and chattering teeth she was trying to disguise. Cold and scared? But she wasn't letting on.

'Hold on then,' he said. 'I'll not be long. Don't go anywhere.'

She clamped her lips tight and he just knew the effort it was taking her not to swear.

To say Jo Conaill was feeling stupid would be an understatement. Jo—Josephine on her birth certificate but nowhere else—was feeling as if the ground had been pulled from under her. Which maybe it had.

Of all the dumb things to do…

She'd landed in Dublin two nights ago, spent twenty-four hours fighting off jet lag after the flight from Sydney, then hired a bike and set off.

It was the first time she'd ever been out of Australia and she was in Ireland. Ireland! She didn't feel the least bit Irish, but her surname was Irish and every time she looked in the mirror she felt Irish. Her name and her looks were her only connection to this place, but then, Jo had very few connections to anything. Or anyone.

She was kind of excited to be here.

She'd read about this place before she came—of course she had. Ireland's bogs were legion. They were massive, mysterious graveyards of ancient forests, holding treasures from thousands of years ago. On the Internet they'd seemed rain-swept, misty and beautiful.

On her lunch break, working as a waitress in a busy café on Sydney Harbour, she'd watched a You Tube clip of a couple walking across a bog just like this. They'd been jumping up and down, making each other bounce on the spongy surface.

Jumping on the bogs of Galway. She'd thought maybe she could.

And here she was. The map had shown her this road, describing the country as a magnificent example of undisturbed bog. The weather had been perfect. The bog looked amazing, stretching almost to the horizon on either side of her bike. Spongy. Bouncy. And she wasn't stupid. She had stopped to ask a local and she'd been reassured.

So she'd jumped, just a little at first and then venturing further from the road to get a better bounce. And then the surface had given way and she'd sunk to her knees. She'd struggled for half an hour until she was stuck to her thighs. Then she'd resigned herself to sit like a dummy and wait for rescue.

So here she was, totally dependent on a guy who had the temerity to laugh. Okay, he hadn't laughed out loud but she'd seen his lips twitch. She knew a laugh when she saw one.

At least he seemed…solid. Built for rescuing women from bogs? He was large, six-two or -three, muscular, lean and tanned, with a strongly boned face. He was wearing moleskin trousers and a khaki shirt, open-necked, his sleeves rolled above the elbows to reveal brawny arms.

He was actually, decidedly gorgeous, she conceded. Definitely eye candy. In a different situation she might even have paused to enjoy. He had the weathered face and arms of a farmer. His hair was a deep brown with just a hint of copper—a nod to the same Irish heritage she had? It was wavy but cropped short and serviceable. His deep green eyes had crease lines at the edges—from exposure to weather?

Or from laughter.

Probably from laughter, she decided. His eyes were laughing now.

Eye candy or not, she was practically gritting her chattering teeth as she waited for him. She was totally dependent on a stranger. She, Jo Conaill, who was dependent on nobody.

He was heading back, carrying a couple of short planks, moving faster now he'd assessed the ground. His boots were heavy and serviceable. Stained from years of work on the land?

'I have a bull who keeps getting himself bogged near the water troughs,' he said idly, almost as if he was talking to himself and not her. 'If these planks can get Horace out, they'll work for you. That is if you don't weigh more than a couple of hundred pounds.'

Laughter was making his green eyes glint. His smile, though, was kind.

She didn't want kind. She wanted to be out of here.

'Don't try and move until they're in place,' he told her. 'Horace always messes that up. First sign of the planks and he's all for digging himself in deeper.'

'You're comparing me to a bull?'

He'd stooped to set the planks in place. Now he sat back on his heels and looked at her. Really looked. His gaze raked her, from the top of her dishevelled head to where her leather-clad legs disappeared into the mud.

The twinkle deepened.

'No,' he said at last. 'No, indeed. I'll not compare you to a bull.'

And he chuckled.

If she could, she'd have closed her eyes and drummed her heels. Instead, she had to manage a weak smile. She had to wait. She was totally in this man's hands and she didn't like it one bit.

It was her own fault. She'd put herself in a position of dependence and she depended on nobody.

Except this man.

'So what do they call you?' He was manoeuvring the planks, checking the ground under them, setting them up so each had a small amount of rock underneath to make them secure. He was working as if he had all the time in the world. As if she did.

She didn't. She was late.

She was late and covered in bog.

'What would who call me?' she snapped.

'Your Mam and Daddy?'

As if. 'Jo,' she said through gritted teeth.

'Just Jo?'

'Just Jo.' She glared.

'Then I'm Finn,' he said, ignoring her glare. 'I'm pleased to meet you, Just Jo.' He straightened, putting his weight on the planks, seeing how far they sank. He was acting as if he pulled people out of bogs all the time.

No. He pulled bulls out of bogs, she thought, and that was what she felt like. A stupid, bog-stuck bovine.

'You're Australian?'

'Yes,' she said through gritted teeth, and he nodded as if Australians stuck in bogs were something he might have expected.

'Just admiring the view, were we?' The laughter was still in his voice, an undercurrent to his rich Irish brogue, and it was a huge effort to stop her teeth from grinding in frustration. Except they were too busy chattering.

'I'm admiring the frogs,' she managed. 'There are frogs in here. All sorts.'

He smiled, still testing the planks, but his smile said he approved of her attempt to join him in humour.

'Fond of frogs?'

'I've counted eight since I've been stuck.'

He grinned. 'I'm thinking that's better than counting sheep. If you'd nodded off I might not have seen you from the road.' He stood back, surveyed her, surveyed his planks and then put a boot on each end of the first plank and started walking. The end of the planks were a foot from her. He went about two-thirds along, then stopped and crouched. And held out his hands.

'Right,' he said. 'Put your hands in mine. Hold fast. Then don't struggle, just let yourself relax and let me pull.'

'I can...'

'You can't do anything,' he told her. 'If you struggle you'll make things harder. You can wiggle your toes if you like; that'll help with the suction, but don't try and pull out. If you were Horace I'd be putting a chain under you but Horace isn't good at following orders. If you stay limp like a good girl, we'll have you out of here in no time.'

Like a good girl. The patronising toerag...

He was saving her. What was she doing resenting it? Anger was totally inappropriate. But then, she had been stuck for almost an hour, growing more and more furious with herself. She'd also been more than a little bit frightened by the time he'd arrived. And cold. Reaction was setting in and she was fighting really hard to hold her temper in check.

'Where's a good wall to kick when you need it?' Finn asked and she blinked.

'Pardon?'

'I'd be furious too, if I were you. The worst thing in the world is to want to kick and all you have to kick is yourself.'

She blinked. Laughter and empathy too? 'S...sorry.'

'That's okay. Horace gets tetchy when he gets stuck, so I'd imagine you're the same. Hands—put 'em in mine and hold.'

'They're covered in mud. You won't be able to hold me.'

'Try me,' he said and held out his hands and waited for her to put hers in his.

It felt wrong. To hold this guy's hands and let her pull... Jo Conaill spent her life avoiding dependence on anyone or anything.

What choice did she have? She put out her hands and held.

His hands were broad and toughened from manual work. She'd guessed he was a farmer, and his hands said she was right. He manoeuvred his fingers to gain maximum hold and she could feel the strength of him. But he was wincing.

'You're icy. How long have you been here?'

'About an hour.'

'Is that right?' He was shifting his grip, trying for maximum hold. 'Am I the first to come along? Is this road so deserted, then?'

'You're not a local?'

'I'm not.' He was starting to take her weight, sitting back on his heels and leaning backward. Edging back as the planks started to tilt.

The temptation to struggle was almost irresistible but she knew it wouldn't help. She forced herself to stay limp.

Channel Horace, she told herself.

'Good girl,' Finn said approvingly and she thought: *What—did the guy have the capacity to read minds?*

He wasn't pulling hard. He was simply letting his weight tug her forward, shifting only to ease the balance of the planks. But his hold was implacable, a steady, relentless pull, and finally she felt the squelch as the mud eased its grip. She felt her feet start to lift. At last.

He still wasn't moving fast. His tug was slow and steady, an inch at a time. He was acting as if he had all the time in the world.

'So I'm not a local,' he said idly, as if they were engaged in casual chat, not part of a chain where half the chain was stuck in mud. 'But I'm closer to home than you are.'

He manoeuvred himself back a little without lessening his grip. He was trying not to lurch back, she realised. If he pulled hard, they both risked being sprawled off the planks, with every chance of being stuck again.

He had had experience in this. With Horace.

'Horace is heavier than you,' he said.

'Thanks. Did you say…two hundred pounds?'

'I did, and I'm thinking you're not a sliver over a hundred and ninety. That's with mud attached,' he added kindly. 'What part of Australia do you come from?'

'S… Sydney.' Sometimes.

'I've seen pictures.' Once more he stopped and readjusted. 'Nice Opera House.'

'Yeah.' It was hard to get her voice to work. He'd released her hands so he could shift forward and hold her under her arms. Once more he was squatting and tugging but now she was closer to him. Much closer. She could feel the strength of him, the size. She could feel the warmth of his chest against her face. The feeling was…weird. She wanted to sink against him. She wanted to struggle.

Sinking won.

'We…we have great beaches too,' she managed and was inordinately proud of herself for getting the words out.

'What, no mud?'

'No mud.'

'Excellent. Okay, sweetheart, we're nearly there. Just relax and let me do the work.'

He had her firmly under the arms and he was leaning back as she forced herself to relax against him. To let him hold her…

The feeling was indescribable—and it worked!

For finally the mud released its grip. Even then, though, he was still in control. He had her tight, hauling her up and back so that she was kneeling on the planks with him, but she wasn't released. He was holding her hard against him, and for a moment she had no choice but to stay exactly where she was.

She'd been stuck in mud for an hour. She was bone-chillingly cold, and she'd been badly frightened. Almost as soon as the mud released her she started to shake.

If he didn't hold her she could have fallen right off the

planks. No, she *would* have fallen. She felt light-headed and a bit sick.

He held and she had to let him hold. She needed him.

Which was crazy. She didn't need anyone. She'd made that vow as a ten-year-old, in the fourth or fifth of her endless succession of foster homes. She'd yelled it as her foster mother had tried to explain why she had to move on yet again.

'It's okay,' she'd yelled. 'I don't need you. I don't need anyone.'

Her foster mother had cried but Jo hadn't. She'd learned to never let herself close enough to cry.

But now she was close, whether she willed it or not. Her rescuer was holding her in a grip so strong she couldn't break it even if she tried. He must be feeling her shaking, she thought, and part of her was despising herself for being weak but most of her was just letting him hold.

He was big and warm and solid, and he wasn't letting her go. Her face was hard against his chest. She could feel the beating of his heart.

His hand was stroking her head, as he'd stroke an injured animal. 'Hey there. You're safe. The nasty bog's let you go. A nice hot bath and you'll be right back to yourself again. You're safe, girl. Safe.'

She hadn't been unsafe, she thought almost hysterically, and then she thought maybe she had been. If he hadn't come… Hypothermia was a killer. She could have become one of those bog bodies she'd read about, found immaculately preserved from a thousand years ago. They'd have put her in a museum and marvelled at her beloved bike leathers…

'There was never a chance of it,' Finn murmured into her hair and his words shocked her into reaction.

'What?'

'Freezing to your death out here. There's sheep wandering these bogs. I'm thinking a farmer'll come out and check them morn and night. If I hadn't come along, he would have.'

'But if you're not…if you're not local, how do you know?' she demanded.

'Because the sheep I passed a way back look well cared for, and you don't get healthy sheep without a decent shepherd. You were never in real danger.' He released her a little, but his hands still held her shoulders in case she swayed. 'Do you think you can make it back to the road?'

And then he frowned, looking down at her. 'You're still shaking. We don't want you falling into the mud again. Well, this is something I wouldn't be doing with Horace.'

And, before she could even suspect what he intended, he'd straightened, reached down and lifted her into his arms, then turned towards the road.

She froze.

She was close to actually freezing. From her thighs down, she was soaking. She'd been hauled up out of the mud, into this man's arms, and he was carrying her across the bog as if she weighed little more than a sack of flour.

She was powerless, and the lifelong sense of panic rose and threatened to drown her.

She wanted to scream, to kick, to make him dump her, even if it meant she sank into the bog again. She couldn't do anything. She just…froze.

But then, well before they reached the road, he was setting her down carefully on a patch of bare rock so there was no chance she'd pitch into the mud. But he didn't let her go. He put his hands on her shoulders and twisted her to face him.

'Problem?'

'I…no.'

'You were forgetting to breathe,' he said, quite gently. 'Breathing's important. I'm not a medical man, but I'd say breathing's even more important than reaching solid ground.'

Had her intake of breath been so dramatic that he'd heard it—that he'd felt it? She felt ashamed and silly, and more than a little small.

'You're safe,' he repeated, still with that same gentleness. 'I'm a farmer. I've just finished helping a ewe with a difficult lambing. Helping creatures is what I do for a living. I won't hurt you. I'll clean the muck off you as best I can, then put your bike in the back of my truck and drive you to wherever you can get yourself a hot shower and a warm bed for the night.'

And that was enough to make her pull herself together. She'd been a wimp, an idiot, an absolute dope, and here she was, making things worse. This man was a Good Samaritan. Yeah, well, she'd had plenty of them in her life, but that didn't mean she shouldn't be grateful. He didn't need her stupid baggage and he was helping her. Plus he was gorgeous. That shouldn't make a difference but she'd be an idiot not to be aware of it. She made a massive effort, took a few deep breaths and tugged her dignity around her like a shield.

'Thank you,' she managed, tilting her face until she met his gaze full-on. Maybe that was a mistake. Green eyes met green eyes and something flickered in the pit of her stomach. He was looking at her with compassion but also…something else? There were all sorts of emotions flickering behind those eyes of his. Yes, compassion, and also laughter, but also…empathy? Understanding?

As if he understood what had caused her to fear.

Whatever, she didn't like it. He might be gorgeous. He might have saved her, but she needed to be out of here.

'I can take care of myself from here,' she managed. 'If you just walk across to the road, I'll follow in your footsteps.'

'Take my hand,' he said, still with that strange tinge of understanding that was deeply unsettling. 'You're shaky and if you fall that's time wasted for both of us.'

It was reasonable. It even made sense but only she knew how hard it was to place her hand in his and let him lead her back to the road. But he didn't look at her again. He watched the ground, took careful steps then turned and watched her feet, making sure her feet did exactly the same.

Her feet felt numb, but the leathers and biker boots had insulated her a little. She'd be back to normal in no time, she thought, and finally they stepped onto the glorious solid road and she felt like bending down and kissing it.

Stupid bogs. The Irish could keep them.

Wasn't she Irish? Maybe she'd disinherit that part of her.

'Where can I take you?' Finn was saying and she stared down at her legs, at the thick, oozing mud, and then she looked at her bike and she made a decision.

'Nowhere. I'm fine.' She forced herself to look up at him, meeting his gaze straight on. 'Honest. I'm wet and I'm dirty but I don't have far to go. This mud will come off in a trice.'

'You're too shaken to ride.'

'I *was* too shaken to ride,' she admitted. 'But now I'm free I'm not shaking at all.' And it was true. Jo Conaill was back in charge of herself again and she wasn't about to let go. 'Thank you so much for coming to my rescue. I'm sorry I've made you muddy too.'

'Not very muddy,' he said and smiled, a lazy, crooked smile that she didn't quite get. It made her feel a bit...melting. Out of control again? She didn't like it.

And then she noticed his feet. His boots were still clean. Clean! He'd hauled her out of the bog and, apart from a few smears of mud where he'd held her, and the fact that his hands were muddy, he didn't have a stain on him.

'How did you do that?' she breathed and his smile intensified. 'How did you stay almost clean?'

'I told you. I'm an old hand at pulling creatures out of trouble. Now, if you were a lamb I'd take you home, rub you down and put you by the firestove for a few hours. Are you sure I can't do that for you?'

And suddenly, crazily, she wanted to say yes. She was still freezing. She was still shaking inside. She could have this man take her wherever he was going and put her by his fireside. Part of her wanted just that.

Um…not. She was Jo Conaill and she didn't accept help. Well, okay, sometimes she had to, like when she was dumb enough to try jumping on bogs, but enough. She'd passed a village a few miles back. She could head back there, beg a wash at the pub and then keep on going.

As she always kept going.

'Thank you, no,' she managed and bent and wiped her mud-smeared hands on the grass. Then she finished the job by drying them on the inside of her jacket. She gave him a determined nod, then snagged her helmet from the back of her bike. She shoved it onto her head, clicked the strap closed—only she knew what an effort it was to make her numb fingers work—and then hauled the handles of her bike around.

The bike was heavy. The shakiness of her legs wouldn't quite support…

But there he was, putting her firmly aside, hauling her bike around so it was facing the village. 'That's what you want?'

'I…yes.'

'You're really not going far?'

'N… No. Just to the village.'

'Are you sure you'll be fine?'

'I'm sure,' she managed and hit the ignition and her bike

roared into unsociable life. 'Thank you,' she said again over its roar. 'If I can ever do anything for you…'

'Where will I find you?' he asked and she tried a grin.

'On the road,' she said. 'Look for Jo.'

And she gave him a wave with all the insouciance she could muster and roared off into the distance.

CHAPTER TWO

AS CASTLES WENT, it seemed a very grand castle. But then, Finn hadn't seen the inside of many castles.

Mrs O'Reilly, a little, round woman with tired eyes and capable, worn hands, bustled into the dining room and placed his dinner before him. It was a grand dinner too, roast beef with vegetables and a rich gravy, redolent of red wine and fried onions. It was a dinner almost fit for…a lord?

'There you are, My Lord,' the housekeeper said and beamed as she stood back and surveyed her handiwork. 'Eh, but it's grand to have you here at last.'

But Finn wasn't feeling grand. He was feeling weird.

My Lord. It was his title. He'd get rid of it, he decided. Once the castle was sold he didn't need to use it. He wasn't sure if he could ever officially abandon it but the knowledge of its existence could stay in the attic at the farm, along with other family relics. Maybe his great-great-great-grandson would like to use it. That was, if there ever was a great-great-great-grandson.

He thought suddenly of Maeve. Would she have liked to be My Lady? Who knew? He was starting to accept that he'd never known Maeve at all. Loyalty, habit, affection—he'd thought they were the basis for a marriage. But over the last twelve months, as he'd thrown himself into improving the farm, looking at new horizons himself, he'd realised it was no basis at all.

But Maeve's father would have liked this, he thought, staring around the great, grand dining room with a carefully neutral expression. He didn't want to hurt the housekeeper's feelings, but dining alone at a table that could fit twenty, on fine china, with silver that spoke of centuries of use, the family crest emblazoned on every piece, with a vast silver epergne holding pride of place in the centre of the shining mahogany of the table… Well, it wasn't exactly his style.

He had a good wooden table back at his farm. It was big enough for a man to have his computer and bookwork at one end and his dinner at the other. A man didn't need a desk with that kind of table, and he liked it that way.

But this was his heritage. His. He gazed out at the sheep grazing in the distance, at the land stretching to the mountains beyond, and he felt a stir of something within that was almost primeval.

This was Irish land, a part of his family. His side of the family had been considered of no import for generations but still…some part of him felt a tug that was almost like the sensation of coming home. Finn was one of six brothers. His five siblings had left their impoverished farm as soon as they could manage. They were now scattered across the globe but, apart from trips to the States to check livestock lines, or attending conferences to investigate the latest in farming techniques, Finn had never wanted to leave. Over the years he'd built the small family plot into something he could be proud of.

But now, this place…why did it feel as if it was part of him?

There was a crazy thought.

'Is everything as you wish?' Mrs O'Reilly asked anxiously.

He looked at her worried face and he gazed around and

thought how much work must have gone into keeping this room perfect. How could one woman do it?

'It's grand,' he told her, and took a mouthful of the truly excellent beef. 'Wonderful.'

'I'm pleased. If there's anything else…'

'There isn't.'

'I don't know where the woman is. The lawyer said mid-afternoon…'

He still wasn't quite sure who the woman was. Details from the lawyers had been sparse, to say the least. 'The lawyer said you'd be expecting me mid-afternoon too,' he said mildly, attacking a bit more of his beef. Yeah, the epergne was off-putting—were they tigers?—but this was excellent food. 'Things happen.'

'Well,' the woman said with sudden asperity, 'she's Fiona's child. We could expect anything.'

'You realise I don't know anything about her. I don't even know who Fiona is,' he told her and the housekeeper narrowed her eyes, as if asking, *How could he not know?* Her look said the whole world should know, and be shocked as well.

'Fiona was Lord Conaill's only child,' she said tersely. 'His Lady died in childbirth. Fiona was a daughter when he wanted a son, but he gave her whatever she wanted. This would have been a cold place for a child and you can forgive a lot through upbringing, but Fiona had her chances and she never took them. She ran with a wild lot and there was nothing she wanted more than to shock her father. And us… The way she treated the servants… Dirt, we were. She ran through her father's money like it was water, entertaining her no-good friends, having parties, making this place a mess, but His Lordship would disappear to his club in Dublin rather than stop her. She was a spoiled child and then a selfish woman. There were one too many parties, though. She died of a drug overdose ten years ago, with only His Lordship to mourn her passing.'

'And her child?'

'Lord Conaill would hardly talk of her,' she said primly. 'For his daughter to have a child out of wedlock… Eh, it must have hurt. Fiona threw it in his face over and over, but still he kept silent. But then he wouldn't talk about you either and you were his heir. Is there anything else you'll be needing?'

'No, thank you,' Finn said. 'Are you not eating?'

'In the kitchen, My Lord,' she said primly. 'It's not my place to be eating here. I'll be keeping another dinner hot for the woman, just in case, but if she's like her mother we may never hear.'

And she left him to his roast beef.

For a while the meal took his attention—a man who normally cooked for himself was never one to be ignoring good food—but when it was finished he was left staring down the shining surface of the ostentatious table, at the pouncing tigers on the epergne, at his future.

What to do with this place?

Sell it? Why not?

The inheritance had come out of the blue. Selling it would mean he could buy the farms bordering his, and the country down south was richer than here. He was already successful but the input of this amount of money could make him one of the biggest primary producers in Ireland.

The prospect should make him feel on top of the world. Instead, he sat at the great, grand dining table and felt… empty. Weird.

He thought of Maeve and he wondered if this amount of money would have made a difference.

It wouldn't. He knew it now. His life had been one of loyalty—eldest son of impoverished farmers, loyal to his parents, to his siblings, to his farm. And to Maeve.

He'd spent twelve months realising loyalty was no basis for marriage.

He thought suddenly of the woman he'd pulled out of the bog. He hoped she'd be safe and dry by now. He had a sudden vision of her, bathed and warmed, ensconced in a cosy pub by a fire, maybe with a decent pie and a pint of Guinness.

He'd like to be there, he thought. Inheritance or not, right now maybe he'd rather be with her than in a castle.

Or not. What he'd inherited was a massive responsibility. It required...more loyalty?

And loyalty was his principle skill, he thought ruefully. It was what he accepted, what he was good at, and this inheritance was enough to take a man's breath away. Meanwhile the least he could do was tackle more of Mrs O'Reilly's excellent roast beef, he decided, and he did.

If she had anywhere else to go, she wouldn't be here. *Here* scared her half to death.

Jo was cleaned up—sort of—but she was still wet and she was still cold.

She was sitting on her bike outside the long driveway to Castle Glenconaill.

The castle was beautiful.

But this was no glistening white fairy tale, complete with turrets and spires, with pennants and heraldic banners fluttering in the wind. Instead, it seemed carved from the very land it was built on—grey-white stone, rising to maybe three storeys, but so gradually it gave the impression of a vast, long, low line of battlements emerging from the land. The castle was surrounded by farmland, but the now empty moat and the impressive battlements and the mountains looming behind said this castle was built to repel any invader.

As it was repelling her. It was vast and wonderful. It was…scary.

But she was cold. And wet. A group of stone cottages were clustered around the castle's main gates but they all looked derelict, and it was miles back to the village. And she'd travelled half a world because she'd just inherited half of what lay before her.

'This is my ancestral home,' she muttered and shivered and thought, *Who'd want a home like this?*

Who'd want a home? She wanted to turn and run.

But she was cold and she was getting colder. The wind was biting. She'd be cold even if her leathers weren't wet, she thought, but her leathers were wet and there was nowhere to stay in the village and, dammit, she had just inherited half this pile.

'But if they don't have a bath I'm leaving,' she muttered.

Where would she go?

She didn't know and she didn't care. There was always somewhere. But the castle was here and all she had to do was march across the great ditch that had once been a moat, hammer on the doors and demand her rights. One hot bath.

'Just do it,' she told herself. 'Do it before you lose your nerve entirely.'

The massive gong echoed off the great stone walls as if in warning that an entire Viking war fleet was heading for the castle. Finn was halfway through his second coffee and the sound was enough to scare a man into the middle of next week. Or at least spill his coffee. 'What the…?'

'It's the doorbell, My Lord,' Mrs O'Reilly said placidly, heading out to the grand hall. 'It'll be the woman. If she's like her mother, heaven help us.' She tugged off her apron, ran her fingers through her permed grey hair, took a quick peep into one of the over-mantel mirrors and then tugged at the doors.

The oak doors swung open. And there was…

Jo.

She was still in her bike gear but she must have washed. There wasn't a trace of mud on her, including her boots and trousers. Her face was scrubbed clean and she'd re-applied her make-up. Her kohl-rimmed eyes looked huge in her elfin face. Her cropped copper curls were combed and neat. She was smiling a wide smile, as if her welcome was assured.

He checked her legs and saw a telltale drip of water fall to her boots.

She was still sodden.

That figured. How many bikers had spare leathers in their kitbags?

She must be trying really hard not to shiver. He looked back at the bright smile and saw the effort she was making to keep it in place.

'Good evening,' she was saying. She hadn't seen him yet. Mrs O'Reilly was at the door and he was well behind her. 'I hope I'm expected? I'm Jo Conaill. I'm very sorry I'm late. I had a small incident on the road.'

'You look just like your mother.' The warmth had disappeared from the housekeeper's voice as if it had never been. There was no disguising her disgust. The housekeeper was staring at Jo as if she was something the cat had just dragged in.

The silence stretched on—an appalled silence. Jo's smile faded to nothing. *What the…?*

Do something.

'Good evening to you too,' he said. He stepped forward, edging the housekeeper aside. He smiled at Jo, summoning his most welcoming smile.

And then there was even more silence.

Jo stared from Mrs O'Reilly to Finn and then back again. She looked appalled.

As well she might, Finn conceded. As welcomes went, this took some beating. She'd been greeted by a woman whose disdain was obvious, and by a man who'd seen her at her most vulnerable. Now she was looking appalled. He thought of her reaction when he'd lifted her, carried her. She'd seemed terrified and the look was still with her.

He thought suddenly of a deer he'd found on his land some years back, a fawn caught in the ruins of a disused fence. Its mother had run on his approach but the fawn was trapped, its legs tangled in wire. It had taken time and patience to disentangle it without it hurting itself in its struggles.

That was what this woman looked like, he thought. Caught and wanting to run, but trapped.

She was so close to running.

Say something. 'We've met before.' He reached out and took her hand. It was freezing. Wherever she'd gone to get cleaned up, it hadn't been anywhere with a decent fire. 'I'm so glad you're…clean.'

He smiled but she seemed past noticing.

'You live here?' she said with incredulity.

'This is Lord Finn Conaill, Lord of Castle Glenconaill,' the housekeeper snapped.

Jo blinked and stared at Finn as if she was expecting two heads. 'You don't look like a lord.'

'What do I look like?'

'A farmer. I thought you were a farmer.'

'I am a farmer. And you're an heiress.'

'I wait tables.'

'There you go. We've both been leading double lives. And now… It seems we're cousins?'

'You're not cousins,' Mrs O'Reilly snapped, but he ignored her.

'We're not,' he conceded, focusing only on Jo. 'Just distant relations. You should be the true heir to this whole place. You're the only grandchild.'

'She's illegitimate,' Mrs O'Reilly snapped and Finn moved a little so his body was firmly between Jo and the housekeeper. What was it with the woman?

'There's still some hereabouts who judge a child for the actions of its parents,' he said mildly, ignoring Mrs O'Reilly and continuing to smile down at Jo. 'But I'm not one of them. According to the lawyer, it seems you're Lord Conaill's granddaughter, marriage vows or not.'

'And…and you?' *What was going on?* She had the appearance of street-smart. She looked tough. But inside… the image of the trapped fawn stayed.

'My father was the son of the recently deceased Lord Conaill's cousin,' Finn told her. He furrowed his brows a little. 'I think that's right. I can't quite get my head around it. So that means my link to you goes back four generations. We're very distant relatives, but it seems we do share a great-great-grandfather. And the family name.'

'Only because of illegitimacy,' Mrs O'Reilly snapped.

Enough. He turned from Jo and faced Mrs O'Reilly square-on. She was little and dumpy and full of righteous indignation. She'd been Lord Conaill's housekeeper for years. Heaven knew, he needed her if he was to find his way around this pile but right now…

Right now he was Lord Conaill of Castle Glenconaill, and maybe it was time to assume his rightful role.

'Mrs O'Reilly, I'll thank you to be civil,' he said, and if he'd never had reason to be autocratic before he made a good fist of it now. He summoned all his father had told him of previous lords of this place and he mentally lined his ancestors up behind him. 'Jo's come all the way from Australia. She's inherited half of her grandfather's estate and for now this castle is her home. *Her* home. I therefore expect you to treat her with the welcome and the respect her position entitles her to. Do I make myself clear?'

There was a loaded silence. The housekeeper tried glaring but he stayed calmly looking at her, waiting, his face impassive. He was Lord of Glenconaill and she was his housekeeper. It was time she knew it.

Jo said nothing. Finn didn't look back at her but he sensed her shiver. If he didn't get her inside soon she'd freeze to death, he thought, but this moment was too important to rush. He simply stood and gazed down at Mrs O'Reilly and waited for the woman to come to a decision.

'I only...' she started but he shook his head.

'Simple question. Simple answer. Welcome and respect. Yes or no.'

'Her mother...'

'Yes or no!'

And finally she cracked. She took a step back but his eyes didn't leave hers. 'Yes.'

'Yes, what?' It was an autocratic snap. His great-great-grandfather would be proud of him, he thought, and then he thought of his boots and thought: *maybe not.* But the snap had done what he intended.

She gave a frustrated little nod, she bobbed a curtsy and finally she answered him as he'd intended.

'Yes, My Lord.'

What was she doing here? If she had to inherit a castle, why couldn't she have done it from a distance? She could have told the lawyer to put up a For Sale sign, sell it to the highest bidder and send her a cheque for half. Easy.

Why this insistence that she had to come?

Actually, it hadn't been insistence. It had been a strongly worded letter from the lawyer saying decisions about the entire estate had to be made between herself and this unknown sort-of cousin. It had also said the castle contained possessions that had been her mother's. The lawyer suggested that decisions would be easier to make with her here, and the estate could well afford her airfare to Ireland to make those decisions.

And it had been like a siren song, calling her…home?

No, that was dumb. This castle had never been her home. She'd never had a home but it was the only link she had to anyone. She might as well come and have a look, she'd thought.

But this place was like the bog that surrounded it. The surface was enticing but, underneath, it was a quagmire. The housekeeper's voice had been laced with malice.

Was that her mother's doing? Fiona? Well, maybe invective was to be expected. Maybe malice was deserved.

What hadn't been expected was this strong, hunky male standing in the doorway, taking her hand, welcoming her—and then, before her eyes, turning into the Lord of Glenconaill. Just like that. He'd been a solid Good Samaritan who'd pulled her out of the bog. He'd laughed at her—which she hadn't appreciated, but okay, he might have had reason—and then, suddenly, the warmth was gone and he was every bit a lord. The housekeeper was bobbing a curtsy, for heaven's sake. What sort of feudal system was this?

She was well out of her depth. She should get on her bike and leave.

But she was cold.

The lawyer had paid for her flight, for two nights' accommodation in Dublin and for the bike hire—he'd suggested a car or even a driver to meet her, but some things were non-negotiable. Two nights' accommodation and the bike was the extent of the largesse. The lawyer had assumed she'd spend the rest of her time in the castle, and she hadn't inherited anything yet. Plus the village had no accommodation and the thought of riding further was unbearable.

So, even if she'd like to ride off into the sunset, she wasn't in a position to do it.

Plus she was really, really cold.

Finn…Lord of Glenconaill?…was looking at her with eyes that said he saw more than he was letting on. But his gaze was kind again. The aristocratic coldness had disappeared.

His gaze dropped to the worn stone tiles. There was a puddle forming around her boots.

'I met Miss Conaill down the bog road,' he said, smiling at her but talking to the housekeeper. 'There were sheep on the road. Miss Conaill had struck trouble, was off her bike, wet and shaken, and I imagine she's still shaken.' He didn't say she'd been stuck in a bog, Jo thought, and a surge of gratitude made her almost light-headed. 'I offered to give her a ride but, of course, she didn't know who I was and I didn't know who she was. I expect that's why you're late, Miss Conaill, and I'm thinking you're still wet. Mrs O'Reilly, could you run Miss Conaill a hot bath, make sure her bedroom's warm and leave her be for half an hour? Then there's roast beef warm in the oven for you.'

His voice changed a little, and she could hear the return of the aristocrat. There was a firm threat to the housekeeper behind the words. 'Mrs O'Reilly will look after you, Jo, and she'll look after you well. When you're warm and fed, we'll talk again. Meanwhile, I intend to sit in your grandfather's study and see if I can start making sense of this pile we seem to have inherited. Mrs O'Reilly, I depend on you to treat Jo with kindness. This is her home.'

And there was nothing more to be said. The housekeeper took a long breath, gave an uncertain glance up at…her Lord?…and bobbed another curtsy.

'Yes, My Lord.'

'Let's get your gear inside,' Finn said. 'Welcome to Castle Glenconaill, Miss Conaill. Welcome to your inheritance.'

'There's no need for us to talk again tonight,' Jo managed. 'I'll have a bath and go to bed.'

'You'll have a bath and then be fed,' Finn said, and there was no arguing with the way he said it. 'You're welcome here, Miss Conaill, even if right now it doesn't feel like it.'

'Th...thank you,' she managed and turned to her bike to get her gear.

If things had gone well from there they might have been fine. She'd find her bedroom, have a bath, have something to eat, say goodnight and go to bed. She'd talk to the lawyer in the morning. She'd sign whatever had to be signed. She'd go back to Australia. That was the plan.

So far, things hadn't gone well for Jo, though, and they were about to get worse.

She had two bags—her kitbag with her clothes and a smaller one with her personal gear. She tugged them from the bike, she turned around and Finn was beside her.

He lifted the kitbag from her grasp and reached for the smaller bag. 'Let me.'

'I don't need help.'

'You're cold and wet and shaken,' he told her. 'It's a wise woman who knows when accepting help is sensible.'

This was no time to be arguing, she conceded, but she clung to her smaller bag and let Finn carry the bigger bag in.

He reached the foot of the grand staircase and then paused. 'Lead the way, Mrs O'Reilly,' he told the housekeeper, revealing for the first time that he didn't know this place.

And the housekeeper harrumphed and stalked up to pass them.

She brushed Jo on the way. Accidentally or on purpose, whatever, but it seemed a deliberate bump. She knocked the carryall out of Jo's hand.

And the bag wasn't properly closed.

After the bog, Jo had headed back to the village. She'd have loved to have booked a room at the pub but there'd been a No Vacancies sign in the porch, the attached cobwebs and dust suggesting there'd been no vacancies for years. She'd made do with a trip to the Ladies, a scrub under cold water—no hot water in this place—and an attempt at repair to her make-up.

She'd been freezing. Her hands had been shaking and she mustn't have closed her bag properly.

Her bag dropped now onto the ancient floorboards of Castle Glenconaill and the contents spilled onto the floor.

They were innocuous. Her toiletries. The things she'd needed on the plane on the way over. Her latest project…

And it was this that the housekeeper focused on. There was a gasp of indignation and the woman was bending down, lifting up a small, clear plastic vial and holding it up like the angel of doom.

'I knew it,' she spat, turning to Jo with fury that must have been building for years. 'I knew how it'd be. Like mother, like daughter, and why your grandfather had to leave you half the castle… Your mother broke His Lordship's heart, so why you're here… What he didn't give her… She was nothing but a drug-addicted slut, and here you are, just the same. He's given you half his fortune and do you deserve it? How dare you bring your filthy stuff into this house?'

Finn had stopped, one boot on the first step. His brow snapped down in confusion. 'What are you talking about?'

'Needles.' The woman held up the plastic vial. 'You'll find drugs too, I'll warrant. Her mother couldn't keep away from the stuff. Dead from an overdose in the end, and here's her daughter just the same. And half the castle left to her… It breaks my heart.'

And Jo closed her eyes. *Beam me up*, she pleaded. Where was a time machine when she needed one? She'd come all this way to be tarred with the same brush as her mother. A woman she'd never met and didn't want to meet.

Like mother, like daughter… What a joke.

'I'll go,' she said in a voice she barely recognised. She'd sleep rough tonight, she decided. She'd done it before—it wouldn't kill her. Tomorrow she'd find the lawyer, sign whatever had to be signed and head back to Australia.

'You're going nowhere.' The anger in Finn's voice made her eyes snap open. It was a snap that reverberated through the ancient beams, from stone wall to stone wall, worthy of an aristocratic lineage as old as time itself. He placed the kitbag he was holding down and took the three steps to where the housekeeper was standing. He took the vial, stared at it and then looked at the housekeeper with icy contempt.

'You live here?' he demanded and the woman's fury took a slight dent.

'Of course.'

'Where?'

'I have an apartment…'

'Self-contained?'

'I…yes.'

'Good,' he snapped. 'Then go there now. Of all the cruel, cold welcomes…' He stared down at the vial and his mouth set in grim lines. 'Even if this was what you thought it was, your reaction would be unforgivable, but these are sewing needles. They have a hole at the end, not through the middle. Even if they were syringes, there's a score of reasons why Miss Conaill would carry them other than drug addiction. But enough. You're not to be trusted to treat Miss Conaill with common courtesy, much less kindness. Return to your apartment. I'll talk to you tomorrow morning but not before. I don't wish to see you again tonight. I'll take care of Miss Conaill. Go, now.'

'You can't,' the woman breathed. 'You can't tell me to go.'

'I'm Lord of Glenconaill,' Finn snapped. 'I believe the right is mine.'

Silence. The whole world seemed to hold its breath.

Jo stared at the floor, at her pathetic pile of toiletries and, incongruously, at the cover of the romance novel she'd read on the plane. It was historical, the Lord of the Manor rescuing and marrying his Cinderella.

Who'd want to be Cinderella? she'd thought as she read it, and that was what it felt like now. Cinderella should have options. She should be able to make the grand gesture, sweep from the castle in a flurry of skirts, say, *Take me to the nearest hostelry, my man, and run me a hot bath...*

A hot bath. There was the catch. From the moment Finn had said it, they were the words that had stuck in her mind. Everything else was white noise.

Except maybe the presence of this man. She was trying not to look at him.

The hero of her romance novel had been...romantic. He'd worn tight-fitting breeches and glossy boots and intricate neckcloths made of fine linen.

Her hero had battered boots and brawny arms and traces of copper in his deep brown hair. He looked tanned and weathered. His green eyes were creased by smiles or weather and she had no way of knowing which. He looked far too large to look elegant in fine linen and neckcloths, but maybe she was verging on hysterics because her mind had definitely decided it wanted a hero with battered boots. And a weathered face and smiley eyes.

Especially if he was to provide her with a bath.

'Go,' he said to Mrs O'Reilly and the woman cast him

a glance that was half scared, half defiant. But the look Finn gave her back took the defiance out of her.

She turned and almost scuttled away, and Jo was left with Finn.

He didn't look at her. He simply bent and gathered her gear back into her bag.

She should be doing that. What was she doing, staring down at him like an idiot?

She stooped to help, but suddenly she was right at eye level, right…close.

His expression softened. He smiled and closed her bag with a snap.

'You'll be fine now,' he said. 'We seem to have routed the enemy. Let's find you a bath.'

And he rose and held out his hand to help her rise with him.

She didn't move. She didn't seem to be able to.

She just stared at that hand. Big. Muscled. Strong.

How good would it be just to put her hand in his?

'I forgot; you're a wary woman,' he said ruefully and stepped back. 'Very wise. I gather our ancestors have a fearsome reputation, but then they're your ancestors too, so that should make me wary as well. But if you can cope with me as a guide, I'll try and find you a bedroom. Mind, I've only just found my own bedroom but there seem to be plenty. Do you trust me to show you the way?'

How dumb was she being? Really dumb, she told herself, as well as being almost as offensive as the woman who'd just left. But still she didn't put her hand in his. Even though her legs were feeling like jelly—her feet were still icy—she managed to rise and tried a smile.

'Sorry. I…thank you.'

'There's no need to thank me,' he said ruefully. 'I had the warm welcome. I have no idea what bee the woman has in her bonnet but let's forget her and find you that bath.'

'Yes, please,' she said simply and thought, despite her wariness, if this man was promising her a bath she'd follow him to the ends of the earth.

CHAPTER THREE

JO HAD A truly excellent bath. It was a bath she might well remember for the rest of her life.

Finn had taken her to the section of the castle where Mrs O'Reilly had allocated him a bedroom. He'd opened five doors, looking for another.

At the far end of the corridor, as far from Finn's as she could be, and also as far from the awesome bedroom they'd found by mistake—it had to have been her grandfather's—they'd found a small box room containing a single bed. It was the only other room with a bed made up, and it was obvious that was the room Mrs O'Reilly wanted her to use.

'We'll make up another,' Finn had growled in disgust—all the other rooms were better—but the bed looked good to Jo. Any bed would look good to Jo and when they'd found the bathroom next door and she'd seen the truly enormous bathtub she'd thought she'd died and gone to heaven.

So now she lay back, up to her neck in heat and steam. Her feet hurt when she got in, that was how cold they were, but the pain only lasted for moments and what was left was bliss.

She closed her eyes and tried to think of nothing at all.

She thought of Finn.

What manner of man was he? He was… what…her third cousin? Something removed? How did such things work? She didn't have a clue.

But they were related. He was…family? He'd defended her like family and such a thing had never happened to her.

He felt like…home.

And that was a stupid thing to think. How many times had she been sucked in by such sweetness?

'*You're so welcome. Come in, sweetheart, let's help you unpack. You're safe here for as long as you need to stay.*'

But it was never true. There was always a reason she had to move on.

She had to move on from here. This was a flying visit only.

To collect her inheritance? This castle must be worth a fortune and it seemed her grandfather had left her half.

She had no idea how much castles were worth on the open market but surely she'd come out of it with enough to buy herself an apartment.

Or a Harley. That was a thought. She could buy a Harley and stay on the road for ever.

Maybe she'd do both. She could buy a tiny apartment, a place where she could crash from time to time when the roads got unfriendly. It didn't need to be big. It wasn't as if she had a lot of stuff.

Stuff. She opened her eyes and looked around her at the absurd, over-the-top bathroom. There was a chandelier hanging from the beams.

A portrait of Queen Victoria hung over the cistern, draped in a potted aspidistra.

Finn had hauled open the door and blanched. 'Mother of… You sure you want to use this?'

She'd giggled. After this whole appalling day, she'd giggled.

In truth, Finn Conaill was enough to make any woman smile.

'And that's enough of that,' she said out loud and splashed

her face and then decided, dammit, splashing wasn't enough, she'd totally submerge. She did.

She came up still thinking of Finn.

He'd be waiting. 'Come and find me when you're dry and warm,' he'd said. 'There's dinner waiting for you somewhere. I may have to hunt to find it but I'll track it down.'

He would too, she thought. He seemed like a man who kept his promises.

Nice.

And Finn Conaill looked sexy enough to make a girl's toes curl. And when he smiled…

'Do Not Think About Him Like That!' She said it out loud, enunciating each word. 'You've been dumb enough for one day. Get tonight over with, get these documents signed and get out of here. Go buy your Harley.'

Harleys should be front and foremost in her mind. She'd never thought she'd have enough money to buy one and maybe now she would.

'So think about Harleys, not Finn Conaill,' she told herself as she reluctantly pulled the plug and let the hot water disappear. 'No daydreaming. You're dry and warm. Now, find yourself some dinner and go to bed. And keep your wits about you.'

But he's to be trusted, a little voice said.

But the old voice, the voice she knew, the only voice she truly trusted, told her she was being daft. *Don't trust anyone. Haven't you learnt anything by now?*

He heard her coming downstairs. Her tread was light but a couple of the ancient boards squeaked and he was listening for her.

He strode out to meet her and stopped and blinked.

She was wearing jeans and an oversized crimson sweater. She'd lost the make-up. Her face was a smatter of freckles and the rest seemed all eyes. She'd towelled her hair dry but it was still damp, the short curls tightly sprung, coiling as much as their length allowed.

She was wearing some kind of sheepskin bootees which looked massively oversized on her slight frame. She was flushed from the heat of her bath, and she looked like a kid.

She was treading down the stairs as if Here Be Dragons, and it was all he could do not to move forward and give her a hug of reassurance.

Right. As if that'd go down well. Earlier he'd picked her up when she needed to be picked up and she'd pretty near had kittens.

He forced himself to stay still, to wait until she'd reached the bottom. Finally she looked around for where to go next and she saw him.

'Hey,' he said and smiled and she smiled back.

It was a pretty good smile.

And that would be an understatement. This was the first time he'd seen this smile full on, and it was enough to take a man's breath away.

He had to struggle with himself to get his voice to sound prosaic.

'Kitchen?' he managed. 'Dining room's to the left if you like sitting with nineteen empty chairs and an epergne, or kitchen if you don't mind firestove and kettle.'

'Firestove and kettle,' she said promptly but peered left into the dining room, at its impressive size and its even more impressive—ostentatious?—furnishings. 'This is nuts. I have Queen Victoria in my bathroom. Medieval castle with interior decorator gone mad.'

'Not quite medieval, though the foundations might be. It's been built and rebuilt over the ages. According to Mrs O'Reilly, much of the current decorating was down to your mother. Apparently your grandfather kept to himself, the place gathered dust and when she was here she was bored.'

'Right,' she said dryly, looking askance at the suits of armour at the foot of the stairs. 'Are these guys genuine?'

'I've been looking at them. They're old enough, but there's not a scratch on them. Aren't they great?' He pointed to the sword blades. 'Note, though, that the swords have been tipped to make them safe. The Conaills of Glenconaill seem to have been into making money, not war. *To take and to hold* is their family motto.' He corrected himself. '*Our* family creed.'

'Not my creed,' she said dryly. 'I don't hold onto anything. Did you say dinner?'

'Kitchen this way. I used your bath time to investigate.' He turned and led her through thick wooden doors, into the kitchen beyond.

It was a truly impressive kitchen. A lord's kitchen.

A massive firestove set into an even larger hearth took up almost an entire wall. The floor was old stone, scrubbed and worn. The table was a vast slab of timber, scarred from generations of use.

The stove put out gentle heat. There was a rocker by the stove. Old calendars lined the walls as if it was too much trouble to take them down in the new year—simpler to put a new one up alongside. The calendars were from the local businesses, an eclectic mix of wildlife, local scenery and kittens. Many kittens.

Jo stopped at the door and blinked. 'Wow.'

'As you say, wow. Sit yourself down. Mrs O'Reilly said she'd kept your dinner hot.' He checked out the firestove, snagged a tea towel and opened the oven door.

It was empty. *What the heck?*

The firestove had been tamped for the night, the inlet closed. The oven was the perfect place to keep a dinner warm.

He closed the oven door and reconsidered. There was

an electric range to the side—maybe for when the weather was too hot to use the firestove? Its light was on.

The control panel said it was on high.

He tugged open the oven door and found Jo's dinner. It was dried to the point where it looked inedible.

'Uh oh,' he said, hauling it out and looking at it in disgust. And then he looked directly at Jo and decided to say it like it was. 'It seems our housekeeper doesn't like you.'

'She's never met me before tonight. I imagine it's that she doesn't…she didn't like my mother.'

'I'm sorry.'

'Don't be. I didn't like my mother myself. Not that I ever met her.'

He stared down at the dinner, baked hard onto the plate. Then he shrugged, lifted the lid of the trashcan and dumped the whole thing, plate and all, inside.

'You realise that's probably part of a priceless dinner set?' Jo said mildly.

'She wouldn't have served you on that. With the vitriol in the woman it's a wonder she didn't serve you on plastic. Sit down and I'll make you eggs and bacon. That is…' He checked the fridge and grinned. 'Eureka. Eggs and bacon. Would you like to tell me why no one seems to like your mother?'

'I'll cook.'

'No,' he said gently. 'You sit. You've come all the way from Australia and I've come from Kilkenny. Sit yourself down and be looked after.'

'You don't have to…'

'I want to, and eggs and bacon are my speciality.' He was already hauling things out of the fridge. 'Three eggs for you. A couple—no, make that three for me. It's been a whole hour since dinner, after all. Fried bread? Of course, fried bread, what am I thinking? And a side of fried tomato so we don't die of scurvy.'

So she sat and he cooked, and the smell of sizzling bacon filled the room. He focused on his cooking and behind him he sensed the tension seep from her. It was that sort of kitchen, he thought. Maybe they could pull the whole castle down and keep the kitchen. The lawyer had told him they needed to decide what to keep. This kitchen would be a choice.

'*To take and to hold.* Is that really our family creed?' Jo asked into the silence.

'*Accipere et Tenere.* It's over the front door. If my schoolboy Latin's up to it…'

'You did Latin in school?'

'Yeah, and me just a hayseed and all.'

'You're a hayseed?'

He didn't mind explaining. She was so nervous, it couldn't hurt to share a bit of himself.

'I have a farm near Kilkenny,' he told her. 'I had a short, terse visit from your grandfather six months back, telling me I stood to inherit the title when he passed. Before that I didn't have a clue. Oh, I knew there was a lord way back in the family tree, but I assumed we were well clear of it. I gather our great grandfathers hated each other. The title and all the money went to your side. My side mostly starved in the potato famine or emigrated, and it sounded as if His Lordship thought we pretty much got what we deserved.'

He paused, thinking of the visit with the stooped and ageing aristocrat. Finn had just finished helping the team milk. He'd stood in the yard and stared at Lord Conaill in amazement, listening to the old man growl.

'He was almost abusive,' he told Jo now. 'He said, "Despite your dubious upbringing and low social standing, there's no doubt you'll inherit my ancient title. There's no one else. My lawyers tell me you're the closest in the male line. I can only pray that you manage not to disgrace our name." I was pretty much gobsmacked.'

'Wow,' Jo said. 'I'd have been gobsmacked too.' And then she stared at the plate he was putting down in front of her. 'Double wow. This is amazing.'

'Pretty impressive for a peasant.' He sat down with his own plate in front of him and she stared at the vast helping he'd given himself.

'Haven't you already eaten?'

'Hours ago.' At least one. 'And I was lambing at dawn.'

'So you really are a farmer.'

'Mostly dairy but I run a few sheep on the side. But I'll try and eat with a fork, just this once.' He grinned at her and then tackled his plate. 'So how about you? Has your grandfather been firing insulting directions at you too?'

'No.'

Her tone said, *Don't go there,* so he didn't. He concentrated on bacon.

It was excellent bacon. He thought briefly about cooking some more but decided it had to be up to Jo. Three servings was probably a bit much.

Jo seemed to focus on her food too. They ate in silence and he was content with that. Still he had that impression of nervousness. It didn't make sense but he wasn't a man to push where he wasn't wanted.

'Most of what I know of this family comes from one letter,' Jo said at last, and he nodded again and kept addressing his plate. He sensed information was hard to get from this woman. Looking up and seeming expectant didn't seem the way to get it.

'It was when I was ten,' she said at last. 'Addressed to my foster parents.'

'Your foster parents?'

'Tom and Monica Hastings. They were lovely. They

wanted to adopt me. It had happened before, with other foster parents, but they never shared the letters.'

'I see.' Although he didn't. And then he thought, *Why not say it like it is?* 'You understand I'm from the peasant side of this family,' he told her. 'I haven't heard anything from your lot before your grandfather's visit, and that didn't fill me in on detail. So I don't know your history. I'd assumed I'd just be inheriting the title, and that only because I'm the next male in line, no matter how distant. Inheriting half this pile has left me stunned. It seems like it should all be yours, and yet here you are, saying you've been in foster homes…'

'Since birth.' Her tone was carefully neutral. 'Okay, maybe I do know a bit more than you, but not much. I was born in Sydney. My mother walked out of the hospital and left me there, giving my grandfather's name as the only person to contact. According to the Social Welfare notes that I've now seen—did you know you can get your file as an adult?—my grandfather was appalled at my very existence. His instructions were to have me adopted, get rid of me, but when my mother was finally tracked down she sent a curt letter back saying I wasn't for adoption; I was a Conaill, I was to stay a Conaill and my grandfather could lump it.'

'Your grandfather could lump it?'

'Yeah,' she said and rose and carried her plate to the sink. She ran hot water and started washing and he stood beside her and started wiping. It was an age-old domestic task and why it helped, he didn't know, but the action itself seemed to settle her.

'It seemed Fiona was a wild child,' she told him at last. 'She and my grandfather fought, and she seemed to do everything she could to shock him. If I'd been a boy I'm guessing she would have had him adopted. My grandfather might have valued a boy so having him adopted away from the family might have hurt him more than having an illegitimate grandchild. But I was just a girl so all she could do to shock him was keep me as a Conaill and grind it into his face whenever she could. So Social Welfare was left with him as first point of contact and I went from foster home to foster home. Because I'd been in foster care for ever, though, there was always the possibility of adoption. But every time any of my foster parents tried to keep me, they'd contact my grandfather and eventually he'd talk to Fiona—and she would refuse. It seemed she wanted to keep me in my grandfather's face.'

'So it was all about what was between Fiona and her father. Nothing about you.'

'It seems I was the tool to hurt him.' She shrugged and handed him the scrubbed frying pan. 'Nothing else. Why he's left me anything… I don't understand.'

'I suspect he ran out of options,' Finn told her. He kept his attention on the pan, not on her. 'I was the despised poor relation who stood to inherit the title whether he willed it to me or not. You were the despised illegitimate granddaughter. I imagine it was leave everything to us or leave it to a cats' home—and there's no sign that he was fond of cats.' He gazed around the kitten-adorned walls. 'Except in here, but I doubt the kitchen was his domain.'

'I guess.' She let the water run away and watched it swirl into the plughole. 'Isn't it supposed to swirl the other way?'

'What?'

'I'm in a different hemisphere. Doesn't the water go round in opposite directions?'

'What direction does it go round in Australia?'

'I have no idea.'

'You've never looked?'

'It's not the sort of thing you notice.'

'We could check it out on the Internet.'

'We could,' she conceded. 'Or we could go to bed.' And then she paused and flushed. 'I mean…' She stopped and bit her lip. 'I didn't…'

'You know, despite the fact that your mother was a wild child, I'm absolutely sure you didn't just proposition me,' he said gently and handed her the dishcloth to wipe her hands. 'You're tired, I'm tired and tomorrow we have a meeting with the lawyer and a castle to put on the market. That is, unless you'd like to keep it.'

She stared at him. 'Are you kidding? What would I do with a castle?'

'Exactly,' he said and took the dishcloth back from her and hung it up, then took her shoulders in his hands and twisted her and propelled her gently from the room. 'So tomorrow's for being sensible and we might as well start now. Bedtime, Jo Conaill. Don't dream of bogs.'

'I wouldn't dare,' she told him. 'I've been stuck in some pretty scary places in my time but the bog's the worst. Thank you for pulling me out.'

'It was my pleasure,' he told her. 'And Jo…'

'Yes?' He'd let her go. She was out of the door but glancing back at him.

'I'm glad I've inherited with you. If we have to be dissolute, unwanted relatives, it's good that it's two of us, don't you think?'

'I guess.' She frowned. 'I mean…we could have done this on our own.'

'But it wouldn't have been as much fun,' he told her. 'Tomorrow promises to be amazing. How many times in your life do you inherit a castle, Jo Conaill?' Then, as she didn't answer, he chuckled. 'Exactly. Mostly none. Go to bed, Jo, and sleep thinking of fun. Tomorrow you wake up as Lady of the Castle Glenconaill. If we have to inherit, why not enjoy it?'

'I'm not a Lady…'

'You could be,' he told her. 'Okay, neither of us belong,

but tomorrow, just for a little, let's be Lord and Lady of all we survey. We might even Lord and Lady it over Mrs O'Reilly and if she gives us burnt toast for breakfast it's off with her head. What do you say?'

She gazed at him, dumbfounded, and then, slowly, her face creased into a smile again.

It really was a beautiful smile.

'Exactly,' he told her. 'Tomorrow this is our place. It's where we belong.'

'I don't belong.'

'Yes, you do,' he told her. 'Your grandfather and your mother no longer hold sway. Tomorrow you belong here.'

'I guess I could pretend…'

'There's no pretence about it. Tomorrow you belong right here.'

She met his gaze. Everything that needed to be said had been said but just for a moment she stayed. Just for a moment their gazes locked and something passed between… Something intangible. Something strong and new and… unfathomable.

It was something he didn't understand and it seemed she didn't either. She gazed at him for a long moment and then she shook her head, as if trying to clear a mist she'd never been in before. As if trying to clear confusion.

'Goodnight,' she said in a voice that was decidedly unsteady.

'Goodnight,' he told her and finally she left.

He stood where he was.

Surely she hadn't guessed that he'd had a crazy impulse to walk across and kiss her?

And surely her eyes hadn't said that that kiss might have been welcome?

His bedroom was magnificent, almost as magnificent as the one the old Lord had slept in. He lay in the vast four-poster bed and thought of the cramped cots he and his brothers had shared as kids, of the impoverished farm his parents had struggled to keep, of a childhood lacking in anything but love.

But he thought of Jo and he knew he'd been lucky. She'd told him little, and yet there was so much behind her words that he could guess. A childhood of foster homes, and anyone who wanted to keep her being unable to do so.

She looked tough on the surface but he didn't need to scratch very deep before seeing scars.

She was…intriguing.

And that was something he shouldn't be thinking, he decided. Wasn't life complicated enough already?

'No.' He said it suddenly, out loud, and it surprised even him. His life wasn't complicated. He'd fought to make their parents' farm prosper. His father had died when he was in his teens and his brothers were younger. His mother had had no choice but to let him have his head. He'd set about changing things, firstly trying to keep them all from starving but in the end relishing the challenge. None of his brothers had had any inclination to stay on an impoverished farm. They'd gone on to have interesting, fulfilling careers but farming seemed to be in Finn's blood. By the time his mother died, twenty years later, the farm was an excellent financial concern.

And then there'd been Maeve, the girl next door, the woman he'd always assumed shared his dreams. The woman he'd thought he'd marry.

'You're loyal to a fault.' Sean, his youngest brother, had thrown it at him on his last visit home. 'You took on the farm when you were little more than a kid and practically hauled us all up. You gave up your dreams for us. You never let our mam down. You've managed to make a go of the farm, and that's great, but Maeve—just because you promised eternal love when you were ten years old doesn't mean you owe her loyalty for life. She doesn't want this life. I'm thinking half what she thought was love for you was loyalty to her dad, but there's more to life than loyalty. She's seen it. So should you.'

Sean was right. The last twelve months had taught him that what he thought of as love was simply loyalty to a friend, loyalty to a way of life, loyalty to his vision of his future.

So where did his future lie now?

He thumped the pillow and then, when it didn't result in immediate sleep, he tossed back the covers and headed to the window. It was a vast casement window, the stone wall almost two feet thick.

Beneath the window the land of Glenconaill stretched away to the moonlit horizon, miles of arable land reaching out to the bogs and then the mountains beyond.

If he'd inherited the whole thing…

'You didn't. This place is money only,' he muttered and deliberately drew the great velvet curtains closed, blocking out the night. 'Don't you be getting any ideas, Lord Finn of Glenconaill.'

And at the sound of his title he grinned. His brothers would never let him live it down. All now successful businessmen in their own rights, they'd think it was funny.

And Maeve…well, it no longer mattered what Maeve thought. He'd accepted it over the last few months and this morning's visit had simply confirmed it. Yes, she was in a mess but it wasn't a mess of his making. Their relationship was well over.

Had she faced her father or gone back to Dublin?

It was none of his business.

He headed back to bed and stared up at the dark and found himself thinking of the wide acres around Castle Glenconaill.

And a girl sleeping not so far from where he lay. A woman.
A woman named Jo.

By the time Jo came downstairs, the massive dining room was set up for breakfast. The housekeeper greeted her with a curt, 'Good morning, miss. Lord Conaill's in the dining room already. Would you like to start with coffee?'

It was pretty much your standard Bed and Breakfast greeting, Jo decided, and that was fine by her. Formal was good.

She walked into the dining room and Finn was there, reading the paper. He was wearing a casual shirt, sleeves rolled past his elbows. Sunbeams filtered through the massive windows at the end of the room. He looked up at her as she entered and he smiled, his deep green eyes creasing with pleasure at the sight of her—and it was all a woman could do not to gasp.

Where was formal when she needed it?

'Did you sleep well?' he asked and somehow she found her voice and somehow she made it work.

'How can you doubt it? Twelve hours!'

'So you'd be leaving the jet lag behind?'

'I hope so.' She sat at the ridiculous dining table and gazed down its length. Mrs O'Reilly had set places for them at opposite ends. 'We'll need a megaphone if we want to communicate.'

'Ah, but I don't think we're supposed to communicate. Formality's the order of the day. You're the aristocratic side of the family. I'm the peasant.'

'Hey, I'm on the wrong side of the blanket.'

'Then I'm under the bed, with the rest of the lint bunnies.'

She choked. The thought of this man as a lint bunny…

Mrs O'Reilly swept in then with coffee and placed it before her with exaggerated care. 'Mr O'Farrell's just phoned,' she told Finn, stepping back from the table and wiping her hands on her skirt as if she'd just done something dirty. 'He's the lawyer for the estate. He's been staying in Galway and he can be here in half an hour. I can ring him if that's not satisfactory.'

Finn raised his brows at Jo. 'Is that satisfactory with you?'

'I…yes.'

'We can see him then,' Finn told her. 'In Lord Conaill's study, please. Could you light the fire?'

'The drawing room would be…'

'The study, please,' Finn said inexorably and the woman stared at him.

Finn gazed calmly back. Waiting.

For a moment Jo thought she wouldn't answer. Finally she gave an angry tut and nodded.

'Yes, My Lord.'

'Mrs O'Reilly?'

'Yes.'

'You haven't asked Miss Conaill what she'd like for breakfast.'

'Toast,' Jo said hurriedly.

'And marmalade and a fruit platter,' Finn added. 'And I trust it'll be up to the excellent standard you served me. You do realise you burned Miss Conaill's dinner last night?'

He was holding the woman's gaze, staring her down, and with a gaze like that there was never any doubt as to the outcome.

'I'm sorry, My Lord. It won't happen again.'

'It won't,' Finn told her and gave a curt nod and went back to his newspaper.

The woman disappeared. Jo gazed after her with awe and then turned back to Finn. He was watching her, she found. He'd lowered his paper and was smiling at her, as if giving the lie to the gruff persona she'd just witnessed.

And it was too much. She giggled. 'Where did you learn to be a lord?' she demanded. 'Or is that something that's born into you with the title?'

'I practice on cows,' he said with some pride. 'I've had six months to get used to this Lordship caper. The cows have been bowing and scraping like anything.' He put his paper down and grinned. 'Not my brothers so much,' he admitted. 'They haven't let me live it down since they heard. Insubordination upon insubordination. You've never seen anything like it.'

'Do you guys share the farm?' She held her coffee, cradling its warmth. The dining room had an open fire in the hearth, the room was warm enough, but the sheer size of it was enough to make her shiver.

'I own my parents' farm outright, but it wasn't much of an inheritance when I started. My brothers all left for what they saw as easier careers and they've done well. Me? I've put my heart and soul into the farm and it's paid off.'

'You're content?'

He grinned at that. 'I'm a lord. How can I not be content?'

'I meant with farming.'

'Of course I am. I don't need a castle to be content. Cows are much more respectful than housekeepers.'

'I'm sure they are,' she said, thinking the man was ridiculous. But she kind of liked it.

She kind of liked him.

'No wife and family?' she asked, not that it was any of her business but she might as well ask.

'No.' He shrugged and gave a rueful smile. 'I've had a long-term girlfriend who's recently decided long-term is more than long enough. See me suffering from a broken heart.'

'Really?'

'Not really.' He grinned. 'I'll live.'

And then Mrs O'Reilly came sniffing back in with toast and he followed her every move with an aristocratically raised eyebrow until she disappeared again. It was a bit much for Jo.

'You do the Lord thing beautifully.'

'You should try.'

'Not me. I'm inheriting what there is to inherit and then I'm out of here.'

'Maybe that's wise,' Finn said thoughtfully. 'From all accounts, your grandpa wasn't the happiest of men. Maybe being aristocratic isn't all it's cut out to be.'

'But being content is,' she said softly. 'I'm glad… I'm glad, Finn Conaill, that you're content.'

The lawyer arrived just as Mrs O'Reilly finished clearing breakfast. Jo had had half a dozen emails from this man, plus a couple of phone calls from his assistant. She'd checked him out on the Internet. He was a partner in a prestigious Dublin law firm. She expected him to be crusty, dusty and old.

He turned up in bike leathers. He walked in, blond, blue-eyed, his helmet tucked under one arm, a briefcase by his side, and she found herself smiling as she stood beside Finn to greet him. There were things she'd been dreading over this meeting. Being intimidated by the legal fraternity was one of them, but this guy was smiling back at her, dumping his gear, holding out his hand in greeting. A fellow biker.

'Whose is the bike?' he asked.

'Mine,' she said. 'Hired in Dublin.'

'You should have let me know. My father would disapprove but I know a place that hires vintage babies. Or there are places that hire Harleys. We could have set one up for you.'

'You're kidding. A Harley?' She couldn't disguise the longing.

'No matter. After this morning, I imagine you'll be able to buy half a dozen Harleys.' He glanced at Finn and smiled. 'And yours will be the Jeep?'

And there it was, the faintest note of condescension. Jo got it because she was used to it, and she glanced up at Finn's face and she saw he got it too. And his face said he was used to it as well.

The lawyer's accent was strongly English. She'd read a bit of Ireland's background before she came. The lawyer would be public school educated, she thought. Finn…not so much. But she watched his face and saw the faint twitch at the edges of his mouth, the deepening of the creases at his eyes and thought, *He's amused by it.*

And she thought, *You'd be a fool to be condescending to this man.*

'I'm the Jeep,' he conceded.

'And the new Lord Conaill of Glenconaill,' the lawyer said and held out his hand. 'Congratulations. You're a lucky man.'

'Thank you,' Finn said gravely. 'I'm sure every Irishman secretly longs for his very own castle. I might even need to learn to eat with a fork to match.'

He grinned to take any offence from the words and Jo found herself grinning back. This man got subtle nuances, she thought, but, rather than bristling, he enjoyed them. She looked from Finn to the lawyer and thought this farmer was more than a match for any smart city lawyer.

'Lord Conaill and I have just been having breakfast,' she said. 'Before he takes me on a tour of the estate.'

'You know you're sharing?'

'And that's what you need to explain,' Finn said and they

headed into her grandfather's study, where John O'Farrell of O'Farrell, O'Farrell and O'Lochlan spent an hour explaining the ins and outs of their inheritance.

Which left Jo…gobsmacked.

She was rich. The lawyer was right. If she wanted, she could have half a dozen Harleys. Or much, much more.

The lawyer had gone through each section of the estate, explaining at length. She'd tried to listen. She'd tried to take it in but the numbers were too enormous for her to get her head around. When he finally finished she sat, stunned to silence, and Finn sat beside her and she thought, *He's just as stunned as I am.*

Unbelievable.

'So it's straight down the middle,' Finn said at last. 'One castle and one fortune.'

'That's right and, on current valuations, they're approximately equal. In theory, one of you could take the castle, the other the fortune that goes with it.' The lawyer looked at Jo and smiled. He'd been doing that a bit, not-so-subtle flirting. But then he decided to get serious again and addressed Finn.

'However, if you did have notions of keeping the castle, of setting yourself up as Lord of Glenconaill and letting Miss Conaill take the rest, I have bad news. This place is a money sink. My father has been acting as financial adviser to Lord Conaill for the last forty years and he knows how little has been spent on the upkeep of both castle and land. He's asked me to make sure you know it. The cosmetic touches have been done—Lord Conaill was big on keeping up appearances and his daughter insisted on things such as central heating—but massive capital works are needed to keep this place going into the future. Lord Conaill told my father he thought your own farm is worth a considerable amount but, in my father's opinion, if you wished to keep the castle, you'd need considerably more.

And, as for Miss Conaill…' he smiled again at Jo '… I suspect this lady has better things to do with a fortune than sink it into an ancient castle.'

Did she?

A fortune…

What would the likes of her do with a fortune?

Finn wasn't speaking. He'd turned and was looking out of the massive casement window to the land beyond.

He'd need time to take this in, she thought. They both would. This was…massive. She tried to think of how it would affect her, and couldn't. She tried to think of how it would affect Finn, but watching his broad shoulders at the window was making things seem even more disconcerting.

So focus on something else. Anything.

'What about Mrs O'Reilly?' she found herself asking, and the lawyer frowned.

'What about her?'

'It's just…there's no mention of her in the will and she seems to have been here for ever. She knew my mother.'

Finn turned and stared at her. She kept looking at the lawyer.

'I believe she has,' the lawyer said. 'There has been… discussion.'

'Discussion?'

'She rang after the funeral,' the lawyer admitted. 'Her husband was the old Lord's farm manager and she's maintained the castle and cared for your grandfather for well over thirty years. My father believes she's been poorly paid and overworked—very overworked as the old Lord wouldn't employ anyone else. My father believes she stayed because she was expecting some sort of acknowledgement in the will. She knew the castle was to be left to you, My Lord,' he told Finn. 'But it would have been a shock to hear the remainder was to be left to a granddaughter he'd never seen.'

He hesitated then but finally decided to tell it how it was. 'The old Lord wasn't without his faults,' he told them. 'My father said he wouldn't be surprised if he'd made promises to her that he had no intention of keeping. It gave him cheap labour.'

'And now?' Jo asked in a small voice.

'Her husband died last year. The place is without a farm manager and I wouldn't imagine you'll be having ongoing use for a housekeeper. She'll move out as soon as you wish.'

'But she's been left nothing? No pension? Nothing at all?'

'No.'

'That sucks,' Jo said.

'She doesn't like you,' Finn reminded her, frowning.

'It still sucks. She took care of my grandfather?'

'I believe she did,' the lawyer told her. 'For the last couple of months he was bedbound and she nursed him.'

'And she hated my mother, so she can't be all bad. How much would a cottage in the village and a modest pension be? Actually, you don't even need to tell me. Work it out and take it from my half.'

'She burned your dinner!' Finn expostulated.

Jo shrugged and smiled. 'If I thought she'd just inherited my home I might have burned her dinner.'

'She called your mother a drug addict.'

'My mother *was* a drug addict.' She turned back to the lawyer. 'Can you set it up?'

'Of course, but…'

'Take it from both sides,' Finn growled. 'We both have a responsibility towards her and we can afford to be generous. A decent house and a decent pension.'

'There's no need…' Jo started.

'We're in this together,' he said.

The lawyer nodded. 'It seems reasonable. A pension

and a local cottage for Mrs O'Reilly will scarcely dent what you'll inherit.

'Well, then,' he said, moving on. 'Irish castles with a history as long as this sell for a premium to overseas buyers looking for prestige. If you go through the place and see if there's anything you wish to keep, we can include everything else with the sale. I'd imagine you don't wish to stay here any longer than you need. Would a week to sort things out be enough? Make a list of anything you wish to keep, and then I'll come back with staff and start cataloguing. You could both have your inheritance by Christmas.' He smiled again at Jo. 'A Harley for Christmas?'

'That'd be…good,' Jo said with a sideways look at Finn. How did he feel about this? She felt completely thrown.

'Excellent,' Finn said and she thought he felt the same as she did.

How did she know? She didn't, she conceded. She was guessing. She was thinking she knew this man, but on what evidence?

'Jo, let me know when you've finished up here,' the lawyer was saying. 'We can advance you money against the estate so you can stay somewhere decent in Dublin. I can lend you one of my bikes. I could take you for a ride up to Wicklow, show you the sights. Take you somewhere decent for dinner.'

'Thanks,' she said, though she wasn't all that sure she wanted to go anywhere with this man, with his slick looks and his slick words.

'And you'll be imagining all the cows you can buy,' he said jovially to Finn and she saw Finn's lips twitch again.

'Eh, that'd be grand. Cows… I could do with a few of those. I might need to buy myself a new bucket and milking stool to match.'

He was laughing but the lawyer didn't get it. He was

moving on. 'Welcome to your new life of wealth,' he told them. 'Now, are you both sure about Mrs O'Reilly?'

'Yes.' They spoke together, and Finn's smile deepened. 'It's a good idea of Jo's.'

'Well, I may just pop into the kitchen and tell her,' the lawyer told them. 'I know she's been upset and, to be honest, my father was upset on her behalf.'

'But you didn't think to tell us earlier?' Finn demanded.

'It's not my business.' He shrugged. 'What you do with your money is very much your own business. You can buy as many milking stools as you want. After the castle's sold I expect I won't see you again. Unless…' He smiled suggestively at Jo. 'Unless you decide to spend some time in Dublin.'

'I won't,' Jo said shortly and he nodded.

'That's fine. Then we'll sell this castle and be done with it.'

CHAPTER FOUR

WHAT HAD JUST happened seemed too big to get their heads around. They farewelled the lawyer. They looked at each other.

'How many people do you employ on your farm?' Jo asked and he smiled. He'd enjoyed the lawyer's attempt at condescension and he liked that Jo had too.

'Ten, at last count.'

'That's a lot of buckets.'

'It is and all.'

'Family?' she asked.

'My parents are dead and my brothers have long since left.' He could tell her about Maeve, he thought, but then—why should he? Maeve was no longer part of his life.

'So there's just you and a huge farm.'

'Yes.'

'But you're not wealthy enough to buy me out?'

He grinned at that. 'Well, no,' he said apologetically. 'Didn't you hear our lawyer? He already has it figured.'

He tried smiling again, liking the closeness it gave them, but Jo had closed her eyes. She looked totally blown away.

'I need a walk.'

And he knew she meant by herself. He knew it because he needed the same. He needed space to get his head around the enormity of what had just happened. So he nodded and headed outside, across the castle grounds, past the dilapidated ha-ha dividing what had once been gardens from the fields beyond, and then to the rough ground where sheep grazed contentedly in the spring sunshine.

The lawyer's visit had thrown him more than he cared to admit, and it had thrown him for two reasons.

One was the sheer measure of the wealth he stood to inherit.

The second was Jo. Her reaction to Mrs O'Reilly's dilemma had blown him away. Her generosity…

Also the smarmy lawyer's attempt to flirt with her. Finn might have reacted outwardly to the lawyer with humour but inwardly…

Yeah, inwardly he'd have liked to take that smirk off the guy's face and he wouldn't have minded how he did it.

Which was dumb. Jo was a good-looking woman. It was only natural that the lawyer had noticed and what happened between them was nothing to do with Finn.

So focus on the farm, he told himself, but he had to force himself to do it.

Sheep.

The sheep looked scrawny. How much had their feed been supplemented during the winter? he asked himself, pushing all thoughts of Jo stubbornly aside, and by the time he'd walked to the outer reaches of the property he'd decided: not at all.

The sheep were decent stock but neglected. Yes, they'd been shorn but that seemed to be the extent of animal husbandry on the place. There were rams running with the ewes and the rams didn't look impressive. It seemed no one really cared about the outcome.

There were a couple of cows in a small field near the road. One looked heavily in calf. House cows? He couldn't imagine Mrs O'Reilly adding milking to her duties and both were dry. The cows looked as scrawny as the landscape.

Back home in Kilkenny, the grass was shooting with

its spring growth. The grass here looked starved of nutrients. It'd need rotation and fertiliser to keep these fields productive and it looked as if nothing had been done to them for a very long time.

He kept walking, over the remains of ancient drainage, long blocked.

Would some American or Middle Eastern squillionaire pay big bucks for this place? He guessed they would. They'd buy the history and the prestige and wouldn't give a toss about drainage.

And it wasn't their place. It was…*his*?

It wasn't, but suddenly that was the way he felt.

This was nuts. How could he feel this way about a place he hadn't seen before yesterday?

He had his own farm and he loved it. His brothers had grown and moved on but he'd stayed. He loved the land. He was good at farming and the farm had prospered in his care. He'd pushed boundaries. He'd built it into an excellent commercial success.

But this… Castle Glenconaill… He turned to look at its vast silhouette against the mountains and, for some reason, it almost felt as if it was part of him. His grandfather must have talked of it, he thought, or his father. He couldn't remember, but the familiarity seemed bone-deep.

He turned again to look out over the land. What a challenge.

To take and to hold…

The family creed seemed wrong, he decided, but *To hold and to honour…* That seemed right. To take this place and hold its history, to honour the land, to make this place once more a proud part of Irish heritage… If he could do that…

What was he thinking? He'd inherited jointly with a woman from Australia. Jo had no reason to love this place and every reason to hate it. And the lawyer was right; even with the wealth he now possessed, on his own he had no hope of keeping it. To try would be fantasy, doomed to disaster from the start.

'So sell it and get over it,' he told himself, but the ache to restore this place, to do something, was almost overwhelming.

He turned back to the castle but paused at the ha-ha. The beautifully crafted stone wall formed a divide so stock could be kept from the gardens without anything as crass as a fence interfering with the view from the castle windows. But in places the wall was starting to crumble. He looked at it for a long moment and then he couldn't resist. Stones had fallen. They were just…there.

He knelt and started fitting stone to stone.

He started to build.

To hold and to honour… He couldn't hold, he decided, but, for the time he was here, he would do this place honour.

Jo thought about heading outside but Finn had gone that way and she knew he'd want to be alone. There was silence from the kitchen. Mrs O'Reilly was either fainting from shock or trying to decide whether she could tell them they could shove their offer. Either way, maybe she needed space too.

Jo started up towards her bedroom and then, on impulse, turned left at the foot of the staircase instead of going up.

Two massive doors led to what looked like an ancient baronial hall. She pushed the doors open and stopped dead.

The hall looked as if it hadn't been used for years. Oversized furniture was draped with dustsheets and the dustsheets themselves were dusty. Massive beams ran the length of the hall, and up in the vaulted ceiling hung generations of spider webs. The place was cold and dank and… amazing.

'Like something out of Dickens,' she said out loud and her voice echoed up and up. She thought suddenly of Miss Havisham sitting alone in the ruins of her bridal finery and found herself grinning.

She could rent this place out for Halloween parties. She could…

Sell it and go home.

Home? There was that word again.

And then her attention was caught. On the walls…tapestries.

Lots of tapestries.

When she'd first entered she'd thought they were paintings but now, making her way cautiously around the edges of the hall, she could make out scores of needlework artworks. Some were small. Some were enormous.

They were almost all dulled, matted with what must have been smoke from the massive blackened fireplace at the end of the room. Some were frayed and damaged. All were amazing.

She fingered the closest and she was scarcely breathing.

It looked like…life in the castle? She recognised the rooms, the buildings. It was as if whoever had done the tapestries had set themselves the task of recording everyday life in the castle. Hunting. Formal meals with scores of overdressed guests. Children at play. Dogs…

She walked slowly round the room and thought, *These aren't from one artist and they're not from one era.*

They were the recording of families long gone.

Her family? Her ancestors?

It shouldn't make a difference but suddenly it did. She hated that they were fading, splitting, dying.

Her history…

And Finn's, she thought suddenly. In her great-great-grandfather's era, they shared a heritage.

Maybe she could take them back to Sydney and restore them.

Why? They weren't hers. They'd be bought by whoever bought this castle.

They wouldn't be her ancestors, or Finn's ancestors. They'd belong to the highest bidder.

Maybe she could keep them.

But Jo didn't keep *stuff*, and that was all these were, she reminded herself. *Stuff*. But still… She'd restored a few tapestries in the past and she wasn't bad at it. She knew how to do at least step one.

As she'd crossed the boundaries of the castle last night she'd crossed a creek. No, a stream, she corrected herself. Surely in Ireland they had streams. Or burns? She'd have to ask someone.

But meanwhile it was spring, and the mountains above Castle Glenconaill must surely have been snow-covered in winter. The stream below the castle seemed to be running full and free. Clear, running water was the best way she knew to get soot and stains from tapestries, plumping up the threads in the process.

She could try with a small one, she decided, as her fingers started to itch. She'd start with one of the hunting scenes, a brace of pheasants without people or place. That way, if she hurt it, it wouldn't matter. She could start with that one and…

And nothing. She was going home. Well, back to Australia.

Yeah, she was, but first she was getting excited. First, she was about to clean a tapestry.

Finn had placed a dozen rocks back in their rightful position and was feeling vaguely pleased with himself. He'd decided he should return to the castle to see what Jo was doing—after all, they were here for a purpose and repairing rock walls wasn't that purpose—and now here she was, out in the middle of the stream that meandered along the edge of the ha-ha.

What was she doing? Those rocks were slippery. Any minute now she'd fall and get a dunking.

'Hey!'

She looked up and wobbled, but she didn't fall. She gave him a brief wave and kept on doing what she was doing.

Intrigued, he headed over to see.

She was messing with something under water.

The water would be freezing. She had the sleeves of her sweater pulled up and she'd hauled off her shoes. She was knee-deep in water.

'What's wrong?'

She kept concentrating, her back to him, stooped, as if adjusting something under water. He stood and waited, more and more intrigued, until finally she straightened and started her unsteady way back to the shore.

'Done.'

He could see green slime attached to the rocks underneath the surface. She was stepping gingerly from rock to rock but even the ones above the surface would be treacherous.

He took a couple of steps out to help her—and slipped himself, dunking his left foot up to his ankle.

He swore.

'Whoops,' Jo said and he glanced up at her and she was grinning. 'Uh oh. I'm sorry. I'd carry you if I could but I suspect you're a bit heavy.'

'What on earth are you doing?'

'Heading back to the castle. All dry.' She reached the shore, jumping nimbly from the last rock, then turned and proffered a hand to him. 'Can I help?'

'No,' he said, revolted, and her smile widened.

'How sexist is that? Honestly...'

'I was trying to help.'

'There's been a bit of that about,' she said. 'It's not that I don't appreciate it; it's just that I hardly ever need it. Bogs excepted.'

'What were you doing?' He hauled himself out of the water to the dry bank and surveyed his leg in disgust. His boot would take ages to dry. Jo, on the other hand, was drying her feet with a sock and tugging her trainers back on. All dry.

'Washing tapestries,' she told him and he forgot about his boots.

'Tapestries...?'

'The hall's full of them. You should see. They're awesome. But they're filthy and most of them need work. I've brought one of the small ones here to try cleaning.'

'You don't think,' he asked cautiously, 'that soap and water might be more civilised?'

'Possibly. But not nearly as much fun.'

'Fun...' He stared at his leg and she followed his gaze and chuckled.

'Okay, fun for me, not for you. I'm obviously better at creeks than you are.'

'Creeks...'

'Streams. Brooks. What else do you call them? Whatever, they'll act just the same as home.' She gestured to the surrounding hills, rolling away to the mountains in the background. 'Spring's the best time. The water's pouring down from the hills; it's running fast and clean and it'll wash through tapestries in a way nothing else can, unless I'm prepared to waste a day's running water in the castle. Even then, I wouldn't get an even wash.'

'So you just lie it in the stream.' He could see it now, a

square of canvas, stretched underwater and weighed down by rocks at the edges.

'The running water removes dust, soot, smoke and any burnt wool or silk. It's the best way. Some people prefer modern cleaning methods, but in my experience they can grey the colours. And, as well, this way the fibres get rehydrated. They plump up almost as fat as the day they were stitched.'

'You're intending to leave it here?'

'I'll bring it in tonight. You needn't worry; I'm not about to risk a cow fording the stream and sticking a hoof through it.'

'And then what will you do?' he asked, fascinated.

'Let it dry and fix it, of course. This one's not bad. It has a couple of broken relays and warps but nothing too serious. I'll see how it comes up after cleaning but I imagine I'll get it done before I leave. How's the stone wall going?'

To say he was dumbfounded would be an understatement. This woman was an enigma. Part of her came across tough; another part was so fragile he knew she could break. She was wary, she seemed almost fey, and here she was calmly setting about restoring tapestries as if she knew exactly what she was talking about.

He was sure she did.

'You saw me working?' he managed and she nodded.

'I walked past and you didn't see me. It feels good, doesn't it, working on something you love. So…half a yard of wall fixed, three or four hundred yards to go? Reckon you'll be finished in a week?' She clambered nimbly up the bank and turned and offered a hand. 'Need a pull?'

'No,' he said, and she grinned and withdrew her hand.

And he missed it. He should have just taken it. If he had she would have tugged and he would have ended up right beside her. Really close.

But she was smiling and turning to head back to the castle and it was dumb to feel a sense of opportunity lost.

What was he thinking? Life was complicated enough without feeling…what he was feeling…

And that's enough of that, he told himself soundly. It behoved a man to take a deep breath and get himself together. This woman was…complicated, and hadn't he decided on the safe option in life? His brothers had all walked off the land to make their fortunes and they'd done well. But Finn… He'd stayed and he'd worked the land he'd inherited. He'd aimed for a good farm on fertile land. A steady income. A steady woman?

Like Maeve. That was a joke. He'd thought his dreams were her dreams. He'd known her since childhood and yet it seemed he hadn't known her at all.

So how could he think he knew Jo after less than a day?

And why was he wondering how he could know her better?

'So do you intend to keep the suits of armour?' Jo asked and he struggled to haul his thoughts back to here and now. Though actually they were here and now. They were centred on a slip of a girl in a bright crimson sweater and jeans and stained trainers.

If Maeve had come to the castle with him, she'd have spent a week shopping for clothes in preparation.

But his relationship with Maeve was long over—apart from the minor complication that she wouldn't tell her father.

The sun was on his face. Jo was by his side, matching his stride even though her legs were six inches shorter than his. She looked bright and interested and free.

Of course she was free. She was discussing the fate of two suits of armour before she climbed back on her bike and headed back to Australia.

'I can't see them back on the farm,' he admitted.

'Your farm is somewhere near a place called Kilkenny,' she said. 'So where is that? You head down to Tipperary and turn…?'

'North-east. I don't go that way. But how do you know of Tipperary?'

'I looked it up on the map when I knew I was coming. There's a song… *It's a Long Way to Tipperary.* I figured that's where I was coming. A long way. And you farm cows and sheep?'

'The dairy's profitable but I'd like to get into sheep.'

'It's a big farm?'

'Compared to Australian land holdings, no. But it's very profitable.'

'And you love it.'

Did he love it?

As a kid he certainly had, when the place was rundown, when everywhere he'd looked there'd been challenges. But now the farm was doing well and promising to do better. With the money from the castle he could buy properties to the north.

If he wanted to.

'It's a great place,' he said mildly. 'How about you? Do you work at what you love?'

'I work to fund what I love.'

'Which is?'

'Tapestry and motorbikes.'

'Tell me about tapestry,' he said, and she looked a bit defensive.

'I didn't just look up the Internet and decide to restore from Internet Lesson 101. I've been playing with tapestries for years.'

'Why?' It seemed so unlikely…

'When I was about ten my then foster mother gave me a tapestry do-it-yourself kit. It was a canvas with a painting of a cat and instructions and the threads to complete it. I learned the basics on that cat, but when I finished I thought the whiskers looked contrived. He also looked smug so I ended up unpicking him a bit and fiddling. It started me drawing my own pictures. It works for me. It makes me feel…settled.'

'So what do you do the rest of the time?'

'I make coffee. Well. I can also wait tables with the best of them. It's a skill that sees me in constant work.'

'You wouldn't rather work with tapestries?'

'That'd involve training to be let near the decent ones, and training's out of my reach.'

'Even now you have a massive inheritance?'

She paused as if the question took concentration. She stared at her feet and then turned and gazed out at the grounds, to the mountains beyond.

'I don't know,' she admitted. 'I like café work. I like busy. It's kind of like a family.'

'Do they know where you are?'

'Who? The people I work with?'

'Yes.'

'Do you mean if I'd sunk in a bog yesterday would they have cared or even known?' She shrugged. 'Nope. That's not what I mean by family. I pretty much quit work to come here. Someone's filling in for me now, but I'll probably just get another job when I go back. I don't stay in the same place for long.'

'So when you said family…'

'I meant people around me. It's all I want. Cheerful company and decent coffee.'

'And you're stuck here with me and Mrs O'Reilly and coffee that tastes like mud.'

'You noticed,' she said approvingly. 'That's a start.'

'A start of what?' he asked mildly and she glanced sharply up at him as if his question had shocked her. Maybe it had. He'd surprised himself—it wasn't a question he'd meant to ask and he wasn't sure what exactly he was asking.

But the question hung.

'I guess the start of nothing,' she said at last with a shrug that was meant to be casual but didn't quite come off. 'I can cope with mud coffee for a week.'

'All we need to do is figure what we want to keep.'

'I live out of a suitcase. I can't keep anything.' She said it almost with defiance.

'And the armour wouldn't look good in a nice modern bungalow.'

'Is that what your farmhouse is?'

'It is.' The cottage he'd grown up in had long since deteriorated past repair. He'd built a large functional bungalow.

It had a great kitchen table. The rest…yeah, it was functional.

'I saw you living somewhere historic,' Jo said. 'Thatch maybe.'

'Thatch has rats.'

She looked up towards the castle ramparts. 'What about battlements? Do battlements have rats?'

'Not so much.' He grinned. 'Irish battlements are possibly a bit cold even for the toughest rat.'

'What about you, Lord Conaill? Too cold for you?'

'I'm not Lord Conaill.'

'All the tapestries in the great hall…they're mostly from a time before your side of the family split. This is your history too.'

'I don't feel like Lord Conaill.'

'No, but you look like him. Go in and check the tapestries. You have the same aristocratic nose.'

He put his hand on his nose. 'Really?'

'Yep. As opposed to mine. Mine's snub with freckles, not an aristocratic line anywhere.'

And he looked at her freckles and thought…it might not be the Conaill nose but it was definitely cute.

He could just…

Not. How inappropriate was it to want to reach out and touch a nose? To trace the line of those cheekbones.

To touch.

He knew enough about this woman to expect a pretty firm reaction. Besides, the urge was ridiculous. Wasn't it?

'I reckon your claim to the castle's a lot stronger than mine,' she was saying and he had to force his attention from her very cute nose to what they were talking about.

They'd reached the forecourt. He turned and faced outward, across the vast sweep of Glenconaill to the mountains beyond. It was easier talking about abstracts when he wasn't looking at the reality of her nose. And the rest of her.

'Your grandfather left the castle to two strangers,' he told her. 'We're both feeling as if we have no right to be here, and yet he knew I was to inherit the title. He came to my farm six months ago and barked the information at me, yet there was never an invitation to come here. And you were his granddaughter and he didn't know you either. He knew we'd stand here one day, but he made no push to make us feel we belong. Yet we do belong.'

'You feel that?'

'I don't know,' he said slowly. 'It's just…walking across the lands today, looking at the sheep, at the ruined walls, at the mess this farmland has become, it seems a crime that no push was made…'

'To love it?' She nodded. 'I was thinking that. The tapestries… A whole family history left to disintegrate.' She shrugged. 'But we can't.'

'I guess not.' He gazed outward for a long moment, as though soaking in something he needed to hold to. 'Of course you're right.'

'If he'd left it all to you, you could have,' Jo said and he shrugged again.

'Become a Lord in fact? Buy myself ermine robes and employ a valet?'

'Fix a few stone walls?'

'That's more tempting,' he said and then he grinned. 'So your existence has saved me from a life of chipping at cope stones. Thank you, Jo. Now, shall we find out if Mrs O'Reilly intends to feed us?'

And Jo thought…it felt odd to walk towards Castle Glenconaill with this man by her side.

But somehow, weirdly, it felt right.

'What are you working on at the moment?' Finn asked and she was startled back to the here and now.

'What?'

'You're carrying sewing needles. I'm not a great mind, but it does tell me there's likely to be sewing attached. Or do you bring them on the off chance you need to darn socks?'

'No, I…'

'Make tapestries? On the plane? Do you have a current project and, if so, can I see?'

She stared up at him and then stared down at her feet. And his feet. One of his boots was dripping mud.

Strangely, it made him seem closer. More human.

She didn't show people her work, so why did she have a sudden urge to say…?

'Okay.'

'Okay?' he said cautiously.

'It's not pretty. And it's not finished. But if you'd really like to see…'

'Now?'

'When your foot's dry.'

'Why not with a wet foot?'

'My tapestry demands respect.'

He grinned. 'There speaks the lady of the castle.'

'I'm not,' she said. 'But my tapestry's up there with anything the women of this castle have done.' She smiled then, one of her rare smiles that lit her face, that made her seem…

Intriguing? No, he was already intrigued, he conceded.

Desirable?

Definitely.

'Are you sure?' she asked and he caught himself. He'd known this woman for how long?

'I'm very sure,' he told her. 'And, lady of the castle or not, your tapestry's not the only thing to deserve respect. I will take my boot off for you.'

'Gee, thanks,' she told him. 'Fifteen minutes. My bedroom. See you there.'

And she took off, running across the forecourt like a kid without a trouble in the world. She looked…free.

She looked beautiful.

Fifteen minutes with his boot off. A man had to get moving.

The tapestry was rolled and wrapped in the base of her kitbag. He watched as she delved into what looked to be the most practical woman's pack he'd ever seen. There were no gorgeous gowns or frilly lingerie here—just bike gear and jeans and T-shirts and sweaters. He thought briefly of the lawyer and his invitation to dinner in Dublin and found himself smiling.

Jo glanced up. 'What?'

'Is this why you said no to our lawyer's invite? I can't see a single little black dress.'

'I don't have a use for 'em,' she said curtly.

'You know, there's a costume gallery here,' he said and she stared.

'A costume gallery?'

'A store of the very best of what the Conaills have worn for every grand event in their history. Someone in our past has decided that clothes need to be kept as well as paintings. I found the storeroom last night. Full of mothballs and gold embroidery. So if you need to dress up…'

She stared at him for a long moment, as if she was almost tempted—and then she gave a rueful smile and shook her head and tugged out the roll. 'I can't see me going out to dinner with our lawyer in gold embroidery. Can you? But if you want to see this…' She tossed the roll on the bed and it started to uncurl on its own.

Fascinated, he leaned over and twitched the end so the whole thing unrolled onto the white coverlet.

And it was as much as he could do not to gasp.

This room could almost be a servant's room, it was so bare. It was painted white, with a faded white coverlet on the bed. There were two dingy paintings on the wall, not very good, scenes of the local mountains. They looked as if they'd been painted by a long ago Conaill, with visions of artistic ability not quite managed.

But there was nothing 'not quite managed' about the tapestry on the bed. Quite simply, it lit the room.

It was like nothing he'd ever seen before. It was colour upon colour upon colour.

It was fire.

Did it depict Australia's Outback? Maybe, he thought, but if so it must be an evocation of what that could be like. This was ochre-red country, wide skies and slashes of river. There were wind-bent eucalypts with flocks of white cockatoos screeching from tree to tree… There were so many details.

And yet not. At first he could only see what looked like burning: flames with colour streaking through, heat, dry. And then he looked closer and it coalesced into its separate parts without ever losing the sense of its whole.

The thing was big, covering half the small bed, and it wasn't finished. He could see bare patches with only vague pencil tracing on the canvas, but he knew instinctively that these pencil marks were ideas only, that they could change.

For this was no paint by numbers picture. This was...

Breathtaking.

'This should be over the mantel in the great hall,' he breathed and she glanced up at him, coloured and then bit her lip and shook her head.

'Nope.'

'What do you do with them?'

'Give them to people I like. You can have this if you want. You pulled me out of a bog.'

And once more she'd taken his breath away.

'You just...give them away?'

'What else would I do with them?'

He was still looking at the canvas, seeing new images every time he looked. There were depths and depths and depths. 'Keep them,' he said softly. 'Make them into an exhibition.'

'I don't keep stuff.'

He hauled his attention from the canvas and stared at her. 'Nothing?'

'Well, maybe my bike.'

'Where do you live?'

'Where I can rent a room with good light for sewing. And where my sound system doesn't cause a problem. I like my music loud.' She shrugged. 'So there's another thing I own—a great speaker system to plug into my phone. Oh, and toothbrushes and stuff.'

'I don't get it.' He thought suddenly of his childhood, of his mother weeping because she'd dropped a plate belonging to her own mother. There'd been tears for a ceramic thing. And yet...his focus was drawn again to the tapestry. That Jo could work so hard for this, put so much of herself in it and then give it away...

'You reckon I need a shrink because I don't own stuff?' she asked and he shook his head.

'No. Though I guess…'

'I did see someone once,' she interrupted. 'When I was fifteen. I was a bit…wild. I got sent to a home for troublesome adolescents and they gave me a few sessions with a psychoanalyst. She hauled out a memory of me at eight, being moved on from a foster home. There was a fire engine I played with. I'd been there a couple of years so I guess I thought it was mine. When I went to pack, my foster mum told me it was a foster kid toy and I couldn't take it. The shrink told me it was significant, but I don't need a fire engine now. I don't need anything.'

He cringed for her. She'd said it blithely, as if it was no big deal, but he knew the shrink was right. This woman was wounded. 'Jo, the money we're both inheriting will give you security,' he said gently. 'No one can take your fire engine now.'

'I'm over wanting fire engines.'

'Really?'

And she managed a smile at that. 'Well, if it was a truly excellent fire engine…'

'You'd consider?'

'I might,' she told him. 'Though I might have to get myself a Harley with a trailer to carry it. Do Harleys come with trailers? I can't see it. Meanwhile, is it lunchtime?'

He checked his watch. 'Past. Uh oh. We need to face Mrs O'Reilly. Jo, you've been more than generous. You don't have to face her.'

'I do,' she said bluntly. 'I don't run away. It's not my style.'

Mrs O'Reilly had made them lunch but Finn wasn't sure how she'd done it. Her swollen face said she'd been weeping for hours.

She placed shepherd's pie in front of them and stood back, tried to speak and failed.

'I can't...' she managed.

'Mrs O'Reilly, there's no need to say a thing.' Jo reached for the pie and ladled a generous helping onto her plate. 'Not when you've made me pie. But I do need dead horse.'

'Dead horse?' Finn demanded, bemused, and Jo shook her head in exasperation.

'Honestly, don't you guys know anything? First, dead horse is Australian for sauce and second, shepherd's pie without sauce is like serving fish without chips. Pie and sauce, fish and chips, roast beef with Yorkshire pud... What sort of legacy are you leaving for future generations if you don't know that?'

He grinned and Mrs O'Reilly sniffed and sniffed again and then beetled for the kitchen. She returned with four different sauce bottles.

Jo checked them out and discarded three with disgust.

'There's only one. Tomato sauce, pure, unadulterated. Anything else is a travesty. Thank you, Mrs O'Reilly, this is wonderful.'

'It's not,' the woman stammered. 'I was cruel to you.'

'I've done some research into my mother over the years,' Jo said, concentrating on drawing wiggly lines of sauce across her pie. 'She doesn't seem like she was good to anyone. She wasn't even good to me and I was her daughter. I can only imagine what sort of demanding princess she was when she was living here. And Grandpa didn't leave you provided for after all those years of service from you and your husband. I'd have been mean to me if I were you too.'

'I made you sleep in a single bed!'

'Well, that is a crime.' She was chatting to Mrs O'Reilly as if she were talking of tomorrow's weather, Finn thought. The sauce arranged to her satisfaction, she tackled her pie with gusto.

Mrs O'Reilly was staring at her as if she'd just landed from another planet, and Finn was feeling pretty much the same.

'A single bed's fine by me,' she said between mouthfuls. 'As is this pie. Yum. Last night's burned beef, though…that needs compensation. Will you stay on while we're here? You could make us more. Or would you prefer to go? Finn and I can cope on our own. I hope the lawyer has explained what you do from now on is your own choice.'

'He has.' She grabbed her handkerchief and blew her nose with gusto. 'Of course…of course I'll stay while you need me but now… I can have my own house. My own home.'

'Excellent,' Jo told her. 'If that's what you want, then go for it.'

'I don't deserve it.'

'Hey, after so many years of service, one burned dinner shouldn't make a difference, and life's never about what we deserve. I'm just pleased Finn and I can administer a tiny bit of justice in a world that's usually pretty much unfair. Oh, and the calendars in the kitchen…you like cats?'

'I…yes.'

'Why don't you have one?'

'Your grandfather hated them.'

'I don't hate them. Do you hate them, Finn?'

'No.'

'There you go,' Jo said, beaming. 'Find yourself a kitten. Now, if you want. And don't buy a cottage where you can't keep one.'

She was amazing, Finn thought, staring at her in silence. This woman was…stunning.

But Jo had moved on. 'Go for it,' she said, ladling more pie onto her fork. 'But no more talking. This pie deserves all my attention.'

* * *

They finished their pie in silence, then polished off apple tart and coffee without saying another word.

There didn't seem any need to speak. Or maybe there was, but things were too enormous to be spoken of.

As Mrs O'Reilly bustled away with the dishes, Jo felt almost dismayed. Washing up last night with Finn had been a tiny piece of normality. Now there wasn't even washing up to fall back on.

'I guess we'd better get started,' Finn said at last.

'Doing what?'

'Sorting?'

'What do we need to sort?' She gazed around the ornate dining room, at the myriad ornaments, pictures, side tables, vases, stuff. 'I guess lots of stuff might go to museums. You might want to keep some. I don't need it.'

'It's your heritage.'

'Stuff isn't heritage. I might take photographs of the tapestries,' she conceded. 'Some of them are old enough to be in a museum too.'

'Show me,' he said and that was the next few minutes sorted. So she walked him through the baronial hall, seeing the history of the Conaills spread out before her.

'It seems a shame to break up the collection,' Finn said at last. He'd hardly spoken as they'd walked through.

'Like breaking up a family.' Jo shrugged. 'People do it all the time. If it's no use to you, move on.'

'You really don't care?'

She gazed around at the vast palette of family life spread before her. Her family? No. Her mother had been the means to her existence, nothing more, and her grandfather hadn't given a toss about her.

'I might have cared if this had been my family,' she told him. 'But the Conaills were the reason I couldn't have a family. It's hardly fair to expect me to honour them now.'

'Yet you'd love to restore the tapestries.'

'They're amazing.' She crossed to a picture of a family group. 'I've been figuring out time frames, and I think this could be the great-great-grandpa we share. Look at Great-Great-Grandma. She looks a tyrant.'

'You don't want to keep her?'

'Definitely not. How about you?' she asked. 'Are you into family memorabilia?'

'I have a house full of memorabilia. My parents threw nothing out. And my brothers live very modern lives. I can't see any of this stuff fitting into their homes. I'll ask them but I know what their answers will be. You really want nothing but the money?'

'I wanted something a long time ago,' she told him. They were standing side by side, looking at the picture of their mutual forebears. 'You have no idea how much I wanted. But now…it's too late. It even seems wrong taking the money. I'm not part of this family.'

'Hey, we are sort of cousins.' And, before she knew what he intended, he'd put an arm around her waist and gave her a gentle hug. 'I'm happy to own you.'

'I don't…' The feel of his arm was totally disconcerting. 'I don't think I want to be owned.' And this was a normal hug, she told herself. A cousinly hug. There was no call to haul herself back in fright. She forced herself to stand still.

'Not by this great-great-grandma,' he conceded. 'She looks a dragon.' But his arm was still around her waist, and it was hard to concentrate on what he was saying. It was really hard. 'But you need to belong somewhere. There's a tapestry somewhere with your future on it.'

'I'm sure there's not. Not if it has grandmas and grandpas and kids and dogs.' Enough. She tugged away because it had to be just a cousinly hug; she wasn't used to hugs and she didn't need it. She didn't! 'I'm not standing still long enough to be framed.'

'That's a shame,' he told her, and something in the timbre of his voice made her feel…odd. 'Because I suspect you're worth all this bunch put together.'

'That's kissing the Blarney Stone.'

He shrugged and smiled and when he smiled she wanted that hug back. Badly.

'I'm not one for saying what I don't mean, Jo Conaill,' he told her. 'You're an amazing woman.'

'D…don't,' she stammered. For some reason the hug had left her discombobulated. 'We're here to sort this stuff. Let's start now.'

And then leave, she told herself. The way she was feeling… The way she was feeling was starting to scare her.

The size of the place, the mass of furnishings, the store of amazing clothing any museum would kill for—the entire history of the castle was mind-blowing. It was almost enough to make her forget how weird Finn's hug made her feel. But there was work to be done. Figuring out the scale of their inheritance would take days.

Underground there were cellars—old dungeons?—and storerooms. Upstairs were 'living' rooms, apartment-sized chambers filled with dust-sheeted furniture. Above them were the bedrooms and up a further flight of stairs were the servants' quarters, rooms sparsely furnished with an iron cot and dresser.

Over the next couple of days they moved slowly through the place, sorting what there was. Most things would go straight to the auction rooms—almost all of it—but, by mutual consent, they decided to catalogue the things that seemed important. Detailed cataloguing could be done later by the auctioneers but somehow it seemed wrong to sell everything without acknowledging its existence. So they moved from room to room, taking notes, and she put the memory of the hug aside.

Though she had to acknowledge that she was grateful for his company. If she'd had to face this alone…

This place seemed full of ghosts who'd never wanted her, she thought. The costume store on its own was enough to repel her. All these clothes, worn by people who would never have accepted her. She was illegitimate, despised, discarded. She had no place here, and Finn must feel the same. Regardless of his inherited title, he still must feel the poor relation.

And he'd never fit in one of these cots, she thought as they reached the servants' quarters. She couldn't help glancing up at him as he opened the door on a third identical bedroom. He was big. Very big.

'It'd have to be a bleak famine before I'd fit in that bed,' he declared. He glanced down at the rough map drawn for them by Mrs O'Reilly. 'Now the nursery.'

The room they entered next was huge, set up as a schoolroom as well as a nursery. The place was full of musty furniture, with desks and a blackboard, but schooling seemed to have been a secondary consideration.

There were toys everywhere, stuffed animals of every description, building blocks, doll's houses, spinning tops, dolls large and small, some as much as three feet high. All pointing to indulged childhoods.

And then there was the rocking horse.

It stood centre stage in the schoolroom, set on its own dais. It was as large as a miniature pony, crafted with care and, unlike most other things in the nursery, it was maintained in pristine condition.

It had a glossy black coat, made, surely, with real horse hide. Its saddle was embellished with gold and crimson, as were the bridle and stirrups. Its ears were flattened and its dark glass eyes stared out at the nursery as if to say, *Who Dares Ride Me?*

And all around the walls were photographs and paintings, depicting every child who'd ever sat on this horse, going back maybe two hundred years.

Jo stared at the horse and then started a round of the walls, looking at each child in turn. These were beautifully dressed children. Beautifully cared for. Even in the early photographs, where children were exhorted to be still and serious for the camera or the artist, she could see their excitement. These Conaills were the chosen few.

Jo's mother was the last to be displayed. Taken when she was about ten, she was dressed in pink frills and she was laughing up at the camera. Her face was suffused with pride. *See*, her laugh seemed to say. *This is where I belong.*

But after her…nothing.

'Suggestions as to what we should do with all this?' Finn said behind her, sounding cautious, as if he guessed the well of emotion surging within. 'Auction the lot of them?'

'Where are you?' she demanded in a voice that didn't sound her own.

'Where am I where?'

'In the pictures.'

'You know I don't belong here.'

'No, but your great-great-grandfather…'

'I'm thinking he might be this one,' Finn said, pointing to a portrait of a little boy in smock and pantaloons and the same self-satisfied smirk.

'And his son's next to him. Where's your great-grandfather? My great-grandpa's brother?'

'He was a younger son,' Finn said. 'I guess he didn't get to ride the horse.'

'So he left and had kids who faced the potato famine instead,' Jo whispered. 'Can we burn it?'

'What, the horse?'

'It's nasty.'

Finn stood back and surveyed the horse. It was indeed…

nasty. It looked glossy, black and arrogant. Its eyes were too small. It looked as if it was staring at them with disdain. The poor relations.

'I'm the Lord of Glenconaill,' Finn said mildly. 'I could ride this nag if I wanted.'

'You'd squash it.'

'Then you could take my photograph standing over a squashed stuffed horse. Sort of a last hurrah.'

She tried to smile but she was too angry. Too full of emotion.

'How can one family have four sets of Monopoly?' Finn asked, gazing at the stacks of board games. 'And an Irish family at that? And what were we doing selling Bond Street?'

'They,' she snapped. 'Not we. This is not us.'

'It was our great-great-grandpa.'

'Monopoly wasn't invented then. By the time it was, you were the poor relation.'

'That's right, so I was,' he said cheerfully. 'But you'd have thought they could have shared at least one set of Monopoly.'

'They didn't share. Not this family.' She fell silent, gazing around the room, taking in the piles of…stuff. 'All the time I was growing up,' she whispered. 'These toys were here. Unused. They were left to rot rather than shared. Of all the selfish…' She was shaking, she discovered. Anger that must have been suppressed for years seemed threatening to overwhelm her. 'I hate them,' she managed and she couldn't keep the loathing from her voice. 'I hate it all.'

'Even the dolls?' he asked, startled.

'All of it.'

'They'll sell.'

'I'd rather burn them.'

'What, even the horse?' he asked, startled.

'Everything,' she said and she couldn't keep loathing

from her voice. 'All these toys… All this sense of entitlement… Every child who's sat on this horse, who's played with these toys, has known their place in the world. But not me. Not us. Unless your family wants them, I'd burn the lot.'

'My brothers have all turned into successful businessmen. My nieces and nephews have toys coming out their ears,' Finn said, a smile starting behind his eyes. There was also a tinge of understanding. 'So? A bonfire? Excellent. Let's do it. Help me carry the horse downstairs.'

She stared, shocked. He sounded as if her suggestion was totally reasonable. 'What, now?'

'Why not? What's the use of having a title like mine if I can't use some of the authority that comes with it? Back at my farm the cows won't so much as bow when I walk past. I need to learn to be lordly and this is a start.' He looked at the horse with dislike. 'I think that coat's been slicked with oils anyway. He'll go up like a firecracker.'

'How can we?'

'Never suggest a bonfire if you don't mean it,' he said. 'There's nothing we Lords of Glenconaill like more than a good burning.' He turned and stared around at the assortment of expensive toys designed for favoured children and he grimaced. 'Selling any one of these could have kept a family alive for a month during the famine. If there was a fire engine here I'd say save it but there's not. Our ancestors were clearly people with dubious taste. Off with their heads, I say. Let's do it.'

CHAPTER FIVE

THE NURSERY WAS on the top floor and the stairway was narrow. The horse went first, manoeuvred around the bends with Finn at the head and Jo at the tail. Once downstairs, Finn headed for the stables and came back with crumbling timber while Jo carted more toys.

While they carried the horse down she was still shaking with anger. Her anger carried her through the first few armfuls of assorted toys but as Finn finished creating the bonfire and started helping her carry toys she felt her anger start to dissipate.

He was just too cheerful.

'This teddy looks like he's been in a tug of war or six,' Finn told her, placing the teddy halfway up the pyre. 'It's well time for him to go up in flames.'

It was a scruffy bear, small, rubbed bare in spots, one arm missing. One ear was torn off and his grin was sort of lopsided.

She thought of unknown ancestors hugging this bear. Then she thought of her mother and hardened her heart. 'Yes,' she said shortly and Finn cast her a questioning glance but headed upstairs for another load.

She followed, carting down a giraffe, two decrepit sets of wooden railway tracks and a box of blocks.

The giraffe was lacking a bit of stuffing. He was lopsided.

He was sort of looking at her.

'It's like the French Revolution,' Finn told her, stacking them neatly on his ever-growing pyre. 'All the aristocracy off to the Guillotine. I can just imagine these guys saying, "Let them eat cake".'

But she couldn't. Not quite.

The horse was sitting right on top of the pile, still looking aristocratic and nasty. The teddy was just underneath him. It was an old teddy. No one would want that teddy.

She was vaguely aware of Mrs O'Reilly watching from the kitchen window. She looked bemused. She wasn't saying anything, though.

These toys were theirs now, to do with as they wanted, Jo thought with a sudden stab of clarity. Hers and Finn's. They represented generations of favoured children, but now...were she and Finn the favoured two?

She glanced at Finn, looking for acknowledgement that he was feeling something like she was—anger, resentment, sadness.

Guilt?

All she saw was a guy revelling in the prospect of a truly excellent bonfire. He was doing guy stuff, fiddling with toys so they made a sweeping pyre, putting the most flammable stuff at the bottom, the horse balanced triumphantly at the top.

He was a guy having fun.

'Ready?' he asked and she realised he had matches poised.

'Yes,' she said in a small voice and Finn shook his head.

'You'll have to do better than that. You're the lady of the castle, remember. It's an autocratic "Off with their heads", or the peasants will sense weakness. Strength, My Lady.'

'Off with their heads,' she managed but it was pretty weak.

But still, she'd said it and Finn looked at her for a long

moment, then gave a decisive nod and bent and applied match to kindling.

It took a few moments for the wood to catch. Finn could have put a couple of the more flammable toys at the base, she thought. That would have made it go up faster. Instead he'd left a bare spot so the fire would have to be strongly alight before it reached its target.

The teddy would be one of the first things to catch, she thought. The teddy with the missing ear and no arm. And an eye that needed a stitch to make his smile less wonky.

She could…

No. These were favoured toys of favoured people. They'd belonged to people who'd rejected her. People who'd given her their name but nothing else. People who'd made sure she had nothing, and done it for their own selfish ends.

The teddy… One stitch…

The flames were licking upward.

The giraffe was propped beside the teddy. There was a bit of stuffing oozing out from his neck. She could…

She couldn't. The fire was lit. The thing was done.

'Jo?' Finn was suddenly beside her, his hand on her shoulder, holding her with the faintest of pressure. 'Jo?'

She didn't reply. She didn't take her eyes from the fire.

'You're sure you want to do this?' he asked.

'It's lit.'

'I'm a man who's into insurance,' he said softly and she looked down and saw he was holding a hose.

A hose. To undo what she needed to do.

The teddy…

Even the evil horse…

She couldn't do it. Dammit, she couldn't. She choked back a stupid sob and grabbed for the hose. 'Okay, put it out.'

'You want the fire out?'

'I'll do it.'

'You'll wet the teddy,' he said reproachfully. 'He'll get hypothermia as well as scorched feet. Trust me, if there's one thing I'm good at it's putting out fires.'

And he screwed the nozzle and aimed the hose. The water came out with satisfactory force. The wood under the teddy hissed and sizzled. Flames turned to smoke and then steam.

The teddy was enveloped with smoke but, before she realised what he intended, Finn stomped forward in his heavy boots, aimed the hose downward to protect his feet, then reached up and gathered the unfortunate bear.

And the giraffe.

He played the water for a moment longer until he was sure that no spark remained, then twisted the nozzle to off and turned back to her.

He handed her the teddy.

'Yours,' he said. 'And I know I said I have too much stuff, but I'm thinking I might keep the giraffe. I'll call him Noddy.'

She tried to laugh but it came out sounding a bit too much like a sob. 'N… Noddy. Because…because of his neck?'

'He's lost his stuffing,' Finn said seriously. 'He can't do anything but nod. And Teddy's Loppy because he's lopsided. He looks like he's met the family dog. One side looks chewed.'

'It'd be the castle dog. Not a family dog.'

'Ah, but that's where you're wrong,' he said, softly now, his gaze not leaving her face. As if he knew the tumult of stupid emotions raging within her. 'These people rejected us for all sorts of reasons but somehow they still are family. Our family. Toe-rags most of them, but some will have been decent. Some will have been weak, or vain or silly, and some cruel and thoughtless, but they were who they were. This…' he waved to the heap of toys spared from the flames '…this is just detritus from their passing.'

'Like us.'

'We're not detritus. We're people who make decisions. We're people who've spared a nursery full of toys and now need to think what to do with them.' He looked doubtfully at his lopsided giraffe. 'You did say you could sew.'

'I… I did.'

'Then I'll ask you to fix him so he can sit in my toolshed and watch me do shed stuff. Maybe Loppy can sit on your handlebars and watch you ride.'

'That'd be silly.'

'Silly's better than haunted.'

She stared at the pile of ancient toys, and then she turned and looked up at the castle.

'It's not its fault.'

'It's not even the horse's,' Finn said gently. 'Though I bet he collaborated.'

'He'd probably sell for heaps.'

'He would. I didn't like to say but there's been one like him in the window of the antique shop in the village at home. He has a three hundred pound price tag.'

'Three hundred… You didn't think to mention that when I wanted to burn him?'

'I do like a good bonfire.'

She choked on a bubble of laughter, emotion dissipating, and then she stared at the horse again. Getting sensible. 'We could give him away. To a children's charity or something.'

'Or we could sell him to someone who likes arrogant horses and give the money instead,' Finn told her. 'Think how many bears we could donate with three hundred pounds. Kids need friends, not horses who only associate with the aristocracy.'

There was a long silence. Mrs O'Reilly had disappeared

from her window, no doubt confused by the on-again off-again bonfire. The sun was warm on Jo's face. In the shelter of the ancient outbuildings there wasn't a breath of wind. The stone walls around her were bathed in sunshine, their grey walls softened by hundreds of years of wear, of being the birthplace of hundreds of Conaills, of whom only a few had been born with the privilege of living here.

'I guess we can't burn the whole castle because of one arrogant grandfather and one ditzy mother,' she said at last, and Finn looked thoughtful. Almost regretful.

'We could but we'll need more kindling.'

She chuckled but it came close to being a sob. She was hugging the teddy. Stupidly. She didn't hug teddies. She didn't hug anything.

'I suppose we should get rational,' she managed. 'We could go through, figure what could make money, sell what we can.'

'And make a bonfire at the end?' he asked, still hopefully, and her bubble of laughter stayed. A guy with the prospect of a truly excellent bonfire…

'The sideboards in the main hall are riddled with woodworm,' she told him, striving for sense. 'Mrs O'Reilly told me. They'd burn well.'

'Now you're talking.'

She turned back to the pile of unburned toys and her laughter faded. 'You must think I'm stupid.'

'I'm thinking you're angry,' Finn told her. He paused and then added, 'I'm thinking you have cause.'

'I'm over it.'

'Can you ever be over not being wanted?'

'That's just the trouble,' she said, and she stared up at the horse again because it was easier looking at a horse than looking at Finn. He seemed to see inside her, this man, and to say it was disconcerting would be putting it mildly. 'I *was* wanted. Three separate sets of foster parents wanted to adopt me but the Conaills never let it happen. But I'm a big girl now. I have myself together.'

'And you have Loppy.'

'I'll lose him. I always lose stuff.'

'You don't have to lose stuff. With the money from here you can buy yourself a warehouse and employ a storeman to catalogue every last teddy.' He gestured to the pile. 'You can keep whatever you want.'

'I don't know…what I want.'

'You have time to figure it out.'

'So what about you?' she demanded suddenly. 'What do you want? You're a lord now. If you could…would you stay here?'

'As a lord…' He sounded startled. 'No! But if I had time with these sheep…'

'What would you do with them?' she asked curiously, and he shrugged and turned and looked out towards the distant hills.

'Someone, years ago, put thought and care into these guys' breeding. They're tough, but this flock's different to the sheep that run on the bogs. Their coats are finer. As well, their coats also seem repellent. You put your hand through a fleece and you'll find barely a burr.'

'Could you take some back to your farm? Interbreed?'

'Why would I do that? Our sheep are perfect for the conditions there. These are bred for different conditions. Different challenges.' And he gazed out over the land and she thought he looked…almost hungry.

'You'd like a challenge,' she ventured and he nodded.

'I guess. But this is huge. And Lord of Glenconaill… I'd be ridiculous. Have you seen what the previous lords wore in their portraits?'

She grinned. 'You could ditch the leggings.'

'And the wigs?'

'Hmm.' She looked up at his gorgeous thatch of dark

brown hair, the sun making the copper glints more pronounced, and she appeared to consider. 'You realise not a single ancestor is showing coloured hair. They wore hats or wigs or waited until they'd turned a nice, dignified white.'

'So if I'm attached to my hair I'm doomed to peasantry.'

'I guess.'

'Then peasantry it is,' he said and he smiled and reached out and touched her copper curls. 'I don't mind. I kind of like the company.'

And then silence fell. It was a strange kind of silence, Jo thought. A different silence. As if questions were being asked and answered, and thought about and then asked again.

The last wisps of leftover smoke were wafting upwards into the warm spring sunshine. The castle loomed behind them, vast and brooding, as if a reminder that something immeasurable was connecting them. A shared legacy.

A bond.

This man was her sort-of cousin, Jo thought, but the idea was a vague distraction, unreal. This man was not her family. He was large and male and beautiful. Yet he felt...

He felt unlike any of the guys she'd ever dated. He felt familiar in a sense that didn't make sense.

He felt...terrifying. Jo Conaill was always in control. She'd never gone out with someone who'd shaken that control, but just standing beside him...

'It feels right,' Finn said and she gazed up at him in bewilderment.

'What feels right?'

'I have no idea. To stand here with you?'

'I'm leaving.'

'So am I. We have lives. It's just...for here, for now... it feels okay.' He paused but there was no need for him to continue. She felt it too. This sense of...home.

What was she thinking? Home wasn't here. Home wasn't this man.

'My home's my bike,' she said, out of nowhere, and she said it too sharply, but he nodded as if she'd said something that needed consideration.

'I can see that, though the bike's pretty draughty. And there's no bath for when you fall into bogs.'

'I don't normally fall into bogs.'

'I can see that too. You're very, very careful, despite that bad girl image.'

'I don't have a bad girl image.'

'Leathers and piercings?' He smiled down at her, a smile that robbed his words of all possible offence. And then he lifted her arm to reveal a bracelet tattoo, a ring of tiny rosebuds around her wrist. 'And tattoos. My nieces and nephews will think you're cool.'

'Your nieces and nephews won't get to see it.'

'You don't want to meet them?'

'Why would I want to?'

'They're family, too.'

'Not my family.'

'It seems to me,' he said softly, 'that family's where you find it. And it also seems that somehow you've found it. Your hair gives you away.'

'If we're talking about my red hair then half of Ireland has it.'

'It's a very specific red,' he told her. 'My daddy had your hair and I know if I've washed mine nicely you can see the glint of his colour in mine.' And he lifted a finger and twisted one of her short curls. His smile deepened, an all-enveloping smile that was enough to make a woman sink into it. 'Family,' he said softly. 'Welcome to it, Jo Conaill. You and your teddy.'

'I don't want…'

'Family? Are you sure?'

'Y…yes.'

'That's a big declaration. And a lonely one.' He turned so he was facing her, then tilted her chin a little so her gaze was meeting his. 'I might have been raised in poverty, but it seems to me that you've been raised with the more desperate need. Does no one love you, Jo Conaill?'

'No. I mean…' Why was he looking at her? Why was he smiling? It was twisting something inside her, and it was something she'd guarded for a very long time. Something she didn't want twisting.

'I won't hurt you, Jo,' he said into the stillness and his words made whatever it was twist still more. 'I promise you that. I would never hurt you. I'm just saying…'

And then he stopped…saying.

Finn Conaill had been trying to work it out in his head. Ever since he'd met her something was tugging him to her. Connecting.

It must be the family connection, he'd thought. Or it must be her past.

She looked stubborn, indecisive, defiant.

She looked afraid.

She'd taken a step back from him and she was staring down at the bear in her arms as if it was a bomb about to detonate.

She didn't want family. She didn't want home.

And yet…

She wanted the teddy. He knew she did.

By now he had some insight into what her childhood must have been. A kid alone, passed from foster family to foster family. Moved on whenever the ties grew so strong someone wanted her.

Learning that love meant separation. Grief.

Learning that family wasn't for her.

A cluster of wild pigeons was fussing on the cobblestones near the stables. Their soft cooing was a soothing background, a reassurance that all was well on this peaceful morning. And yet all wasn't well with this woman before him. He watched her stare down at the teddy with something akin to despair.

She wanted the teddy. She wanted…more.

Only she couldn't want. Wanting had been battered out of her.

She was so alone.

Family… The word slammed into his mind and stayed. He'd been loyal to Maeve for so many years he couldn't remember and he'd thought that loyalty was inviolate. But he'd known Jo for only three days, and somehow she was slipping into his heart. He was starting to care.

'Jo…' he said into the silence and she stared up at him with eyes that were hopelessly confused, hopelessly lost.

'Jo,' he said again.

And what happened next seemed to happen of its own volition. It was no conscious movement on his part, or hers.

It was nothing to do with them and yet it was everything.

He took the teddy from her grasp and placed it carefully on the ground.

He took her hands in his. He drew her forward—and he kissed her.

Had he meant to?

He didn't have a clue. This was unchartered territory.

For this wasn't a kiss of passion. It wasn't a kiss he'd ever experienced before. In truth, in its beginning it hardly felt like a kiss.

He tilted her chin very gently, with the image of a wild creature strongly with him. She could pull away, and he half expected her to. But she stayed passive, staring mutely up at him before his mouth met hers. Her chin tilted with the pressure of his fingers and she gazed into his eyes with an expression he couldn't begin to understand. There was a sort of resigned indifference, an expression which should have had him stepping back, but behind the indifference he saw a flare of frightened…hope?

He didn't want her indifferent, and it would be worse to frighten her. But the hope was there, and she was beautiful and her mouth was lush and partly open. And her eyes invited him in…

It was the gentlest of kisses, a soft, tentative exploration, a kiss that understood there were boundaries and he wasn't sure where they were but he wasn't about to broach them.

His kiss said *Trust me*. His kiss matched that flare of hope he was sure he'd seen. His kiss said, *You're beautiful and I don't understand it but something inside is drawing me to you.* And it said, *This kiss is just the beginning.*

Her first reaction was almost hysterical. Her roller coaster of emotions had her feeling this was happening to someone other than her.

But it was her. She was letting the Lord of Glenconaill kiss her.

Was she out of her mind?

No. Of course she wasn't. This was just a kiss, after all, and she was no prude. She was twenty-eight years old and there'd been men before. Of course there had. Nothing serious—she didn't do serious—but she certainly had fun. And this man was lovely. Gorgeous even. She could take him right now, she thought. She could tug him to her bed, or maybe they should use his bed because hers was ridiculously small. And then she could tear off his gear and see his naked body, which she was sure would be excellent, and she was sure the sex would be great…

Instead of which, her lips were barely touching his and her body was responding with a fear that said, *Go no fur-*

ther. Go no further because one thing she valued above all others was control, and if she let this man hold her...

Except he was holding her. His kiss was warm and strong and true.

True? What sort of description was that for a kiss?

But then, in an instant, she was no longer thinking of descriptions. She wasn't thinking of anything at all. The kiss was taking over. The kiss was taking her to places she'd never been before. The kiss was...mind-blowing.

It was as if there'd been some sort of shorting to her brain. Every single nerve ending was snapped to attention, discarding whatever it was they'd been concentrating on and rerouting to her mouth. To his mouth. To the fusing of their bodies.

To the heat of him, to the strength, to the feeling of solid, fierce desire. For this was no cousinly kiss. This wasn't even a standard kiss between man and woman or if it was it wasn't something Jo had ever experienced before.

She was losing her mind. No, she'd lost it. She was lost in his kiss, melting, moulding against him, opening her lips, savouring the heat, the taste, the want—and she wanted more.

Her body was screaming for more. That was what all those nerve endings were doing—they'd forgotten their no doubt normally sensible functions and they were screaming, *This is where you're meant to be. Have. Hold.*

This is your...your...

No.

Whatever it was, whatever her body had been about to yell, she was suddenly closing down in fright. She was tugging away, pushing, shoving back. He released her the instant she pushed. She stood in the silent courtyard and stared at him as if he had two heads.

He didn't have two heads. He was just a guy. Just a stranger who happened to be vaguely related.

He was just the guy who'd saved her teddy.

She stared down at the bear at her feet, gasped and stooped to grab it. But Finn was before her, stooping to pick it up before she did. Their gaze met on the way up, and he handed over the bear with all solemnity.

'Was that why we stopped?' he asked. 'Because you'd dropped your bear?'

'Don't…don't be ridiculous.'

'Then don't look scared. Sweetheart, it was just a kiss.'

'I'm not your sweetheart.'

'No.'

'And I couldn't care less about the teddy.' But she did, she realised.

Why?

Because Finn had offered to burn it for her?

Because Finn had saved it?

The stupid twisting inside her was still going on and she didn't understand it. She didn't want it. It felt as if she was exposing something that hurt.

'We can give these things to charity,' she managed. 'That'd be more sensible than burning.'

'Much more sensible,' he agreed. Then he picked up the giraffe. 'I'll still be keeping this lad, though. No one would be wanting a stuffed giraffe with a wobbly neck.'

'I'll mend him for you.'

'That would be a kindness. But he's still not going to charity. How about Loppy?'

'I guess… I'm keeping him as well.' She was still wary, still unsure what had just happened. Still scared it might happen again.

'Then here's a suggestion,' he said, and the cheerful ordinariness was back in his voice, as if the kiss had never happened. 'There's a trailer in the stables. I'll hook it up and cart these guys—with the exception of Loppy and Noddy—into the village before the night dew falls. That'll stop us needing to cart them upstairs again. Meanwhile, you do some mending or take a walk or just wander the parapets and practice being Lady of the Castle. Whatever you want. Take some space to get to know Loppy.'

'I…thank you.' It was what she needed, she conceded. Space.

'Take all the time you need,' Finn said and then his smile faded and the look he gave her was questioning and serious. 'We're here until the documents can be signed. We do need to figure if there's anything in this pile to keep. But Jo…'

'Y… Yes?'

'Never, ever look at me again as if you're afraid of me,' he told her. 'We can organise things another way. I can stay in the village, or you can if that makes you feel safer. Whatever you like. But I won't touch you and I won't have you scared of me.'

'I'm not.'

'Yes, you are,' he said gently. 'And it needs to stop now.'

It took a couple of hours to link the trailer, pack the toys and cart them into the village. In truth, it was wasted time—there was so much in the castle to be sorted and dispersed that taking one load to the local charity shop was a speck in the ocean.

But he knew Jo needed him to leave. He'd kissed her, he'd felt her respond, he'd felt the heat and the desire—and then he'd felt the terror.

He wasn't a man to push where he wasn't wanted. He wasn't a man who'd ever want a woman to fear him.

And then there was the complication of Maeve and her father's expectations. He was well over it. The whole thing made him feel tired, but Maeve had left loose ends that needed to be sorted and they needed to be sorted now.

He was almost back at the castle but somehow he didn't

want to be taking the complication of Maeve back there. He pulled to the side of the road and rang.

'Finn.' Maeve's voice was flat, listless. Normally he'd be sympathetic, gently pushing her to tell him what was happening but today things felt more urgent.

'Have you told him?'

'I can't. I told you I can't. That's why I came to see you. Finn, he'll be so upset. He's wanted us to marry for so long. He's already had a heart attack. It'll kill him.'

'That's a risk you have to take. Keeping the truth from your father any longer is dumb.'

'Then come and tell him with me. You can placate him. He's always thought of you as his son.'

'But I'm not his son,' he said gently. 'Maeve, face it.'

'Give me another week. Just a few more days.'

'By the time I come home, Maeve.' His voice was implacable. 'It has to be over.'

There was a moment's pause. Then… 'Why? You've met someone else?' And, astonishingly, she sounded indignant.

And that was what he got for loyalty, he thought grimly. An ex-fiancée who still assumed he was hers.

'It's none of your business, Maeve,' he told her and somehow forced his voice back to gentleness. 'Whatever I do, it's nothing to do with you.'

He disconnected but he stayed sitting on the roadside for a long time.

Loyalty…

It sat deep with him. Bone-deep. It was the reason he couldn't have walked away from his mam and brothers when his dad died. It would have been far easier to get a job in Dublin, fending for himself instead of fighting to eke out an existence for all of them. But the farm was his home and he'd fought to make it what it was, supporting his family until the need was no longer there. And by then the farm felt a part of him.

And Maeve? Maeve was in the mix too. She'd been an only child, his next door neighbour, his friend. Her father dreamed of joining the two farms together, and Finn's loyalty to that dream had always been assumed.

Maeve had smashed that assumption. He should be sad, he thought, but he wasn't. Just tired. Tired of loyalty?

No.

He could see the castle in the distance, solid, vast, a piece of his heritage. A piece of his country's heritage. Could old loyalties change? Shift?

His world seemed out of kilter. He wasn't sure how to right it but somehow it seemed to have a new centre.

A woman called Jo?

It was too soon, he told himself. It was far too soon, but for now…for now it was time to return to the castle.

Time to go…to a new home?

CHAPTER SIX

JO SEEMED TO spend the next three days avoiding him as much as she could. The tension between them was almost a physical thing. The air seemed to bristle as they passed, so they spent their time doing what their separate skills required, separately.

Finn took inventory of the farm, working his way through the flocks of sheep, looking at what needed to be done before any sale took place. Inside the castle, the personal stuff was deemed to be Jo's, to do with what she wanted. She, after all, was the granddaughter of the house, Finn said firmly. She wanted none of it—apart from one battered bear—but things needed to be sorted.

She had three categories.

The first contained documents that might be important and photographs she decided to scan and file electronically in case someone in the future—not her—needed to reference them.

The second was a list of the things that seemed to go with the castle—the massive furnishings, the tapestries, the portraits.

The third contained items to be sold or given to museums. That included the storeroom full of ancient clothes. At some point in the far distant past, one of their ancestors had decided the amazing clothes worn on ceremonial occasions by generations of Conaills were worth preserving. A storeroom had been made dry and mothproof. The clothes smelled musty and were faded with age but they were still amazing.

'A museum would kill for them,' Jo told Finn.

He'd come in to find her before dinner. She was on the storeroom floor with a great golden ballgown splayed over her knees. The white underskirt was yellowed with age, but the mass of gold embroidery worked from neckline to hem made it a dazzle of colour.

'Try it on,' Finn suggested and Jo cast him a look that was almost scared. That was what he did to her, he thought ruefully. One kiss and he had her terrified.

'I might damage it.'

'I will if you will,' he told her. He walked across to a cape that would have done Lord Byron proud. 'Look at this. Are these things neckcloths? How do you tie them? I'd have to hit the Internet. I'm not sure of the boots, though—our ancestors' feet seems to have been stunted. But if I can find something… Come on, Jo. We're eating dinner in that great, grand dining room. Next week we'll be back to being Finn the Farmer and Jo the Barista. For tonight let's be Lord and Lady Conaill of Castle Glenconaill. Just for once. Just because we can.'

Just because we can. The words echoed. She looked up at him and he could see the longing. Tattoos and piercings aside, there was a girl inside this woman who truly wanted to try on this dress.

'Dare you,' he said and she managed a smile.

'Only if you wear tights.'

'Tights?'

'Leggings. Breeches. Those.' She pointed to a pair of impossibly tight pants.

'Are you kidding? I'll sing falsetto for ever.'

'Dare you,' she said and suddenly she was grinning and so was he and the thing was done.

* * *

He was wearing a magnificent powder-blue coat with gilt embroidery, open to just above his knees. He'd somehow tied an intricate cravat, folds of soft white linen in some sort of cascade effect that was almost breathtaking. He looked straight out of the pages of the romance novel she'd read on the plane. His dark hair was neat, slicked, beautiful. And he was wearing breeches.

Or pantaloons? What were they called? It didn't matter. They clung to his calves and made him look breathtakingly debonair. He looked so sexy a girl's toes could curl.

She forced herself to look past the sexy legs, down to his shoes. They looked like slippers, stretched but just on. More gilt embroidery.

More beauty.

'If you're thinking my toes look squashed you should feel everything else,' he growled, following her gaze. 'How our ancestors ever fathered children is beyond me. But Jo...' He was staring at her in incredulity. 'You look... beautiful.'

Why that had the power to make her eyes mist she had no idea. He was talking about the clothes, she told herself. Not her.

'You're beautiful already,' he told her, making a lie of her thoughts. 'But that dress...'

She was wearing the dress he'd seen on her knee and why wouldn't she? This was a Cinderella dress, pure fantasy, a dress some long ago Conaill maiden had worn to a ball and driven suitors crazy. She'd have to have had warts all over her not to drive suitors crazy, Jo thought. This dress was a work of art, every inch embellished, golden and wondrous. It was almost more wondrous because of the air of age and fragility about it.

But it fitted her like a glove. She'd tugged it on and it had slipped on her like a second skin. The boned bodice pushed her breasts up, cupping them so their swell was accentuated. She'd powdered her curls. She'd found a tiara in her grandfather's safe, and a necklace that surely wasn't diamonds but probably was. There were earrings to match.

She, too, was wearing embroidered dancing slippers. She needed a ball, she thought, and then she thought, no, she had enough. She had her beautiful gown.

She had her Prince Charming.

And oh, those breeches…

'Our ancestors would be proud of us,' Finn told her and offered his arm, as befitted the Lord of the Castle offering his arm to his Lady as they approached the staircase to descend to the dining hall.

She hesitated only for a moment. This was a play, she told herself. It wasn't real.

This was a moment she could never forget. She needed to relax and soak it in.

She took his arm.

'Our ancestors couldn't possibly not be proud of us,' she told him as they stepped gingerly down the stairs in their too-tight footwear. But it wasn't her slippers making her feel unsafe, she thought. It was Finn. He was so big. He was so close.

He was so gorgeous.

'Which reminds me…' He sounded prosaic, but she suspected it was an effort to make himself sound prosaic. She surely couldn't. 'What are we going to do with our ancestors?'

'What do you mean?'

'All the guys who wore these clothes. All the pictures in the gallery.'

'I guess…they'll sell with the castle. They can be someone else's ancestors.'

'Like in Gilbert and Sullivan? Do you know *The Pirates of Penzance*?' He twirled an imaginary moustache and lowered his voice to that of a raspy English aristocrat. 'Major General Stanley, at your service,' he said, striding ahead down the staircase and turning to face up to her. Prince Charming transformed yet again. 'So, My Lady,' he growled up at her. 'In this castle are ancestors, but we're about to sell the castle and its contents. So we don't know whose ancestors they will be. Mind, I shudder to think that an unknown buyer could bring disgrace upon what, I have no doubt, is an unstained escutcheon. Our escutcheon. We'll have to be very careful who we sell it to.'

'Escutcheon?' she said faintly and he grinned.

'Our unblemished pedigree, marred only by you not appearing to have a daddy, and me being raised surrounded by pigs. But look at us now.' He waved down at the grand entrance and the two astonishing suits of armour. 'Grand as anything. Forget Major General Stanley. I'm dressed as Lord Byron but I believe I aspire to the Pirate King. All I need is some rigging to scale and some minions to clap in irons.'

'I vote not to be a minion.'

'You can be my pirate wench if you like,' he said kindly. 'To scrub decks and the like.'

'In this dress?'

He grinned. 'You could pop into a bucket and then swish across the decks with your wet dress. The decks would come up shiny as anything.' And then he paused and smiled at her, a smile that encompassed all of her. Her beautiful dress with its neckline that was a bit too low and accentuated her breasts. Her powdered curls. Her diamond necklace and earrings and tiara.

But somehow his smile said he saw deeper. His smile made her blush before he said anything more.

'Though I'd have better things to do with my wench than have her scrubbing decks,' he said—and he leered.

How could she blush when there was a bubble of laughter inside? And how could she blush when he was as beautiful as she was?

And suddenly she wanted to play this whole game out to its natural conclusion. She wanted to play Lady to his Lord. She wanted Finn to sweep her up in her beautiful ballgown and carry her upstairs and…

And nothing! She had to be sensible. So somehow she lifted her skirts, brushed past him and hiked down the remaining stairs and across the hall. She removed her tiara and put it safely aside, lifted the helmet from one of the suits of armour and put it on her head. Then she grabbed a sword and pointed it.

'Want to try?' she demanded. 'This wench knows how to defend herself. Come one step closer…'

'Not fair. I don't have my cutlass.' He glanced ruefully at his side. 'I think there's a ceremonial sword to go with this but I left it off.'

'Excellent.' Her voice was sounding a bit muffled.

'Jo?'

'Yep.'

'Can you see in that thing?'

'Nope.'

'So if I were to come closer…'

'I might whirl and chop. Or…'

'Or?'

Or…uh oh… She bent—with difficulty—boned bodices weren't all that comfortable—and laid the sword carefully on the floor. She raised her hands to the helmet. 'Or you might help me off with this,' she said, a bit shakily. 'It sort of just slid on. Now…it seems to be heavy.'

'A Lady of the Castle pretending to be a pirate wench, in a suit of armour?' He stood back and chuckled. 'I think I like it.'

What was she doing, asking this man for help? What a wuss! She bent to retrieve her sword, an action only marred by having to grope around her swirling skirts. With it once more in her hand, she pointed it in what she hoped was his general direction. 'Help me or the giraffe gets it,' she muttered.

'Noddy?' he demanded, astounded. 'What's Noddy done to you?'

'Nothing, but we knights don't skewer lords. We hold them to ransom and skewer their minions instead.'

'So how will you find my…minion? Noddy's up in my bedroom.' He was smiling at her. It was a bit hard to see through the visor but she knew he was smiling.

'With difficulty,' she conceded. 'But I stand on my principles.' She tried again to tug her helmet off and wobbled in her tight slippers but she held onto her defiance. 'If you're the pirate king, I insist on equal status.'

'We can go back to being Lord and Lady of our real life castle.'

'I guess.' She sighed. Enough. She had to confess. 'Finn, this may look like a bike helmet but it seems the helmet manufacturers of days of yore had a lot to learn. Help me get this off!'

He chuckled. 'Only if you guarantee that Noddy's safe.'

'Noddy's safe.'

'And no ransom?'

'Not if I don't have to play wench.'

'Are you in a position to negotiate?'

'I believe,' she said, 'that I still have a sword and I stand between you and your dinner.'

'That's playing mean.'

'Help me off with the helmet or we'll both starve,' she said and he chuckled again and came forward and took the sword from her hands and gently raised her helmet.

She emerged, flushed and flustered, and it didn't help that he was only inches away from her face and he was smiling down at her. And he did look like the Lord of His

Castle. And her skirts were rustling around her and his dangerous eyes were laughing, and how they did that she didn't know but it was really unfair. And the look of him… The feel of his coat… The brush of his fingers…

The odds were so stacked in this man's favour.

He was Lord to her Lady.

Only, of course, he wasn't. He wasn't hers. He wasn't anyone's and she didn't want anyone anyway. In less than a week this fantasy would be over. She'd be on the road again, heading back to Australia, and she'd never see him again and that was what she wanted, wasn't it?

Goodbyes. She was really good at them.

Goodbyes were all she knew.

'Jo?'

She must have been looking up at him for too long. The laughter had faded, replaced by a troubled look.

'I…thank you.' She snatched the helmet from his hands and jammed it back on its matching body armour. Which should have meant she had her back to him, but he took the sword and came to stand beside her, putting the sword carefully back into a chain-meshed hand.

He was too close. She was too flustered. He was too…

'Dinner! And don't you both look beautiful!' Mrs O'Reilly's voice was like a boom behind them. How long had she been standing there? Had Finn known she was standing there? Okay, now it was time for her colour to rise. She felt like grabbing the sword again and…

'Knives and forks at noon?' Finn said and the laughter was back in his voice. He took her hand and swung her to face the housekeeper, for all the world like a naughty child holding his accomplice fast for support. 'Are we late, Mrs O'Reilly?'

'I'll have you know those clothes haven't been touched for hundreds of years. And, as for that armour, it's never been moved.'

'See,' Finn told Jo mournfully. 'I told you we're more interested in finance than war. Ours is not a noble heritage.'

'Just as well we're selling it then.'

'Indeed,' he said but his voice didn't quite sound right. She flashed him a questioning glance but he had himself together again fast. 'We're sorry, Mrs O'Reilly. It's to be hoped nothing's come to any grief.'

'It does suit you both,' the housekeeper admitted. 'Eh, you look lovely. And it's yours to do with what you want.'

'Just for a week,' Finn told her. 'Then it's every ancestor for himself. Off to the highest bidder. Meanwhile, Lady of the Castle Glenconaill, let's forget about war. Let's eat.'

'Yes, My Lord,' she said meekly, but things had changed again and she didn't know how.

After that they went back to their individual sorting but somehow the ridiculous banter and the formal dinner in the beautiful clothes had changed things. A night dressed up as Lord and Lady had made things seem different. Lighter? Yes, but also somehow full of possibilities. Finn didn't understand how but that was the way his head was working.

Through the next couple of days they reverted to practicalities. Jo still worked inside. He drafted the sheep into age and sex, trying to assess what he had. He brought the two cows up to the home field. One was heavy with calf and looked badly malnourished.

'They're not ours,' Mrs O'Reilly told him when he questioned her at breakfast. 'They were out on the road a couple of weeks back and a passing motorist herded them through the gate. Then he came here and harangued us for letting stock roam. I let them stay. I didn't know what else to do.'

'You've been making all the decisions since my grandfather became ill?' Jo demanded.

'I have.'

'Then I think we need to increase Mrs O'Reilly's share of the estate,' she declared.

'There's no need to do that,' the housekeeper said, embarrassed. 'There's nothing else I need.' She paused mid-clearing and looked around the massive dining room with fondness. Finn's suggestion that they eat in the kitchen had been met with horror so they'd decided for a week they could handle the splendour. 'Though I would like more time here. Do you think a new owner might hire me?'

'In a heartbeat,' Jo said soundly and the woman chuckled.

'Get on with you. But, if it happens, it'd be lovely.' She heaved a sigh and left and Finn turned impulsively to Jo.

'Come with me this morning.'

'What? Why?'

'Because I want you to?' There was little time left, he thought. Tomorrow the lawyer was due to return. They could sign the papers, and Jo could leave. He'd need to sort someone to take care of the livestock but Jo didn't need to stay for that. So the day after tomorrow—or even tomorrow night—Jo could be on her way back to Australia.

'I've found a bouncy bog,' he told her.

'A bouncy bog…?'

'Our south boundary borders the start of bog country. I checked it out yesterday. There's a patch that quakes like a champion.'

'You mean it sucks things down like it nearly sucked me?'

'I jumped,' he told her. 'And I lived to tell the tale. And Jo, I did it for you. The Lady of Castle Glenconaill would like this bog, I told myself, so here I am, my Lady, presenting an option. Sorting more paperwork or bog jumping.'

'There is…'

'More paperwork,' he finished for her. 'Indeed there is. I looked at what you've done last night and I'm thinking you've done a grand job. But surely the important stuff's sorted and maybe you could grant yourself one morning's holiday. No?'

She should say no.

Why?

Because she didn't trust him?

But she did trust him and that was the whole problem, she decided. He was so darned trustworthy. And his smile was so lovely. And he was so…

Tempting.

Go and jump on a bog with Finn Conaill?

Go with Finn Conaill?

This guy might look like a farmer but she had to keep reminding herself who he was.

He was Lord Conaill of Castle Glenconaill.

And worse. He'd become…her friend?

And he'd kissed her and maybe that was the crux of the problem. He'd kissed her very thoroughly indeed and, even though he'd drawn away when she wanted and there'd been no mention of the kiss ever since, it was still between them. It sort of hovered…

And he'd worn breeches. And he'd looked every inch the Lord of Glenconaill.

And she was going home tomorrow! Or the next day if the lawyer was late. What harm could a little bog jumping do?

With a friend.

With Finn.

There was no harm at all, she told herself, so why were alarm bells going off right, left and centre?

'I don't think…' she started and he grinned.

'Chicken.'

'I'd rather be a chicken than a dead hen.'

'Do they say that in Australian schoolyards as well?' He was still smiling. Teasing.

'For good reason.'

'Bogs don't swallow chickens. Or not unless they're very fat. I'll hold you up, Jo Conaill. Trust me.'

And what was it that said a man who looked totally trustworthy—who *felt* totally trustworthy, for her body was still remembering how solid, how warm, *how much a woman*, this man made her feel—what was it that made her fear such a man assuring her he could be trusted?

What made her think she should run?

But he was still smiling at her, and his smile was no longer teasing but gentle and questioning, and it was as if he understood how fearful she was.

It was stupid not to go with him, she thought. She had one day left. What harm could a day make?

'All right,' she said ungraciously, and the laughter flashed back.

'What, no curtsy and "Thank You, Your Lordship, your kind invitation is accepted"?'

'Go jump,' she said crossly and he held out his hand.

'I will,' he said. 'Both of us will. Come and jump with me.'

For the last couple of days the amount of sorting had meant every time they came together there was so much to discuss there was little time for the personal. But now suddenly there wasn't. Or maybe there was but suddenly it didn't seem important.

Jo was no longer sure what was important.

She'd never felt so at ease with anyone, she thought as they walked together over fields that grew increasingly rough the nearer they were to the estate boundaries. But right now that very ease was creating a tension all by itself.

She didn't understand it and it scared her.

She needed to watch her feet now. This was peat country and the ground was criss-crossed with scores of furrows where long lines of peat had been dug. That was what she needed to do before she went home, she thought. Light a peat fire. Tonight? Her last night?

The thought was enough to distract her. She slipped and Finn's hand was suddenly under her elbow, holding her steady.

She should pull away.

She didn't.

And then they were at a line of rough stone fencing. Finn stepped to the top stone and turned to help her.

As if she'd let him. She didn't need him.

She stepped up and he should have got out of the way, gone over the top, but instead he waited for her to join him.

There was only a tiny section of flat stone. She had no choice but to join him.

His arm came round and held her, whether she willed it or not, and he turned her to face the way they'd come.

'Look at the view from here.'

She did and it was awesome. The castle was built on a rise of undulating country, a vast monolith of stone. It seemed almost an extension of the country around it, rough hewn, rugged, truly impressive.

'For now, it's ours,' Finn said softly and Jo looked over the countryside, at the castle she'd heard about since childhood and never seen, and she felt…

Wrong.

Wrong that she should be signing a paper that said sell it to the highest bidder.

Wrong that she should be leaving.

But then she always left, she thought. Of course she did. What was new?

She tugged away from Finn, suddenly inexplicably angry. He let her go, but gently so she didn't wrench back but had time to find the footholds to descend to the other side.

To where the bog started.

'Beware,' Finn told her as she headed away from the wall, and she looked around her and thought, *Beware is right.*

It was the same sort of country she'd been caught in when Finn first found her. This wall wasn't just a property boundary then. It was the start of where the country turned treacherous.

For here were the lowlands. The grasses were brilliant green, dotted with tiny wildflowers. There were rivulets of clear water, like rivers in miniature. The ground swept away to the mountains beyond, interrupted only by the occasional wash of sleet-coloured water.

There were no birds. There seemed no life at all.

'I've been out on it,' Finn told her. 'It's safe. Come on; this is fun.'

And he took her hand.

Her first impulse was to tug away. Of course it was. Since when did she let anyone lead her anywhere? But this was Finn. This was Ireland. This was…right?

'I'm not hauling you anywhere you don't want to go,' Finn told her. 'This is pure pleasure.'

So somehow she relaxed, or sort of relaxed, as he led her across the stone-strewn ground to where the ground ceased being solid and the bog began. But his steps were sure. All she had to do was step where he stepped. And leave her hand in his.

Small ask.

'It doesn't hurt,' he said softly into the stillness.

'What doesn't hurt?'

'Trusting.'

She didn't reply. She couldn't. Her hand was in his, enveloped in his strength and surety.

Trust...

'That first day when I picked you up,' he said softly. 'I

pretty near gave you a heart attack. I pretty near gave *me* a heart attack. You want to tell me what that was about?'

'No.'

'Okay,' he said lightly and led her a bit further. She was concentrating on her feet. Or she should be concentrating on her feet.

She was pretty much aware of his hand.

She was still pretty much aware of his question.

'I couldn't handle it,' she told him. 'I had a temper.'

'I guessed that,' he said and smiled. But he wasn't looking at her. He was concentrating on the ground, making sure each step he took was steady, and small enough so she could follow in his footsteps. It was the strangest sensation… 'So what couldn't you handle?'

'Leaving.'

'Mmm.' The silence intensified. There were frogs, she thought. There'd been frogs in the last bit of bog but there were more here. So it wasn't silent.

Except it was.

'Will you tell me?' he asked conversationally, as if it didn't matter whether she did or not, and then he went back to leading her across the bog.

If he left her now, she thought… If he abandoned her out here…

He wouldn't. But, even if he did, it wasn't a drama. He was stepping from stone to stone and she understood it now. If he left she wouldn't be in trouble.

She could leave. She could just turn around and go.

Will you tell me?

'I got attached,' she said softly, as if she didn't want to disturb the frogs, which, come to think of it, she didn't. 'Everywhere I went. I think…because my mother was overseas, because she didn't want anything to do with me, because no one knew who my father was, it was assumed I'd eventually be up for adoption. So I was put with people who were encouraged to love me. To form ties. And of course I grew ties back.'

'That sucks.'

'It was only bad when it was time to leave.'

'But when it was…'

'It was always after a full-on emotional commitment,' she told him. 'I'd stay for a couple of years and we'd get close. My foster parents would apply for adoption, there'd be ages before an answer came but when it did it was always the same. My mother didn't want me adopted. She'd say she was currently negotiating taking me herself so she'd like me transferred close to Sydney, Melbourne, Brisbane—always the city that was furthest from my foster parents. She said it was so she could fly in quickly from Ireland to pick me up. I got stoic in the end but I remember when I was little, being picked up and carried to the car, and everyone I loved was behind me and my foster mum was crying… I'm sorry, but the day you first saw me I'd been stuck in the bog for an hour and I was tired and jet-lagged and frightened and you copped a flashback of epic proportions. I'm ashamed of myself.'

Silence.

He felt his free hand ball into a fist. Anger surged, an anger so great it threatened to overwhelm him.

'Let's revisit our bonfire idea,' he said. 'I'd kind of like to burn the whole castle.' He was struggling to make his voice light.

'We've been there. I couldn't even burn the horse.'

'Mrs O'Reilly said it made three hundred and fifty pounds for the local charity shop,' he told her. 'For kids with cancer.'

'As long as the kids with cancer don't have to look into its sneering face.'

'But that's what you're doing,' he said gently. 'Coming back to Ireland. You're looking at a nursery full of toys owned by kids who were wanted. You're looking into its sneering face.'

'I don't want to burn it, though,' she said. She turned and gazed back across the boundary, back to the distant castle. 'It's people who are cruel, not things. And things can be beautiful. This is beautiful and the people are gone.'

'And so's the horse,' he said encouragingly. 'And we can go put thistles on Fiona's grave if you want.'

'That'd be childish. I'm over her.'

'Really?'

'As long as you don't pick me up.'

'I won't pick you up. But, speaking of childish… You don't want childish?'

'I…'

'Because what I've found here is really, really childish.' He took her hand again and led her a little way further to the base of a small rise. The grassland here looked lush and rich, beautifully green, an untouched swathe.

'Try,' he said, and let go her hand and gave her a gentle push. 'Jump.'

'What—me? Are you kidding? I'll be down to my waist again.'

'You won't. I've tried it.'

She stared at it in suspicion. 'The grass isn't squashed.'

'And there's no great holes where I sank. There's a whole ribbon of this, land that quakes beautifully but doesn't give. Trust me, Jo. Jump.'

Trust him. A man who wore leggings and intricate neckties and looked so sexy a girl could swoon. The Lord of Glenconaill Castle.

A man in work trousers and rolled-up sleeves.

A man who smiled at her.

She stared back at him, and then looked at the grassy verge. It looked beautiful.

The sun was shining on her face. The sound of a thousand frogs was a gentle choir across the bog.

Trust me.

She took a tentative step forward and put her weight on the grass.

The ground under her sagged and she leaped back. 'I don't think…'

'You're not sinking into mud. This is a much thicker thatch of grass than where you got stuck. I've tried it out. Look.' And he jumped.

The ground sagged and rose again. Jo was standing two or three feet away from him. The grasses quivered all the way across to her and she rode a mini wave.

She squealed in surprise, then stared down in astonishment. 'Really?'

He jumped again, grinning. 'I found it just for you. Try it.'

She jumped, just a little.

'Higher.'

'It'll…'

'It won't do anything. I told you before; I've tried it. I was here yesterday, scouting a good bit of bog to show you.'

'You did that…for me?'

'I can't have you going back to Australia thinking all Irish bogs are out to eat Australians.' He reached out and caught her hands. 'Bounce.'

'I…'

'Trust me. Bounce.'

Trust him. She looked up at him and he was smiling, and he was holding her hands and the warmth of him… the strength of him…

He wouldn't let her down. How did she know it? She just knew it.

'Bounce,' he said again, encouragingly, and she met

his gaze and his smile said *Smile back* and somehow she felt herself relax.

She bounced and the lovely squishy grasses bounced with her and, to her amazement, she felt Finn do a smaller bounce as the quaking ground moved under him as well.

'It's like a water bed,' she breathed.

'I've never tried a water bed,' Finn admitted. 'I always thought they'd be weird.'

'But fun.'

'You've slept in one?'

'One of my foster mums had one. She had three foster kids and we all bounced. She was out one day and we bounced too much and she came home to floods. She wasn't best pleased.'

'I'd imagine,' Finn said, chuckling, and jumping himself so Jo bounced with him. 'Gruel and stale bread for a week?'

'Mops at twenty paces.' She bounced again, starting to enjoy herself. 'Foster parents are awesome.'

'Until you have to leave.'

'Let's not go there.' She bounced again, really high. The ground sagged but bounced back, so she and Finn were rocking with each other. The sun was on their faces. A couple of dozy sheep were staring over the stone wall with vague astonishment. A bird—a kestrel?—was cruising high in the thermals above them, maybe frog-hunting?

'I hope we're not squashing frogs,' she worried out loud and he grinned.

'Any self-respecting frog will be long gone. That was some squeal.'

'I don't squeal.'

'You did.'

'I might have,' she conceded, jumping again just because she could, just because it felt good, just because this man was holding her hands and for now it felt right. She felt right. She felt…as if this was her place. As if she had every right in the world to be here. As if this was her home?

'I had…provocation,' she managed. She was trying to haul her thoughts back to whether or not she'd squealed, but her thoughts were heading off on a tangent all of their own.

A tangent that was all about how this man was holding her and how good it felt and how wonderful that when she jumped he jumped, and when he jumped she jumped. And suddenly it had nothing to do with the bog they were jumping on but everything to do with how wonderful it was. With how wonderful *he* was.

'I should warn you, you're seeing the bog at its best,' Finn told her. 'Tomorrow it'll be raining. In fact this afternoon it may be raining. Or in half an hour. This is Ireland, after all.'

'I like Ireland.'

'You've seen approximately nought point one per cent of Ireland.'

'Then I like nought point one per cent. I like this part.'

'Me, too,' he said and jumped again and suddenly they were grinning at each other like idiots and jumping in sync and the world felt amazing. The world felt right.

'You want to explore a bit further?' he asked and her hands were in his and suddenly she thought no matter where he wanted to take her she'd follow. Which was a stupid thought. She didn't do trust. She didn't…love?

There was a blinding thought, a thought so out of left field that she tugged her hands back and stared at him in confusion. She'd known this guy for just over a week. You couldn't make decisions like that in a week.

Could you?

'What's wrong?' he asked gently and she stared at him and somehow the confusion settled.

He wasn't asking her to love him. He was asking her to explore the landscape.

With him.

'You know I won't let you sink,' he told her and she looked up at him and made a decision. A decision based on his smile. A decision based on the gentleness of his voice.

A decision not based one little bit on how good-looking he was, or how big, or how the sun glinted on his dark hair or how the strength of him seemed like an aura. He was a farmer born and bred. He was a farmer who was now the Lord of Glenconaill. Who could transform at will…

No. The decision wasn't based on that at all. It was simply that she wanted to see more of this amazing country before she left.

'Yes, please,' she said and then, because it was only sensible and Jo Conaill prided herself on being sensible, she slipped her hands back into his. After all, he was her guarantee…not to sink.

'Yes, please,' she said again. 'Show me all.'

He wished he knew more about this country.

If you drove quickly across bog country you could easily take it for a barren waste. But if you walked it, as he and Jo were walking it, taking care to stick to ground he knew was solid but venturing far from the roads, where the ground rose and fell, where the streams trickled above and below ground, where so many different plants eked out a fragile life in this tough terrain…if you did that then you realised the land had a beauty all its own. He knew the artist in Jo was seeing it as it should be seen.

And she was asking questions. She'd tighten her hold on his hand and then stoop, forcing him to stoop with her. 'What's this?' she'd ask, fingering some tiny, delicate flower, and he didn't know what it was and he could have kicked himself for not knowing.

He knew what grew on his farm. He didn't know this place.

But it was fascinating and Jo's enjoyment made it more so.

'I need to sketch,' she whispered, gazing around her with awe. 'I never knew...'

But she was going home, he thought, and more and more the thought was like grey fog.

They'd had their week at the castle. They'd had their fairy tale. After tomorrow they'd go back to their own lives. The castle would be nothing more than an eye-watering amount in their bank accounts.

And, as if on cue, the sun went under a cloud. He glanced up and saw the beginnings of storm clouds. You didn't expect anything else in this country. The land was so wet that as soon as it was warm, condensation formed clouds and rain followed.

It was kind of comforting. A man knew where he was with this weather—and if he had to feel grey then why not let it rain?

'We need to get back,' he told her. 'It'll be raining within the hour.'

'Really?'

'Really.'

She paused and gazed around her, as if drinking in the last view of this amazing landscape. Her hand was still in his.

Her hand felt okay. It felt good.

The feeling of grey intensified. Tomorrow it'd be over. He'd be back on his farm, looking towards the future.

He'd be rich enough to expand his farm to something enormous. He could do whatever he liked.

Why didn't that feel good?

'Okay,' Jo said and sighed. 'Time to go.'

And it was.

CHAPTER SEVEN

EXCEPT THERE WAS the cow.

They reached the home field behind the castle just as the first fat raindrops started to fall. Jo's hand was still in his—why let it go? Finn helped her climb the last stile and then paused.

He'd brought the two stray cows into the paddock nearest the stables so he could give them extra feed and watch the younger cow who he thought was close to calving. She was very young, he'd decided as he'd brought her to the top field, barely more than a calf herself. The cow she was with was probably her mother.

And now she was definitely calving, heaving with futile effort. The older cow was standing back, watching, backing off a little and then edging nearer, as if not knowing what was happening but frightened regardless.

She had reason to be frightened, Finn acknowledged as he got a clear look at what was going on. The ground around the little cow was flattened, as if she'd been down for a while. Her eyes were wild and rolling back.

Damn.

'Calving?' Jo asked and Finn nodded grimly. He approached with caution, not wanting to scare her more than she already was, but the little cow was too far gone to be scared of anything but what was happening to her body.

'Lord Conaill?'

Mrs O'Reilly was standing on the castle side of the field's stone wall underneath a vast umbrella. 'Thank heaven you've come. She's been down for two hours and nothing's happening. I didn't know where you were so I telephoned the veterinary. He's away. The lad who answers his calls says there's nothing he can do. If it's a stray cow, the kindest thing would be to shoot her, he said, so I took the liberty of unlocking your grandfather's gun cabinet. Which one would you be wanting to use?'

She was holding up guns. Three guns!

This was a stray cow, with no known lineage. It was a straggly, half starved animal and its mother looked little better. She'd fetch little at market, maybe a small amount for pet food.

He glanced back at Jo. Her face was expressionless.

'I've used the shotgun on the sheep when I had to,' Mrs O'Reilly said, sounding doubtful. 'But it made a dreadful mess. Would you be knowing more about them?'

Finn had been stooping over the cow. Now he straightened and stared at her. 'You shot…'

'Two sheep,' she told him. 'One got some sort of infection—horrid it was, and the old lord wouldn't let me get the veterinary—and then there was an old girl who just lay down and wouldn't get up. After two days I felt so sorry for her.'

'You've had no help at all?'

'He was very stubborn, the old lord. When my husband died he said it was no use spending money on the estate when it was just to be owned by…' She hesitated.

'By what?' Finn asked, still gentle.

'*Tuathánach*,' she muttered. 'I'm sorry but that's how he saw you. Which gun?'

'No gun,' Finn said grimly. 'We may be *tuathánach* but sometimes that's a good thing. Put the guns away, Mrs O'Reilly, and remind us to increase what we're giving you. You've been a hero but, *tuathánach* or not, we're in charge now. Jo, get yourself inside out of the rain. Mrs

O'Reilly, could you fetch me a bucket of hot soapy water, anything I might be able to use for lubricant and a couple of old sheets and scissors? I'll see what I can do.'

'I'm staying,' Jo said and he shrugged.

'As you like, but it won't be pretty.'

'Then isn't it good that pretty's not my style.'

'So what's *tuathánach*?'

Mrs O'Reilly had disappeared, off to replace gun with soap and water. Finn was gently moving his hands over the little cow's flank, speaking softly—in Gaelic? Did cows understand Gaelic? Jo wondered. Or maybe it was cow talk. This man was so big and so gentle…

Did she have a cow whisperer on her hands?

She didn't go near. When she'd gone near any of the livestock on the place they'd backed with alarm, but Finn seemed to be able to move among them with ease. When he'd approached the little cow she'd heaved and tried to rise but the effort had been too much. She'd slumped again but the moment he'd touched her, the moment the soft Gaelic words began, she seemed to have lost fear.

Maybe I would too, Jo thought, and then thought maybe she had. She thought back to Finn walking towards her over the bog, to Finn speaking in his soft Irish brogue, to Finn smiling at her, and she remembered how the terror of her situation had disappeared. She'd still been cold and humiliated and stuck but the moment he'd opened his mouth she'd stopped being afraid.

He was just plain lovely, she decided, wiping rain from her face. She was so wet now she was almost past noticing, or maybe it was that she was only noticing Finn. He was kind and he was funny and he was wise and he was strong—and it didn't hurt that he was so darned good-looking as well.

Did the little cow think he was good-looking?

'*Tuathánach* means peasant,' Finn told her. He'd taken a while to answer her question but she was forced to forgive him. You could forgive a lot of a dripping-wet man with his arm up a cow. 'That's what I am.'

'You're Lord of Glenconaill.'

'Who's just ruined a perfectly good shirt. Is that a lordly thing to do?'

'It's definitely a lordly thing to do,' she declared. 'Can I help?'

'If you must stay then you could rip sheets,' he told her. 'Do you faint at the sight of blood?'

'Excuse me?'

He grinned. 'Sorry. I forgot you're *tuathánach*, too. We peasants come from strong stock. But Jo, this'll get messy, I can't guarantee a happy ending and you must be wet and cold. You might want to go inside and wait.'

'Like a lady. Huh? What's the Irish for bastard?'

'Jo...'

'Tell me.'

'*Bastaird*,' he said reluctantly.

'Well, there you go,' she said, and hauled herself up on the stone fence, close enough to watch but not so close as to worry the little cow and the older cow still hovering close. 'A *tuathánach bastaird*. That's not the class who gets to block out the nasties of the world. You do what you have to do. I'm the support team. I might not be much help but I'm cheering from the sidelines.'

She hesitated and then looked at the little cow and the terror that was unmistakable in the creature's eyes. 'Do you really think you can help her?'

'If not, I do know how to use a gun,' Finn told her. 'I won't push past my limitations but I'll do my best.'

Jo sat on her fence in the rain and cut sheets into strips, as instructed, on the diagonal to give them more strength.

'I could use ropes but sheets will be cleaner and I don't have time to forage in the stables looking for the right type of rope,' Finn told her. So she sat and cut her sheets with care, as if it was very important that she get each line exactly straight. Mrs O'Reilly had brought an armload of linen. She tested each sheet and decided on the coarsest for strength and then worried that it might be too coarse.

She could go inside and do it but she didn't want to. This was a small job but she was focusing fiercely because it was the only thing she could do and she was desperate to help. She was hardly noticing that it was raining.

'Tell me what's happening,' she asked quietly, and she wouldn't have asked at all but Finn was speaking slow and steady to the little cow, as if to reassure her that he was no stranger but a man who knew his job, who was here to help her.

And it was surely working, Jo decided. The more she listened to his soft, reassuring brogue, the more she decided the calf would slip out to listen.

But of course the calf didn't.

'It's a big calf,' Finn told her, still softly, as if still talking to the little cow, though changing from Gaelic to English. Did cows understand Gaelic better?

Gaelic sounded…sexier.

'I'm thinking she's been got at by a bull that's not her breed.' Finn was lying flat in the mud. She couldn't see what he was doing from the angle where she sat but she could see enough to know it was hard. She could see the cow tense with contractions and she could tell by the way Finn's voice changed that the contractions were squeezing his arm.

'I'm suspecting the older cow's someone's house cow,' he said. 'She'll have got out with her nearly grown calf and wandered the roads. Somehow the younger one's been got at by a bull. I'm betting they'll belong to a hobby farmer, someone who spends weekends down here, doesn't care for the land. Doesn't search for missing stock. These two would have starved if Mrs O'Reilly hadn't agreed to take them. And now we get to pick up the pieces.'

'You love it,' she said slowly, hearing the anger in his voice.

'What, this?'

'No, farming.'

'I do.' He gave a grunt of pain. 'This calf has a big head and the legs are tucked back. I'm trying to haul the hooves forward between contractions but there's so little room.'

'Could I help?'

'You!'

' I have small hands. Plus you don't ride bikes like I do without gaining shoulder muscles. Try me.'

'Jo, you don't want…'

'Try me.'

So then it was Jo, lying in the mud, following Finn's directions.

'You need to wait until the contraction backs off to try and bring the hooves forward. But you're doing two things,' he told her. 'While the contraction hits, you need to hold the head back. Feel before the contraction hits, work out how you can cup the skull and push back. As soon as the contraction eases then try and hook the hooves forward. It's tight, and you only have until the next contraction. My hands just won't do it.'

'I'll try.'

'Of course you will,' he said. '*A mhuirnín*. I'm starting to think you can do anything.'

And what was there in that to make her feel warm despite any amount of mud? And determined to do this.

She concentrated. She held the head and rode out a contraction and then manoeuvred her fingers until she felt what she was sure was a leg. Or almost sure. She got a grip and tugged, and the leg slid forward. The hoof was suddenly in front of the little nose.

'I did it,' she breathed but then the next concentration hit and she went back to holding the head because she could still only feel one hoof in front. And the contraction hurt!

But Finn was holding her shoulders and it was okay.

It was okay as long as Finn was holding her.

'You're amazing,' Finn told her and because he said it she decided she was. 'You can do it,' he said and she took a deep breath and tackled the other side. And when the hoof slid up and she had two hooves facing forward she felt as if she were flying.

'I think we're ready,' she said unsteadily.

'Both hooves forward?'

'Yes.'

Finn lubricated his arm and she backed off. He checked, and his face broke into a grin that made her heart twist and the pain in her bruised arm fade to nothing.

'Now it's time for your sheets,' he said and she had to forget about his smile and hand him her strips of sheets and watch as he fashioned ties around the little hooves. Then she watched and waited as he pulled back at every contraction.

She watched as finally the little calf slipped out into the world, as Finn's face broke into the widest grin she'd ever seen.

She had to wait as he cleared the calf's nose and mouth. As he checked her and found her flawless. As he lifted her and carried her round so her exhausted mother could see her, smell her and then tentatively start the first lick of cleaning, of caring, of starting to be…family.

And then she had to hold her breath as Finn turned back to her. For a moment she thought he was getting on with the job of cleaning up.

Instead of which, he drew her gently to him.

And he kissed her.

'Jo Conaill, you are awesome.'

'So are you, Finn Conaill.'

'Yes, we are,' he said and kissed her again. 'You want a shower? It's stopped raining.'

So it had. She hadn't noticed.

Did she want a shower? She drew back and looked down at herself and laughed.

'Maybe.'

'Together?'

And that took her breath away.

She did, she thought. Of course she did. She could let herself sink into this man, into his body, into his smile, into his life.

She wanted to.

But at her feet the little cow mooed softly and struggled to shift so she could lick her calf more effectively and somehow a sliver of sense was gleaned from the pair of them.

Actions had consequences.

She was a loner for a reason.

'I think…separate showers,' she managed, and he hesitated and then nodded.

'That's probably wise.'

It was, but she was having a whole lot of trouble staying wise.

They had a very late lunch, interrupted by constant visits to the window to check how mother and baby were doing. The sun had come out again and they were looking fine.

Even Mrs O'Reilly detoured past the window every time she brought anything to and from the dining room, and she seemed to find a lot of excuses to come to and from the dining room.

'Eh, you've done well, the pair of you,' she said as she served them coffee. She beamed at them as if she was their grandma and all their useful attributes were due to inheritance from her side of the family. Then she whisked herself off and closed the door behind her.

'We did,' Jo said, suddenly just a little self-conscious. Actually, she always was self-conscious in this room. Mrs O'Reilly loved serving them here. She wouldn't hear of them eating in the kitchen but it was so ostentatious. If she had to stay here longer she'd insist on eating somewhere else, she thought. *Tuathánachs* should eat in the kitchen.

Tuathánach bastairds probably ate on the back step.

Which reminded her...

'*A mhuirnín*,' she said out loud and Finn stared.

'Sorry?'

'That's what you called me. What does it mean?'

He coloured, just a bit, which she liked. She liked it when he was disconcerted.

'My sweetheart,' he mumbled. 'Figure of speech.'

'I guess it's better than *tuathánach bastaird*.'

'I guess.' He was blushing, Jo thought with delight. Blushing! But, she reminded herself, she had refused the shower. She needed to get things back on an even keel.

'What will you do with them?' she asked, but he was still distracted.

'Who?'

'The cows.'

'I guess that's for both of us to decide.'

'I can't decide the fate of cows.'

'They won't sell. They're a motley collection of breeds. The calf's a heifer but she's a weird wee thing and they're all scrawny.'

'They could stay here until the farm sells.'

'I guess. I doubt Mrs O'Reilly will want the responsibility. We need to find an overseer until transition.'

'Because we're leaving,' she said flatly and he nodded.

'Because we're leaving.'

Silence.

What was happening? Jo thought. Things should be straightforward. This was an amazing inheritance. They'd sorted almost everything that had to be sorted. Tomorrow the lawyer would come, the papers would be signed and they'd be on their way, an enormous amount richer.

The doorbell pealed and they both started, then looked at each other and grinned. Two identical smiles.

'Are we expecting anyone—dear?' Finn asked, and Jo chuckled. They were sitting at an absurdly formal dining table, sipping coffee from heirloom china, waiting for their housekeeper to open the doors and announce whoever it was. It really was ridiculous.

'I can't think,' she murmured. 'But if it's a gentleman… dear…you'll need to take him into the study for port. The lady needs to retire to her needlework.'

His chuckle matched hers, but he rose and opened the dining room doors, to find Mrs O'Reilly welcoming a rotund little man, bald, beaming and sporting a clerical collar.

'Lord Conaill, this is Father…'

'Adrian,' the little man said, beaming and holding out his hand in welcome. 'No need to stand on ceremony, My Lord.'

'Then it's Finn,' Finn said, taking his hand. Jo watched as the little man pumped Finn's hand with pleasure and then beamed through to her.

'And this must be the castle's new lady. Fiona's daughter. You look like your mother, girl.'

'I'm Jo,' she said shortly.

'Lovely,' the priest said. 'Now, I know you're busy. So much to sort out. So sad about your…grandfather? I've let you be until now, knowing you need time to settle, but I thought I'd pop in now and let you know the whole village is eager to meet you. And when you're ready to join the community…' His beam faded a little. 'Well, your presence will be keenly felt. There's so much need. You know you're the biggest landholder here, and half the village pays you rent. But the land's bad. If you can possibly see your way to do something about the drainage…'

Whoa, Jo thought, but Finn was before her.

'The castle's for sale,' he said and the little man's face dropped.

'Really?'

'Really.'

And he slumped. The life seemed to drain out of him. He closed his eyes for a moment, then took a deep breath and tried to regroup. When he opened his eyes again, his shoulders went back as if bracing and he managed a weak smile to both of them.

'Well,' he said, 'I've heard rumours of the way the old lord treated you both so maybe I'm not surprised, but it's such a shame. I imagine the castle will be bought by foreigners. They almost all are, our stately homes. Corporates, mostly, where company executives can bring colleagues and clients for an Irish jaunt. They do the castles up, but the countryside…' He sighed. 'Well, if you're sure… It's no business of mine to be making you change your mind.'

Silence. Then…

'What's the story on the empty cottages on the road in?' Jo asked, and she said it even before she knew she was going to ask. Why was she asking? Mrs O'Reilly should usher the priest out, she thought, and then she and Finn should get on with sorting the last few things that needed to be done before the lawyer arrived tomorrow.

'The cottages…' the priest repeated and Mrs O'Reilly suddenly sprang to life, like a hunting spaniel at first sight of duck.

'I've just made coffee, Father,' she said. 'Would you be liking some?'

'Well, I would,' the priest told her, and Finn glanced at Jo, startled, and she shrugged because she didn't regret asking. Not really. She was walking away from this place. Surely she should understand what she was walking away from?

Once ensconced in a dining chair, in the midst of the absurd formality of the room, the priest seemed to relax. He took his time with his first couple of sips of coffee, seeming to consider what was best to say and then started. 'There used to be a village much closer to the castle,' he told them. 'That was before the clearing, though.'

'The clearing?' Jo asked, carefully not looking at Finn. She still wasn't sure why she was doing this.

'Nineteenth century,' the priest told her. 'The landlords found they could make a much greater profit if the land was rolled into one holding. The tenants were cleared, and of course the potato famine hit. These cottages seem to stand for ever, though. No lord's ever thought of pulling them down. There was a church here too, though that was pulled down to be used for the making of the church in Killblan. And a school, though that's rubble. I've often thought it would be grand to restore them, put in tenants, like an artists' community or somesuch. Something that could bring life to the district. Something...'

He searched for the right word and finally found it. 'Something fun,' he said at last. 'There's been little fun for a long, long time. No disrespect, but the old lord was a terrible landlord, as was his father and his father before him. I was so hoping...'

But then he stopped. He pushed back his cup as if he'd just realised he was speaking his own dream. The dream had already been dashed. He closed his eyes and then opened them and gave a brisk nod. Moving on to what was possible.

'But it's naught to do with you,' he said, gently now. 'You'll have your own lives to lead, and what's happening here is our business. I'm sorry to have bothered you. I'll let you get on. Bless you both, the pair of you, with what you decide to do with the proceeds of this place, though I'd be remiss if I didn't say a donation to the building fund of our church in Killblan would be very welcome. But if that's as far as you can manage…' He dredged a smile. 'Well, we're thankful for what we can get.'

And he was gone, with a warm word for Mrs O'Reilly, and not a backward glance at the pair of them. And Finn and Jo were left sitting at the dining table feeling…

Rotten, Jo thought. Really rotten.

Which was unfair. This had nothing to do with her. The family in this castle had rejected her out of hand. She'd been unwanted. The paintings, the tapestries on the walls, had no place for an illegitimate child of the daughter of the house. Neither had they a place for a man who was the descendant of an unwanted 'spare to an heir'.

But…

'What would you do if you stayed?' Finn asked.

CHAPTER EIGHT

*W*HAT WOULD YOU *do if you stayed?*

The question didn't make sense. Jo stared at Finn across the table and thought…actually the words did make sense. It was only everything else that didn't.

'What do you mean?' she managed.

'Just what I said.' But he wasn't looking at her. He was staring into the dregs of his coffee cup. 'Just for a moment, just for…fun. As the priest said. Think out of the box. If the lawyer wasn't coming tomorrow, what would you do?'

There was only one answer to that. 'I'd start a tapestry of you with the cows,' she flashed. 'You should be on these walls.'

He smiled, but his smile was strained. 'It'd need to be a portrait of both of us. You with your arm elbow-deep in cow. You could have a caption underneath: "I may need to clean my watch".'

'I'm right, though,' she muttered. 'You should be on the walls.'

'As should you. It's only an accident of birth that we're not. But we don't have a place here, Jo. It's not ours.'

'No.'

'But if it was…'

'What would *you* do?' she asked curiously, and was surprised by the look of passion that flooded his face.

'Drains,' he said. 'As Father Adrian said. I'd see to the drainage here on the castle land but, as he said, on the tenants' land as well. I haven't had time to even look at the tenanted farms but the land's a mess that could be fixed. If I had my way…' And then he stopped and the room was filled with silence.

'What would you do with the cows?' she asked at last.

'The cows?'

'There are three generations of cow looking in the window at us right now.' It wasn't true. They were half a field away but in her imagination Jo had them staring straight at them, knowing their fate was in their hands.

'The sensible thing…'

'You said we're not talking sensible,' she retorted. 'We're talking fun. What would you do…for fun?'

'Keep them to keep the grass down?' He grinned. 'No, okay, the sheep could do that. But we have a newly calved cow who'll produce more milk than her calf needs. It'd be fun to milk her once a day, to have fresh milk whenever we need it. And to watch the calf grow. Those little cows have had a pretty lean time of it. It'd be good to watch them fatten up.'

'But not for the knackery.'

'As you said, I'm talking fun, not sense.' He stared out of the window, across the fields. In the distance were the ruins of the old village settlement the priest had been talking of. 'You know…'

'They'd be great with people in them,' Jo finished for him because that was what she was thinking and maybe he was too? 'What did the priest say? An artists' colony, or somesuch? Wouldn't that be a fun project to bring people to the district? Maybe this castle could even be part bed and breakfast. An upmarket one. Maybe we could cash in on tourists wanting local colour.'

'It'd take a serious amount of money.'

'There is a serious amount of money,' she whispered. 'And we wouldn't have to do it all at once.'

They were staring at each other over the table. Jo could almost see their thoughts bouncing back and forth. There were things she was thinking that she didn't need to say—she could see the reflection of them in his eyes.

'We couldn't,' she said at last, but the frisson of thought kept flashing.

'Why not?' It was taking a while between sentences. They needed space between truly enormous thoughts.

'Your farm…'

'I could sell my farm if I had this one. It'd be a shift in loyalties but I could do it. But you… Jo, we couldn't do this apart. The castle needs the fortune that goes with it. It'd have to be a partnership. You'd have to stay here. You'd have to…settle.'

And there it was, out in all its enormity. Jo was gazing at Finn and he was gazing back. His look wasn't challenging, though. It was…

No. She didn't know what it was, but she did know that there was understanding behind his gaze. As if he knew how torn this whole thing could make her.

If they stopped talking of this as a fantasy… If they decided to make it real…

'You know,' he said thoughtfully when the silence seemed as if it might extend into the middle of next week—when the enormity of what was between them was starting to seem overwhelming— 'we don't need to decide right now.'

'What…what do you mean? The lawyer's coming tomorrow.'

'But I'm the Lord of Glenconaill,' he told her and his grin suddenly flashed out again. 'I'm a man with two suits of armour—okay, one if we share, but maybe one's enough. I believe the Lord of Castle Glenconaill, with or without armour, can decree when and if a lowly Dublin lawyer can and can't visit this castle.'

And Jo thought back to the smooth-speaking, supercilious Dublin lawyer who'd treated them both as if he knew what was best for them and she couldn't help it. She giggled.

'Would you phone him and say, "This is Lord Conaill speaking"?'

'I could do that.'

'Grandpa has a brocade dressing jacket in his room. One of those would be just the thing for such a phone call.'

'And I could say, "Myself and Lady Jo—" for if the priest is referring to you as the lady of the castle, who am I to argue and we're sharing, right? "—Our High and Mightinesses have mutually decided we wish for more time to decide on the fate of our heritage. So please delay your travel…"'

'"My good man",' Jo finished for him and giggled again and then she stopped giggling because what was happening was far bigger than a delay in a lawyer's visit.

Suddenly what was between them was huge.

'We've kissed,' she said, because the kisses were with her still, the way he'd touched her, the way her body had responded. 'It didn't…it doesn't…'

'It might,' Finn told her. He smiled across the table and his smile was enough to make her gasp. His smile was a caress all by itself. 'I guess this would give us a chance to see.'

And that took her breath away. *A chance to see…*

She didn't get attached. She couldn't get attached. She didn't have a home and she didn't want one.

So how had she ended up here, with a castle and a tattered teddy bear and three cows and… Finn?

The concept was terrifying. The concept was exhilarating.

'One day at a time,' Finn said very gently, and she thought, *He does understand. He won't be rushing me.*

But she almost wished he was. She almost wanted him to round the table and take her in his arms and say, *This is where you belong. You're staying here for ever. With me.*

Only that was the siren song. They were the words she'd been waiting a lifetime to hear, only when she had heard them they'd always turned into a lie.

'You want me to make the call?' Finn asked and she tried to think logically but his gentleness shook her logic.

His gentleness that made her want to stay.

'Only if you can do it without the dressing jacket,' she managed. 'Only if you can do it as you.'

'Then it should be a three-way call,' he told her. 'If I'm not doing it as the autocratic Lord of Glenconaill then it should be from you and me, from Finn and Jo, telling him we've decided to stay.'

'But only...'

'Only for a while,' he said, still gently. 'Only until we... see what might happen.'

'You wouldn't sell your farm straight away?'

'I have a manager and staff,' he told her. 'No one else needs me.'

Except someone did.

The call to his manager was tricky.

'I won't be home for a while,' he told Rob and there was a lengthy silence on the end of the phone while Rob thought about it. His manager was a friend of long-standing, and a man of few words. He wasn't a man to rush things. Maybe he'd buy the farm, Finn thought. He could make it easy for him. But that was for the future. Meanwhile...

'What about your Maeve?' Rob asked. 'Her father was here today.'

'Martin came? Did Maeve come with him?'

'She's back in Dublin. People are saying it's over between you, but her father talks like he's still expecting a wedding.'

'It is over,' he said heavily. 'But it's up to Maeve to tell him. I don't know why she won't.'

'Finn…'

'What would you have me do?' he demanded. 'Walk into Martin's living room and say, "I'm not marrying your daughter"? Maeve came over the day I left and asked me to give it a bit more time before she tells him. To be honest, I no longer know what Maeve wants, but it needs to be settled. It was only just okay to pretend before I met…'

And then there was silence.

'Before you met…?' Rob said at last and Finn tried to think of something to say and couldn't.

'This Jo,' Rob ventured. 'The woman you've inherited with. Your cousin?'

'We share the same great-great-grandfather. That's hardly a bar…'

'To what?' Finn could almost see his manager's eyebrows disappearing into his receding hairline. 'Marriage? Whoa.'

'Whoa's right. I hardly know her.'

'You've been in the same castle for a week.'

'It's a very big castle.'

'I'm sure it is.' And his manager was laughing. 'You seem to have yourself in the midst of a love triangle.'

Where was respect when you needed it? he thought. This was what happened when you employed friends. Surely the Lord of Glenconaill should be immune from ribbing. 'That's not the way it is,' he said bluntly. But he thought of Maeve, laying claim to him even now. And he thought of Jo, not laying claim to a thing.

Jo would never claim. She didn't think she had the right.

'There's nothing like that in it,' he said sharply. 'But Rob, the sheep here… I've not seen anything like the quality of their coats. Someone's put a huge amount into their breeding. I'll get you up to see them. I'd like your advice.'

'About breeding?' And Rob was still laughing. 'Of course,' he told him. 'Well, well. We live in interesting times but I think I need to avoid Maeve's father, don't you?'

'Raye?'

It was the first call Jo had made to Australia since she'd arrived; the only call she had to make. Raye was part owner of the last café she'd worked at. She had Jo's bike in the back of her shed.

'Jo!' Raye was brisk and practical and she sounded rushed. 'Good to hear from you, girl. When can we expect you back?'

'I've been delayed,' Jo told her. 'I'm sorry but I'm not sure when I'm arriving.'

'You know Caroline's heading back to the States next week. She's your fill-in, honey. If you're not back by then I'll have to employ someone else.'

'I know.'

'It's a pity. You're good. But it can't be helped,' Raye said. 'And I can't keep the bike much longer. My son and his mate are driving down from Brisbane next week. I told them they could use the shed for their car. What do you want me to do with it?'

'I'll find a storage place on the Internet and have them pick it up.'

'That'll cost you.'

'Yeah.' She said it flatly. It wasn't Raye's business what she did. It was no one's business but her own.

'It'll have to be collected between eight and ten, one morning before the kids arrive next week,' Raye said, moving on. 'That's the only time I'm here to hand over the keys. Let me know when.'

'I'll do that.'

'Right then. See you later,' Raye told her and disconnected and Jo stood still and thought Raye had been her boss for six months and hadn't asked why she was staying longer in Ireland or whether she was having a good time or…anything.

She had no personal connection.

That was what she wanted, Jo thought. Wasn't it? It was the background she'd carefully cultivated since the last disastrous foster home.

But still…

She was sitting on the bed in her Spartan little bedroom. The bald little teddy was sitting beside her. She picked him up and stared down into his lopsided eyes.

'I do like being alone,' she whispered, but she still held him and then Finn's voice shouted along the corridor.

'Jo, I'm heading out to check our calf before bedtime. You want to come?'

'Yes,' she called and then she smiled down at her scruffy, moth-eaten teddy. 'Yes, I do.'

The calf was fine.

The storm was well past and the night was warm and still, so Finn had decreed the threesome were best left in the field rather than ushered into the sheds. The little cow was placidly nosing her calf while her udder was being prodded and tugged, and the older cow was standing benignly beside them in the moonlight, to all appearances like a doting grandma.

'We've done well,' Finn said. They didn't go close, just stood back and watched. 'A couple of bruised arms for us and a happy ending all round.'

'It is a happy ending,' Jo said softly and then Finn caught her hand in his and held. Strong and warm and fast.

'It could be,' he said and there was all the meaning in the world in those three words.

She didn't pull away. She couldn't, even if she wanted to—which she didn't.

'It's too soon,' she murmured.

'Much too soon,' he agreed. 'But we're giving ourselves time. How long does it take to make the tapestry you're talking of?'

'Months.'

'There you go, then.' He sounded smug.

'Once I draw it I can finish it back in Australia.'

'I can't draft sheep anywhere but here.'

'You could always put in a farm manager and travel back and forth from your home to supervise.'

'So I could,' he said easily. 'If that's what I wanted.'

'Finn…'

'Mmm.'

'It is too fast.'

'It is and all,' he said and then he didn't say anything for a while. They simply stood, hand in hand, in the moonlight while thoughts, feelings, sensations zinged back and forth between them. Things changed. Things grew.

'I should…go to bed,' Jo said at last and the zinging increased a little.

A lot.

'So should I,' Finn told her. 'Noddy's waiting.'

'Your giraffe?'

'And your teddy's waiting for you,' he told her placidly, and she could hear the smile in his voice, even if she couldn't see it in the dark. 'So you'll be sleeping in your tiny bed with your teddy, and I'll be sleeping in my grand bed with my giraffe. Jo…'

'Mmm?' She was almost afraid to breathe.

'My bed's big enough for four.'

'It's…too soon.'

'Of course it is.' He was instantly contrite. 'Sorry I ever mentioned it. It's just that I thought Noddy and Loppy might sleep better with company.' His hand still held hers, and it felt…okay. 'Same with us,' he told her. 'I'm sure this castle has its share of ghosts. *Taibhse.* I thought I heard them last night, clanking round in the basements. I'm sure I'd sleep better with company.'

'Just to keep the *taibhse* at bay.'

'That's it,' he said cheerfully. 'I'm a 'fraidy cat.'

'I'm very sure you're not.'

'And you, Jo Conaill?' And suddenly his voice lost all trace of laughter. He turned and took her other hand so he had them both and he was gazing down at her in the moonlight. His grip was strong and sure, and yet she knew if she pulled back he'd let her go in an instant. 'Are you afraid, my Jo?'

'I'm not…your Jo.'

'You're not,' he told her. 'As you say, it's too soon. Too fast. Too…scary?'

And yet it wasn't. What was scary about leaving her hands between his? What was scary about taking this giant step into the unknown?

A step towards loving?

Why not? Why on earth not?

'I…it'd be only for Loppy and Noddy,' she ventured, and his smile played out again but it was a different smile, a smile full of tenderness, of promise. Of wonder.

'Only for the children,' he agreed. 'Jo…'

'Mmm?' She could hardly make her voice work.

'Will you let me carry you to our bedroom?'

Our bedroom. There it was, just like that. *Ours.*

She'd never had an *ours.*

And to be carried as she'd been carried before, heart-broken, kicking and screaming, being carried away…

But this time she'd not be carried away, she thought. She'd be carried to a bed with Loppy and Noddy. And Finn.

He was waiting for her answer. He'd wait, she thought,

this big, gentle man who was the Lord of Glenconaill and yet he wasn't. This man who was just… Finn.

Finn, the man who was holding her hands and smiling down at her and waiting for her to find the courage to step forward.

Only she didn't need to step forward. He was waiting to carry her. If she could just find the breath to speak.

'Yes, please,' she managed and his grip on her hands tightened. He knew how big this was for her. He knew her fear.

She felt exposed to him, she thought, in a way she'd never let herself be exposed before. This man held her heart in his hands. She'd laid herself open.

She trusted.

'You're sure, *a mhuirnín*?'

'Are you sure that means *my sweetheart*?'

'My sweetheart. My darling. My love. Take your pick.'

'I think,' she said, and her voice was so trembly she had trouble making it work at all, 'that I choose them all.'

And then there was no need for words for Finn's grip on her tightened. Before she knew what he was about he'd swung her up into his arms.

And she didn't fight him. Why would she? There was no need for fighting.

As three little cows basked peacefully under the moonlight, the Lord of Glenconaill carried his lady back into his castle, up the grand staircase and into his bed.

Into his heart.

CHAPTER NINE

THIS WAS A secret world. This couldn't possibly be real—and yet it was.

She was the Lady of the Castle. Castle Glenconaill was hers to wander at leisure, explore, to think about what could be done with all these treasures.

A week ago she'd been going from room to room deciding what was to be kept for some vague family archive—some family that wasn't hers.

Now she and Finn were hauling off dust covers, bouncing on sofas, saying, 'Let's keep this one…no, this one… how about both? How about all?'

She was a kid in a sweet shop, suddenly knowing every sweet could be hers. This world could belong to her and to Finn, and as the days went on it felt more and more wonderful.

It felt right.

Castle or not, it felt like home.

And it had nothing at all to do with the fact that this was a castle, part of an inheritance so large she could hardly take it in. It had everything to do with the way Finn smiled at her, laughed with her, teased her. With the way Finn took her to his bed and enfolded her body with a passion that brought tears to her eyes.

With the way Finn loved her…

And there was the heart of what was happening. Finn loved her.

It's hormones, she told herself in the moments when she was trying to be sensible. She'd read somewhere that no one should ever make a long-term relationship decision in the first few months of hormonal rush, and yet the decision seemed almost to have been made.

For Finn loved her and she was sure of it. In the closeness of the night he held her and he whispered words to her, sometimes in Gaelic, sometimes in words she knew, but, either way, the meaning was as obvious as the way he held her.

She was loved.

She was…home.

And surely that was the most seductive word of all. Jo Conaill had finally found a place she trusted, a place where she couldn't be turned out on the whim of her ditzy mother or the problems of a troubled foster parenting system. This was a place that was hers. Or, okay, it was half hers but it didn't matter that it was half hers because the other half was Finn's and Finn loved her.

And she loved him.

She loved everything about him. She loved that he was his own man. She loved that even on that first morning, after a night of lovemaking that made her feel as if her world had been transformed entirely, he'd pushed back the covers and smiled down at her and left.

'I need to check the cows.' He'd kissed her and went to check on the newborn calf, and she'd looked out of the window and seen him turn from the cows and gaze out over the land to the sheep grazing in the distance. She knew he cared about so much more than just her.

But then he'd come back to her and they'd showered together and made love again. Afterwards she'd taken more tapestries down to the stream. Life had started again, only rebooted with a different power source.

Rebooted with love and with trust.

It was almost dark now. She was sitting by the fire sorting threads she'd bought by mail from Dublin. She had enough to start her tapestry.

She could stay here until she finished it, she thought dreamily. She could walk the hills with Finn during the day. She could help him with the stock. They could put off contacting the lawyer until…until…

She didn't want to know until when. She just wanted to *be*.

'Hey.' He'd entered silently. She looked up and smiled, at her Lord of Castle Glenconaill in his stockinged feet, his worn trousers, his sleeves rolled to reveal his brawny arms. Her man of the land. Her lord and her lover.

'Sewing a fine seam, My Lady?'

'Help me sort the threads,' she said calmly. 'I want the blues sorted left to right, pale to dark.'

'Yes, ma'am,' he said and sat and sorted and she sat by the massive fireplace and thought she'd never been so at peace. She could never be any happier than she was right at this moment.

And then, when the blues were in a neat line, he looked up at her and his eyes gleamed in the firelight.

'Threads sorted, My Lady,' he told her. 'The work of the world is done. The castle's at peace and it's time for the lord of the castle to take his lady to bed. Are you up for it?'

And she grinned like an idiot, smiling into his laughing eyes, falling deeper and deeper.

And when he lifted her into his arms, as he did most nights now, there was no panic.

She was home.

Only of course she wasn't.

Paradise was for fools. How many times had she learned that as a child? Trust was what happened just before the end.

* * *

Finn was out with the sheep when he came. It was mid-morning. Jo had taken the farm truck into town to pick up feed supplement for the cows. They'd thought to go together but one of the sheep had caught itself on a fence and lacerated its hind quarters.

'I'm not good with blood,' Jo had said, looking at the sheep with dismay. 'I managed with the calf but that was because I could do it by feel, with my eyes closed. Yikes. Will you need to put it down?'

'I can stitch it.'

'You!'

'There's no end to my talents,' he'd told her, grinning. 'I wasn't always Lord Conaill, able to ring whoever and say, "Stitch it, my good man". Needs must.'

'Can you stop it hurting?' she said dubiously and he'd shown her the kit he always carried in the back of his truck and she'd shuddered and headed for the village so she didn't have to watch.

The sheep wasn't as badly injured as the amount of blood suggested. Finn cleaned, stitched, loaded her with antibiotic and set her free, then stood for a while looking out over the land, thinking of everything he could do with this place. Thinking of everything he and Jo could do with this place.

The prospect almost made him dizzy. This farm and Jo.

He'd never met anyone like her. His loyalties had somehow done a quantum shift. His castle, his lady. Jo made him feel…

'My Lord?' It was Mrs O'Reilly, calling from the top of the ha-ha. She refused to call him anything other than *My Lord* and lately she'd even started calling Jo *My Lady*. Much to Jo's discomfort.

He turned and saw the housekeeper and then he saw who was beside her.

Martin Bourke.

Maeve's father.

Mrs O'Reilly waved and Martin negotiated the ha-ha and came across the field towards him, a stocky, steady man, grizzled from sixty years of farm life, a man whose horizons were totally set on his farm and his daughter.

Finn's heart sank as he saw him. Now what?

'Martin,' he said, forcing his greeting to be easy-going. He held out his hand. 'Good to see you.'

'It's not good to see you,' Martin snapped and stood six feet back from him and glared. 'You're sitting pretty here all right. Lord of Glenconaill. Think you're better than us, do you?'

'You know me better than that, Martin.' He should. Martin Bourke had been his neighbour all his life. Finn and Maeve were the same age. They'd started school together, had been firm friends, had been in and out of each other's houses since childhood.

Maeve had been a friend and then, somehow, a girlfriend. There'd always been an assumption that they were destined to be a pair. But then things had changed…

'You'll come home and marry her,' Martin snapped and Finn thought, *Whoa, that's pushing things to a new level.*

'Martin…'

'I couldn't get any sense out of her. Nothing. That day you left… She came home weeping and went straight back to Dublin and have I got a word of sense out of her since? I have not. I thought there's been a tiff, nothing more, that it was more of this nonsense of giving her space, but yesterday I'd had enough. So I went to Dublin and I walked into this fine bookshop she's been working in and she was standing side on to the door. And I saw… She's pregnant. Pregnant and never a word to me. Her father. Did you know? Did you?'

'I knew,' he said heavily. 'She told me the morning I left.'

'So…'

'Martin, it's not…'

'Don't tell me,' he snapped. 'She says it's nothing to do with you and she'll come home at the weekend and we'll talk about it. Nothing to do with you? When she's been loving you for years? I know she's got cold feet. Women do, but if a child's on the way it's time to forget that nonsense. Look at you in your grand castle with your grand title. If you think you can walk away from your responsibilities… You'll come home and marry her or I'll bring her here, even if I have to pick her up and carry her. You'll make an honest woman of her, Finn Conaill, or I'll… I'll…'

'You'll what?' Finn said quite mildly. 'Martin, Maeve loves you. That's the only reason she'd marry me—to make you happy. I know that now. Will you push her into marrying a man she doesn't love because she loves you?'

The man stared at him in baffled fury. 'She wants to marry you. The farms… She wants that as much as I do.'

But she didn't. It was the curse of loving, Finn thought. Maeve's mother had died giving birth to the much wanted son who'd been stillborn, and Maeve had been trying to make it up to her father ever since. Until she'd fled to Dublin she'd never had the courage to stand up for what she wanted.

'I'm guessing this woman you have here is the reason,' Martin snapped. 'I saw her in the village when I asked for directions. "Where's the castle?" I asked, and they pointed to this trollop with piercings and hair cut like a boy and said she's the lady of the castle and would I be looking for her or for her man? And by her man they meant you. And your housekeeper says she's living here. Is that why Maeve's crying her eyes out? If you think you can leave her with a child…'

Finn raked his hair and tried to sort it in his head. He

thought of all the things he could say to this man. He thought of all the things he should say.

He could say nothing. It had to come from Maeve. She'd been his friend for ever. She was in trouble and he wasn't about to cut her loose.

'I'll go and see her,' he told him.

'You'll come with me to Dublin. Now.'

'No,' Finn snapped. 'What's between Maeve and me is between Maeve and me. You point a shotgun at the pair of us and it'll make no difference. Leave it, Martin. Go home.'

'You'll leave this trollop and fetch Maeve home?'

'If you ever refer to Jo as a trollop again you'll find your teeth somewhere around your ankles,' he said quite mildly. 'Go home and wait for Maeve.'

Martin left. Finn went inside and cleaned up and thought of what he should do.

Wait until tomorrow? Tell Jo what was happening? But it sounded sordid, he thought. *Jo, I'm going to Dublin to tell my ex-girlfriend to tell her father she's having a baby that's not mine.*

The words made him feel vaguely grubby. And angry. How was he in this mess? He should walk from the lot of them.

But his loyalty held him. Martin had helped him when his father died. Without Martin's help, the farm would have gone under.

And Maeve had been his friend for ever.

He could do this, he thought. He'd make a fast trip to Dublin, sort it out, bang their thick heads together if need be and be back late tonight.

Should he leave a note for Jo? How could he? How to explain the unexplainable?

He swore.

And then he lightened. This was the last obligation, he thought. The last link tying him to his old life.

He could do this and then come home to Jo. He could tell her what had happened face to face, and then they could move on with their life together. Here.

This was the start of a new loyalty, to this castle and to each other.

'He's had to go to Dublin on family business. He'll be back late tonight. He said don't worry and he'll explain things when he gets back.'

Jo stared at Mrs O'Reilly in bemusement. She wasn't so much worried about what the housekeeper was saying. There were any number of reasons why Finn could suddenly be called away. After all, he'd left his farm for longer than he'd intended. Things could go wrong. But it was the way the housekeeper was saying it, as if there was a well of titillating facts behind the words.

She wouldn't enquire, she decided. Finn's business was Finn's business.

She headed for the stairs. She needed to wash. One of the bags had split when she'd hauled it out of the truck. She'd scooped it back together but cow food supplement stank.

But Mrs O'Reilly didn't move and then she spoke again.

'He's got another woman and she's in the family way.' The housekeeper's words came out as a gasp. 'I shouldn't say, but girl, it's true. Her father came today, shouting, threatening, mad as fire. Five months gone, she is, and when's he going to marry her? That's what her dadda's demanding! And it seems she's in Dublin, all alone, and your man's saying it's naught to do with him. And I shouldn't have heard but sound carries across the fields and such anger… Two bulls at each other's throats. "You make an honest woman of her", her father said and loud enough to be heard from Dublin itself. So off they went, separate though, His Lordship looking grim as death and her father looking like he wanted his gun. And I don't like to break it to you, when you've been so good to me, but hiding things behind your back… Well, it's best you know. I'm sorry.'

Silence. Jo didn't say a word.

She couldn't.

What was there to say?

He's got another woman and she's in the family way.

This had been a fairy tale, she thought in the tiny part of her brain that wasn't filled with white noise. This inheritance, this castle, this…love story? This fantasy that she could possibly have found her home.

But fairy tales came to an end, and happy ever after… Well, that was just part of the fantasy. What happened to Cinderella after she married her prince? Did he go on being a prince while she went back to sitting by the fireside waiting for the snippets of time he was prepared to give her?

There was so much rushing through her head. Hammering at her were the times as a kid when she'd started feeling secure, feeling loved. '*Would you like to be our child? Would you like this to be your home?*'

She should never, ever have trusted.

'He'll be back for a late dinner,' Mrs O'Reilly said, sounding frightened. 'He said he just needed to sort things at home. He said not to worry. He'll be back before you know he's been gone.'

'You're…sure?' she managed. 'That there's another woman.'

'"My Maeve…"' Mrs O'Reilly told her, and she was quoting verbatim. 'That's what her dadda said. "You've been sweet on each other for ever," he said. "Look at you in your grand castle with your grand title and if you think you can walk away from your responsibilities… You'll come home and marry her or I'll bring her here, even if I have to pick her up and carry her."'

And there was that word again. Home.

It was such a little word, Jo thought bleakly. It was thrown around by those who had such things as if it didn't even matter.

You'll come home.

He'd said he'd had a long-term girlfriend, she thought dully, but she hadn't asked for details. It wasn't her business. But how could he make love to her, knowing what was in the background?

A woman called Maeve.

A baby.

'I'll make you some lunch,' Mrs O'Reilly said uneasily. 'Things always look better when you're fed.'

Right, Jo thought. *Right?*

She wanted, suddenly, desperately, to go home.

Home?

Home was her bike, she thought. Home was Australia—all of Australia. Home was wherever her wheels took her.

Home was certainly not in some great castle.

Home was not with Finn.

'I need to take some tapestries out of the stream,' she said and was inordinately pleased with the way her voice sounded. 'I'll set them out in the long room—the sun's warm in there. Would you mind turning them for me as they dry? Every couple of hours or so. I dry them flat but they need a wee shake every couple of hours just to get them ventilated underneath.'

'Why can't you do it?' the housekeeper asked, but by the look on her face she already knew.

'Because I don't belong here,' Jo told her. 'Because it's time I went...home.'

It was a long journey to Dublin, a fraught time, and then an even longer journey back to the castle.

Why couldn't they have sorted it between them? Still, at least it was done. Maeve's Steven was a wimp, Finn decided. He was even weaker than Maeve. No wonder they'd feared facing Maeve's father. He should have taken the two of them in hand a month ago and made them face the music. But at least it was now out in the open. Maeve's father was still blustering, but Finn was out of the equation.

'At least now I can organise a wedding,' Maeve had sobbed and he'd managed a smile. He knew Maeve. Now her father's distress had been faced, pregnant or not, she'd have a dozen bridesmaids and she'd have a glorious time choosing which shade of chiffon they'd all wear.

Jo wouldn't be into chiffon. The thought was a good one and he was smiling as he entered the castle, smiling at the thought of lack of chiffon but smiling mostly because Jo was here and he'd been away all day and she'd smile at him…

Only she wasn't.

'She's left,' Mrs O'Reilly said, and handed him an envelope before stalking off towards the kitchen. She slammed the door behind her so hard the castle seemed to vibrate.

He stood in the entrance hall staring down at the envelope, thinking, *What the...?*

Read it, he told himself but it took a surprising amount of resolution to slit the envelope.

It was brief.

I should have asked about your background. That's my dumb fault. You know all about me and I was so happy I didn't want to know that you had happy families playing in the background. But now Mrs O'Reilly says you have a woman called Maeve and she's five months pregnant. Happy families? I don't know what this is all about but you know what? I don't need to know. All I know is that nothing's solid. Nothing's true. I've known it for ever, so how dumb can I be for forgetting? For hoping things could change?

Finn, I know you want to farm the castle land and, thinking about it, I want you to have it. You're the Lord of Glenconaill and it seems right that your place is here. I know you can't maintain the castle without the fortune, but I don't need a fortune. I mean that, Finn. I'm no martyr, but I have a bike and I make good coffee. I'm free and that's the way I like it.

So I'll write to the lawyer from Australia. I won't be a total doormat—I'd like enough to buy myself a small apartment so if I ever fall off my bike I have security, and I'd like to upgrade my bike, but the rest is yours. It's the way it should be. For you're part of a family, Finn, in a way I never can be. In a way I don't want to be. Being a family is a promise I don't know how to keep.

So that's it. Don't feel guilt over what's happened. I'm over it already and I'm used to moving on. Keep the cows safe. Oh, and I'll do some research and send you details of someone who can be trusted to restore the tapestries.

Despite all this, I wish you all the best, now and for ever.

Jo

He stood in the entrance hall and stared blindly at the letter.

All the best, now and for ever.

Jo.

For ever.

Then he swore so loudly that Mrs O'Reilly came scuttling back from the kitchen.

'I need to go to Dublin,' he snapped.

'There's no use.'

'What do you mean, no use?'

'I heard her on the phone. She got one of the last tickets on tonight's flight to Sydney. That's why she had to rush.' She glanced at her watch. 'Her plane would be leaving now. Poor girl.'

The door crashed closed again and Finn stood where he was, letting his emotions jangle until he felt as if his head was imploding. Then he walked out to the field where the little cows stood. The calf was suckling. The light was fading and the mountains in the background were misty blue.

This place was heaven. This place called him as nothing ever had before.

Except Jo.

He should have told her. He should have talked of his problems. Even though what was between him and Maeve was essentially private, essentially over, even, he conceded, essentially humiliating, he should have shared.

He could phone her, he thought. As soon as she reached Sydney…

Did he have a number? No.

Email then? No.

Follow her? Catch the next flight? Pick her up and bring her home?

Home. The word was a sudden jolt, tumbling through his jumbled thoughts. Where was home?

Home could be here, he thought, gazing out at the land of the Conaills, of the land of his forebears. He could make this wonderful. This place should be where his loyalty lay.

But Jo…

Being a family is a promise I don't know how to keep.

How could Jo fit into his vision of home? Into his vision of loyalty?

He couldn't pick her up and carry her anywhere.

Did he want to?

He was suddenly thinking back over twenty years, to

the night of his father's funeral, sitting in the flower-filled living room trying to stem his mother's inconsolable weeping. He was the oldest and he'd been thought of as the bright one of the family. There'd even been talk of him going to university. But never after that night.

'Please don't leave us,' his mother had sobbed. 'If you leave the farm I'll never be able to support the young ones. Finn, I need you to be loyal to this farm. It's our home.'

So he'd built it up until he could survey it with pride. He'd thought he loved it but now…

He stood in the stillness and wondered whether it was the farm he'd loved or was it the people who lived there? He'd thought of selling it to move to the castle. Love, then, wasn't so deep.

And Maeve? Had he loved Maeve or was it home and place that she represented? She'd been his friend and that friendship had morphed into something more. But caught up in his relationship was his love for the land and Maeve's loyalty to her father. And overriding everything was her father's unswerving loyalty to his farm.

Maeve's father had encouraged their courtship since they were teenagers, aching for the farms to be joined. He'd almost lost his daughter because of it.

The night wore on. His thoughts were jumbled, confusing jolts of consciousness he was having trouble sorting, but he was getting there.

He was moving on from Maeve…sorting the mess that loyalty to place had caused…

He was focusing on this castle and Jo.

He'd fallen for the two of them. From the time he'd first seen the castle he'd felt a deep, almost primeval urge to work on this land, to restore this estate to what it could be. But part of that urge was the fact that Jo was in the deal. He knew it now because Jo wasn't here and the place felt empty. Desolate.

His thoughts moved back, to Maeve and her father and the not too subtle blackmail.

'If you love me you'll never leave,' Martin had told his daughter. 'This is our farm. Our place. Marry Finn and we'll join the boundaries. It's our home.'

He'd thought this castle could be home. He'd thought this place could hold his loyalty.

He thought of Jo, heading back to Australia. With no home.

Her home should be here.

And then he thought, *Why?* Why should it be here?

What cost loyalty?

He stood and stared at the distant mountains and he felt his world shift and shift again.

Jo.

Home?

CHAPTER TEN

THREE WEEKS LATER saw Jo running a beach café on the south coast of New South Wales.

She hadn't returned to work in Sydney—why would she? She didn't want work colleagues asking how her trip went. Instead she'd ridden south, to a small holiday resort gearing down for the Australian winter. The owners had a new baby, the baby was colicky and when Jo answered the advertisement she was offered as much work as she wanted. She took a vacant room above the shop and got on with her life.

Except she missed things. Things she wasn't allowed to miss?

She worked long hours, from breakfast to dinner. At night she'd pull out her partly done tapestry, of Finn beside cow and calf, with the castle in the background. She wanted it done but she couldn't work on it for long.

It was because she was tired, she told herself, but she knew it was more than that. She could hardly bear to look at it.

Sleep was elusive and her dreams were always the same.

Now, three weeks after she'd arrived back in Australia, she woke at dawn feeling as if she hadn't slept. But work was calling. Even this early, she knew she'd have locals waiting for the café to open. By now she knew them all and they treated her as a friend.

But she wasn't a friend.

'Don't get too attached,' she muttered to herself as she headed downstairs and saw them waiting through the glass doors. 'I'm itinerant. I should have a sign round my neck that says Born To Move On.'

And then she paused because it wasn't just her usual locals waiting. There was someone behind them. Someone with deep brown hair with hints of copper. A big man, half a head taller than anyone else. A man with green eyes that twinkled in the early morning light. Strikingly good-looking. Gorgeous!

A man called Finn.

Her heart did some sort of crazy backflip and when it landed it didn't feel as if it was in the right position. She stopped on the stairway, trying to breathe.

She should head back upstairs, grab her things and run. For a dizzy moment she considered the logistics of hurling her bag from the window, shimmying down the drainpipe and leaving.

But Finn had come and her locals were looking up at her in concern.

'Jo?' Eric-the-retired-librarian called through the glass door, no doubt worried that she'd stopped dead on the stairway and wasn't rushing to cook his porridge. 'Are you okay? Should we wake Tom and Susy?'

Tom and Susy were the owners and she'd seen their light on through the night. She knew they'd been up with their baby daughter. She couldn't do that to them.

So no shimmying down drainpipes.

Which meant facing Finn.

'You can do this,' she muttered to herself and somehow she put on a cheery smile and headed down and tugged the doors open.

It was brisk outside, with the wind blowing cold off the ocean. Her locals beetled to their normal tables clustered round the embers of last night's fire. Eric started poking the embers and piling on kindling.

None of them seemed to notice that Finn Conaill had walked in after them.

'Good morning,' he said, grave as a judge, and she almost choked.

'What are you doing here?'

'I'm here for coffee,' he told her. 'And a chat but maybe it should wait until we're fed. Eric tells me you make excellent porridge and great coffee. Could I help you in the kitchen?'

'No!' she said, revolted, and then she looked closer and realised he was wearing leathers. Bike leathers?

He looked…cold.

'Where have you come from?' she managed and he smiled at her then, a tentative smile but it was the smile she remembered. It was the smile that told her her world could never be the same now this man had entered it.

'From Ireland three days ago,' he told her. 'But it's taken me all that time to organise a bike. I wanted the biggest one but hiring one's impossible, so I had to buy. I picked it up from a Sydney dealer last night.'

'You rode from Sydney this morning?'

'I did.' He even looked smug.

'On a bike.'

'Yes.'

'I didn't know you rode.'

'There's lots of things we don't know about each other yet,' he told her and smiled again, and oh, that smile…

He was tugging his gloves off. She reached forward and touched his fingers, a feather-touch, just to see. His fingers were icy.

'Wh…why?' How hard was it to get that one word out? And of course she knew the answer. He wouldn't come from Ireland to Australia without a reason. He'd come to see her.

Maybe this was the Lord of Glenconaill being noble, she thought wildly. Maybe he was objecting to the letter she'd sent to the lawyer. She'd listed what she could use from the estate and she'd stated that the rest was Finn's. He could do what he wanted with it, with or without a woman called Maeve.

'I've come home,' he told her, and the jumble of thoughts came to a jarring halt.

Home?

The word hung. Behind them the locals had abandoned tending the fire. They weren't bothering to peruse the menu they always perused even though they must have known it off by heart for years, but instead they were looking at them with bright curiosity.

They lived here, Jo thought wildly. She didn't.

Home was nowhere.

'What do you mean, you've come home?' she demanded and if she sounded snappish she couldn't help it. Of all the stupid things to say…

'It seems a good place,' Finn said, looking around the cosy café with approval. 'Nice fire, or it will be. Warm. Good view. And porridge, I'm told. What's not to like? This'll do us until we move on.'

'Finn!'

'Jo.' He reached forward and took her hands. His really were freezing. She should tug him forward to the fire, she thought. She should…

What she should do was irrelevant. She couldn't move. She was standing like a deer caught in headlights, waiting to hear what this man would say.

'I should have told you about Maeve,' he said. 'It was dumb not to tell you. When I first came to the castle, when I first met you, I had a worry about Maeve in the background. In retrospect, I should have shared that worry with you.'

'You should have shared that worry with her,' she managed and it really was a snap now. 'You're having a baby and you don't even talk about it? You don't mention it? Like it's no big deal. That's like my mother…'

'It's not like your mother.' She copped a flash of anger from him then. 'I know your mother thought a baby was no big deal.' The grip on her hands tightened and she could hear his anger in his voice. 'Have a baby, head back to Ireland, refuse to sign adoption papers? Your mother used the fate of her child to try and shame her father, and that seems a very big deal to me. I wish she was alive so I could tell her.'

'But you and Maeve…'

'Jo, it's not my baby.' He paused and his anger faded. His voice became gentle. 'Maeve and I have been best of friends since we were five years old. We always assumed we'd marry. Why not? We loved each other. We always have and we still do. But Maeve's dad is the worst kind of emotional blackmailer. Her mum died when she was seven, and she spent her childhood trying to make him happy. But making her father happy was always a huge ask. He dreamed that we'd marry, that I'd be the son he lost when his wife died in childbirth. We'd join our two farms together, make the empire he'd always dreamed of. It made me uneasy, but I loved Maeve and there was no point in fighting it.'

'You loved Maeve…' She was struggling. They should find somewhere private to talk, she thought. Somewhere like the kitchen. But her onlookers seemed fascinated. Keep the punters happy, she decided, and then she decided she was pretty close to hysteria.

'When you grow up with someone, you do love them,'

Finn told her. 'They become...family. I know you don't get that, Jo. I'm hoping I can teach you.'

'But Maeve...'

'Maeve and I loved as best friends,' he told her, smiling down at her with a smile that did her head in. 'And Maeve's father used her loyalty to him and to his farm to coerce her. I never guessed the pressure. More fool me, but then...' He shrugged. 'I was one-eyed about my farm as well so maybe I was part of the problem. Marrying Maeve was just an extension of that loyalty. But over a year ago she found the strength to run. She told her father—and me—that she needed time out before marrying and she took a job in a bookshop in Dublin. And promptly met the owner and fell in love. Really, truly in love. She was so much in love that for the first time in our lives she didn't want to talk to me about it. But her father's emotional blackmail continued. He's had one heart attack and terrified her with the thought of another. She kept telling both of us that she just wanted space.'

'Which broke your heart?' she ventured. She was finding it hard to breathe here. He was so close. He was here. *Finn.*

He grinned at that. 'Um...no,' he conceded. 'Sure, I was puzzled, and yes, my pride was hurt, but we've been apart for over twelve months now. And in truth I wasn't all that upset. Maybe a part of me was even relieved. But then she told me she was pregnant and she wanted me to face her father with her. She thought it might make things better if I was there when she told him, but I thought it'd make things worse. I thought she should face him with Steven, the father of her baby, and I told her so.'

'Oh...' She'd forgotten her audience. She'd forgotten everything. 'Oh, Finn...'

'So that's where it was when I came to the castle,' Finn told her. 'Maeve and I were over. That's when I met you and that's when I knew for certain that Maeve was right. What she and I had was nothing compared to how I felt about you.'

And what was a girl to say about that? Nothing, Jo decided. Nothing seemed to be working. Certainly not her voice. She seemed to be frozen.

'She still didn't have the gumption to face her father,' Finn told her. 'But he finally discovered she was pregnant. Instead of confronting her, he came to find me.'

'And you went…'

'To knock some sense into the three of them,' he told her. 'Yes, Maeve was still terrified but I collected the family doctor on the way back to her father's farm. It was insurance, and her father turned purple with rage and distress, but there wasn't a twinge of heart trouble. They survived and it's sorted. They're about to live happily ever after; that's assuming they have enough gumption to find their way out of a paper bag. But enough of Maeve. Jo, I came here to talk about you. About us. And even about marriage?'

There was a concerted gasp behind them. Jo tried to speak. She couldn't.

And then her locals took over.

'You've come all the way from Ireland to propose?' It was a snap out of left field. Eric had abandoned his fire lighting and now he stalked up to Finn like a small, indignant cockerel. 'So who are you to be asking?' He poked him in the chest. 'You can't just sweep in here and carry her off.'

'Ooh, maybe he can,' one of the ladies behind him twittered. 'He's beautiful.'

'He's a biker. A biker!'

'So's she.'

'Yes, but…'

But she was no longer listening to her locals. She was only listening to Finn.

'Jo, I'm not here to carry you anywhere,' he said softly, smiling at her now, his lovely, gentle smile that kick-started her heart and had it doing handsprings. 'I wasn't so much thinking of me carrying you off but us riding into the sunset together. But there's no rush.' His grip on her hands was infinitely gentle. They were warming, she thought. She was feeding him warmth.

It was a two-way street. The zing between the two of them…

'I'm not here to take you back to the castle,' Finn told her. 'Jo, I'm not here to take you anywhere. I'm here because I'm home.'

'What…?' It was so hard to make her voice work. 'I don't understand.' When her voicc finally did work it camc out as almost a wail.

'Because where you are is my home,' he said softly and he drew her a little closer so his lips could brush her hair. 'That's what I figured. And I also figured how I'd loved you back in Ireland was dumb. I just assumed you'd be part of the package. Castle and Jo. We'd marry, I hoped, and live in our castle for ever. But then you were gone and I looked around the castle and thought: I don't love the castle. It's just a thing. It's just a place. How can I love a thing or a place when the only way I can truly love is to love you?'

Then, as she said nothing—for how could she think of a single thing to say?—his grip on her hands became more urgent. 'Jo, you said you don't know how to do family. You said you don't do home. But, the way I see it, home is us. Family is us. As long as you and I are together we don't have to strive for anything else. No castles. No farms. Nothing. Not even our bikes if we don't want them.'

Bikes. It was a solid word, the one tangible thing she

was able to get her head around. She looked out through the door and saw a great, gleaming Harley parked to the side.

'I don't… I don't have a Harley yet,' she managed which, in the circumstances, made no sense at all.

'We can fix that. We don't have to but we can if we want. Jo, if you'll let me stay we can do anything we want.'

'You want the castle,' Jo whispered.

'Not as much as I want you.'

'Your farm…'

'I'm selling the farm. Where you go, that's where I belong.'

'So you'd follow me round like a stalker…' She was fighting to keep things light but she was failing. Miserably.

And Finn got serious.

'I wouldn't do that to you, Jo,' he said softly. 'If you say the word I'll go back to Ireland. Or I'll get on my bike and ride around Australia to give you more time to think about it. The decision's yours, love. I won't carry you anywhere and I won't follow unless you want. All I ask is that I love you but that love's dependent on nothing but your own beautiful self. Not on location, loyalty, history. Simply on you.'

'So…' She was starting to feel almost hysterical. How could she believe this? It was a dream. How could she make her thoughts work? 'You'll just abandon the castle? The sheep?'

'That's why it's taken me three weeks to be here. That and the fact that you weren't kind enough to leave a forwarding address. I had to take our slimy lawyer out to dinner and ply him with strong drink before he'd give me your mail address and it took sheer force of personality to make your last employer tell me who'd checked recently on your references. And then I had to find someone to take care of the livestock because I don't like Mrs O'Reilly's cure by gun method. Luckily she has a nephew who's worked the land with his dad and he seems sensible. So our castle's secure in case we ever wish to come back, but if we decide we don't want to come back then we can put it on the market tomorrow. The world's our oyster. So love... As your astute customer suggested, I'm here to propose, but there's no rush. While you're thinking about it...maybe you could teach me to make porridge?'

'Excellent,' Eric said darkly but he was punched by the lady beside him.

'Eric'll make the porridge,' she said. 'You two go outside and have your talk out. Though can I suggest you head to the side of the shed because the wind's a killer.'

'He can't go down on one knee behind the shed,' Eric retorted. 'It's gravel. And I don't know how to make porridge.'

'That's what the instructions on the packet are for,' the woman retorted. 'And it's only you eating it.' She turned to face Finn. They were all facing Finn. 'So, young man, do you want to pick her up and carry her somewhere you can propose in privacy?'

'I'll carry her nowhere she doesn't wish,' Finn said and his smile was gone and the look he gave Jo was enough to make her gasp. 'Do you wish me to take you outside and propose?'

And there was only one response to that. Jo looked up at Finn and she smiled through unshed tears. She loved this man so much.

He'd given up his castle for her.

He loved her.

'I do,' she whispered and then, because it wasn't loud enough, because it wasn't sure enough, she said it again, three times for luck.

'I do, I do, I do.'

* * *

They stayed until the owners' baby had outgrown her colic. They stayed until Jo had not a single doubt.

She woke each morning in the arms of her beloved and she knew that finally, blessedly, she'd found her home.

The two bikes sat outside waiting, but there was little chance—or desire—to use them. Finn refused wages. 'I'm a barista in training,' he told the owners when they demurred. 'Jo's teaching me to make the world's best coffee.' But they worked side by side and they had fun.

Fun was almost a new word in Jo's vocabulary and she liked it more and more.

She loved the way Finn watched her and copied her and then got fancy and tried new ways with the menu and new ways of attracting punters. She loved the way he made the customers laugh. She loved the way he failed dismally to make decent porridge. She loved the way the locals loved him.

She loved him.

And each night she loved him more, and finally she woke and knew that a line had been crossed. That she could never go back. That she truly trusted.

She was ready for home.

'Surely a man's home is his castle,' she told him. 'Let's go.'

'Are you sure?' He was worried. 'Jo, I'm happy to be a nomad with you for the rest of my life.'

'Just as I'm starting to love not being a nomad,' she chuckled and then got serious. 'Finn, I've been thinking... We could do amazing things with our castle. We could run it as an upmarket bed and breakfast. We could ask Mrs O'Reilly to help us if she wants to stay on. We could make the farm fantastic and set up the little cottages for rent by artists. We could work on the tapestries...'

'*We?*'

'If you want.'

'I'm bad with a needle,' he told her. They were lying in bed, sated with loving, and their conversation seemed only partly vocal. What was between them was so deep and so real that it felt as if words hardly needed to be said out loud.

'You're dreadful at porridge too,' she said lovingly. 'What made you try a porridge pancake? Eric'll never get over it.'

'It was a new art form,' he said defensively. 'It stuck on the bottom. I'd made a crust so I thought I'd use it.'

She chuckled and turned in the circle of his arms. 'Finn Conaill, I love you but I've always known you're not a maker of porridge. You're a farmer and a landowner. You're also the Lord of Glenconaill, and it's time the castle had its people. It's time for us to make the castle our home.'

'It's up to you, love. Home's where you are,' he said, holding her close, deeply contented. And she kissed him again and the thing was settled.

They went back to Ireland. They returned to Castle Glenconaill. Lord and Lady ready to claim their rightful place.

And three months later they were married in the village church, with half the district there for a look at this new lord and his lady.

And they decided to do it in style.

In the storeroom were wedding dresses, the most amazing, lavish wedding gowns Jo had ever seen. Soon they'd give them to a museum, they'd decided, but not until they'd had one last use from them.

She chose a gown made by Coco Chanel, worn by her grandmother, a woman she'd never met but whose measurements were almost exactly hers. It was simplicity itself, a wedding gown straight out of the twenties, with a breast-line that clung, tiny slips of silk at the shoulders and layered flares of creamy silk with embroidery that shimmered and sparkled and showed her figure to perfection.

Its nineteen-twenties look seemed as if it was her natural style. With her cropped curls, a dusting of natural make-up and a posy of wild flowers, she was stunning. All the villagers thought so.

So did Finn.

But Jo wasn't the only one who'd dressed up. Finn had dressed up too, but the twenties were a bit too modern, they'd decided, for a true Lord of Glenconaill. 'Breeches,' Jo had decreed and he'd groaned and laughed and given in. They'd chosen a suit that was exactly what Jo imagined her hero should wear. Crisp white shirt and silk necktie. A magnificently tailored evening jacket in rich black that reached mid-thigh. Deep black breeches that moulded to his legs and made Mrs O'Reilly gasp and fan herself.

A top hat.

It should have looked foppish. It should have looked ridiculous. It didn't. Bride and groom stood together as they became man and wife and there was hardly a dry eye in the congregation.

'Don't they look lovely,' their housekeeper whispered to the woman beside her in the pew. 'They're perfect. They're the best Lord and Lady Glenconaill we've ever had.'

'That's not saying much.' The woman she was talking to was dubious. 'There's been some cold souls living in that castle before them. Kicking out younger sons, disowning daughters, treating their staff like dirt.'

'Yeah.' Mrs O'Reilly's nephew was standing beside them, looking uncomfortable in a stiff new suit. He'd spent the last three months working side by side with Finn and if he had his way he'd be there for ever. 'But that's what toffs do and Finn and Jo aren't toffs. They might be lord and lady but they're… I dunno…okay.'

'Okay' in Niall's view was a compliment indeed, Mrs

O'Reilly conceded, but really, there were limits to what she thought was okay. And something wasn't.

For the bride and groom, newly married, glowing with love and pride, were at the church gate. Jo was tossing her bouquet and laughing and smiling and they were edging out of the gate and then the rest of the gathering realised what Mrs O'Reilly had realised and there was a collective scandalised gasp.

For they'd grabbed their helmets and headed for Finn's bike, a great beast of a thing, a machine that roared into life and drowned out everything else.

And Jo was hiking up her wedding dress and climbing onto the back of the bike and Finn was climbing on before her.

'Ready?' he yelled back at her, while the crowd backed away and gave them room. Roaring motorbikes did that to people.

'I'm ready,' she told him. 'Ready for the road. Ready for anything. Ready for you.'

And he couldn't resist. He hauled off his helmet and turned and he kissed her. And she kissed him back, long and lovingly, while the crowd roared their approval.

'Ready for the rest of our lives?' Finn asked when finally they could speak.

'Ready.'

'Ready for home?'

'I know I am,' Jo told him and kissed him again. 'Because I'm already there.'

* * * * *

"You want *us* to be exclusive? That *is* what you're talking about here, right?"

She groaned at that. "See? I'm a mess when it comes to this relationship stuff. I just asked you to be my *friend* and ten minutes later I'm grilling you about other women, making you think I'm demanding exclusivity."

"But you do want exclusivity, don't you?" He had no doubt that she did. "See, that's the thing, Tessa. You have to tell me what you want."

She blew out her cheeks with a hard breath. "Well, how about if you could be exclusive for the next two weeks, anyway?"

Carson tried not to grin. "Even though we're just friends?"

She covered her face with her hands. "We shouldn't even be talking about this right now. It's too *early* to be talking about this."

He suggested, "How about this? I promise not to seduce any strange women for the next two weeks—present company excluded."

She let her hands drop to her lap, revealing bright spots of red high on her cheeks. "Maybe you shouldn't warn me ahead that you'll be trying to seduce me."

"Why not? We both know that I will, so the least I can do is be honest about it."

* * *

Montana Mavericks:
The Baby Bonanza—
Meet Rust Creek Falls' newest bundles of joy!

MARRIAGE, MAVERICK STYLE!

BY
CHRISTINE RIMMER

First Published in Great Britain 2016
By Mills & Boon, an imprint of HarperCollins*Publishers*
1 London Bridge Street, London, SE1 9GF

Special thanks and acknowledgement to Christine Rimmer for her contribution to the Montana Mavericks: The Baby Bonanza continuity.

ISBN: 978-0-263-91999-8

23-0716

Our policy is to use papers that are natural, renewable and recyclable products and made from wood grown in sustainable forests. The logging and manufacturing processes conform to the legal environmental regulations of the country of origin.

Printed and bound in Spain
by CPI, Barcelona

Christine Rimmer came to her profession the long way around. She tried everything from acting to teaching to telephone sales. Now she's finally found work that suits her perfectly. She insists she never had a problem keeping a job—she was merely gaining "life experience" for her future as a novelist. Christine lives with her family in Oregon. Visit her at www.christinerimmer.com.

For MSR,
always.

Chapter One

Carson Drake was ready to go home to LA.

As president and CEO of both Drake Distilleries and Drake Hospitality, Carson enjoyed luxury cars, willing, sophisticated women and very old Scotch, not necessarily in that order. As for small country towns where everybody knew everybody and every holiday included flag-waving and a parade?

Didn't thrill him in the least.

So what, really, was he doing here on the town hall steps in a tiny dot on the Montana map called Rust Creek Falls? Carson pondered that question as he watched the Rust Creek Falls Baby Bonanza Memorial Day Parade wander by. All around him flags waved. And there were babies. A whole bunch of babies.

Carson had nothing against babies. As long they belonged to someone else, babies were fine with him. But did he have any interest in watching a parade that *featured* babies?

The answer would be no.

Beside him, Ryan Roarke, a lawyer and Carson's friend of several years, said, "That's Emmet DePaulo." Ryan waved at a tall, thin older man on the Rust Creek Falls Medical Clinic float as it rolled by. The man was dressed in a white coat and had a stethoscope slung around his neck. "Emmet runs the local clinic with the help of Callie Crawford, who's—"

"Nate Crawford's wife, I remember," Carson finished for him. The Crawfords were one of the town's first families. Nate had a lot of influence in Rust Creek Falls, which meant he was someone Carson had made it a point to get to know.

Not that all the connections he'd forged in the past two weeks had done him much good, Carson thought glumly as he settled into a slouch against one of the pillars that flanked the steps. It had been a crazy idea, anyway. And he shouldn't let his lack of progress get him down. Not every gamble ended up in the win column. Sometimes a man simply had to accept that he was out of his element and going nowhere fast.

Carson was no quitter, but the plan wasn't happening. He needed to—

His mind went dead blank as he shoved off the pillar and snapped to his full height.

Who's that? he almost demanded of Ryan.

But he shut his mouth over the eager words and simply stared instead.

Damn. She was something. Just the sight of her had emptied his brain of rational thought and slammed all his senses straight into overload.

She rode one of the floats and was dressed as a stork.

Had anyone asked him a moment before if a woman in a stork costume could be hot, he would have laughed. But she *was* hot.

Her thick brown hair poked out from under the long orange stork bill, escaping the white fluffy stork hood to curl around her flushed cheeks. She was perched on a box covered in white cotton batting—to make it look like a cloud, he assumed. In her wings, she held a tiny squalling baby wrapped up in a blue blanket. Her slim legs, encased in orange tights, ended in platterlike webbed orange feet. She should have looked ridiculous—and she did.

Ridiculous. Adorable.

And hot.

Giant pink-and-blue letters sprinkled with glitter proclaimed the float "The Rust Creek Falls Gazette."

"That's Kayla, Kristen's twin," Ryan said, which made zero sense to Carson.

But then he ordered his brain to start working again and noticed the other woman standing beside his beautiful stork. Rigged out to look like the Statue of Liberty, holding her torch high and wearing a pageant-style sash that read, "The Rust Creek Rambler," Miss Liberty waved and smiled as the float drifted past. *She* was the one Ryan had just called Kayla. Carson deduced this because the woman with the torch was a double for Ryan's wife, Kristen.

Ryan kept talking. "Kayla is the recently outed mystery gossip columnist known as—"

"Judging by the sash, I'm thinking the Rust Creek Rambler?"

"Right. Kayla had us all fooled. No one suspected she could be the one who knew everyone's secrets and put them in the *Gazette*. Kayla's quiet, you know? She's the shy one. Nothing like my Kristen."

Carson tuned his friend out. The sweet stork with the wailing blue bundle had all his attention once again.

As he stared, she actually seemed to *feel* his gaze on her; her slim body went perfectly still. Then, slowly, she turned her white, billed head his way—and bam! Just like in some sappy, romantic movie, their eyes collided and locked. And damned if it didn't feel exactly as they always made it seem in the movies. As though she had reached out and touched him. As though they'd just shared a private, way-too-intimate conversation.

As if they were the only two people in the world.

He gaped, and she stared back at him with her sweet mouth hanging open, clearly oblivious in that moment to everything but him, though the band across the street played loudly and badly and some kid nearby had set off a chain of firecrackers and the baby in her arms continued to wail.

What was it about her?

Carson couldn't have said. Maybe it was those big, shining eyes, or that slightly frantic look on her incomparable face—a face that reminded him of his perfect girl-next-door fantasy *and* some bold gypsy woman, both at the same time. Maybe it was the stork costume. Most of the women he knew wouldn't be caught dead dressed as a stork.

But whatever it was about her that had him gaping like a lovesick fool, he *had* to meet her.

Her float rolled on past. Next came the Veterans of Foreign Wars float, with men and women in uniform holding babies in camo and waving way too many flags. As the band launched into "The Ballad of the Green Berets," Carson tried to figure out what had just happened to him.

Slowly, reality crept in—reality wrapped in a blue blanket and wailing.

The woman had a *baby*, for God's sake. Carson liked his women free and unencumbered. And there was not only the baby to consider but also the real possibility of a husband.

Was he losing his mind? He would never make a move on a woman with a baby. If she had a husband that would simply be wrong. And if she didn't, well, there would still be the baby. If he'd wanted kids, he wouldn't be divorced.

You'd think he'd been sampling the magic moonshine that had brought him to Montana in the first place, the magic moonshine created by a local eccentric named Homer Gilmore. Carson wanted the moonshine formula for Drake Distilleries. So far, he'd gotten nowhere near his admittedly out-there goal.

Which was why he'd just about convinced himself to give up and go home.

But the sight of the girl changed all that. The sight of the girl had him thinking that he didn't really want to give up. He just needed something to go right; that was all. He needed a win.

Meeting the adorable girl in the stork costume would definitely cheer him up, even with the damn baby—as long as there was no husband involved.

So then. First and foremost, he needed to find out if she was already taken.

At least that was easily done.

He asked Ryan, "Did you see the girl in the stork costume?"

Ryan gave it right up. "Tessa Strickland. Lives in Bozeman. She's visiting her grandparents at their boardinghouse."

Tessa. It suited her. "Married to…?"

Ryan shot Carson a narrow-eyed, you-can't-fool-a-lawyer look. "You're interested in Tessa. Why?"

"Ryan, is she married or not?"

His friend shoved back that shock of sable hair that was always falling over his forehead. "Tessa's single."

"But with a baby."

"You *are* interested."

"Would that somehow be a problem?"

Ryan smirked. "No problem at all. And Tessa's got no baby." *She's single, no baby.* Things were definitely looking up. Ryan added, "The baby is Kayla's—you remember, Kristen's sister, the Rust Creek Rambler in the Lady Liberty costume?"

Not that it really mattered but… "How do you know who that baby belongs to?"

"I will repeat, Tessa doesn't have a baby, whereas Kayla *is* married to Trey Strickland, and they have a son. Little Gilmore is just two months old. Kayla gave up her job writing the gossip column last year. She and Trey live down in Thunder Canyon now, but they come back to visit often. Somebody else writes the Rambler column now. Nobody knows who, but apparently someone talked Kayla into riding on the float. For old time's sake would be my guess."

"Props to you, man. You're here six months and you know everything about everyone."

Ryan extended both arms wide. "Welcome to my new hometown." Actually, Ryan and Kristen lived in nearby Kalispell, but why quibble over mere facts? And Ryan was smirking again. "The baby's named Gilmore. Get it?"

Carson stared at him, deadpan. "You're not serious."

"As a guilty verdict."

"They named their baby after Homer Gilmore?"

"Yes, they did."

"Who names their kid after a crazy old homeless guy?"

Ryan leaned closer and lowered his voice. "Kayla and Trey first got together last Fourth of July..." He arched a dark eyebrow as he let the sentence trail off.

Carson took his meaning. "You're telling me that they 'got together' over a glass of Homer's moonshine and in the biblical sense?"

"You said it—I didn't." The previous Fourth of July, a lot of women had drunk the famous moonshine, left their inhibitions behind and ended up pregnant—thus, the current Baby Bonanza. Ryan added, "As for why Tessa was holding Kayla's baby, I'm guessing that managing the torch *and* the baby was too much for Kayla, so she got Tessa to carry Gil—and you're definitely interested. Just admit it."

"I have another question."

"Carson. Admit it."

"Wait. Listen. Kayla's husband is a Strickland, you said, same as Tessa. So then, Trey Strickland must be Tessa's brother, right?"

"Wrong. Trey and Tessa are cousins and—Carson, what are you up to here? We've been friends a long time. I'm happy to introduce you around and tell you everything you need to know. But you've got to be up front with me. I *care* about what happens in this town. What do you want with Tessa?"

Carson met Ryan's eyes—and admitted the truth. "I think she's gorgeous, and I want to meet her. Is there something wrong with that?"

Ryan made a low, self-satisfied sound. "I knew it. Rust Creek Falls is getting under your skin."

"No, it's not."

"Yes, it is. You're just like the rest of us."

"Uh-uh."

"Oh, yeah. You'll fall in love with Tessa, and you'll never want to leave."

Carson had to make an effort not to scoff. "I just want to meet the girl. Can you make that happen?"

"Consider it done."

Tessa rocked the crying baby and ordered her racing heart to slow down.

But baby Gil kept right on bawling, and Tessa's heart kept beating way too fast and much too hard. Dear God, she was horrible with babies. They were so small and vulnerable and she always felt like she was holding them wrong. And boy, did little Gil have a set of lungs on him. How could someone so tiny make such a racket?

"Shh now, it's okay. Shh, sweetie, shh…" She tried to sound soothing as her heart galloped a mile a minute and a voice in her brain ordered her to toss the baby to his mother, leap right down off the moving float and run away from Main Street as fast as her webbed feet would carry her.

She really did need to get out of there. And she needed to do it ASAP, before *he* found her—and, no, she didn't know him. She'd never seen the man before in her life. She had no idea who he was or what he was doing in town.

What she did know, what she'd known at the first sight of him, was that he would be looking for her.

She had to make certain that he didn't find her. Because that man was nothing but trouble for someone like her.

Oh, yeah. One look at him and she knew it all.

Because he *had* it all. Tall, broad-shouldered and

killer-hot, he had dark, intense eyes and thick brown hair, chiseled cheekbones and a beautiful, soft, dangerous mouth. He'd looked like he owned the place—the steps he stood on, the town hall behind him, the whole of Rust Creek Falls and the valley and mountains around it.

Tessa could tell just from the perfect cut of his jacket and the proud set of those broad shoulders that he had money to burn.

Just the sight of him, just the way he'd looked at her…

Oh, she knew the kind of man he was, knew that look he gave her. That look was as dangerous as that beautiful mouth of his.

The last time she'd met a man who gave her that kind of look, she'd thrown away her job, her future, *everything*, to follow him—and ended up two years later running home to Bozeman to try to glue the shattered pieces of her life back together.

No way could she afford a disaster like that again.

Kayla glanced down at her. "You doing okay, Tessa?"

"Fine," she lied and rocked the howling Gil some more.

"Just hold on. We're almost there."

There was Rust Creek Falls Elementary School, where the parade had started and would end after a slow and stately procession up one side of Main Street and back down the other.

Why couldn't they hurry a little?

At this pace, he would probably be waiting for her, standing there in the parking lot, the sun picking up bronze highlights in his thick brown hair, looking like a dream come true when she knew very well he was really her worst nightmare just waiting to happen all over again.

Yes, she'd been instantly and powerfully attracted to

him. The look on that too-handsome face had said he felt the same. And that was the problem.

Tessa knew all too well where such powerful attractions led: to the complete destruction of the life she'd so painstakingly built for herself. She would not make that mistake twice. *Uh-uh. No way.*

Five minutes later—minutes that seemed like forever—they turned into the school parking lot. As soon as the float stopped rolling, Tessa jumped to her feet. Taking pity on her, Kayla set down her Lady Liberty torch and reached for the baby.

Gil stopped crying the second his mother's arms closed around him. "Thanks, Tessa." Kayla gave her a glowing, new-mommy smile.

Tessa was already jumping to the blacktop, headed for her battered mini-SUV on the far side of the lot. "No problem. Happy to help," she called back with a quick wave.

"We'll see you at the picnic," Kayla called after her.

Tessa waved again but didn't answer. She wouldn't be going to the Memorial Day picnic in the park, after all. *He* was far too likely to show up there, all ready to help her ruin her life for a second time.

She hurried on, grateful beyond measure that she'd thought to drive her car. It wasn't that far to her grandmother's boardinghouse, but her stupid webbed stork feet would have really slowed her down. Not to mention, she was far too noticeable dressed as a big white bird.

Yes, she realized it was absurd to imagine that the dark-eyed stranger with whom she'd exchanged a single heated glance might be coming to find her, might even now be on her trail, determined to run her to ground. Absurd, but still…

She knew he would be looking for her, knew it in the

shiver beneath her skin, the rapid tattoo of her pulse, the heated rush of her blood through her veins. She could taste it on her tongue with every shaky breath she drew.

It was ridiculous for her to think it, but she thought it, anyway. He *would* be coming after her.

And she needed to make sure he didn't find her. Getting to the safety of the boardinghouse was priority number one.

Main Street was packed with parade-goers, so she took North Broomtail Road. Tessa had her windows down. As she rolled along, she could smell the burning hickory wood from the big cast-iron smokers trucked to Rust Creek Falls Park before dawn. The giant racks of ribs and barbecue would have been slow-smoking all day long. The picnic in the park would go on for the rest of the day and into the night.

At Cedar Street she turned left. A minute later, she was pulling into the parking lot behind a ramshackle four-story Victorian—her grandmother's boardinghouse. Strickland's Boarding House was purple, or it used to be years ago. The color had slowly faded to lavender gray.

Tessa parked, jumped out and headed for the steps to the back porch, her ridiculous orange stork feet slapping the ground with each step. She didn't breathe easy until she was inside and on her way up the narrow back stairs.

In her room, she shut and locked the door and wiggled out of the stork suit. She felt sweaty and nervous and completely out of sorts, so she put on her robe, grabbed her toiletries caddy and went down the hall to the bathroom she shared with the tenant in the room next to hers. It was blessedly empty—the whole house felt empty and quiet. Everyone was probably celebrating on Main Street or over at the park.

She took her time, had a nice, soothing shower, slathered herself in lotion afterward and put real care into blowing her unruly curls into smooth, silky waves. She put on makeup, too—which didn't make a lot of sense if she planned to hide in her room for the rest of the day.

But that was the thing. By the time she got around to applying makeup, an hour had passed since she'd locked eyes with the stranger on Main Street. As the minutes ticked by, her panic and dread had faded down to a faint edginess mixed with a really annoying sense of anticipation.

Come on. He was just a guy—yeah, a really hot guy with beautiful, intense eyes and a mouth made for kissing. But just a guy, nonetheless. It was hardly a crime to be hot and rich and look kissable, now, was it?

She'd overreacted—that was all. And it was silly to let a shared glance with a stranger ruin her holiday. The more she considered the situation, the more determined she became not to run away from this guy.

She was not hiding in her room.

She was taking this out-of-nowhere attraction as a good sign, a sort of reawakening, an indication that she really had recovered—from the awful, depressing way it had ended with Miles *and* from the loss of the hard-earned, successful life that she'd so cavalierly thrown away to be with him.

Tessa returned to her room and dressed in a white tank that showed a little bit of tummy. She pulled on skinny jeans and her favorite red cowboy boots. She looked good, she thought. Confident. And relaxed.

On the way out the door, she grabbed her Peter Grimm straw cowboy hat with the studs and rhinestones, the leopard-print accents and the crimson cross overlay. The park was half a block from the boardinghouse, so she left her car in the boardinghouse lot and walked.

She was going to have a good time today, damn it. The past didn't own her. Not anymore.

A single shared glance during the parade didn't mean a thing. That man was a complete stranger, and he'd probably forgotten all about her by now.

Most likely, she'd never see the guy again.

Chapter Two

Tessa left the sidewalk and started across the rough park grass. She strode confidently toward the rows of coolers filled with ice and canned soft drinks.

Halfway there, Ryan Roarke caught her arm. "Tessa. Come on over here. There's someone I want you to meet."

She turned—and there *he* was, not twenty feet away under a cottonwood, with Kristen, Kayla and Trey. *He* stared right at her, a sinful look in those beautiful eyes and a smile playing at the corners of his too-tempting mouth. She half stumbled at the sight of him.

Ryan steadied her. "Whoa. You okay?"

She was. Absolutely. She was meeting Mr. Tall, Dark and Dangerous, and it would be fine. Because he was not Miles and now was not then. "Whoa is right. I think I stepped in a gopher hole."

Ryan, who was playful and smooth and a little bit

goofy all at the same time, gave her a knowing grin. "Gotta watch out for those."

"Tell me about it."

Ryan led her to the group under the cottonwood. She gave Kristen and Trey each a hug and touched Kayla's arm in greeting.

And then the moment came. *He* spoke to her. "Hello, Tessa." She lifted her chin and met those dark eyes—really, he was much too tall. Six-four, at least. Too tall, too hot, too…everything. She felt breathless all over again, felt that hungry shiver slide beneath her skin.

Ryan said, "Tessa, this is Carson Drake. He's up from LA on business. I've known him for years, used to do legal work for him now and then."

Tessa swallowed her breathlessness and teased, "Are you telling me he's harmless and I should trust him?"

Ryan hesitated. "Harmless. Hmm. Don't know if I'd go that far."

"Don't listen to him," the man himself cut in gruffly. Then he stage-whispered to Ryan, "You're supposed to be on my side, remember?"

"Well, I am on your side, man. I'm just not sure if *harmless* is the right word for you."

Kristen moved in close to her husband. She tipped her head up and pressed a kiss to Ryan's square jaw. "Sweetheart, Tessa's all grown up. She can handle Carson."

Tessa made a show of rolling her eyes. "Why am I feeling like I'm being set up here?"

"Because I asked to meet you." That deep, velvety voice rubbed along her nerve endings like an actual caress. Her stomach hollowed out as she stared into his eyes. The warning bells in her head started ringing again, loud and clear.

She ignored them. They were getting no power over

her. It was a beautiful day, and she meant to have fun. She looked straight at Carson again, took the full force of those dark eyes head-on. "So, Carson. What kind of business is it that brings you to Rust Creek Falls?"

Ryan volunteered, "He's here to try and make a deal with Homer Gilmore."

She kept looking at Carson. He stared right back at her. "What could Homer possibly have that you would want?"

"I want to talk to him about that famous moonshine of his."

"You want to buy some moonshine?"

"I want to buy the formula."

"Had any luck with that?"

"Not a lot. I've been here two weeks trying to set up a meeting with the man. It's not happening—though Homer *has* called me four times." Carson's brow furrowed. "At least, I think it was him. But then, I understand he's homeless. Does he even have a phone? And how did he get my cell number, anyway? Maybe someone's just pranking me." He sent Ryan a suspicious glance.

Ryan put up both hands. "Don't give me that look. If you've been pranked, it wasn't me."

Kayla suggested, "Homer always knows more than you'd think. He's a very bright man, and he has a big heart. He's just a little bit odd."

Tessa asked Carson, "So what did Homer—if it even *was* Homer—say when he called you?"

He gazed at her so steadily. A ripple of pleasure spread through her at the obvious admiration in his eyes. "Homer told me that he knew I was looking for him and he was 'working' on it."

"Working on what?"

Carson lifted a shoulder in a half shrug. "Your guess

is as good as mine. He said he *might* be willing to talk business with me. Soon."

Trey prompted, "And?"

"And that's it."

"He called you four times and that's all he said?" Kristen asked.

"Pretty much. It was discouraging. You'd think a homeless person would be eager to meet with someone who only wants to make him rich. Not Homer Gilmore, apparently."

"You're serious?" Tessa didn't really get it. "You want to buy Homer's moonshine formula and that's going to make him rich?"

"That's right." Carson reached out and took her hand. His touch sent warmth cascading through her. He pulled her closer—and she let him. "Come on. Let's get a drink." He wrapped her fingers around his arm. She felt the pricey fabric of his sport coat, the rock-hard muscles beneath, and she didn't know whether she was scared to death or exhilarated. Carson Drake was even more gorgeous and magnetic close up than from a distance. And he smelled amazing. He probably had his aftershave made specifically for him—bespoke, no doubt, from that famous perfumer in London, at a cost of thousands for a formula all his own.

And it was worth every penny, too.

He gave her a smile.

Pow! A lightning strike of wonderfulness, a hot blast of pure pleasure. It felt so good, to have this particular man looking at her as though there was no one else in the world—*too* good, and she knew it.

She'd been here before and she should get away. Fast.

But she did nothing of the sort. Instead, she said, "I'll have a drink with you—but only if you tell me more about how you're going to buy Homer's moonshine formula and then make him rich."

"Done."

They waved at the others and he led her to the row of coolers, where he grabbed a Budweiser and she took a ginger ale. Arm in arm, they wandered beneath the trees looking for a place to sit—and stopping to visit with just about everyone they passed. Two weeks he'd said he'd been in town. He certainly hadn't wasted any time getting to know people.

Eventually, they found a rough wooden bench at the foot of a giant fir tree. They sat down together, and Carson told her about his clubs and restaurants in Southern California and about Drake Distilleries.

"I know your products," she said. "High-end Scotch, rye and whiskey. Vodka and gin, too. And are you telling me you're hoping to bottle and sell Homer's moonshine in liquor stores all over the country?"

"All over the world, as a matter of fact."

"Wow."

"My family has been making good liquor for nearly a hundred years. When the story of the magic moonshine popped up on the wire services and the web, I read all about it. That was when it happened. I got the shiver."

"Which shiver is that?"

"The one I get when I have a great idea—like packaging Homer's moonshine for international distribution under the Drake label."

"Sounds a little crazy to me."

"Sometimes the best ideas are kind of crazy. I called Ryan. He gave me more details. Homer's famous formula is supposed to be delicious. I want to find out if it's as good as everyone seems to think—and if it is, I want it."

"Be careful," she warned. "Last Fourth of July, people drank Homer's moonshine and then did things they didn't even remember the next morning."

"I take my business seriously," he replied, his eyes level on hers. "And there are a lot of laws governing the bottling and distribution of alcoholic spirits. If I ever get my hands on Homer's formula, there will be extensive testing and trials before the finished product ever reaches the marketplace."

She tipped her head down and found herself staring at his boots. They were cowboy boots. Designer cowboy boots. The kind that cost as much as a used car. She sighed at the sight and lifted her gaze to him again. "It is kind of magical, what happened last year. I wasn't here, but everyone said people had the best time of their lives. There was a lot of hooking up."

"Thus, the Baby Bonanza."

"Exactly. People behaved way out of character, lost all control. Homer put the moonshine in the wedding punch, which was only supposed to have a small amount of sparkling wine in it. Nobody knew what they were drinking."

"I heard about that, too. The old fool is lucky nobody sued his ass."

"At first no one knew how the punch got spiked. For a while, there was talk about tracking down the culprit and putting him in jail. It was months before Homer confessed that he was the one."

"Was he ever arrested or even sued?"

"Nope. By then, folks were past wanting him to pay for what he'd done. It was getting to be something of a town legend, one of those stories people tell their kids, who turn around and tell *their* kids. It was as if Homer's moonshine allowed people to be…swept away, to do the things they would ordinarily only dream of doing. I mean, this little town is not the kind of place where people go to a wedding reception in the park and then wake up the next morning with a stranger, minus their clothes."

He leaned closer, so his forehead almost touched the brim of her hat, bringing the heat of his big body and the wonderful, subtle scent of his skin. "The whole aphrodisiac angle could be interesting—for marketing, I mean."

"Marketing." She put some effort into sounding less breathless and more sarcastic. "Because sex sells, right?"

"You said it—I didn't." His mouth was only inches from hers.

She thought about kissing him, and wanted that. Too much. To get a little distance, she brought up her hands and pushed lightly at his chest. "You're in my space."

One corner of that sinful mouth kicked up. "I think I like it in your space."

She kept her hands on that broad, hard chest, felt the strong, even beating of his heart—and slowly shook her head.

He took the hint, leaning back against the bench again and sipping his beer. "Ryan tells me you're from Bozeman."

"Born, bred and raised."

"You have a job there in Bozeman, Tessa?"

"I'm a graphic designer. I freelance with a small Bozeman firm—and I mean very small, so small the owner closes it down every summer."

"And that gives you a chance to have a nice, long visit in beautiful Rust Creek Falls every year?"

"Exactly. I also take work on my own. I have a website, StricklandGraphix.com—that's an *x* instead of a *cs*, in case you'd like to pay me a whole bunch of money to design your next marketing campaign."

"Are you good?"

"Now, how do you think I'm going to answer that?"

"Tell me you're terrific. I like a woman with confidence."

She took off her hat and dropped it on the bench between them. "Glad to hear it. Because when it comes to design, I know my stuff." *Even if I was blackballed from the industry and am highly unlikely to work in a major design firm or ad agency ever again.*

"Where did you study?"

"The School of Visual Arts."

"In New York?"

She poked him with her elbow. "Your look of complete surprise is not the least flattering."

"That's a great school." He said it with real admiration.

She shouldn't bask in his approval. But she did. "One of the best. I worked in New York for a while after I graduated."

"What brought you home to Bozeman?"

"Now, *that's* a long story. One you don't need to hear right this minute."

"But I would love to hear it." He was leaning close again, his arm along the back of the bench behind her, all manly and much too exciting. "You should tell me. Now."
How did he do that? Have her longing to open her mouth and blather out every stupid mistake she'd ever made?

Uh-uh. Not happening. "But I'm not telling you now—so let it go."

"Maybe you'll tell me someday?" He sounded almost wistful, and that made her like him more, made her think that he was more than just some cocky rich guy, that there was at least a little vulnerability under the swagger.

"I guess anything's possible," she answered, keeping it vague, longing to move on from the uncomfortable subject.

Again, he retreated to his side of the bench. She drank

a sip of ginger ale. Finally, he said, "You looked amazing in that stork costume."

"Oh, please."

"You did. You looked dorky and sweet and intriguing and original."

"Dorky, huh?"

"Yeah. Dorky. And perfect. Almost as perfect as you look right now. I couldn't wait to meet you. And now I never want to leave your side."

"I'll bet."

He put up a hand as though swearing an oath. "Honest truth."

She let out a big, fake sigh. "Not so perfect with babies, unfortunately. Poor little Gil—that's Kayla and my cousin Trey's baby, the one I was holding during the parade."

"I remember."

"Did you hear him wailing?"

"I did. Yes."

"He's probably scarred for life after having *me* hold him for the whole parade."

"I'm not much of a baby person, either," Carson confessed with very little regret.

She teased, "So you're saying that we have something in common?"

"I'll bet we have a lot in common." He sounded way too sincere for her peace of mind. She tried to think of something light and easy to say in response, but she had nothing. He picked up her hat, tipped it back and forth so the rhinestone accents glittered in the sunlight, and then set it back down between them. "Any particular reason you rode the *Gazette*'s float?"

"Two reasons. One, I need work and I'm trying to get in good with the paper's editor and publisher. I love Rust Creek Falls and I'm considering moving here permanently—if I can pull enough business together from my website and locally to make ends meet, that is."

"And the second reason?"

She leaned closer and whispered in his ear, "The stork costume fit me."

He chuckled at that. Then he asked about her family. "Ryan told me that you're staying at your grandmother's boardinghouse."

She explained that she had two sisters, one of whom still lived in Bozeman, as did their mom and dad. "My other sister, Claire, her husband, Levi, and Bekka, their little girl, live here at the boardinghouse. Levi manages a furniture store in Kalispell and Claire is the boardinghouse cook."

Carson listened to her ramble on. He really seemed to want to know everything about her. She found his interest flattering.

Maybe too flattering. Was she playing with fire?

Of course not. She'd met an interesting, attentive man, and she was enjoying his company.

Nothing wrong with that.

Eventually, they got up and each took a beer from the coolers. They visited with friends and family until the barbecue came off the smokers; then they sat together at a picnic table with Ryan and Kristen, Trey and Kayla. Tessa's sister Claire and her husband, Levi, joined them, too.

Tessa was having a fabulous time.

Her original fears about Carson seemed so silly now. He *liked* her. *She* liked *him*.

It was a beautiful day, and she was spending it with a handsome, hunky guy. It would go nowhere, and she was happy with that. Before very long he would return to his glamorous life in LA. She would stay right here in

Rust Creek Falls, enjoying her summer break and trying to figure out what to do with the rest of her life.

Later, as twilight fell, she and Carson got a blanket from his car. They spread the blanket on the grass, got comfortable and talked some more.

She confessed that she was kind of at a crossroads, trying to decide where to take her graphic design career. There was her nice, safe job in Bozeman and the growing business she was building through her website. "I kind of want to try leaving the Bozeman job and focusing on freelancing independently, but it's tricky."

He stuck his long legs out in front of him and crossed them at the ankles. "I thought you said you wanted to move here, to Rust Creek Falls."

"I do, but that doesn't really fit with my ambitions for work. I'm slowly accepting that eventually I need to choose between trying again for a more ambitious career and a move here."

"Go big," he suggested.

"And what, exactly, does that mean?"

He shrugged. "You need to be where the action is. Why don't you move to LA?"

She set her hat on the blanket between them and stretched out on her back. Folding her hands on her stomach, she stared up at the darkening sky. "You weren't listening to me."

He leaned over her and touched her chin with a light brush of his finger, causing a bunch of small, winged creatures to take flight in her belly. "I would be there. To help you get settled."

She tried to keep it light. "Oh, I just bet you would."

"Can you dial back the sarcasm?" He held her eyes.

"Carson, you hardly know me."

"And that's my point. I want to know you better."

There was a moment—a long, sweet one—when he gazed down at her and she looked up at him. The world seemed wide-open at that moment, bright and so beautiful, bursting with hope and limitless possibility.

He whispered, "It's just a thought."

"Don't tempt me." She meant it to sound teasing. Flirtatious. But somehow, it came out too soft. Too full of yearning.

But then the band started playing over by the portable dance floor beneath the warm glow of the party lights strung between the trees.

"Come on." He took her hand and pulled her to her feet. "Let's dance."

And they did dance. For over an hour, they never left the floor. He was more than a foot taller than her, but when he wrapped his big arms around her, it felt only… right. He knew the two-step and how to line dance.

When she told him she hadn't expected an LA boy to know the cowboy dances, he laughed. "You oughta see my disco moves."

"Okay, Carson. Now you're starting to freak me out."

Eventually, they got bottles of water from the coolers and returned to the blanket. Theirs was a great spot, out of the way of the action, shadowed and private, with only the thick swirl of the stars and the waning moon overhead for light.

They whispered together like a couple of bad children plotting insurrections against unwary adults. He told her that he'd been married to his high school sweetheart, Marianne. "Marianne wanted to start a family right away."

"And you didn't want kids, right?"

"Right. I realized I'd married too young. We divorced.

She remarried a couple of years later. Her husband Greg's a great guy. They have four kids."

She stretched out on her back again and stared up at the stars. "So you're saying she's happy?"

"Very. I don't see much of her anymore, but it's good between us, you know? We're past all the ugly stuff. She ended up finding just what she wanted."

"And what about you?"

"I'm happy, too. I like my life. It's all worked out fine." He leaned over her, bending closer.

It just seemed so natural, so absolutely right, to offer her mouth to him, to welcome his kiss.

His lips settled over hers, light as a breath. They were every bit as soft and supple as they looked. She sighed in welcome as little prickles of pleasure danced through her, and she was glad, so glad, that she'd denied her silly fears and come to the park, after all. That she'd met this charming man and was sharing a great evening with him.

When he pulled back, his eyes were darker than ever. "What is it about you, Tessa? I can't take my eyes off you. I feel like I've known you forever. And how come you taste so good?"

She laughed. "Oh, you silver-tongued devil, you." She was trying to decide whether or not to kiss him again when a raspy throat-clearing sound came from a clump of bushes about ten feet away.

Tessa sat up. "What was that?"

Carson challenged, "Who's there?"

Branches rustled—and an old man emerged from right out of the center of a big bush. He wore baggy black jeans, a frayed rope for a belt, battered lace-up work boots and the dingy top half of a union suit as a shirt. Bristly gray whiskers peppered his wattled cheeks. What was left of his hair stood up at all angles.

Tessa recognized him instantly. "Homer Gilmore, were you eavesdropping on us?"

Chapter Three

Homer Gilmore blinked as though waking himself from a sound sleep—and then he grinned wide, showing crooked, yellowed teeth. “Well, if it ain’t little Tessa Strickland. Stayin’ at your grandma’s place for the summer?”

“Yes, I am. And you didn’t answer my question.”

Homer scratched his stubbly cheek. “Me? Eavesdropping?” He put on a hurt expression. “Tessa, you know me better than that.”

Beside her, Carson rose smoothly to his feet and held down a hand for her. She took it, and he pulled her up to stand beside him.

Homer came toward them.

Carson seemed bemused. “Homer Gilmore. Face-to-face at last.”

Homer recognized him. “Carson Drake.” He accepted Carson’s offered hand and gave it a quick pump before letting go. “Told you I’d be in touch.”

"So then, that really was you on the phone?"

"'Course it was." Homer had a mason jar of clear liquid in his left hand. "Here." He shoved it toward Carson.

Carson eyed the jar doubtfully. "What's this?"

"*This* is what you came here to get." Homer grabbed Carson's hand and slapped the jar into it.

"No kidding." Carson held the jar up toward the party lights in the distance. "Homer Gilmore's magic moonshine?"

"The one and only." Homer spoke proudly, puffing out his scrawny chest. "Truth is, I like your style, kid. And here's what I want you to do. Try a taste or two. See what you think. Then we can talk."

"I'm sorry." Carson actually did sound regretful. "It doesn't work that way." He tried to hand the jar back.

Homer refused to take it. "*I* say how it works. Taste it."

"Look, we need a meeting. A real meeting. Yes, there should be sampling, but formal sampling, in a professional setting. And chemical analysis, of course—but all that comes later. First, how about we meet for dinner and we can discuss—"

"Hold on." Homer put up a hand. "We'll get to the talk and the dang *analysis*. But first, you try it. This deal goes nowhere until you do."

"Homer, you're not listening to me. I can't just—"

"Nope. Stop. You heard what I said. Have yourself a taste. After that, we'll talk."

"When, exactly, will we talk?"

"Don't get pushy, kid. I'll be in touch."

Carson opened his mouth to say something else—but then shut it without saying anything. Tessa got that. What was the point? Homer wasn't listening. With a wink and a nod in her direction, the old man turned and walked away. Tessa and Carson stared after him as he vanished into the darkness of the trees.

Baffled, Carson stared down at the jar in his hand. "I don't believe this."

Tessa dropped to the blanket again. "It's Homer. What can you expect?"

"You think he might be crazy?"

"Of course not. He's a little peculiar, that's all. Being an oddball doesn't make you crazy. Kayla had it right. He really does have a good heart."

"If you say so." But he seemed far from convinced. She patted the space beside her. He folded his tall frame down next to her. "So…" He set the jar on the blanket next to her hat. For several seconds, they stared at it together. Over near the dance floor, the band launched into the next number.

Tessa laughed when she recognized the song. "That's 'Alcohol' by Brad Paisley. Perfect, huh?"

Carson slanted her a look full of mischief and delicious badness. "Want to try it?"

She *did* want to try it. She was really, really curious—just to know how it might taste, to maybe get a sense of whether or not any of the outrageous rumors about it might be true.

"Tessa?" he prompted when she failed to answer him.

She tried to remind herself of all the reasons that taking a chance on Homer's moonshine was not a good idea. "It could be dangerous…"

"You really think it's all that bad?"

"I didn't say bad. But you've heard the stories."

He flapped his arms. "Bok-bok-bok."

She laughed and gave his shoulder a playful shove. "Don't make chicken sounds at me. I'm being responsible."

He leaned a little closer. “And what fun is that?”

Oh, she did like him. She liked him a lot—liked him more and more the longer she was with him. He was not only hot. He was fun and smart and perceptive.

And a very good kisser.

Did he see in her eyes that she was thinking about kissing him? Seemed like he must have, because he leaned even closer and brushed a second kiss against her mouth.

So good.

His lips settled more firmly on hers. She sighed in pure delight and had to resist the sharp desire to slide a hand up around his neck and pull him closer still.

She was probably in big trouble.

But the more she got to know him, the less she feared her attraction to him and the more it just felt right to be sitting beside him under the stars with the band playing country favorites. The night had a glow about it, even here in the shadows on their private little square of blanket. She was having so much fun with him, loving every minute of this night. She never wanted it to end. She wanted to sit here and enjoy the man beside her and maybe, a little later, to get up and dance some more. And after that, to steal another kiss.

And another after that.

He reached for the mason jar and unscrewed the lid.

She leaned close and whispered, “You shouldn’t have done that. It’s all over now. Our lives will never be the same.”

He arched an eyebrow at her. “The temptation is just too great. I can’t resist.” He sniffed at the open jar. “Smells like a peach.” He tipped his head to the side, his expression suddenly far away. “I’ve always loved peaches.”

“Peaches? No, really?”

"Really." He offered her the jar.

She took it and sniffed the contents for herself. "Hmm. Smells like summer."

"What'd I tell you?"

"But not peaches. Blackberries. Just a hint." She *really* wanted to taste it now. "I adore blackberries. They're my favorite fruit."

He wrapped his big hand over hers, and they held the jar together. He sniffed again, then insisted, "Admit it. It smells like peaches."

"No, Carson." She shook a finger at him. "Blackberries."

"Peaches."

"Blackberries. And look." She pulled the jar free of his grip and held it up to the party lights. "It even has a faint purple tint. Can't you see it?"

He took it from her hand and raised it high to decide for himself. "Looks more golden to me." He faked a serious expression. "And really, it *would* be a bad idea to taste it. Right?"

"Right. Bad idea to—Carson!" She let out a silly shriek as he took a careful sip from the jar. And then she leaned closer and asked, wide-eyed, "Well?"

He swallowed. Slowly. "That's good. Really good."

"Yeah?"

"Oh, yeah."

"Blackberries, right?" She nodded, holding his gaze, certain she could get him to nod along with her.

But his head went the other way—side to side. "Peaches. Definitely. And a hint of a moonshine burn going down. Gives it a nice kick."

"You're just playing with me."

He looked slightly wounded. "Never."

Only one way to make sure. "Give me that."

He held it away. "You'd better not. You never know what might happen."

"Knock it off, Carson. Hand it over."

"Whoa. Suddenly you're a tough girl."

"That's right. You don't want to mess with me."

"Never, ever would I mess with you." His voice was so smooth and manly, with just the perfect hint of roughness underneath. He gazed at her so solemnly. She really wanted to kiss him again.

Better not.

She reached for the moonshine instead. That time, he surrendered it. She put the jar to her lips and took a teeny, tiny sip.

Flavor bloomed on her tongue. A hint of sweet, summer fruit, and then wonderful heat going down. "Oh, yes. It's good."

"Told you so."

She gave a fist-pump. "Blackberry! Yes!" She sipped a little more, savoring the taste, relishing the lovely burn—and then handed it back to him.

A wonderful, sexy laugh escaped him. She laughed, too, the sound husky to her own ears.

He was watching her so closely, as though he couldn't get enough of just looking at her. She stared right back at him, a warm glow all through her. It was beautiful. Perfect.

She was lost in his eyes.

Chapter Four

Tessa woke slowly, smiling a little. All cozy and safe in bed, she was curled on her side, the blankets tucked up close under her chin.

But then she opened her eyes and felt her smile melt away.

What was this place?

The room was rustic, but richly so. She blinked and stared at an antique bronze mission-style glass lamp by the side of the bed. It sat on a night table made of gorgeous burled wood. Across the room—which was quite large—she saw a pair of French doors that looked out on a redwood deck with plush, padded furniture and a view of evergreen-blanketed mountains beyond. In the far distance, rugged snowcapped peaks poked the sky. It was clear, that sky, and very blue.

Daylight blue.

It must be morning.

But hadn't it been nighttime just a moment ago, nighttime at the Memorial Day picnic in Rust Creek Falls Park?

She shut her eyes and waited. Surely when she opened them again…

Nope. Nothing had changed. Same big, beautifully appointed room. Same morning light.

She pulled the covers tighter under her chin and whispered, "Where am I?" not really expecting an answer.

Then things got worse.

A sleepy male voice asked from behind her, "Tessa?"

She knew that voice—didn't she?

Carefully, slowly, clutching the covers close, she rolled to her back. With great reluctance, she turned her head. And there he was, Carson Drake, hair all rumpled, the scruff on his lean cheeks thicker than last night, his devastating mouth sexier than ever.

With a tiny squeal of distress, she lifted the covers enough to confirm her suspicions.

Yep.

Naked under there.

She grabbed the covers close again. "This cannot be happening."

He looked as bewildered as she felt. "Tessa, I don't…" Dark eyebrows drew together. Now he looked worried. About her. "Look, are you okay?"

She turned her gaze to the beautiful beamed ceiling above. Staring at it really hard, she whispered, "No, Carson. I am not okay." Panic rose. *Breathe.* She did, slowly, and exhaled with care. "I've…got nothing. I have no idea what we did for a least half of last night. I don't know how we got here." And then she went ahead and confessed the awful truth. "This is exactly like what everyone said happened to people last July Fourth. I've had a blackout,

I think. Last thing I remember, we were in the park sampling Homer's moonshine." She gulped and stared even harder at the ceiling overhead. "Do you, um, happen to know where we are and how we got here?"

"Hey. Look at me. Come on. Please?" He spoke so gently. As though her ears were tender and wounded—like her heart right now, like her self-respect and her very soul. She made herself face him again. He captured her gaze. "I didn't know—I promise you. I didn't believe that a jar of moonshine could really—"

"It's okay."

"No, it's not."

"Carson, what I mean is I didn't believe it, either. Just...would you answer my question, please? Where are we and how did we get here?"

"We're in my suite at Maverick Manor. But as to how we got here, I don't have a clue. I remember we drank the moonshine. And there are...flashes of memory after that. Us laughing on the blanket, staring up at the stars. I kissed you. And we danced."

"That was earlier."

"Yeah, and then we danced again, later. And...well, it all starts to go hazy after that."

"But did we...?" It seemed silly to even ask the question. They were here, together, naked. Almost certainly, they *had*.

He reached out a bare, beautifully muscled arm and scooped some bits of foil off the nightstand. "Looks like it."

"What do you mean?"

He opened those long fingers to reveal three empty condom wrappers. They crackled on his palm as the foil relaxed.

"Omigod." How could she? She didn't even *know* this

man. And yet here she was naked in bed with him, staring at empty condom wrappers with no recollection of using them. It was awful and embarrassing and not the kind of thing she would ever do—well, except with Miles. She'd fallen straight into bed with Miles the night she met him, too. But at least she was conscious when she did it. At least it had been her choice, and she'd loved every minute of it.

This, on the other hand…

No. Just...no.

This was all wrong. She didn't remember making a choice. She couldn't recall anything after those first few sips of moonshine.

Okay, she'd been attracted to him from the instant her eyes met his. Wildly so. But falling into bed with him? *Uh-uh. No way.*

"God. Tessa. Your face is dead white. Are you sure you're all right?" He was watching her as though he feared she might shatter.

Well, she wouldn't. Not a chance. She was tougher than that. Yeah, she'd messed up royally. But that didn't mean she couldn't hold it together. She let out a shaky little sigh. "I just can't believe that this is happening, that's all."

"At least we were safe about it," he offered sheepishly.

She played along, because she was not going to lose it right here in front of him. "Yeah. I guess that's something, right?"

"Right." He pushed himself to a sitting position.

She did the same, careful as she scooted up against the headboard to keep the blankets close. They leaned against the headboard side by side. She stared hard at the far wall and wished that the floor would just open up beneath her and swallow her whole.

The silence, weighted so heavily with regret and embarrassment, went on forever.

Finally, she murmured shakily, "I want to go home."

He looked at her again then. His eyes were so sad. "Tessa, I'm so sorry..."

She showed him the hand and aimed her chin high. "Don't. It's no more your fault than mine. I don't blame you. I drank that moonshine of my own free will." It had tasted so good. And she'd never really believed the stories about it. Until now. Slow fury rose in her. "I might have to kill Homer Gilmore, though." She spoke through clenched teeth. "Seriously. It's like we were roofied."

He made a low sound of agreement. "So much for my big plans to get the formula for Drake Distilleries. That stuff is way too dangerous."

She pressed a hand to her queasy stomach. "I may never drink anything with alcohol in it again."

"Believe me, I understand."

They shared a wry, weary glance, and she said, "I really do want to go now."

"All right."

She looked away, toward the balcony and the snow-capped mountains in the distance. The covers shifted as he left the bed. More fabric rustled.

He said, "I'll just use the bathroom." Footsteps padded away.

As soon as she heard the bathroom door close, she jumped from the bed, grabbed her wrinkled clothes from the bedside chair and put them on. Once she was fully dressed, including her socks and red boots, she went looking for her hat.

She found it on the coffee table in the sitting room—next to a sketch pad and a bunch of pastels and colored pencils. "What in the...?" She picked up the pad and turned the pages slowly.

The drawings were her own, though she had zero memory of creating them. And as to where she got the pad and pencils, who knew? But apparently, not only did she and Carson use three condoms last night; she'd also whipped him up an ad campaign for Homer's magic moonshine.

For the first time that morning, she almost smiled.

Not bad. Not bad at all. Clean, clear, imaginative and well executed, if she did say so herself. Even her domineering, tough-as-nails former boss, the legendary Della Storm of Innovation Media in New York, would approve. Tessa especially liked her rendering of a frosty-blue bottle with a sliver of silver moon on it and the words *Blue Muse* in a retro font. She also thought the sketch of a golden bottle with a lightning strike on the front was really good. That one was called *Peach Lightning* in bold copperplate Gothic. And the way she'd managed to work the Drake Distilleries logo of a rearing dragon into both designs? *Damn good.*

Glancing up from the pad in her hand, she stared into the middle distance, remembering how much fun she and Carson had had in the park, how they'd bantered back and forth over whether the 'shine was blackberry or peach. She'd loved every moment with Carson yesterday—at least, every moment that she could recall.

She heard the bathroom door open. With a hard sigh, she tossed the sketchbook back on the low table.

He appeared in the doorway to the bedroom, fully dressed in jeans, a knit shirt and a different pair of high-priced boots than he'd worn the day before. Dear Lord, he was a fine-looking man. Regret dragged at her heart that there couldn't be more between them.

But no. It had all gotten way too complicated too fast. She didn't need complications with a man, not until she had her own life figured out. She needed him to take her back to her grandmother's boardinghouse. After that, she never wanted to see that amazing face of his again.

Across the room, he stared her somberly. Probably trying to think of something to say to her.

She knew exactly how he felt. "I'll just use the bathroom and then I'm ready to go."

Carson found his car in his usual space in the parking lot. He'd had his keys in yesterday's jeans, so he must have driven them there. It freaked him the hell out to think that he'd gotten behind the wheel so drunk on moonshine he had no memory of the trip.

The ride back to town was a silent one.

Carson despised himself the whole way. And he couldn't stop thinking about the condom wrappers, couldn't stop asking himself if they were fools to depend on those empty wrappers as proof that they'd played it safe.

When he pulled in at the curb in front of the boardinghouse, she grabbed her hat off the seat with one hand and the door handle with the other. He should just let her go. It was obvious she wanted to get as far away from him as possible.

But he couldn't let her walk away. Not yet. First, they needed to deal with the consequences of their actions—whatever the hell those actions had actually been.

"Wait, Tessa. Please." She froze and stared at him, her dark hair a wild tangle of curls around her unforgettable gypsy-girl face. He made himself ask, "Are you on any kind of contraception?"

She winced and then confessed bleakly, "No. I had an

implant, but when it expired last time, I didn't replace it. And… I know, I know. Way more information than you needed."

His gut twisted at her news, but he kept his voice gentle and low. "I'm sorry, but I can't stop thinking that those condom wrappers don't really prove we were as careful as we needed to be." For that, he got a soft, unhappy groan.

She put her face in her hands. "You're right. You're absolutely right." With a ragged intake of breath, she lifted her head and squared her shoulders. "Don't worry about it. I'll take care of it. I'll get the morning-after pill today."

Rust Creek Falls had one general store. That store had no pharmacy area that he could remember. "Can you get it at Crawford's?"

She chuckled, a sound with very little humor in it. "No. I'll drive over to Kalispell. It's a quick trip, not a big deal."

He didn't want her doing that all alone. "I'll take you. We can go right now."

She looked at him for a long count of five. And then she answered firmly, "No, thank you. I appreciate the offer. You're a stand-up guy. But I really need to get through the rest of this walk of shame on my own." She grabbed the door handle again and was out on the sidewalk before he could think of some way to change her mind. "Goodbye, Carson," she said. The word had all the finality of a death sentence. She shut the door.

He watched her climb the boardinghouse steps and knew that it was over between them—over without really even getting started.

Tessa's grandmother Melba Strickland was waiting for her in the foyer just inside the front door.

"There you are." Melba reached out her long arms for

a hug. Tessa went into them. Her grandmother always smelled of homey, comforting things. Right now it was coffee and cinnamon toast and a faintly floral perfume. "When you didn't come down for breakfast at seven as usual, I got a little worried. I knocked on your door. No answer. I tried calling you, but your phone went straight to voice mail."

"Sorry." She'd left her phone in her room the night before. Because she'd only been running down the street to the park and she'd expected to return within a few hours. It must have died.

Her grandmother took her by the shoulders. "Are you all right?"

"I'm fine." Tessa resisted the urge to make up a lie that explained her whereabouts last night. Yes, her grandmother had old-fashioned values and wouldn't approve if Tessa said where she'd really been. But Tessa was a grown woman and her mistakes were her own to work out. Her grandma didn't need to hear it. "I want to grab a shower. Then I need to drive into Kalispell and pick up a few things." *You know, like the morning-after pill. Because I'm an idiot, but I'm trying to be a responsible one.*

Melba searched her face. "I just want you to know that I'm ready to listen anytime you need to talk."

Tessa's empty stomach hollowed further with a mixture of equal parts love and guilt. "I do know, Grandma. And I'm grateful."

Melba gave her shoulders a squeeze. "You need to eat."

"I really want to get going."

"Humor me. An egg, some toast, a nice cup of hot coffee..."

So Tessa followed Melba to the kitchen, where eighteen-month-old Bekka sat in a booster seat at the table, drinking from her favorite sippy cup and munching on Cheerios and grapes. It was after nine, so Levi was off at work in Kalispell.

"Auntie Tess, Auntie Tess! Kiss!" Bekka made loud smacking sounds until Tessa bent close and let the little girl press her plump, sticky lips to her cheek. Tessa might not be good with most babies, but at least her niece seemed to like her well enough. Bekka offered a fistful of Cheerios.

They were limp and soggy. Tessa ate one anyway as Bekka beamed her approval.

Then Tessa got herself some coffee, pausing to pat her sister's shoulder as she went by. Claire sent her a questioning look, and Tessa gave a rueful shrug in response. She set herself a place at the table, and Claire whipped her up some scrambled eggs. The food helped. Tessa felt a little better about it all once she'd eaten.

Upstairs, she hung her hat on the peg by the door, had a shower and paid no attention to the mild tenderness between her legs. She ignored the love bite on her left breast. It would fade to nothing in a day or two. She let the water run down over her, soothing her shaky nerves. And she tried not to regret what she couldn't even remember.

Not too much later, dressed in a short denim skirt and a soft plaid shirt, she was on her way to Kalispell. At the first drugstore she came to, she bought a root beer and the hormone pill she needed. She took the pill the moment she got back behind the wheel, sipping the root beer slowly as she drove back to town.

That taken care of, she helped Claire in the kitchen for a while and then went upstairs to check email and dig into some projects she'd acquired through her website. Last Friday, when she'd agreed to ride the *Gazette* float, she'd told Dawson Landry, the paper's editor and publisher, that she was looking for design work. Dawson had said that if she came by, he would put her to work. She'd said she would, on Tuesday.

Well, it was Tuesday. And follow-through mattered.

So once she'd made sure she was on top of her other projects, she called Dawson. He said to come on over.

At the *Gazette*, she spent a couple of hours punching up the layout for the next edition. Once she got absorbed in the work, she was glad she'd come. It helped to keep busy.

As for Carson, well, whatever they'd done last night, it wouldn't be happening again. Last night was clear proof that she should have followed her first instinct when it came to him, should have stayed at the boardinghouse and out of his way.

She wouldn't be seeing him anymore. She would get past her own stupid choices yet again. Everybody made mistakes and life went on.

And if Homer Gilmore knew what was good for him, he'd keep the hell away from her for the next hundred years.

Carson didn't notice the sketchbook until late that afternoon.

He'd driven into Kalispell, too. He'd had a late breakfast at a diner he found. And then he'd wandered around the downtown area, checking things out, seeing what the larger town had to offer.

Was he hoping he might run into Tessa?

A little. Maybe.

But it didn't happen.

It was so strange, the way he felt about her. He missed her. A lot. He'd met her less than twenty-four hour ago, yet somehow he felt as though he knew her. She had a kind of glow about her, an energy and warmth. Already he missed that glow.

His world was dimmer, less vibrant, without her.

As he drove back toward Rust Creek Falls, he realized that he hadn't felt this way about a woman in years. Not since he was fifteen and fell head over heels for Marianne.

He wished he could remember making love with Tessa. Somehow, even though he couldn't remember what they'd done late in the night, the clean, sweet scent of her skin and the lush texture of her hair were imprinted on his brain.

At the Manor, he spent a couple of hours catching up with email and messages. He got on the phone to a number of employees and associates in Southern California. When asked how the moonshine project was going, he said that it had fallen through.

He didn't, however, mention flying back to LA, though he might as well pack up and go. There was no reason to stay. So far, though, he'd failed to start filling suitcases. Nor had he alerted the pilot on standby in Kalispell to file a flight plan and get his plane ready to go.

At a little after four, Carson dropped to the sofa in the suite's sitting room and reached for the TV remote on the coffee table in front of him.

He noticed the two dozen colored pencils and bright, fat, chalklike pastels first. For several seconds, he frowned at them, wondering where they might have come from. Then he saw the sketchbook. The maids had been in and placed it just so on top of the complimentary stack of magazines.

Tessa. The sketchbook must be hers. But he didn't remember her carrying any art supplies with her yesterday. Where had the pad, the pencils and the pastels come from?

He had no idea. It was yet another lost piece of last night. Curious and way too eager to see what might be inside, he grabbed the sketch pad and started thumbing through it.

Instantly, at the first drawing of a series of different-shaped jars and bottles, he was impressed. Each design was unique. The jars were mason-style, the kind with raised lettering manufactured into the glass. Each one made him feel that he could reach out and grab it, that he could trace the pretty curves of the lettering with the pad of a finger. She had great skill with light and shadow, so the bottles almost seemed to have dimension, to be smooth and rounded, made of real glass.

Carson got that shiver—the one that happened whenever he had a really good idea.

These drawings of Tessa's gave him ideas.

She gave him ideas. Because beyond being gorgeous and original, with all that wild, dark hair and a husky laugh he couldn't get out of his head, Tessa Strickland had real talent. He slowly turned the pages, loving what he saw.

She knew how to communicate a concept; her execution was brilliant. Unfortunately, now that a deal with Homer was off the table, he wouldn't be able to use what she'd come up with here.

But you never knew. Homer Gilmore didn't have the moonshine market cornered. If Drake Distilleries developed their own, less dangerous brand of 'shine, the *Blue Muse* and *Peach Lightning* flavors might well have a future, after all.

And even if he gave up on making moonshine completely, Drake Distilleries could benefit from a talent like

Tessa's. And so could his restaurants and nightclubs. Targeted, carefully executed advertising and effective promotion were a lot of what made everything he put his name on successful. Adding Tessa to the firm that promoted his brand could work for him in a big way.

And for her, too. Before last night faded into oblivion, they had talked about her career, about where she might be going with it. He'd said she should go big. Now that he'd seen her work, he knew he'd been right. If he could make her a tempting enough offer, maybe he could convince her to come to LA, after all.

All at once he felt vindicated. He hadn't told his people he was returning to Southern California because he *wasn't*. Not yet.

Not until he'd convinced Tessa Strickland to move to LA, where he could help her have the kind of successful design career she so richly deserved. He knew he could give her a big boost professionally.

And if it went somewhere personal, too, he would be more than fine with that.

First thing the next morning, Carson called Jason Velasco, his contact at Interactive Marketing International in Century City. He was about to explain that he'd found a brilliant graphic designer and he was hoping she might be a fit for IMI. He planned to tell Jason that he wanted Tessa working on the various ad campaigns that IMI developed for both Drake Distilleries and Drake Hospitality, which was the mother company for Carson's clubs and restaurants.

But then he caught himself.

True, Jason knew where his bread was buttered. If Carson wanted Tessa working at IMI, Jason would damn well do all in his power to make that happen.

But how would Tessa react to Carson's setting her up for an interview without consulting her first?

Quite possibly not well.

Given that she'd walked away from him yesterday without a backward glance, he really couldn't afford to take the chance of pissing her off in any way.

And Jason was still waiting on the line, probably wondering if he'd hung up. Carson said lamely, "Hey! Just thought I'd call and check in, see how we're doing with the new campaign." Drake Distilleries was preparing to launch a series of flavored brandy-based liqueurs.

Jason gave him a quick rundown. Then he asked, "So you're still in the wilds of Montana on that supersecret new acquisition of yours?"

"Still in Montana, yes. And the project did start out as a secret. But this is a small town, and it's hard to keep a secret around here." He explained about Homer's moonshine, and how he'd thought it might work for Drake Distilleries. "But it was a long shot and it didn't pan out. The downstroke is it's a no go."

"That's too bad."

"Can't win 'em all."

"So you'll be on your way back now?"

"Not yet. I have a few more things I need to look into here first." *Things like how to convince a certain adorable brunette that California is the place for her.*

"But we'll see you on the twentieth?" On the twentieth, Jason and his team would be presenting the game plan for the liqueur campaign. It was an important meeting. In fact, Carson had more than one meeting he couldn't miss during that week. He would have to return to LA by then.

That gave him two and a half weeks to get through to Tessa. Ordinarily he had limitless confidence in his powers of persuasion. Not so much in this case.

"Carson? You still with me?"

"Right here. And of course I'll be there on the twentieth."

Once he hung up with Jason, Carson called Strickland's Boarding House. Tessa's sister Claire answered, politely identifying herself. He almost told her who he was. But then he remembered the look on Tessa's face when she'd left him the morning before. If Tessa knew he was calling, would she even come to the phone?

He decided to take no chances. "I'd like to speak with Tessa Strickland."

"Hold on."

A moment later, she came on the line. "This is Tessa."

Just the sound of her voice made his chest feel tight. He wanted to see her, wanted it a lot. "You probably won't believe this, but I can't stop thinking about you."

A silence. Not a welcoming one. "Hello, Carson."

"I was thinking maybe lunch. We could drive over to—"

"Carson, I don't think so."

He lowered his head and stared at his boots. "It's just lunch."

She spoke again, her voice almost a whisper. "Please don't worry. I went to Kalispell yesterday and took care of it."

"It?" And then he caught on. He swore low. "Come on, Tessa. Don't. I'm not calling about the damn morning-after pill."

A silence on her end. A long, gruesome one. Then finally, "It's just…not a good time for me to get anything started, you know?"

"Fine." Though it wasn't. Not fine in the least. "This isn't a personal call, anyway." That was only half a lie. He wanted to get close to her, absolutely. But he also wanted to help her have the career she deserved. "Did you know you left sketches in my suite?"

"Yeah. I saw the sketch pad on the coffee table and looked through it. I don't remember how or when it happened, but apparently we plotted out a moonshine campaign." She paused, then, "Wait a minute. You're going ahead with the moonshine thing after all?" Now she sounded surprised—and not in a good away.

"No."

She sighed. "Glad to hear it. You had me worried there for a minute."

"This isn't about the moonshine. It's about you, about your future. Those sketches are amazing. I want you to think about—"

"Carson."

He stared at his boots some more and knew he was getting nowhere. Feeling desperate and pitiful—emotions with which he'd never been the least familiar—he took one more stab at getting through to her. "You have so much talent. I only want to—"

"No, thank you," she said softly, with utter finality. "I have to go now. Goodbye."

Chapter Five

Tessa hung up the phone and hated herself.

She wanted to see Carson so much she could taste it, like a burning sensation on her tongue. She'd hurt him, blowing him off like that. She didn't want to hurt him.

She just…

She needed to keep her head about her, needed to remember that getting swept off her feet by a killer-handsome, charismatic rich guy didn't work for her.

Been there, done that. Not going there again.

She wanted *real* now—a down-to-earth life in this beautiful little town full of people she cared about. And if she couldn't make that happen here, she would come up with a workable compromise, one wherein she could build a satisfying career and still visit Rust Creek Falls at least a few times a year. Eventually, once she figured out how to make the life she wanted for herself, she might even start looking for a guy who wanted the same things she did.

Carson Drake was not that guy. And it really was for the best that she'd told him goodbye.

At first, after Tessa hung up on him, Carson was seriously pissed off. He spent half the day on the phone, keeping up with things in LA, asking himself constantly why he hadn't packed his bags and called his pilot.

That evening, he went downstairs to the hotel bar for a drink and ran into Nate Crawford, the owner of Maverick Manor. Nate said his wife, Callie, was working late at the medical clinic. "And I've been here at the hotel all day. How about a change of scenery? Follow me into town. We'll grab a beer at the Ace in the Hole." The no-frills saloon was the only bar inside the town limits.

At the Ace in the Hole, Carson had a longneck, played a little pool and talked business with Nate, who was always promoting investment opportunities in Rust Creek Falls. Nate wanted him to meet with some guy named Walker Jones who owned a number of day care centers all over the western states and was apparently on track to open a new day care in town—to cope with the recent baby boom, Carson assumed. Nate said Walker Jones might be willing to take on a silent partner or two.

"I'm in liquor and hospitality," Carson reminded the other man. "I know nothing about child care centers."

Nate shrugged. "Why not just meet with the guy? He'll be in town in a couple of weeks."

Carson should have said that he would be long gone by then. But he didn't.

Because he was going nowhere—not until he absolutely had to. Not until he'd found a way to get Tessa to spend a little more time with him, not until he'd gotten his chance to make her see that LA was the right move for her. He really had a thing for her. And he just couldn't walk away from that. Not until he was certain that it was never going anywhere.

Yeah, it didn't make a lot of sense. He'd spent the last decade carefully avoiding anything remotely resembling an actual relationship with a woman and he'd planned on keeping it that way.

But then there was Tessa. Just the sight of her in her silly stork costume, looking like she'd rather be anywhere else than on that float holding Kayla's baby…

One look at her and he'd known his plans were about to change.

He said, "I have meetings I can't miss in LA the week of the twentieth. But if your guy is here before then, sure. Let's have a drink at the Manor Bar, the three of us."

Nate set down his beer. "I'll let you know. Meanwhile, I've been meaning to ask…"

"Yeah?"

"Whatever happened with Homer Gilmore and that moonshine project of yours? You ever get him to meet with you?"

"I spoke with him briefly Monday night at the picnic."

Nate chuckled. "That Homer. One of a kind. And judging by the look on your face, the moonshine project is on hold?"

"You could say that."

"Don't want to talk about it, huh?"

"You could say that, too."

Nate got off his stool and clapped Carson on the shoulder. "Gotta tell you, Carson, I'm not surprised. Callie and I had a little of that wedding punch spiked by Homer last Fourth of July. I'm talking one small paper cupful each. It was a wild night for us—and that's just what I can remember of it."

"I hear you—believe me."

Nate looked at him sideways. "You did try it, then?"

"Yeah, I tried it. And I've learned my lesson. Homer's moonshine is powerful stuff. Drake Distilleries has no plans to unleash it on an unsuspecting world."

"I suppose that's wise." Nate stepped back to take his leave. "I need to head home. Callie should be done at the clinic by now." His green eyes gleamed with eagerness. The man couldn't wait to get home to his wife.

Carson felt a hot little stab of envy. He was eager, too. He wanted to see Tessa again, to watch her smile, hear her voice, brush a quick kiss against her wide mouth.

But that wasn't happening.

Not tonight, anyway.

The next morning, he admitted to himself that he needed help. He called Ryan.

"What's up?" Ryan demanded.

Carson cleared his throat. "I have a question."

"I'm here for you, man."

"Say, just for instance, that I wanted to get to know Tessa Strickland better..."

Ryan played along. "Okay, let's say you do."

"But Tessa's a little...reluctant." *Okay, fine.* She was a *lot* reluctant, but Ryan didn't need to know that.

"A woman actually capable of resisting *the* Carson Drake? Never been born."

Carson rubbed his temple where a headache was forming. He'd been on the phone for less than a minute and already he regretted making this call. "I need help, smart-ass, and you're giving me attitude."

"Really gone on her, huh? That was quick. Damn near instantaneous, as a matter of fact. But I'm not surprised."

"I swear to you, Ryan, if you start in about how I'm

destined to fall in love because this is Rust Creek Falls and that is what people do here, I will hang up on you."

"Go right ahead, man. And who will you ask for help next?"

Carson swore. "Very funny."

"Well, *I* kind of thought so—but okay. I've tortured you enough for one phone call. What do you need?"

"Ways to get closer to Tessa."

"You're turning stalker on me now?"

"I thought you said you were finished torturing me."

"That's not torture. That's just messing with your head."

"Ryan. Are you going to help me or not?"

Ryan heaved a big, hard sigh. "I suppose I have no choice. You're a victim of love, and you really need me."

He was so eager to get on with the conversation, he didn't even bother to argue about Ryan's indiscriminate use of the L word. "Terrific. Let's move forward. Got any suggestions?"

"Melba," said Ryan.

"Come again?"

"Melba Strickland, Tessa's grandmother? Owns the boardinghouse where Tessa is staying?"

"I remember. What about Melba Strickland?"

"You need to get friendly with her. You need to salt the old cow to get to the calf."

"What is that you just said?"

"It's an old country saying."

"Right. Because you're so damn country now."

"You put out a salt lick for the cow," Ryan patiently explained, "and her calf comes with her and then you can catch the calf—for whatever purpose. Tick removal. Branding…"

"How am I going to get friendly with Tessa's grandmother?"

"How do you get friendly with anyone? You get an introduction. Or you go to the places where they hang out."

"Like…?"

"Somehow you imagine I know where to look for Melba Strickland?"

"Well, this *is* your idea."

"Look. It's a really small town. Try the places everybody goes. Church, for instance."

"That's not till Sunday. It's Thursday."

"Carson Drake, you're a very impatient man. I think there's some kind of Bible study class at the community church tonight, as a matter of fact."

Bible study. Was he up for that? He supposed he would have to be. "Are you sure Melba will be there?"

"No. It was just a suggestion of somewhere she might possibly go. Let's see. What about Crawford's? Everyone goes to the general store at some point during the week."

"You want me to lurk around Crawford's General Store?"

"I'm assuming you'll be subtle about it." Ryan made a thoughtful sound. "There's the library. But I have no idea how often Melba goes there, if ever. Plus, a library is not the place to strike up a conversation. You're supposed to be quiet there… Let me think. Where else? Maybe the donut shop or Wings to Go. But I think church or Crawford's is a better bet for Melba. She's a busy older woman without a lot of time to waste munching donuts in coffee shops."

"What do I do once I actually figure out a way to meet the woman?"

"I already told you. You charm her. You make friends

with her, and she invites you home and Tessa will be there."

"I have to say, Ryan. This is about the weakest idea you've ever come up with."

"Sorry. That's all I've got for you. You need to spend some time coming up with your own ideas. And you need *not* to be in such a hurry."

"I live in Malibu. I have two corporations to run. I can't stay here forever."

"See, now? That's your problem. The women, as a rule, just fall in your lap. You're not used to having to work for something you want."

"I work damn hard, thank you."

"You know very well I'm not talking about business here. I'm talking about romance. I'm talking about—"

"Do. Not. Say. That. Word."

"I wouldn't dream of it. Now, get to work on Melba. And try to remember, Carson. This will be good for you. This will be character building."

Carson hung up from the call with Ryan and realized that he had no idea what Melba Strickland even looked like. He picked up his phone again to call Ryan back—and then set it back down. Hard.

He'd had more than enough of Ryan's advice for one day. He would find Melba Strickland on his own, thank you. How hard could that be?

Too hard, he realized in no time at all.

At first, he thought maybe he would just try asking a few people. Like Nate. Or maybe the mayor, Collin Traub. Or the sheriff, Gage Christensen. But the more he considered that approach, the more truly weird he realized he was going to sound. Because, seriously, what possible interest could a guy like him believably have in the elderly lady who ran the boardinghouse?

When he tried to picture himself explaining to Gage or Nate or Collin that he wanted to get to know Melba so he could get closer to Tessa Strickland…well, how was that going to look? Men in Rust Creek Falls were protective of women. He would come off as just what Ryan had jokingly called him: a stalker.

Ryan had suggested he try the library. He could go there and look through old copies of the *Rust Creek Falls Gazette*. Maybe he'd find a mention of Melba, hopefully with a photograph included.

But okay, say he got lucky with a nice, clear headshot of Tessa's grandmother to go by? Then what? It could take days of churchgoing and donut eating and lurking at the general store before he would even catch his first glimpse of the woman.

He didn't have days to waste. He had to be in LA on the twentieth, for God's sake. He needed to get things going with Tessa right away in order to have the next two weeks to convince her to give LA a shot.

Damn Ryan. He was no help at all.

Carson flopped back onto the sofa in his sitting room and scowled at the ceiling, mentally calling his longtime friend a whole bunch of bad names—and right then, just like that, the solution popped into his head.

Just like that, it all became crystal clear.

He knew what to do, and it was priceless.

A half an hour later, he marched up the front steps of Strickland's Boarding House and knocked on the door.

An old man in baggy trousers and a plaid shirt answered. "Howdy."

"I'm Carson Drake, in town on business."

The old guy took his offered hand and gave it a pump. "I'm Gene Strickland. Folks call me Old Gene." He ran a wrinkled hand over what was left of his hair and then moved back. "Come in, come in." Carson stepped over the threshold into a dark, old-fashioned entry hall with stairs rising up in the center of it. Old Gene shut the door. "You're that liquor fella, aren't you? The one trying to bottle Homer Gilmore's 'shine?"

Was there anyone in this town who didn't know more about his business than he did? He doubted it. "I'm the one."

"How's that workin' out for you?"

"Not well."

The old guy let out a cackle. "Why am I not surprised? What brings you to Strickland's?"

"I'm hoping you have a room available."

The wrinkles in Old Gene's forehead got even deeper. "I thought I heard you were stayin' out there at Maverick Manor with all the other rich folks?"

"I have been staying at the Manor, yes. But I've decided I would rather be here on Cedar Street, right in the thick of things." *And closer to Tessa*, he thought but didn't say.

"And that's gonna help you how?" Gene had very sharp eyes, and they were trained hard on Carson.

Carson almost asked the old coot what business it was of his. But he had a feeling that wouldn't go well for him. He punted for all he was worth. "I really like this town. And I've got about two more weeks here before I return to the rat race in LA. I want to…immerse myself in the real Rust Creek Falls experience, and that's not going to happen out at Maverick Manor."

More cackling from Old Gene. "*Immerse* yourself, huh?"

Carson gave a half shrug. "Hey. I'm from LA. We're big into immersion."

"Oh, I'll just bet." Old Gene gave him a long, measuring look. Then, finally, "Well, you'd better come on back to the office and I'll get my better half, Melba. She handles check-in."

Five minutes later, Carson stood at a check-in window in the boardinghouse office at the back of the building. He turned at the sound of footsteps. A sturdy-looking old woman in a button-front dress and sensible black shoes came through the door to the central hallway. She introduced herself. "Hello, I'm Melba, Gene's wife." His first thought—beyond how brilliantly he'd handled this—was that neither she nor her husband looked at all like Tessa. But then Melba smiled—a warm, wide smile.

Maybe there was a similarity, after all.

"Excuse me, young man."

He stepped aside, and Melba opened the door with the check-in window in it and entered the office cubicle on the other side. "Now," she said with another echo-of-Tessa smile. "I have a nice room on the third floor that has just come vacant. It's next to my granddaughter Tessa's room, as a matter of fact." Melba gave him a look from under her eyelashes, and he was absolutely certain she knew *everything* about Monday night—which, come to think of it, would be a hell of a lot more than *he* knew. She asked, "How's that sound?"

He opened his mouth, and the truth popped right out. "Just about perfect." Could he really be getting this lucky?

"You and Tessa will have to share a bath. All the rooms do. Gene says you're from LA and you were staying at the Manor before. You really don't mind sharing a bathroom?"

He kept his face harmlessly blank. "I'm sure it will be fine." And he whipped out his platinum card before she could tell him she'd changed her mind and she didn't want him anywhere near her granddaughter.

Melba ran the card through one of those ancient credit card sliders and then passed him his receipt, rattling off meal and snack options as she did it. Next, she reached to the side and grabbed something—a white plastic caddy—which she plunked on the office check-in window ledge in front of her. "You'll need this to carry your shampoo and shaving gear to and from the bathroom. Here's your key."

He couldn't quell his wide grin as he took the key and grabbed the white caddy. "Thank you."

She eyed him with what seemed to be vague suspicion. "Any questions?"

Now that he thought about it, he did have a question. "Do you have Wi-Fi?"

Melba made a disapproving sound, as though she thought internet access was just pure foolishness. "Gene likes his internet, my grandchildren say they have to have it when they come to visit and most folks these days can't get along without it. We do have it now, though service can be a bit spotty."

Spotty. Not good. But he would keep his suite at the Manor and stay in electronic communication with LA from there.

Melba gave him a small white card. "Here's the password."

"Terrific."

"Enjoy your stay."

"I'm sure I will."

Tessa sat in Emmet DePaulo's cramped office at the Rust Creek Falls Medical Clinic.

Emmet, a nurse practitioner who'd been running the

clinic for as long as Tessa could remember, held out his hand across the desk to her. Tessa rose to shake it. Emmet said, "We really appreciate this, Tessa. It's just me, Callie and Dawn." Callie Crawford was also a nurse practitioner. "Thank the good Lord for Callie. And Dawn. She's a lifesaver." An RN, Dawn Laramie had recently joined the clinic staff. "With all the babies born in the last few months, we need a pediatrician and we need one yesterday."

Tessa shut her laptop and tucked it under her arm. "I'll work up the material we talked about and email it to you tomorrow for approval." She would create a few eye-catching ads as well as simple text-only listings using the information Emmet had just given her. Once Emmet approved her work, she would place the ads for him online in medical forums and on job sites where doctors and nurses looked for employment. "You'll have that new doctor you need in no time."

Emmet came around the desk and walked her out to the waiting area, where every chair was taken. Babies were crying and Brandy, the clinic receptionist, looked about at the end of her rope. Tessa felt really good to be able to help in a good cause. Plus, due a lot to Callie Crawford's husband, Nate, who had plenty of money and put a fair amount of it into worthy causes, the clinic was well funded. Tessa would actually get paid for creating and placing the ads. Win-win in a big way.

Outside, it was cool and sunny. A gorgeous day. Tessa paused before ducking into her trusty Honda CR-V. She turned her face toward the mountains—and thought of Carson with a sharp little stab of what could only be called longing.

She'd been thinking of Carson a lot, way too much, really, since yesterday morning when she'd made it painfully clear to him that this thing between them was over. *Goodbye*, she'd told him. And that should have been the end of it.

Except for how her mind wouldn't stop turning back around to wondering about him and what he might be doing now. Except for the ache in her solar plexus that kept reminding her she missed him.

It was absurd. How could you miss a guy you hardly knew?

Yanking open her door, she dropped her shoulder bag and laptop on the passenger seat and slid in behind the wheel. She hauled the door shut—and then, with a sad little groan, sagged forward until her forehead met the wheel.

Okay, she kind of wished she'd given him more of a chance. Yeah, he was cocky and too rich and too good-looking, totally dangerous to her poor heart and her emotional equilibrium.

Still, she liked him. A lot. She loved being with him. And what could it hurt to enjoy his company for the few more days he might be in town? Just because he reminded her too much of Miles—well, how was that *his* fault?

And as for the craziness that had happened with the moonshine? Again, as she'd reminded herself more than once already, not Carson's fault. She'd drunk that stuff of her own free will—and he'd been just as knocked out by it as she had.

And then she'd freaked and blown it with him. *Way to go, Strickland.*

There was something…not really right about her. She was socially stunted, and she probably ought to get help. She felt powerfully drawn to Carson. She wanted to get to know him better—and so what had she done about that?

Told him to get lost. *Ugh.*

She longed to call him back and tell him she'd been all wrong to end things before they even really got started. She wanted to ask him for another chance.

Not that she would do that.

No. Better to accept her own idiocy, leave bad enough alone and try to do better next time.

A sad little laugh escaped her. Yeah, because killer-handsome, cocky guys who made her laugh, knew the two-step, thought her work was brilliant and turned her knees to jelly were so easy to come by.

Tessa lifted her forehead off the steering wheel, squared her shoulders and muttered, "Get over it," to the empty car.

He was probably long gone back to LA by now, anyway. She needed to let it go.

She started up the car and drove to the boardinghouse—where she found Carson's rented Cadillac SUV parked in the lot behind the building.

Chapter Six

Carson had just finished hanging his shirts in the closet and putting his underwear in the ancient bowfront bureau when the tap came on the door. He shoved the drawer shut, tossed his empty suitcase in the closet and went to answer, hoping that just maybe it might be Tessa.

Score.

She looked amazing, eyes wide and somber, mouth twisted ruefully, standing right in front of him on the threadbare runner in the narrow hallway. She wore a soft pink shirt, black jeans with rolled cuffs and high-heeled sandals with ties that wrapped around her slim ankles. Her hair was loose, corkscrew curls wild and thick around that gypsy face. Just the sight of her raised his blood pressure and hollowed him out down low. He had to order his hungry arms not to reach for her.

"Tessa," he said prayerfully. "At last."

She cleared her throat, a thoroughly enchanting, nervous little sound. "I saw your car in the lot. When I went looking for you downstairs, my grandma shared the big news that you had taken the empty room next to mine..." Her voice trailed off. They stared at each other. Finally, she spoke again. "We should talk."

He stepped back, clearing the doorway.

When she entered, he shut the door and enjoyed the view as she walked to the bed and sat down on the bright red, white and blue quilt. When she patted the space beside her, he couldn't get over there fast enough.

He dropped down next to her and sucked in a slow breath through his nose. She smelled like a rose. A rose and some wonderful, sweet spice.

"What are you doing here?" Her words demanded answers, yet her eyes were soft.

He wanted to touch her, to brush her arm, take her hand. But he didn't dare. "I couldn't give up. Sorry. It's just not in me. Ryan suggested that I make friends with your grandmother."

She blinked in surprise. "My grandmother? What for?"

"As a way to get close to you."

She pondered that for a moment. Then, "That's a little..."

"Out there?" he volunteered when she seemed to have trouble coming up with the right words.

"Yeah."

"Well, Ryan's always been a little out there. But I had nothing, so I went with his suggestion. I was knocking myself out trying to come up with ways to become BFFs with your grandmother. And then I thought of just taking a room here." She looked at him so steadily, he could see gold flecks in those coffee-brown eyes of hers. And dear God, that mouth. He couldn't wait to kiss her again.

She sent a quick glance around the room. "Kind of a step down from Maverick Manor—wouldn't you say?"

"No way. I love it here. This is a terrific room. It has everything I need. A bed, a dresser. A bathroom down the hall..."

"I am making an effort *not* to roll my eyes."

He *had* to ask. "So does your grandmother know you spent Monday night with me? I swear, while I was talking to her, I got the feeling she knew it all."

Tessa actually chuckled. The sound warmed him through and through. "Let's play it smart and never ask her what she knows."

"Because she's one of those old ladies who doesn't believe in hot, sexy times outside of marriage?"

Tessa laughed again, a snorting little burst of sound that had him feeling downright hopeful about his chances with her, after all. "Actually, I don't think my grandma believes in hot, sexy times under any circumstances. But you never know. Did you meet my grandpa, too?"

"I did. And as you can see, I lived to tell about it."

"And Claire?"

"I haven't seen her yet. But I remember you mentioned that she lives here, too."

"There are two full apartments downstairs. My grandparents have one. My sister and her family have the other."

"And Claire and Levi have a little girl, right?"

"Yeah. Bekka. I love Bekka. She's the only baby who ever liked me." Her beautiful smile trembled a little. She lowered her gaze.

He resisted the urge to tip up her chin and make her meet his eyes again. "So you're not mad at me for moving in here?"

And then she did look at him. *God.* He wished she

would never look away. "No, Carson. I'm not mad. How long are you staying?"

"Till the nineteenth. I have meetings in LA the week of the twentieth."

She touched him then, just a quick brush of her hand on the bare skin of his forearm. Heat curled inside him, and he could have sworn that actual sparks flashed from the point of contact. Then she confessed, her voice barely a whisper, "I regretted saying goodbye to you almost from the moment I hung up the phone yesterday."

"Good." The word sounded rough to his own ears. "Because I'm going nowhere for the next two weeks."

She slanted him a sideways glance. "You mean that I'm getting a second chance with you whether I want one or not?"

All possible answers seemed dangerous. He settled on, "Yes."

"I...um. I want to take it slow, Carson. I want to..." She glanced down—and then up to meet his eyes full-on again. "Don't laugh."

He banished the smile that was trying to pull at his mouth. "I'm not laughing."

"I want to be friends with you. Friends first. And then we'll see."

Friends. Not really what he was going for. He wanted so much more. He wanted it all—everything that happened Monday night that he couldn't remember. He wanted her naked, pressed tight against him. Wanted to coil that wild, dark hair around his hand, kiss her breathless, bury himself to the hilt in that tight, pretty body of hers, make her beg him to go deeper, hear her cry out his name.

But none of that was happening right now. So he said

the only thing he could say, given the circumstances. "However you want it, Tessa."

"You're sure about that?"

"I am."

"Because, I'm…" She ran out of steam. Or maybe courage.

And that time he did reach out to curl a finger beneath her chin. She resisted at first, but then she gave in and lifted her gaze to his once more. He asked, "You're what?"

"I'm not good at this, you know?" She stared at him, her mouth soft and pliant, all earnestness, so sweetly sincere. "I'm kind of a doofus when it comes to romance and all that."

He laughed at that, though she'd warned him not to. "A doofus? No way, not you."

"Yes, me. Growing up, I wasn't even interested in boys."

Damn. He wanted to kiss her. Instead, he wrapped an arm around her and pulled her in snugly against his side. She didn't resist—on the contrary, she laid her head on his shoulder. He took total advantage and pressed a quick kiss into the dark cloud of her hair. "Not interested in boys?" he teased. "That can't be normal."

She nudged him with her shoulder. "You're just asking for trouble." But then she settled close again and continued. "I was obsessed, but not with boys. All I cared about was art. I was a total nerd about it. I spent hours drawing every day, and I never slacked on my schoolwork. I needed straight As so I could go to the best design school on scholarship. I got what I was after, a full ride to the college of my choice. I moved to New York, and I never looked back."

"But then, somehow, you ended up back in Bozeman?"

Several seconds ticked by before she answered. "Really, it's a long story and not all that interesting."

"That's pretty much what you said Monday night. And then you clammed up. But now that we've decided we're going to be friends, I think it's only fair that you go ahead and tell me."

"Oh, right. Because you're all about what's fair."

"Come on," he coaxed. "Tell me."

She tipped her head and looked up at him, her dark eyes turned darker, her mouth softer, more vulnerable. "Carson, I..."

"I really do want to know."

She rested her head on his shoulder once more. And finally, she confessed, "I messed up."

"Messed up how?"

"You're not going to give up, are you?" she grumbled. "Not until you know it all."

He smiled to himself. "No, I'm not. You might as well just tell me everything—get it over with so that we can move on."

"You're impossible."

"I've been called worse, believe me. So, you got a full scholarship to the School of Visual Arts and..."

She hesitated, but then she forged ahead with it. "I did well there. In my last year of college, I got a great internship with a small Brooklyn firm. Two months later, they gave me a real job. And I was hired away from them by *the* Della Storm, who is as close to legendary as anyone gets in the world of graphic design."

Carson stroked her hair, loving the feel of it, so thick and wild and warm. He coiled a few strands around his finger as she explained that Della Storm was not only a legend in her field but also tough, uncompromising and difficult to work for. At the age of twenty-four, Tessa had already been given a lot of responsibility and creative say in the projects she took on under Della's supervision. But then she met Della's ex-boyfriend, an archeologist named Miles Rutherford.

"It was insane, how fast I fell for him," Tessa said. "One look in those blue eyes of his, and I was just gone. In the space of a glance, I went from zero interest in love and romance to head over heels."

Already, Carson hated this Miles character, though for all he knew, the guy hadn't done a thing but be the man Tessa fell in love with. "Lucky Miles Rutherford. Let me guess. You were inseparable from that moment on."

"Pretty much."

"Tell me more about him."

She lifted her head from his shoulder. "Do we really need to go into all the gory details?"

He wanted to know everything about her—including the difficult stuff she was reluctant to share. "Come on. Just tell me."

"What can I say? He was from a wealthy Montana family and I felt this instant connection with him."

"How did you meet him?"

"It was one of those big charity events at the Waldorf, the women in full evening dress, the men looking sharp in black tie. We struck up a conversation and talked for hours—about Montana, about design, about Miles's life traveling the world. Then we went to his place and I stayed the night. I moved in with him the next day." She glanced up and scanned his face as though looking for clues as to what he might be thinking. "Go ahead. Say it."

He gave a half shrug. "That was quick."

"I know. And I knew it then, that it was all happening much too fast. But I didn't even care. From the first moment I saw him, he was everything to me. After that first night, I didn't care about my job, didn't give a damn about the career I'd spent my whole life up to that point building. I got sloppy. We were working on an important project, and Della trusted me to run it. I just blew the whole thing off. I messed up everything I'd worked so hard for. I let a lot of people down. It really was all on me. I chose some guy I didn't even know over my life and my responsibilities."

"You said that this Miles was your boss's ex?"

She shifted against him with a tiny sigh. "Caught that, did you?"

He kissed her hair again. "Not a lot gets by me."

"I'll bet. Yeah, Miles was Della's ex. He was completely over her."

"But *she* wasn't over *him*."

"Shh. This is *my* story."

"Am I right?"

"Yes, you are. Della wasn't over him. And I never had the guts to tell her that he and I were together. She found out about Miles and me around the same time I blew up that project she'd trusted me to run. She was furious with me on so many levels. She had no claim on Miles. But she did have every right to come after me for going AWOL on the job. She fired me and she promised me that she would see to it I never worked in a major firm again."

Carson thought about IMI. *The* Della Storm and her jealous vendetta aside, Tessa would have a job at IMI if he wanted her there—well, she would if he could talk her into going to work for them. "How long ago was it that this Storm woman fired you?"

"Four years. And when Della blackballed me, I have to tell you, I didn't even care. All I cared about was Miles. After that, I didn't pick up a sketchbook or open a graphic design program for a year and a half. I was with Miles, and that was plenty for me. He worked in South America, in Egypt and in Spain. When he wasn't on a dig, we lived in luxury in hotels in Paris, London, Rome, Marrakech—you name it. At first, it was like a fairy tale, but over time, the magic began to fade."

"How long were you with him?"

"Two years."

"Why did you break up?"

"He got over me, just like he got over Della before me. I'm pretty sure he was cheating on me before the end. And I was…well, I was starting to admit to myself that what we had wasn't really working for me, either. That I needed my *own* life, you know? I regretted tossing my career in the crapper like that. And then one day I walked in on Miles in bed with two gorgeous women, identical twins."

"Whoa."

"Exactly. That was a real eye-opener. I will never forget what he said to me. 'Darling. Join us.' He was smiling like it was nothing, daring me to make a scene."

"And you…?"

"I didn't say a word. I knew exactly what he was trying to tell me. He was done with me. I turned and left the room. Then I packed my stuff and flew home to Bozeman. The really sad part is, by then, I didn't even care. Seeing him with those two women was just the final nail in the coffin of our bad romance. I'd screwed up my life for some guy I didn't really even know."

"And I…remind you of him, of Miles?"

She eased free of his hold and scooted away a little. He wanted to pull her back but thought better of it. "I love Montana, Carson. I missed Montana during the years I was in New York. And then, with Miles, living from one hotel to the next, I missed home even more."

"Tessa." He waited until she looked at him. "Do I remind you of Miles?"

"You really, truly want me to answer that?"

He didn't, not really. But he needed to know. "Yes."

"Fine." She threw up both hands and then let them drop. "The more I'm around you, the less you remind me of him, the more you're just...you. But yeah. When I first saw you, standing on the town hall steps looking like you ruled the world, it was pretty much Miles all over again."

He got up, went to the window and stared out over the street below. When he faced her again, he made his position very clear. "I don't cheat. Yeah, I wanted to be free when my marriage ended. But I never got near another woman until I had my divorce."

"But there have been a *lot* of other women, right?"

"Is that somehow a crime?"

"Now who's not answering the question, Carson?"

He knew he was busted. "Okay. Yeah. There have been a lot of women. But I'm not seeing anyone now." Truthfully, in the past year or so, he'd started to feel edgy and dissatisfied again, just as he had when his marriage was ending. He'd had his years of freedom, and it had been a great ride. But spending his nights with a series of beautiful women he would never really know—didn't even want to know—just wasn't as exciting as it used to be.

Tessa prodded, "You sure there's no part-time girlfriend thinking she means more to you than she does?"

"Absolutely not."

"No good-time girls waiting at your Beverly Hills mansion for you to return and join them in the hot tub?"

"No. I live in Malibu, and I live alone."

She glared at him intently for a long count of five, as though if she only looked hard enough, she might see inside his skull and know with certainty his level of truthfulness. Finally, she nodded. "Okay, then," she said on a soft little sigh.

He had more questions—about a thousand of them. "Were you and Miles ever married?"

"No."

"But you were exclusive with him?"

"I thought so. But I thought a lot of things, and you see how well that turned out for me."

"You want *us* to be exclusive? That *is* what you're talking about here, right?"

She groaned at that. "See? I'm a mess when it comes to this relationship stuff. I just asked you to be my friend, and ten minutes later I'm grilling you about other women, making you think I'm demanding exclusivity."

"But you do want exclusivity, don't you?" He had no doubt that she did. "See, that's the thing, Tessa. You have to tell me what you want."

She blew out her cheeks with a hard breath. "Well, how about if you could be exclusive for the next two weeks, anyway?"

He tried not to grin. "Even though we're just friends?"

She covered her face with her hands. "We shouldn't even be talking about this right now. It's too early to be talking about this."

He suggested, "How about this? I promise not to seduce any strange women for the next two weeks—present company excluded."

She let her hands drop to her lap, revealing bright spots of red high on her cheeks. "Maybe you shouldn't warn me ahead of time that you'll be trying to seduce me."

"Why not? We both know that I will, so the least I can do is be honest about it."

"Hmm. Well, okay. I'm all for honesty." Her soft mouth

was trying not to smile. "And I admit that I *am* a little strange."

"But in a thoroughly captivating way."

She bent her dark head again and said almost shyly, "Every now and then, you say just the right thing."

"Tessa?"

"What?"

"Look at me." He waited until she met his eyes directly before asking, "Are you absolutely determined to stay in Montana? You wouldn't consider LA, even if you could get your dream job there?"

She hitched up that firm chin. "You're pushing too fast."

"I'm going home in two weeks."

"So then, could you maybe wait a few days at least before trying to talk me into moving to California when I've just said I want to be here? Besides, didn't you hear me say I was blackballed from my own industry?"

"With the right connections, anything is possible."

Her wide mouth tightened. "You mean *your* connections."

"That is exactly what I mean. You know IMI?"

She actually gaped. "You're telling me you think you can get me a job as a graphic designer with Interactive Marketing International?"

"I don't think it. I *know* it. And a *real* job, one that makes full use of your talent, one that's exciting and challenging. You would be a full member of the team."

"Right. Just like that."

"Yeah. Just like that. Don't stare at me as though this is something I should be ashamed of. I have connections, and I'm willing to use them to get what I want."

She glared at him. "Just when I start thinking how

great you are, you make me want to hit you with a large, blunt object."

She was really cute when she was mad. But he had a feeling telling her so wouldn't help his case. He gentled his tone. "You're right. It's only fair that I wait a few days before bullying you into taking a great job with a big paycheck in sunny Southern California."

A scoff escaped her. "Did you just say that you'll let it be for now? Because somehow I'm not feeling it."

He tried his best to look solemn and sincere. "I'm leaving it alone. For now."

She stood. "Thank you." And she turned for the door.

His heart sank to his boots. "Wait. Where are you going?"

"To my room."

"I just got you talking to mc again, and now you want to leave?"

She paused with her hand on the doorknob. "I have some work I need to do. But I'll meet you downstairs at noon in the dining room. We can grab a couple of sandwiches and have a picnic in the park."

He'd been hoping at the very least to steal a kiss before he let her escape. *Have patience*, he told himself. But patience wasn't his strong suit—especially not where she was concerned. "A picnic sounds good."

"All right, then." And she pulled open the door and left him standing there alone by the window wishing it was noon already.

For lunch, Strickland's offered a variety of sandwich choices. The guests gathered in the dining room, where Melba served them beverages and took their orders.

As part of the family, Tessa went straight to the kitchen. She always made her own lunch, careful not to get in Claire's way. Today, she led Carson in there with her. Claire greeted them both and went back to work assembling a trio of club sandwiches.

"Roast beef? Turkey? Ham?" Tessa asked him.

Carson chose roast beef on rye. She made his sandwich and a turkey on whole wheat for herself. They grabbed two individual bags of chips, a couple of Claire's to-die-for chocolate chip cookies and a bottled water each, and headed for the park just down the street.

It was nice out, the day cool and bright. They found an empty picnic table under a big tree and sat down across from each other.

He'd no sooner unwrapped his food than he wanted her to share specifics about Della Storm, about what exactly had happened when Della fired her. He was pushing too hard again, and Tessa almost let her temper flare.

But then she caught herself. She took a moment to gaze at him across from her, heartbreaker handsome in a buff-colored jacket that hugged his broad shoulders over a white knit shirt that showed off his tan skin. And he was not only way too good-looking. He really did want to know about her, about her life, about what had made her the person she was.

How could she get mad at him?

She'd shut him down twice. Still, he'd knocked himself out to try to get close to her. He'd moved from the luxury and comfort of Maverick Manor to her grandmother's no-frills boardinghouse just for a chance to get to know her better.

If he wanted all the awful details of her past failures at life, work and love, well, so be it.

"I was no innocent victim, Carson. Don't even try to paint me as one. Yeah, Della was wildly jealous over Miles and vindictive about it. But I blew off a major project when I fell in love with him. It was as if my brain and ambition went on a long holiday, and all I wanted was to spend every moment with Miles. I'd never been in love before, never understood what other people thought was so important about finding 'the one.'" She dropped her sandwich to air-quote that for him. "And then I met Miles and—boom! I got it. I had no balance, you know? I went from being all about my career to being all about Miles, with no middle ground. I really messed up, and I fully deserved to suffer serious professional consequences."

He sipped from his water bottle. "You're too hard on yourself."

She loved that he defended her. But she couldn't agree. "You're entitled to your opinion. Even when you're wrong."

"So you're telling me you think you should be punished forever because of one mistake?"

"Well, Carson, it really was a doozy of a mistake. And I made it in a competitive field where second chances don't come easily."

"Just answer the question."

"Bossy much?" She opened her chips. "No, I don't think I should be punished forever. But I get why the big ad and design firms are going to be reluctant to hire me."

"Can you say with certainty that you would never screw up like that again?"

She felt pressured again and had to hold back a flippant response. It really was a good question, so she gave him a carefully considered reply. "I can say that I have definitely learned my lesson. I'll never leave colleagues or clients high and dry again. Life sometimes gets in the way of business, but if for some reason I couldn't hold up my end of a project, I'd be damn sure to keep communication open and find a way that the job would get done without me." She popped a chip in her mouth.

"All right. I have one more question."

"Of course you do." She waved another chip dramatically. "Go ahead. Hit me with it."

"Come to dinner with me in Kalispell tonight? Ryan told me about this great little Italian place."

She went with him.

How could she not? He charmed her and he challenged her. Every hour she spent with him, she found herself liking him more. And hey, the man was really easy on the eyes.

He ordered a nice bottle of Chianti and they shared an antipasto. She had ravioli. She also had a great time. He told her about his parents, who divorced when he was in his teens. His mother had remarried. Andrea VanAllen Drake Rivas had no other children. She now lived in Argentina with her second husband. His dad had died of a heart attack five years before.

She wanted to know more. "What about grandparents, aunts and uncles, cousins?"

"No grandparents living. I'm the only son of an only son. My mother has a sister, I think."

"You *think*?"

"They were never close, and I never met my aunt."

"I can't imagine being the only one. I have two sisters and grandparents on both sides. I have three uncles on my dad's side, aunts on my mother's side and a whole bunch of cousins. A Strickland family reunion is a thing of beauty, let me tell you. How long have you been running Drake Distilleries?"

"I took over when my father died. But I opened my first club two years before that. I wanted my own company, something I'd created from the ground up. Drake Hospitality has always been all mine."

"Clearly, there's nothing wrong with your work ethic, Carson."

"I like working, making things happen. My father encouraged me to get out there and see what I could do. He bankrolled my first club without even stopping to think it over. He used to talk about how rich kids often grew up lazy, lacking ambition. He said that I'd never had that problem and he was glad."

She could hear real affection in his voice. "You loved your father."

"Yeah. He was tough. Always one step ahead of the competition. And fearless. He loved the great outdoors, all the macho stuff—hunting and mountain climbing, sailing and stock-car racing. When he went after something, he got it. He taught me to shoot, took me hunting all over the world. I can't say I enjoyed it as much as he did, but if the day ever comes when I need to use a rifle to bring down some dinner, I'll be able to hit what I'm aiming at and take proper care of my weapon, as well. Maybe my dad was a little *too* driven. I think he lost my mother because he didn't have much time for her. And his doctors had been telling him to slow down for at least a decade before he had the heart attack that killed him."

"Would you say that you're like him?"

"In a lot of ways, yes. And proud to be. But I'm better at delegating, better at letting at least some things go." He gave her a smile that did something crazy to her heart. "So, tiramisu? Cannoli?"

"No, thanks. I couldn't eat another bite."

He waved her refusal away and ordered one of each. She ate some of each, too. More than a little. The desserts were too tempting to ignore.

Kind of like the guy across from her.

When they left the restaurant, the sun was half an orange ball sliding slowly behind the tall mountains. They got in his Cadillac, and she automatically went to latch her seat belt.

Carson's big, hot hand settled over hers. She glanced up sharply into those gleaming dark eyes.

One side of his sinful mouth kicked up. "Don't look so suspicious."

But she *was* suspicious. That very morning they'd agreed on friendship first. Not even twelve hours later, she knew from that look in his eye that he was about to kiss her.

Worse, she was about to let him.

Chapter Seven

"Carson," she said sternly—or at least she meant to sound stern. Actually, it came out on a soft hitch of breath.

"I can't stop myself," he whispered.

"Yes, you c—"

His lips took the word away before she finished saying it.

And an unfinished word wasn't all he took. He also laid claim to her will to resist him. He lifted his hand from hers and placed those long, strong fingers gently, carefully, along the side of her face, holding her. Capturing her with a caress.

Sweet heaven, the man could kiss. His mouth brushed across hers, teasing, coaxing, enticing her to let him take the kiss deeper.

She longed only to surrender to the feel of him, the heat of him.

With a small, hungry cry, she did what he wanted, opening to him, letting him in.

She would pay for this, and she knew that. She was giving ground too quickly. And for a man like Carson, that would only mean one thing: she would give some more.

It was all so simple, really. Awakened by the taste of him, her body, her heart, her foolish mind—they would all conspire to betray her for another kiss.

And another.

Easy. She was so easy. Half a day into this new "friendship" of theirs and she was kissing him like a whole lot more than just a friend. She should have more integrity, should stick by her plan to take things nice and slow.

But he'd blown right on by all her carefully erected boundaries. And it felt fabulous: the scent of him, the warmth of him so close, the flavor of him on her tongue. He tasted of coffee and chocolate, whipped cream and wonder, all wet and warm.

He was getting to her, stirring buried memories of Monday night. Sweet, sexy memories that hovered and swooped, taunting her, tempting her, just out of reach as his naughty tongue slid past her teeth and teased the wet places within.

A breathy moan escaped her as she gave to him further, letting her head drop back against the headrest. He didn't miss a beat, kept his mouth fused to hers. He leaned across the console, his fingers moving across her cheek, to her temple. He stroked her hair, soothing her, petting her. He traced the outer shell of her ear, caught her earlobe and rubbed it between his thumb and forefinger.

She moaned a little louder, and he shamelessly drank that sound from her parted lips.

Oh, she really shouldn't put her hands on him and she knew that.

But she did it anyway, bringing her palms up between them, easing them under the lapels of his jacket to press them against the hard, hot wall of his chest, telling herself she only meant to push him away.

That didn't happen.

Those traitorous hands of hers slid upward, loving the muscled feel of him beneath his white shirt, moving over the powerful shape of his shoulders to wrap around the back of his neck, to thread up into his hair.

The kiss went on and on. She didn't ever want it to end.

At the same time, she kept promising herself that she was going to stop it, put her hands back on his chest and gently push him away. She was doing that any minute now.

Very, very soon.

But in the end, she couldn't even manage that tiny triumph.

Oh no. He had her pressed against the seat back, his mouth locked to hers. And she had her arms around his neck as passionate echoes of Monday night drifted just out of reach in her reeling mind.

Lord help her, she never wanted to let him go.

And then *he* pulled back.

Just like that.

He broke the press of their lips, causing her eyes to pop wide-open. She stared straight into his. They were darker than ever, those eyes, full of heat and the promise of delicious pleasure.

"I know," he said ruefully, his voice so low and hot it could set the Cadillac on fire. "It's too soon."

She tried to pull herself together and somehow managed to mutter darkly, "Damn right it is."

"I was supposed to be giving you space, learning how to be your friend."

"That *was* the agreement."

"Tessa, I couldn't stop myself." His eyes smoldered—but she saw the gleam of humor in them, too, didn't miss the way he tried to keep those amazing lips from turning up at the corners.

She pressed her palms to his chest then and pushed him back a few inches more. "You didn't *want* to stop yourself."

"Can you ever forgive me?"

She regarded him patiently. "Stop messing with me."

"Kiss me again and prove you forgive me." He tried to swoop in.

But she was ready for him that time, stiffening her arms, keeping him at bay. "Not a chance. Get back in your seat. Drive the car."

He retreated behind the wheel—and started in about what they should do next. "So, how about the nightlife in Kalispell, Montana? I've been meaning to check out Moose's Saloon or maybe Scotty's Bar and Steakhouse..."

She slanted him a glance. Even from the side, he looked much too pleased with himself. "I think I've had enough thrills for one night. Home to the boardinghouse, please."

He turned those dark-velvet eyes to her and asked hopefully, "Scoreboard Pub and Casino?"

"Keep it up and I *will* make you pay."

"I am so looking forward to that." His eyes burned into hers, causing her skin to heat and the blood to race a little faster through her veins.

And then, finally, just before she blew it completely and reached across the console to grab his jacket in her fists and yank him close for another kiss, he pushed the start button and the Caddy hummed to life.

Tessa got downstairs for breakfast at six the next day. She grabbed a bagel and coffee and ran back up to work, hoping to get a few hours in before Carson came knocking on her door.

At a quarter of eight, she heard him leave his room. She waited for his knock.

It didn't come. He went on down the hall, and she went back to work, thinking he'd be upstairs again in no time.

But as far as she knew, he never came back up. She worked in her room all that morning, getting the ads Emmet needed emailed to the clinic, tackling a few other projects, then placing the ads and notices online as soon as Emmet gave the go-ahead.

At noon when she went down for lunch, she paused at Carson's door and debated whether or not to knock. When she gave in and tapped her knuckles against the wood, he didn't answer.

"Carson?" she called.

Nothing. Apparently, he wasn't in there.

She went down to the kitchen.

Claire, her clever fingers flying as she assembled sandwiches and garnished plates, asked, "So. You and Carson Drake, huh?"

Tessa got herself a cranberry juice from the fridge. "Friends. We are friends."

"How long's he in town for?" It was an innocent enough question.

Tessa felt defensive, anyway. But she took care to answer pleasantly. "A couple of weeks, I think."

"Ah," replied Claire, lining up plates.

Tessa couldn't stop herself from adding with a definite trace of sarcasm, "We have a good time hanging out together—you know, like *friends* do?"

"Well, all righty then." Claire scooped a pair of crispy golden Reuben sandwiches from the two-sided grill, sliced them in half diagonally and plated them.

"Auntie Tess! Hi there!" Bekka, sitting in her booster seat at the table enjoying crackers, banana slices and bits of chicken breast for lunch, slapped a plump hand on the table for attention.

Tessa went to her and got a gooey kiss, after which she couldn't stop herself from asking Claire, "And speaking of Carson, did you, um, happen to see him this morning?"

Before Claire could answer, their grandmother bustled through the open doorway from the dining room and announced, "He came down and had breakfast at a little before eight and left the house soon after." Melba pinned another order to the board above Claire's work area.

Grandma, you've got to stop lurking in the hallway, Tessa thought but didn't say. *And did he happen to mention when he'd be back?* She somehow kept herself from asking. "Thanks, Grandma."

"You're welcome, dear." Melba's smile was downright angelic.

Tessa took a plate, plunked a hunk of cheese on it, grabbed a knife, a napkin, a box of Triscuits and an apple, and went back upstairs to answer some queries that had come in through her website.

She worked for two more hours, with thoughts of Carson lurking in the back of her mind the whole time like a bad habit, the kind you were trying to quit, the kind that refused to let you go. She longed to dart out to the hallway and tap on his door, just to check and see if he might have returned without her hearing him come in. But somehow she kept herself from surrendering to that temptation. The poor man had a right to a little time to himself. And she had plenty to do, anyway.

Except for how she was getting downright stir-crazy. She'd been in her room for most of the day. Maybe a walk—to the park or over to Crawford's General Store. Anything to get out into the fresh air.

She walked to Crawford's, where she chatted with Natalie, Nate Crawford's lively younger sister, who was working the register that day. Tessa bought a five-gallon jar of Crawford's giant dill pickles. Claire liked to use them at lunch. Guests loved them.

Tessa hauled the heavy jar of pickles back to the boardinghouse and helped unload the dishwasher. She wiped down counters and pitched in to get the dining room set up for dinner.

Then she went down to the basement, where piles of clean linens waited for someone to fold them.

She was reaching for the next one from a pile of clean towels, when Carson asked from behind her, "Miss me?"

At the sound of his beautiful, warm, deep voice, Tessa felt the sudden hot press of tears behind her eyes. They burned at the back of her throat. Tears, of all the crazy things. She clutched the still-warm towel to her chest, stared at the concrete wall a few feet away and admitted with a forthright honesty that made her stomach clench, "Yes." She said it quietly, without turning. "I did."

His warm hand touched her shoulder, a brushing touch. She bit the inside of her cheek and swallowed the silly tears down. "Tessa. Hey." When she still didn't turn, he clasped her arm and slowly guided her around. Not a single tear had fallen; she'd called them back before they could. But still, her eyes were misty. She had no doubt he saw. "Tessa…" He looked at her so tenderly.

Always and forever, she would remember this moment. Standing in her grandmother's basement, clutching a warm white towel, while Carson Drake looked at her as though she was the only other person in the world.

"I should be more careful than this," she said. "I should know better than this. I hardly know you—"

"Tessa," he whispered, and that was all.

Just her name. It was enough. It was everything. Because of the way he said it—with so much promise, with hope. As though he wanted to reassure her that everything would work out right for them, even though she felt way too much for him, too soon. Even though she'd been here before and it had gone so badly.

Gently, he took the towel from her and tossed it back on the pile behind her. Then he gathered her close.

She went into his arms with no more than a surrendering sigh, cuddling against him much too eagerly, even going so far as to rest her cheek against the hard wall of his chest.

He kissed the crown of her head and explained, "My virtual meeting software doesn't get along very well with your grandmother's Wi-Fi."

She tipped her head back to look up at him. "I know. It's spotty. I wait forever for things to load."

He kissed her nose, right on the tip. She not only let him; she loved it. They shared one of those smiles, the kind that made her feel like they had about a hundred special secrets known only to the two of them. "I still have my suite at the Manor, so I went over there to get some work done."

"You need a room here *and* your suite at the Manor?"

"I thought I might need it for work. And I do. Plus, when I took the room next to yours, I wasn't sure how you'd react."

"Needed somewhere to run if I chased you out of here?"

"Exactly."

She thought that over and shrugged. "Hey. Makes perfect sense to me."

"You can join me there anytime, use the Wi-Fi, get your work done faster."

"Thanks. So far I'm managing, but I'll definitely keep your offer in mind."

"I grabbed a sandwich at the Manor Bar, where I ran into Mayor Traub, who invited me up to his house on Falls Mountain for dinner tomorrow. He promised to give me a tour of his saddle-making workshop. Did you know the guy makes these amazing custom saddles?"

"I did."

"The mayor also promised barbecued ribs—some special family recipe, he said. He told me that one of his cousins is *the* DJ Traub of DJ's Rib Shack fame."

Tessa had met *the* DJ Traub several times. "I know DJ. He lives down in Thunder Canyon now, with his wife and children. And did *you* know that Mayor Traub used to be plain old Collin Traub, who was about the baddest bad boy Rust Creek Falls has ever seen? No one could believe it when he and Willa Christensen fell in love. They'd been at odds practically since they were in diapers. Oh, and Collin and Nate Crawford grew up sworn enemies, too."

"Not possible. Those two are thick as thieves now, always plotting new ways to bring more business opportunities to this burg."

"Burg?" She shoved at his chest for that. "You'd better not let Collin or Nate hear you call our town a burg. They'll truss you up on Main Street in front of the town hall and let everyone throw rotten fruit at you."

He put up both hands and pretended to be terrified. "Don't let them hurt me."

"I won't be able to stop them. You need to remember to show some respect."

"I will, absolutely." He tried to look regretful. But he mostly just looked handsome and far too appealing for her peace of mind. "Collin said I should bring a friend tomorrow night. That would be you. Will you come?"

"Thank you, I will." She turned back to the table and picked up that towel again.

"Tessa…" He moved in closer and nuzzled her hair.

It felt simply glorious, just to have him near—and if she didn't keep her wits about her, she'd end up on her back with him on top of her faster than she could say the word *moonshine*. She faced him and put on her tough-girl voice. "Watch yourself there, friend."

"Tessa…" He said her name in a teasing whisper that time and tried to pull her close again. She snapped him with the towel. "Ow!"

"Go on upstairs. I'll be there in a few minutes. I just need to finish folding these."

He failed to obey, which didn't surprise her. Instead, he picked up a towel and folded it. No way had she expected that.

"Just being helpful," he said in response to her surprised glance.

They folded in silence, side by side, and she reminded herself not to get all dewy-eyed because the big-shot CEO was giving her a hand with the laundry.

That night, they stayed in and ate in the dining room. Later, they hung around in the downstairs sitting room with her grandparents. Carson seemed comfortable. He even agreed to play hearts when her grandfather pulled out a dog-eared deck and started shuffling. Tessa hauled the card table out of the hall closet, and Carson set it up for them.

Her grandma had a thousand and one questions for Tessa's new friend and she wasn't shy about asking them. Melba not only just *had* to know about his parents' divorce and his mother's remarriage, his father's death and the names of his nightclubs and restaurants, she also wanted to know if he'd ever been married.

Tessa tried to intervene at that point. "Grandma. Give the poor guy a break."

But Carson stepped right up. "It's okay, Tessa." He told her grandma, "I married my high school sweetheart the summer after our junior year at UCLA."

"But you got a divorce." Melba pursed her lips disapprovingly, as though just saying the D word left a bad taste in her mouth.

Carson explained how Marianne had wanted a family right away. "But I didn't. We keep in touch, though. And she's happy now, with the way it all turned out."

"I don't believe in divorce," declared Melba, as though that was going to be news to anyone. "But it appears you've had the best possible outcome of a failed marriage."

Tessa stifled a groan of embarrassment, but again, Carson didn't seem bothered in the least. He said, "My ex is a happy woman, and my life is good. It could have been a whole lot worse."

Her grandfather grunted. "Melba, your turn."

By the time Melba decided which card to play, the subject of Carson's ex-wife had been left behind.

Later, they sat out on the front porch, just Tessa and Carson, and talked until well past midnight. Then they walked up the stairs hand in hand. The whole way up, she thought about how much she wanted to kiss him.

But it was only the second day of their new "friendship," after all. She needed to keep the brakes on or she'd end up zipping right through the friend zone, headed straight for a full-blown affair.

Maybe she wanted that. Maybe they *would* end up in bed together again.

But not tonight.

When they reached her door, she wished him goodnight and ducked quickly into her room.

The next evening, they drove up Falls Mountain, past the spectacular wall of falling water that gave the mountain its name, to Collin and Willa Traub's beautiful, rustic house. Collin had inherited the house from a bachelor uncle and enlarged it, taking out walls, adding rooms and lots of windows. One wall of windows gave a spectacular view of the pine- and fir-covered mountains and of Rust Creek Falls, looking so small and quaint and charming in the valley below.

Collin led Carson down to his saddle-making workshop in the basement. Tessa stayed upstairs with Willa, a kindergarten teacher at RCF Elementary, and their baby boy who'd been born at the end of March. His name was Robert Wayne.

Willa insisted that Tessa hold him.

"Really, I'm just bad with babies," she tried to protest.

"No one is 'just bad with babies,'" Willa said. "Here."

Tessa gave in and took the baby. The second she curved her arms around him, little Robbie started wailing. "See? I warned you." Tessa handed the red-faced bundle back to his mom. "Babies hate me."

Willa smiled knowingly as she gathered Robbie close. "Wait till it's your own."

Oh, I plan to. Indefinitely. "I'm sure you're right,"

Tessa agreed. Because seriously, why argue? Babies were adorable and she totally loved them—they just didn't love her.

Willa cooed at her baby, and he settled right down. Tessa set the table as Robbie nursed. Then Willa took him to his room to change him and put him down.

"Out like a light," Willa said when she returned to the kitchen. "He's a good baby. If we're lucky, we'll get through dinner."

As they put the food on the table, Tessa explained how she was on the lookout for graphic design projects. "I'll take any job, no matter how small. I design everything from websites to yard sale ads to community car wash flyers. I'm hoping to get enough business going that I can move to Rust Creek Falls."

Willa suggested she check in at the high school. Maybe Tessa could teach a summer workshop in graphic design to boost her profile in the community. "And Kalispell isn't far. I'm sure you could find work there."

At dinner, the talk was mostly of plans Collin had to bring jobs and services to Rust Creek Falls. "Gotta tell you, Carson," he said. "I'm disappointed that you changed your mind about buying Homer's moonshine for Drake Distilleries."

Carson shook his head. "Sorry. Drake Distilleries is getting nowhere near that stuff."

Collin served himself another helping of ribs. "I was kind of hoping that the publicity might bring us more investors for our various projects around town."

"Trust me," Carson said. "Nobody needs *that* kind of publicity."

Tessa stuck a rib bone in the air. "Allow me to second that."

Willa and Collin shared a long look. Then Willa asked, "So, you guys tried it?"

Tessa glanced across at Carson. A little thrill shivered through her and she realized that somehow, in the past few days, the awful thing that had happened to them Monday night didn't seem so bad anymore.

Oh, she would never stop wanting to kick Homer's butt for being such an irresponsible, crazy old fool. But still.

The past couple of days had done a lot to change her mind about the whole thing. Now, no matter what happened between the two of them in the end, even if he flew back to LA tomorrow and she never saw him again, she would remember with fondness the night of the moonshine and how hard he'd worked afterward to get another chance with her. She would be glad that she'd known him. And that included her hazy recollections of what had happened in his bed.

"Okay, you two," Collin chided indulgently. "Your ribs will get cold."

Tessa realized she'd been sitting absolutely still, holding that same chewed-clean rib bone, staring into Carson's eyes for way longer than necessary. "Ahem." She set down the bone and blotted her lips with her napkin.

Willa prompted, "So, did you try the moonshine or not?"

Carson glanced Tessa's way again. At her quick nod of permission, he answered, "We did."

"And?"

"I'll say this. I don't think either of us will ever forget the experience—even though that stuff basically knocked us out cold."

Willa was nodding. "We had some, too. We drank the punch at the wedding picnic last Fourth of July."

She turned to look at her husband again, and her cheeks flushed pink.

Collin stared right back at her. "It tasted good. Really good."

Tessa asked, "Did it knock you out?"

"No, it didn't." Collin's voice had turned a little gruff, and his gaze was still locked on his wife. "I remember everything about that night. We went home early."

And then Willa chuckled. "Best Fourth of July ever."

Tessa just had to ask. "Robbie?"

Collin's bad-boy grin was slow and full of satisfaction. "Yep. Our little man's a Bonanza baby and that is no lie."

The next day, Sunday, Carson's cell rang at seven in the morning. He fumbled for the phone on the nightstand, peeled his eyes open and looked at the display. "What now, Ryan?"

"Kristen heard that you moved to Strickland's."

Carson yawned and shifted to get more comfortable in the slightly lumpy bed. "You said that Melba Strickland was the key. I went with that, more or less."

"Bold move. Clever."

"I try."

"Making progress with Tessa?"

"Last night I took her to dinner up at Collin and Willa's. It was great." She'd kissed him at her door when they said good-night, going on tiptoe, her soft hands sliding up and hooking around his neck, her high, firm little breasts pressing into his chest, her pliant mouth tasting of coffee and Willa's apple cobbler and the promise of more.

Ryan interrupted the sweet memory with a suggestion. "Feel free to thank me with a little Drake Imperial." The fifty-year-old special-edition Scotch sold for thirteen K a bottle.

"Your advice does not come cheap, my friend."

"Good advice never does. So what are you doing today? Kristen and I have an invite to her parents' place." The Daltons owned a ranch not far from town. "Bring Tessa. Dress for riding. We'll go up into the mountains and be back down in time for dinner with the folks."

Carson tapped on Tessa's door ten minutes later. She answered in a short satin robe, her hair loose on her shoulders, eyes a little droopy, lazy from sleep. It was a great look for her. She made his empty arms ache to hold her.

But he restrained himself.

"Ryan just called. He invited us to spend the day out at the Dalton Ranch. There will be horseback riding and then dinner with Kristen's family later."

She had her door partway open, leaning out to him, her slim body braced between the door and the frame. "Sounds like fun. I would love to go."

"Excellent. But you're crinkling your forehead. Is there a problem?"

"Well, I was just wondering if you've ever been on a horse."

It was so nice to feel smug. "I own a horse ranch. It's not far from Santa Barbara. I don't get out there as much as I'd like to. But it's a beautiful property. We raise and train Morgans and Thoroughbreds, mostly."

"So besides owning a *ranch* in *Santa Barbara*—" she drew out the emphasized words in a snooty tone "—you're saying you know how to ride a horse?"

"Yeah."

She wrinkled that beautiful nose at him. "Is there anything you don't know how to do?"

"Let me think it over. I'm sure there must be something."

"Humph. Dibs on the bathroom first."

"Wait a minute. Didn't you have it first yesterday morning?"

"Of course. I'm the *girl*. Girls get the bathroom first. They also take their time while they're in there. Deal with it." She tried to shut the door on him.

But he stuck his boot in it. "This is not a fair rule."

"Fair schmair. Sometimes life is just that way. Now get your foot out of my door so I can grab my caddy and have my shower."

He gave in and went downstairs to get a coffee while he waited for the use of the bathroom. It was ridiculously inconvenient.

And he couldn't remember ever having so much fun.

Tessa thoroughly enjoyed that day.

They spent most of it on horseback with Ryan and Kristen, riding up into the mountains, stopping often to enjoy the great views of the valley down below. When they got back down to the ranch late in the late afternoon, Kristen's mother had cold drinks waiting.

They all pitched in to set the table. Dinner was beer can chicken—you propped up the seasoned birds in a covered grill with a half-full can of beer in the cavity. The meat came out tender, juicy and full of flavor. Later, they all sat out on the Daltons' long front porch as the sun disappeared behind the mountains.

Tessa dropped off to sleep on the way back to town. When they got to the boardinghouse, Carson woke her with a kiss. Inside, they stopped to chat for a little with her grandparents and a few guests who were gathered in the sitting room.

Upstairs, Tessa got the bathroom first. He didn't even give her a hard time about it. Once her teeth were brushed and her face freshly washed, she lay in her bed in the dark and thought how she hadn't been this happy in years.

It was like they were roomies, but with a delicious, special edge of shared excitement and attraction. She wished it would never end.

Of course, she knew that it had to. She knew that she would stay in Montana and he had a life and a couple of companies to run in Southern California. They might think they could keep their connection, might promise each other they would stay together in their hearts, that thirteen hundred miles between them was nothing.

But realistically, long-distance relationships were impossible to maintain.

The next week went by way too fast. Tessa cut back on her efforts to scare up work and refused to feel bad about it. She wanted more time with Carson, and she took it.

He wouldn't be in town all that long, after all. And she decided to savor every minute she might have with him.

They hiked just about every day, taking his SUV to the edge of the forest and then setting out on foot, carrying snacks and cold drinks in their backpacks, heading up the trails into the big trees.

Carson had a real understanding of the wilderness—things his father had drilled into him, he said. He could distinguish deer tracks from elk, tell coyote tracks from a dog's. Once, they found bear tracks preserved in dried mud. They were left by a black bear, he said. Grizzly prints would be larger, with longer claw marks, the toes closer together. The bear was long gone, he told her. No scat and no fresh bear sign. She teased him that if he ever got tired of running Drake Distilleries, he could always hire out as a tracker or wilderness guide.

On Saturday, as that week drew to a close, they rented horses from a local stable and rode out east, into the valley. Sunday, they did the same, riding toward the southwest that time, finding a nice spot on Rust Creek not far from the Crawford family ranch, where they went for a swim.

The water was icy cold. Still they laughed and splashed and dunked each other. And then they spread a blanket on the creek bank in the sun, wrapped their arms around each other and cuddled and kissed for over an hour.

Finally, he whispered against her parted lips, "We need to stop."

In response, she did exactly what she knew she shouldn't. She pressed her body closer to his, feeling the fine, hard ridge of his arousal against her belly. She wished she could melt right into him, hold on tight and never let go. She nibbled on his lower lip. "I don't ever want to stop."

He kissed a hot path down the side of her throat, smoothing her still-wet hair out of his way as he went. She moaned as he sank his teeth into the crook of her shoulder. "Come to the Manor with me. Stay there with me tonight." He breathed the words against her skin.

Oh, she wanted to. She was more than ready to spend a whole night with him. And this time, there would be no magic moonshine to leave her wondering what had really happened. This time, she would remember every moment, every touch, every thrilling, hungry sigh.

She kissed him eagerly, sifting her fingers through the damp silk of his hair.

When he lifted away that time, he levered back on his knees and reached for the shirt he'd thrown there when they went swimming. She lay in the sun and watched the play of light and shadow against the beautiful musculature of his chest until he went and covered it all up with that shirt.

"Tonight?" he asked again.

"Let me think about it."

And she did think about it, all the rest of that day. She thought how much she wanted the whole night with him—and the night after that. And after that.

She also reminded herself that spending a string of hot, sexy nights with him would only make it harder in the end to let him go.

That evening, after dinner, after a nice, long walk together in Rust Creek Falls Park, she told him she wouldn't be going to the Manor with him that night.

He didn't argue, just took her arm when they reached the edge of the park and pulled her under the shelter of a big oak. She waited with way too much anticipation for him to kiss her.

But he didn't. Instead, for the first time in a full week, he brought up the subject of that interview he wanted her to agree to, an interview with one of the biggest advertising firms in LA.

"Let me call them and set it up," he coaxed. "What do you have to lose? I'll fly you down there so you can check them out."

She laughed. "That's a good one. I think the idea is that *they* check *me* out—and I can buy my own plane ticket, thank you."

"Get there however you want to. Just promise you'll come if I get you the interview. And all I'm saying is that it doesn't have to cost you a thing. Just a little of your time. And you can stay with me in Malibu."

Okay, now *that* was tempting. To visit him in Malibu, to be with him there, where he lived…

She might be constantly telling herself not to get too close to him, but who did she think she was kidding? The minute he left her to return to his own life, she was going to start missing him. It was going to be tough.

"Say yes—" He framed her face in his big, warm hands. "To the trip, to the interview, to staying with me." He dropped a kiss in the middle of her forehead. "It's not a lifetime commitment. You can just say no to the job if it's not going to work for you."

She searched those dark eyes of his and found only tenderness and hope that she might give it a chance—both the job *and* this thing they had together.

Why not? asked a brave little voice deep down inside her.

He'd been nothing but wonderful to her. She needed to quit making up reasons to push him away.

And as for the job, she should stop being so negative. She wanted another chance at the career she'd trained for, apprenticed for, worked her butt off for. If she really could get a great job in LA, why shouldn't she go for it? Why shouldn't she try again? It wouldn't kill her to put off her dream of living in Rust Creek Falls for a few more years.

She needed to buck up, stop throwing away a great opportunity. She needed to be braver. To stand tall and take a real chance or two in life again—and just maybe in love, as well.

"Tessa?" He was watching her, looking more than a little worried. "You're too quiet. What are you thinking?"

She went for it. "I'm thinking I need to thank you, Carson."

He looked more wary than flattered. "Thank me for what?"

"For pushing me to take a damn chance again."

His mouth twitched with the beginnings of a smile. "You're welcome."

"Go ahead and call your guy at IMI. Set up the interview. I'll come visit you in Malibu, and we'll see how it goes."

Chapter Eight

The next morning after breakfast, Carson went to Maverick Manor where the Wi-Fi was dependable. He had a virtual meeting scheduled for ten o'clock with the Drake Distilleries management team.

But before that, he called Jason Velasco at IMI. After the usual how're-you-doing chitchat, he told Jason about Tessa and said he'd seen her work, considered her brilliant and talented and wanted Jason to take a look at her for IMI.

He gave Jason her website address. "Tessa worked in New York for a couple of years, but then moved back to her hometown of Bozeman, Montana. And I have some examples of her work here with me," he added, meaning the sketchbook from the night of the moonshine. "She drew up a whole moonshine campaign for me on the fly."

"You mean the moonshine campaign that isn't going to happen?" Jason asked.

"That's the one. But I thought it might be useful to you. It'll give you another angle on how damn good she is. I'll get that to you overnight."

"How, exactly, do you see us proceeding with this?"

"Look over her stuff. Vet her. Then have her in for an interview and see where it goes from there."

"She's now in Bozeman, Montana, you said? What's the name of her firm there?"

"She works freelance. I'll have her fly down to you when you're ready to interview her." Carson really didn't want to get into the part about Della Storm firing her. What if Tessa had overestimated the problem? He didn't want to make her look bad if Jason didn't even need to know.

Then again, Jason would be hiring her to a large degree on Carson's say-so. The man had a right to know the basic story as Tessa had explained it.

So he told Jason a generalized version of what Tessa had told him, excluding any mention of that douche canoe, Miles Rutherford, instead citing "personal issues" as the reason Tessa had lost focus on her work and ended up being discharged.

Carson also left out the part about how the Storm woman had blackballed her. Legally, Della Storm could do nothing of the sort, and four years had passed since all that had gone down. Maybe Tessa's former boss was willing to let bygones be bygones by now.

When Carson finished the story, Jason said he'd heard of Della Storm, that she was a household name in the ad game. Then he asked, "And since Della Storm let her go, Tessa Strickland has only worked freelance, you said?"

"Look at it this way. Now you know she's a find. Della Storm wouldn't work with anyone second-rate."

"That's an interesting take on the situation." At least

Jason chuckled when he said it. “Okay, Carson. I’ll do my homework on this, and we’ll go from there.”

“Can’t ask for more.”

“I’ll get back to you if I have questions.”

“Please do. I’ll mail you these sketches.”

“And I’ll let you know when we’re ready to move on to the next step.”

“Meaning the interview,” Carson clarified.

“Yes. Meaning the interview.”

“Terrific. I appreciate this, Jason. And I can’t wait to see what you and your team have for us next week.”

Jason went on for a few minutes about how excited he was to show off the campaign for the flavored liqueur launch. Carson made the right noises in response and then, finally, they said goodbye.

After Carson took his virtual meeting, which lasted two hours, he packed up Tessa’s sketchbook to send to Jason and added it to the stack of outgoing mail in the foyer of his suite. The Manor’s concierge would take care of it from there.

By the time he finally got back to the boardinghouse, Melba told him that Tessa was down in the basement dealing with laundry. He ran down the backstairs, eager to see her.

She was bent at the waist, stuffing wet sheets in a dryer when he found her.

“Don’t straighten up,” he advised. “Things look great from here.”

She called him a bad name under her breath and did exactly what he’d asked her not to do, rising to her full five-foot-three, shoving the door shut and starting the machine. The sheets inside began to tumble as she turned to face him. He grabbed her hand and pulled her close, wrapping his arms around her, burying his nose against her throat so he could breathe in the scent of her.

She sighed and let her hands slide up to hook around his neck. "Hello, Carson."

They shared a kiss. God, he loved the taste of her.

When he lifted his head, she asked, "Busy morning?"

He bent close again and rubbed his cheek against her hair. "I had a long online meeting." He sighed. "And I miss my assistant. I had to address several envelopes all by myself."

She faked a sympathetic look, not a very good one. "Oh, you poor thing. You must be exhausted."

"My fingers are worn to the bone." He held them out to her. "Kiss them." Wearing a very serious expression, she did just that, one by one. He watched those soft lips brush his fingertips and wished he could freeze time in that moment, with her standing so close, her gold-flecked eyes shining up into his. "Thank you," he said once she'd kissed all eight fingers and his thumbs, as well. "I feel so much better now."

"Good. Help me." She grabbed a sheet from the table by the machines. He helped her fold, taking one side, following her cues, until the large sheet was a tidy square. They started on the next one. "So...did you talk to your guy at IMI about me?"

He brought her up to speed on that situation. "I hope you're not pissed that I said you fell down on the job."

She gave him a glowing smile for that. "Are you kidding? A little honesty is never a bad thing."

"Good." Relief released the slight knot of tension between his shoulder blades. He *had* been worried she'd be upset that he'd said so much. "I left that Miles character completely out of it, just said you had 'personal issues,' so when it comes to the interview, you can take that in whatever direction you want. And I never said anything about your being blackballed, either."

She tipped her head sideways and gave him a thoughtful look. "You're sure there will even be an interview?"

"I am, absolutely."

A low, amused sound escaped her. "It must be wonderful being you. You just say jump, and all your minions ask how high."

He gave her a shrug. "Someone has to rule the world. I think I should get another kiss for being so helpful to your career."

She handed him one end of yet another sheet. "You're always finding some reason that you should get another kiss."

He reached out, wrapped an arm around her and hauled her close. "Give me my kiss."

She whipped her side of the sheet quickly around her other arm before it could hit the concrete floor. "Oh, fine. Take it."

So he did. A long one. Until she pushed against his chest and demanded, "Get folding." He stepped back, and the whole process began again.

As they came together and then stepped away, she said softly, "I feel kind of bad."

"Why?"

"I think I've made Miles seem worse than he was."

"Worse? How could that bastard be worse? He cheated on you, and he set you up so you walked in on him in the act. He rubbed your nose in it. The man gives new meaning to ugly."

"He, um, he did propose to me. Several times."

"So? He still cheated. You made the right choice to tell him no."

"All I'm saying is, maybe he got tired of waiting for me to say yes."

"So what? He didn't deserve a yes."

"But, Carson, at the end, after I caught him with the twins, when I was packing my bags to go, he told me that he'd given up on me because I kept turning him down."

"He actually said that?" At her sad little nod, he said exactly what he thought of Miles Rutherford's excuses. "If he was so damned upset that you wouldn't say yes, he should have told you so then, and tried to work it out with you. After that, if you still wouldn't meet him half-way, he should have broken it off. Relationships aren't rocket science, Tessa. A guy needs to stand up and be-have with integrity. If he doesn't, he gets what he damn well deserves." He saw the gleam in her eyes and went on before she could start in on him. "And yeah, I've been with more women than I probably should have. I blew up my marriage to a wonderful wife. I wasn't ready to be married, and I damn well should have figured that out before I broke Marianne's heart. I'm not perfect. But I don't tell lies, and I don't cheat." He moved close and gave her his side of the mostly folded sheet.

She made the last few folds and set it on the stack. "You're right," she said at last. "I didn't really trust Miles, not deep in my heart. I felt so inexperienced. I *was* in-experienced. I didn't want to make some huge mistake, you know? And it turned out he wasn't worth trusting, anyway."

"Now you're seeing what really happened there."

"Which doesn't say a whole lot for my judgment, does it?"

He gave her a stern look. "Name me one person on earth who hasn't been guilty of bad judgment at one time or another."

She hummed low in her throat. "I do feel bad that I screwed Della over, though. She was tough as nails, but she was fair. I think she would have gotten over my relationship with Miles if I hadn't left her high and dry on that last project."

"So get a message to her. Apologize."

She gave him a wide-eyed look. "Seriously? Won't she just think I'm kissing up when IMI contacts her?"

"Tessa, it's what *you* think that matters."

Her smile bloomed then, a wide one. "You know, I just might do that."

"Good."

He backed her up against the folding table and claimed another kiss, after which they finished folding the rest of the sheets and went upstairs for lunch.

Once they'd eaten, she said she had work to do and shut herself in her room for a few hours. He let her go reluctantly.

They had six days left until he had to return to LA. Yeah, he had high hopes that she'd agree to take the job with IMI. He couldn't wait to show her how much she was going to love living in California.

But who knew how long it would take to get the job thing settled, to get her moved so she lived nearby? He could be weeks without her. Months, even.

So right now, while he had the chance, he wanted to spend every possible minute with her. Was he falling too damn fast and way too hard for her?

So what if he was?

The way he saw it, his strong feelings for her were all the more reason to steal every second he could with her.

That evening, he'd agreed to meet for drinks at the Manor bar with Walker Jones, the millionaire entrepreneur who was opening a new day care center in Rust

Creek Falls. Tessa went with him. Both Nate Crawford and Collin Traub were there, too. Nate had brought his wife, Callie, which worked out great. She and Tessa were already casual friends and happy for a chance to catch up.

Walker Jones's day care empire was called Just Us Kids, and the one in Rust Creek Falls would be opening the second week of July. Nate joked that Just Us Kids was "just in time." The only other day care in town, Country Kids, had a waiting list now, what with all the babies born that spring.

Walker was a good-looking, confident guy who seemed a little more interested in empire building than in the particulars of how the new Rust Creek Falls day care center would be run. But Carson was big into empire building himself, so he didn't fault Jones for having a lot of ambition. They exchanged contact info and promised to stay in touch.

Afterward, when everyone left, it was just Carson and Tessa. They ordered burgers right there in the bar.

Their food had just arrived when she said, "Thanks for the pep talk this afternoon."

He leaned close. The way he saw it, the closer he got to her, the better. Her hair shone in the glow from the lights above and he didn't think he'd ever seen eyelashes as thick and silky as hers. "It wasn't a pep talk. I just said what I believe."

She dredged a French fry in ketchup and popped it into her mouth. "Well, I appreciate it. And I took your advice about Della. I wrote her a letter—you know, on actual stationery. I don't know why exactly, but on nice paper, it all seemed more serious, more sincere somehow."

"I get that, yeah."

"I told her how much I respect her and how much I learned from her and also how much I regret blowing that last account. I apologized for that and wished her well. And then I mailed it before I could think of a thousand reasons not to."

"Well done." He stared at her for a solid count of five and thought that he would never grow tired of looking at her.

She leaned a little closer. "I really like you, Carson. I mean, I really, *really* like you."

He couldn't resist, so he didn't. He leaned closer still, brushed a kiss across her soft cheek and whispered in her ear, "I like you more."

She giggled. It was about the most beautiful sound he'd ever heard. And then she said, "Look. Down here." She dipped that dark head toward her lap, where she held her small purse wide-open between her hands. Inside, he saw a toothbrush and a bit of cream-colored satin.

His chest felt suddenly tight. So did his pants. He leaned in again and whispered, directly into her ear that time. "Panties? You brought panties?"

She backed away a fraction, enough that she could meet and hold his gaze. "A girl needs clean panties. And a toothbrush, too. At least she does if she's planning on staying the night."

Chapter Nine

Tessa stood in the doorway from the bathroom in Carson's suite. She wore only a black lace bra and panties to match. She'd never been so nervous in her life.

"Come here." Carson's voice was deep, a little bit rough—and very sure. He'd gotten undressed while she used the bathroom, and now he rose from the bedside chair and faced her in only a pair of dark boxer briefs.

Oh, my Lord. The man was so beautiful. How did he have time to keep a honed, cut body like that while running two corporations and chasing down crazy moonshine makers in the wilds of Montana?

He held out his hand to her.

A sound slipped from her—half sigh, half moan. She could not believe this was actually happening. It didn't feel quite real.

Oh, but it was. Her bare feet whispered across the polished wide-plank floor and then were silenced completely when she reached the thick pile of the bedroom rug. Three more steps and she stood before him.

"Tessa." Her name came out on a low husk of breath. And then he touched her. With one slow, deliberate finger, he traced a line from the hollow of her throat straight down to the little black bow between her small breasts. "I've waited forever for this." That finger went roaming, stirring a trail of heat and hunger in its wake, up the gentle curve of one breast, back down, and up over the other.

She somehow couldn't stop her mouth from arguing. "It hasn't been *that* long. We've only known each other—oh!" The breathless sound escaped her as he took her by the shoulders and pulled her tight against that big, hard body of his. It felt so good. That hardness. That heat.

He bent his head and rubbed his deliciously scruffy cheek against hers. "You are perfect."

"Well, no, I'm—"

"Don't argue." His hand strayed behind her.

"But…" She forgot whatever it was she meant to say as she felt the quick brush of his knuckles against the middle of her back right before her bra came undone. She barely had time to gasp in surprise before he had the straps sliding along her arms and was pulling it down from between them, whipping it up and tossing it over his shoulder.

"Perfect." He clasped her waist and then eased both hands upward along her rib cage to cover her breasts with his big palms. His thumbs dipped in to rub her nipples, making them ache, bringing a long, breathy moan from her. "I've never known anyone like you," he whispered. "I hardly know what to do with you. I only know that from the first minute I saw you, Tessa, in that stork suit on that silly float, holding Kayla's baby, looking adorable and miserable and too cute for words, I knew I *had* to meet you, to know you, to hold you like this."

She stared down at his hands. They felt so good engulfing her breasts. With a slow sigh, she lifted her gaze to meet his. "I was so scared that day when you saw me, when you stared at me and I stared back at you. I felt as though you and I were the only two people in the world, as though Main Street and the Baby Bonanza Parade and every single citizen of Rust Creek Falls had vanished. There was just us, and I was terrified."

"Terrified?" He frowned down at her, dark eyes velvet soft. "Why?"

"The attraction I felt for you was so strong, so… instantaneous. It really scared me. It was too much like what had happened with—"

He cut her off with a quick shake of his head.

She understood. She didn't want to say another man's name right now, anyway. Because there *was* no other man. Just this one. Just Carson. "I…didn't want to go there again."

He made a chiding sound. "This is nothing like what happened before. You're with me now. I've told you I won't cheat." He repeated, "This is nothing like before."

But how long will it last? And what if it ends badly? What if you break my poor heart?

The questions tumbled over themselves in her mind. And why wouldn't they? After all, she was doing exactly what she'd promised herself she wouldn't do, taking the kind of emotional risk she'd sworn never to take again. And, no, Carson really wasn't like Miles. Except for being too good-looking and having too much money—oh, and giving off an air of undeniable power and self-confidence.

And the women. Even if he'd promised not to cheat

and she actually believed him, he'd admitted openly that he'd been with a whole bunch of women.

He bent close, caught her earlobe between his white teeth and worried it gently, unleashing a flood of sensation inside her, hot little shivers that skittered down her nerve endings. "You're thinking too much. Stop."

And then he banded those big arms around her, hard. Her bare breasts pressed flat against his broad, hot chest. She could feel everything, every beautiful muscle, including the long, thick hardness between his muscular thighs.

"Oh!" she gasped again—her vocabulary reduced to one silly exclamation—as he grasped her bottom in both hands and lifted her. "Yes," she sighed, raising her legs, wrapping them around him nice and tight.

His mouth came down on hers. She opened to him instantly, kissing him with eager yearning as he carried her to the bed. His tongue skimmed the wet surfaces beyond her parted lips. She sucked on it shamelessly, rolled her own tongue around it. He tasted so good. She could kiss him forever.

She loved the way he touched her, so tenderly and yet with such hunger. He laid her down on the bed so carefully, as though she were infinitely precious to him. And then he took his mouth from hers and looked into her eyes. "I need to see you. All of you. I need you bare."

She couldn't agree fast enough. "Yes. Bare. Please. You first."

That took about a second. He lifted the waistband of his boxer briefs over the bulge of his erection, shoved them down his legs and kicked them off.

He was so fine. A smile trembled across her lips.

He smiled back, slowly, a naughty smile that promised a whole night full of sweet, hot delights. And then he took her panties by the elastic and guided them down.

She lifted her head from the pillow and watched as he slid them past her thighs, over her knees, all the way clear of her lavender-painted toes. He tossed them off the end of the bed.

"So damn pretty," he declared, gently easing her thighs apart, revealing her most secret, intimate flesh to his gaze. "Beautiful."

It had been so long since a man had looked at her this way, so possessively, with a hunger that promised he would devour her. Not for years. *No, wait.*

The night of the moonshine. Carson had looked at her that way then. But how could that count when she could only remember it in a vague and hazy way?

A horrible thought occurred to her. She gasped and bounced up onto her elbows.

He stopped tickling the back of her knee to ask, "What's the matter?"

"Condoms. I forgot to ask. I just assumed you would have them."

"Shh." His hand went roaming. He caressed his way up to the top of her thigh.

She gasped again, partly in response to his touch and partly because there was no way they were going any further without condoms, no way she was driving to Kalispell for the morning-after pill again. "But, Carson—"

"You assumed right. I have them. Now, lie back."

Relieved, she dropped her head onto the pillows again as his hand strayed higher. He traced a slow path inward and then up even higher, over the narrow strip of dark hair she'd left when she'd groomed herself so carefully to be ready for him tonight.

And then, at last, he parted her, touching her where she wanted him most. "Wet," he whispered approvingly. Followed by, "Finally, Tessa. Finally."

She might have said yes. She might have said anything as he parted her, stroking her, making her wetter still, dipping one finger in and then another. She moved with him, her body rocking in rhythm with his knowing touch. No way could she keep herself from lifting, opening her legs wider, offering him more.

When he lowered his mouth to her, she cried out.

He made soft, soothing sounds as he kissed her there, where she burned for him. Oh, it was so good. So fine. Just what she'd needed from him for so long now—for these past two weeks of too-brief days that also somehow felt like forever.

He guided her knee up, eased those wide shoulders under her thigh and settled between her parted legs. He kissed her some more, deeply, thrillingly, using his hands, too, to take her higher and higher, until she cried out as fulfillment found her. Clutching his dark head, holding him there, she lost herself completely, her climax drawing down to a pinpoint of heated light and then flaring, spreading out from the center of her like the spokes in a burning wheel.

He stayed with her, touching her, kissing her, drawing the pleasure out, so that it kept pulsing through her for the longest, sweetest time.

At the end, she wanted him closer, wanted to feel him all along her yearning body, skin to skin. She fumbled, grabbing for him, pulling on his shoulders, stroking his hair.

Finally he freed himself from the cage of her open thighs and slid up her body. He gathered her close to him, wrapping her up in those big, hard arms of his. She breathed in the scent of him, soap and that subtle aftershave he wore. And man.

All man.

It was wonderful. Exactly right. She laid her head against his chest and listened to the strong, steady beat of his heart as he cradled her close.

And then she was ready all over again, yearning for more.

Because really, who knew how long this thing with them would last? Who could say?

She only knew she was in it now, her hungry heart open, wanting. Needing. Hoping for more.

Better not to waste a moment.

She ran her seeking fingers downward, over the hard curves of his chest, along the rocklike ripples of those beautiful abs until she found him and wrapped her hand around him.

She stroked him, learning the beautiful shape of him.

"Harder," he commanded in a low growl.

She was only too eager to comply, squeezing him tighter, sliding her hand roughly up and down the shaft, rubbing her thumb over the sleek flare, spreading the moisture that wept at the tip.

He kissed her as she stroked him, kissed her hard and deep and wild.

And then, with a feral groan, he reached between them and stilled her hand. She tried to override him, to keep stroking, keep pleasuring him.

But he wouldn't have it. "Not like this." He kissed the words onto her parted lips. "Together."

Still, she held on. It felt so good to claim him that way, to have the power to make him wild.

"Behave." He growled the word. He pressed his forehead to her forehead. And then, a little raggedly, "Please."

Reluctantly, she released him. He reached across her to the nightstand on her side, slid open the drawer and took out a condom. She watched as he tore off the top foil strip with his teeth, got it free of the packet with a quick twist of his long fingers.

He rolled it down over himself.

And then he was reaching for her again, turning her to her side, facing him. His mouth took hers as his warm hand slid down over the curve of her back, one long stroke over her hip to her thigh. He lifted her leg, guiding it over to wrap around him, positioning her for him so that he slid into her waiting heat in one smooth, thrilling glide.

They kissed endlessly, their mouths fused as though sealed together, never, ever to let go. And then he started to move, withdrawing so slowly, then returning, only to withdraw once more. Each time he retreated, she almost lost him.

More than once, he chuckled against her mouth, cruel and tender, as she begged him with her lips and her body, with her arms around him and her leg wrapping him hard and tight, holding him to her.

Please, please don't go.

Never go.

Stay.

He picked up the rhythm, pulsing faster against her, going deeper, retreating farther, though surely that wasn't possible. Each time, she knew she would lose him. Until he came back to her, filling her so perfectly, going deeper still. She felt him all through her, into the heart of her. He claimed her, all of her, thrilling her, carrying her away to a place where there was only pleasure. Only him. His big body taking her, his eyes searing into hers, his touch burning her in the most shocking, delicious way.

Like a wave, he rolled over her, rising, crashing into her, filling her so full with him, so that all she wanted was the feel of him, the touch of his mouth on her skin, the warmth of his breath in her ear.

Carson, I love you.

Dear, sweet Lord in heaven, she'd almost said it. How totally foolish would that have been? She'd known him for exactly two weeks as of that very night. Nowhere near enough time to start talking about love.

But some shred of sanity remained to her. She kissed him harder and kept those words in.

And he kept on moving, pushing so deep within her, driving her higher, until she was lost again, the coil of heat and wonder opening wide within her. She let out a cry as her climax rolled through her.

He guided her onto her back then. She lifted her legs and twined them around him. He levered up on those muscled arms and moved harder and faster, went deeper than ever.

Dazed, dreamy, her own finish still rocking her in thrilling aftershocks, she saw the shudder of greater pleasure sweep through him, felt him pulsing within her as his climax took him down.

They made love again an hour later. Tessa thought it was even more beautiful than the first time.

More tender, less desperate, the hungry edge not quite so sharp. He filled her body and her heart.

Love. Dear Lord, I love him.

She wasn't supposed to do that, had thought she'd learned her lesson, had promised herself never again to fall so hard and so fast.

Later, she decided. She would think about it later. He was leaving in five days. She would enjoy every second she had with him till then.

And after that, well, they would see, wouldn't they?

Maybe there would be a job offer from IMI, as he kept insisting was guaranteed to happen. By then, she would have a better idea of what to do.

Or at least, she hoped she would.

"Tessa." He nuzzled her neck, wrapped her hair around his fist. "God. I can't get enough of you. The scent of you, the feel of your skin, those soft little sounds you make when I touch you, all of it, all you do. You drive me wild."

And then he was kissing her, touching her all over, turning her onto her stomach, doing very naughty things to her…

Twenty minutes later, he left her just long enough to get rid of the condom. When he returned to her in the tangled bed, he wrapped her close, pulling her back against him, spoon-style. "Sleep now."

"Umm…" She was already drifting off.

Long after midnight, he woke her again with slow, drugging kisses. She moaned and told him to go back to sleep.

At first.

But he only kept kissing her, kept touching her, arousing her. Soon enough, she was every bit as eager as he to make love yet again.

They didn't get to sleep again until almost four.

Sometime later, she woke to the smell of coffee. He was bending over her, wearing unbuttoned jeans and a tempting smile. "Eggs and bacon?"

"Perfect."

He served her breakfast in bed, after which they greeted the morning with more lovemaking, her slight soreness from the night before quickly turning to excitement and pleasure.

After that, she took a long, slow bath in the suite's

huge jetted tub as he made a few calls to LA and caught up on his messages.

They returned to the boardinghouse for lunch, taking sandwiches to the park the way they liked to do. Later, after she'd put in a couple of hours helping her grandmother and Claire, they hiked into the mountains, where they spread a blanket in the sun and made love beneath the wide Montana sky.

That night they returned to the Manor and went to bed early, though not to sleep.

After that, the days settled into a glorious rhythm. Mornings were for working. And the afternoons, evenings and late into the night were for the two of them. The hours flew by. She wished she could grab each moment and hold it close, so that this precious time they shared would never end.

On Thursday afternoon, Carson told Tessa that IMI would be calling her. On Friday, she got that call. She agreed to an interview at their Century City offices on the following Thursday.

Too soon, it was Saturday. Carson would leave for Los Angeles on Sunday.

That night they had dinner at the Manor bar and then went up to his suite, where they fell on the bed together, kissing desperately, popping more than a few buttons in their eagerness to eliminate the flimsy barrier of their clothing. They made love as though they would never see each other again.

And then, as they lay together afterward, holding each other close, he tipped up her chin, stared hard into her eyes and said, "Come with me tomorrow. Move in with me in Malibu. You can work from there as well as here. And there will be a great job for you with IMI, anyway."

She opened her mouth to speak.

But he shook his head and went right on. "I want you with me. I know it's fast, but I don't give a damn. I haven't felt like this since…oh, who am I kidding? I've *never* felt like this. I don't want to walk away from it. I want us together."

Yes! cried her hungry heart. But she needed to be smarter than that. She needed not to make the same mistakes she'd made with Miles. "Carson, I—"

His eyes flashed with angry heat. "No. Don't start with the excuses. Don't compare me to that cheating loser who didn't have sense enough to take care of what mattered, who was too much of an idiot to treat you right."

"I'm not comparing you to him."

"The hell you're not."

"I'm not. I just can't go with you now."

"You *can*."

"I can't. Not right now. I really can't just throw over all my plans so suddenly. I need to do this my way. I'll come down for the interview with IMI, I promise. That's less than a week from now. I'll stay a day or two with you then. But we have to slow down a little. Please try and understand."

He dragged her close and kissed her, a hot, angry, punishing kiss, a kiss she reveled in—until he ended it by grabbing her arms again and pushing her away. "No," he said much too softly. "I don't understand." And then he shoved back the covers and left her.

Clutching the sheet against her chest, she watched him stride naked to the bathroom. He shut the door behind him harder than he needed to.

Tessa waited, feeling miserable, having to hold herself in place there in the bed, to keep herself from tiptoeing to the bathroom door, from tapping on it gingerly, from promising to do whatever he wanted if only he would let her in.

He came out on his own a few minutes later and rejoined her in the bed.

And then he apologized. "I was out of line. I'm sorry. I just… I don't want to leave you, but my businesses aren't going to run themselves."

She kissed him and stroked the hair at his temples, pressed her palm against his scruff-rough cheek. "I hate that you're going. I only want to be with you, but I need to take this slower. Please."

Reluctantly, he agreed to do it her way.

In the morning, he checked out of Maverick Manor and they returned to the boardinghouse. He packed up his things there.

They'd already agreed that he would drive himself to Kalispell where his plane waited. He said goodbye to her grandparents and her sister.

She followed him out to the Cadillac. He kissed her one last time right there in the parking lot, a long, slow one that she wished might never end.

Much too soon, he was pulling away and getting behind the wheel. "I'm sending a plane for you next Wednesday. You can stay with me Wednesday night, be fresh for the interview Thursday. Don't argue with me about it."

She gave him a trembling smile. "Thank you." And then she stood in the bright late-morning sunshine and watched him drive off, her heart aching as though she'd just ripped it in two.

Chapter Ten

The next few days were awful. Tessa missed him terribly. Her whole body seemed to ache with longing for him—which, really, was ridiculous. She would be seeing him again in three days, on Wednesday, when he flew her to him in LA.

And he kept in close touch, carrying on a constant conversation with her via text. Plus, two or three times a day, one or the other of them would find a reason they just *had* to talk to the other immediately. Then they would play phone tag until whoever couldn't talk was available—often that would be at night, when his long workday was through. Those calls inevitably ended in really good phone sex.

She truly was never out of contact with him. But she yearned for him, anyway. And every minute she wasn't on the phone with him dragged by in slow motion.

There was another slight problem, too. As of Monday, her period was officially late.

But she refused to worry over it, reminding herself that it had been late before and always came eventually. And hello! Three condom wrappers *plus* the morning-after pill. How could she possibly be pregnant? It made no sense.

It was the excitement, that was all, of being wildly in love, of longing for Carson. Not to mention the upheaval of not really knowing what to do about it all.

Should she follow her heart to LA, change her life for him—as she'd done for Miles? Or should she stick with one of her earlier plans, which weren't all that solid, either: stay in Bozeman, or try to make a go of it in Rust Creek Falls?

Finally, Wednesday morning came. At nine fifteen, she boarded Carson's plane at the Kalispell airport. When the plane touched down in Santa Monica, he had a car waiting for her. Forty-five minutes later, she was greeted at his front door by his housekeeper, Sharon, who took her suitcase to the master suite and gave her a quick tour of Carson's gorgeous, modern house, one whole side of which—the one facing the Pacific—was made of glass.

There was a gym in the basement and an infinity pool beyond the wall of windows—a whole section of which rolled up like a big garage door, making it possible to combine the living room and the massive deck into one beautiful indoor-outdoor room. The kitchen was enormous, all stainless steel and stark white cabinetry, with top-of-the-line appliances.

Sharon explained that dinner was ready to be popped into the oven and an assortment of cheeses and meats, fresh fruits and crudités, along with fresh-baked bread and several varieties of crackers, were all ready and waiting for her should she feel like a snack.

If none of those suited, the pantry was full and there

was more to choose from in the fridge. Sharon jotted her number on the pad at the end of the counter. "Just in case you need anything that I might be able to help you with. The beach is lovely today," she added. "Simply take the stairs down at the edge of the deck. Should you need a suit, check the cabinets in the cabana."

Then, with a warm smile, Sharon left. She was barely out the door when Tessa's cell rang.

It was Carson. "How was your flight?"

"Smooth." She pressed a finger to the side of her throat, where her pulse had quickened at the sound of his voice. "The limo driver was there waiting for me when I arrived. I feel thoroughly spoiled. And Sharon is a treasure."

"I need to see you." His voice had gone darker. It burned in her ear.

Heat flooded her, a lovely heaviness down low made up of longing and delicious anticipation. "Come home, then. I'm right here."

He arrived an hour later, swept her into his arms and took her to bed, where they remained for three hours. Then he had to go back to the office for a late meeting. She found a bikini in the cabana and went down to the water for a long stroll along the beach.

Carson returned a little after seven. They ate the dinner Sharon had prepared for them, and he opened a bottle of very expensive champagne he'd bought to celebrate their reunion.

She thought of her period that hadn't come yet and took a pass on the bubbly.

"You okay?" he asked, watching her much too closely.

"I'm fine. I..."

"What?"

No. Uh-uh. She was not discussing her menstrual

cycle now. She rallied with, "Remember how I told you after the night of the moonshine that I would never drink again?"

He gave her his most patient look. "Tessa, this is a 1996 Krug Clos d'Ambonnay."

She took his glass from him and had a sip. "Delicious. Spectacular." She handed it back. "I'm honored you would open it for me. And that's all I'm having."

He shrugged then and teased, "More for me," and let it go at that, for which she was grateful.

They went to bed early, ostensibly so that she could get her beauty sleep. That didn't happen.

Not that she cared. His touch not only set her on fire; it pushed back all her worries—about where to go from here, about the real reason she'd turned down his expensive champagne.

In the morning, he asked her again if something was bothering her. She said she was just nervous, with the interview in a couple of hours. He kissed her, told her she was going to knock their socks off and got her to promise to call him as soon as she left IMI.

Once she was alone in his big house by the ocean, she took her time getting ready, making sure her hair and makeup were just right. She wore a gray pencil skirt and jacket to match, with a burnt-orange silk blouse underneath for the perfect pop of color. Sky-high taupe heels completed the outfit, a fabulous pair of shoes that still looked amazing five years after she'd bought them at Stuart Weitzman in New York. She'd had her mother get the outfit from her closet in Bozeman and overnight it to her in Rust Creek Falls so she could look her best.

The driver was waiting in front of the house. He took her straight to the IMI building on Century Park East. The man at the podium by the elevator took her name and sent her to the tenth floor. There, a beautiful receptionist led her to a small conference room.

Ten minutes later, she sat across from Carson's associate, Jason Velasco, two other ad executives and the top designer at the firm. After a minimum of cheerful chitchat, it got serious.

There was praise. They'd seen her work on her website and they were all impressed with her designs from the night of the moonshine. She might have laughed at that if she'd felt at all comfortable.

But she didn't feel comfortable, even though they thoroughly surprised her by telling her that Della Storm had a lot of good things to say about her.

Good things? Della? Really? She wasn't sure that she believed them. But then she thought about the letter she'd written and mailed last week. Could her apology have actually made a difference to Della?

Jason Velasco then cleared his throat and tiptoed into a mention of the "difficulties" of Tessa's last month with Della and the fact that she had been "terminated abruptly."

Tessa went with the "personal problems" explanation, keeping it general. There was nothing to be gained by getting specific. When they asked if those problems were resolved, she answered firmly that they were.

At the end, they thanked her and said they would be in touch. As Jason saw her to the elevator, he told her how much he loved working with Carson, as did everyone at IMI. He asked her to give Carson his best.

She promised that she would.

Again the car was waiting for her outside the building. As the driver took her back to Malibu, she stared out the tinted window and tried not to feel too discouraged.

Carson called when she was halfway there. "I thought you said you'd call me the minute you left IMI."

"Sorry. I was thinking about the interview, obsessing on it really."

"What happened? Are you okay?" He sounded so worried for her.

She got busy reassuring him. "I'm fine—I promise you. And I think it went pretty well."

"I know they'll make an offer."

They probably would. For his sake. That shouldn't have depressed her, but it did. She really didn't want to get a job because she happened to be sleeping with a powerful man. Somehow, that would be almost as bad as throwing over her career for one. "We'll see."

There was a lengthy silence on the line. Then finally he said, "Tessa, won't you tell me what's wrong?"

She lied and said, "Nothing," and hated herself for it. But really, were they going to discuss this now, on the phone?

No way. It had to wait till later.

She wasn't sure exactly when. But not right now.

He said he would be back at the house by five, and he was taking her out someplace nice to celebrate.

Celebrate what? she thought. *Ugh.* Surely she'd become the gloomiest person on the planet. "Can't wait," she replied, trying really hard to inject a little enthusiasm.

At Carson's house, she changed into the bikini she'd found in the cabana the day before, grabbed a towel, a bottle of sunscreen and a dog-eared paperback she'd taken from the sitting room at her grandma's boardinghouse and brought along to read on the plane. She swam several laps in the pool, slathered on the sunscreen and stretched out on a chaise with her book.

After an hour of reading, she wandered back inside

for lunch, then put on a beach cover-up and went down the stairs to the sand. She walked for two hours. When she returned to the house, she stretched out on Carson's California king.

He woke her right on time, at five, joining her in the bed for a while. That was good. Perfect even. If she could make love to Carson all day and night, she would never have to decide where her life was going.

Later, they went out to a gorgeous restaurant and ate on a wide deck in the glow of a thousand party lights, with a beautiful view of the ocean. He ordered an excellent cabernet and she had none of it.

He didn't ask her why—and he didn't ask her what was wrong. Apparently, he'd figured out by then that she wasn't going to tell him.

That night, she couldn't sleep. She crept quietly from his enormous bed, pulled on the filmy beach cover-up she'd left in the bathroom and went downstairs.

The pool deck shone silver in the moonlight. She pushed open the sliding door from the kitchen and went out.

A while later he found her there, sitting on the edge of the pool, her feet dangling in the water. "Are you ever going to talk to me?" He stood gazing down at her, wearing only a pair of track pants that rode low on his hard hips, the sculpted planes of his chest so beautiful in the moonlight. "Come on." He held out his hand.

She took it and let him pull her up into his waiting arms. "I'm sorry I'm such awful company. I just…need a little time. Everything's happening too fast, that's all."

He kissed her and then gazed down at her, unsmiling, a thousand questions in his eyes. "I can't make it right if you won't tell me what's wrong."

"That's just it. It's not your job to make it right. It's mine. And I…well, what I really need is to go home."

Surprisingly, he didn't argue. "When?"

"Tomorrow—or rather, today."

"I'll arrange for the plane. Rust Creek Falls or Bozeman?"

"Rust Creek Falls."

"Done. Come back to bed." He took her hand again and led her toward the glass doors. She followed him willingly up the stairs and climbed back beneath the covers with him, scooting close against him, her back to his broad chest. Really, she loved everything about him—the scent of his skin, the heat of him at her back, the strength in him. The will to win. His limitless confidence in his ability to mold the world to his liking. And his tenderness, too.

She just…wasn't ready; that was all. Not ready for the fabulous job he'd arranged for her. Not ready to decide which way her life should go. And definitely not ready to be having his baby.

Uh-uh. No way was she ready for that. If only her period would come. She would feel so much better about everything.

He wrapped his arm around her, smoothed her hair.

Eventually, she slept.

Carson had no damn clue what was going on with her.

He also didn't know how to find out what the problem was so they could work through it. She wasn't the least forthcoming lately. And asking got him nowhere. She'd shut him out.

The next morning they were careful with each other. He asked her to call him when she heard from IMI. She promised that she would, though she said nothing about when they might see each other again.

He didn't bring it up, either. Was he getting a little pissed at her? Oh, yes, he was.

But he was trying to be patient, an activity at which he'd never especially excelled. He was trying to give her time to come to him with the truth.

Whatever the hell that was.

He had a meeting at ten that he couldn't get out of. Her flight was set for noon, and he'd ordered a car to get her to the airport. He kissed her goodbye and left the house at nine.

At three that afternoon, he got a text from her. Home safe. Thanks for everything.

He had to actively resist the urge to throw his phone against the far wall of his office just to watch it shatter.

She wanted to play it cryptic? He could do that.

You're welcome, he texted back.

And nothing more.

Carson was angry with her. Tessa totally got that. She didn't blame him, either. She'd been cool and distant and completely uncommunicative, while he'd been charming and attentive and knocked himself out to make her LA visit a good one.

If only her period would come. As soon as it did, as soon as she knew there was no baby on the way, she would call him. They would work things out.

But her period didn't come. And she still had no idea what to say to him. So she didn't call. Or text. Or email. He returned the favor. There was a large and cold silence between them.

The weekend went by.

When Monday finally came, she couldn't stand it anymore. She went to Kalispell and bought a test, which she took first thing Tuesday morning.

Positive.

She stared at the little result window in complete disbelief. How was a positive result even possible? Okay, yes. She could see how it wouldn't have been wise to count on the condom wrappers they'd found the morning after the night of the moonshine. Not when they'd had no clear memory of what they'd actually done with the condoms themselves. One might have torn. Or maybe they'd been so out of it, they'd unwrapped them and then not bothered to use them.

Who could ever say?

But shouldn't she have been able to count on the morning-after pill, at least?

A little online research on that subject had her discovering the pill was about 95 percent effective if taken in the first twenty-four hours.

So, a 5 percent chance of failure.

Maybe the test had been wrong.

Wednesday, she took a second test. The result didn't change. Apparently, she'd somehow managed to fall into that lonely 5 percent.

Tessa sat at the window of her room at the boardinghouse and stared out over Cedar Street below.

A baby. She was having Carson's baby.

She was terrible with children. As for Carson, he'd made it much too clear that he didn't want children.

Where did that leave them?

Nowhere good.

She had no idea what to do, how to tell him. As she pondered the impossibility of breaking the big news to him, her phone rang.

It was Jason Velasco. "Tessa, hello!"

"Jason." It came out on a weary sigh.

"Is this a bad time?"

Terrible. "No. No, not at all." Somehow, she pulled it together and managed to inject at least a little enthusiasm. "What a…nice surprise. How are you doing?"

"Fine, fine." He told her about the weather in California, about the vacation he had coming up. He and his family were going to Hawaii.

And then he got down to it. He said he'd wanted to call her personally with IMI's offer, though human resources would be calling soon, too. The paperwork was on the way, all the terms laid out clearly, in detail.

He gave her the gist of it. She would be a full-fledged graphic designer, a midlevel position with an excellent salary, a generous benefit package and great potential for advancement.

As he chattered excitedly in her ear, a sort of calm settled over her.

She knew two things: She didn't want this job. And she was keeping her baby.

As soon as Jason paused for a breath, she told him where she stood. "I appreciate your calling me, Jason. I appreciate all the effort that you and your team put into making a place for me at IMI. But the truth is I just don't think we're a good fit."

Jason sputtered a bit, but he quickly recovered. He asked what her issues were, specifically, so that he could address them.

She stalled. "Exactly how frank would you like me to be?"

He didn't give up. "You feel…uncomfortable—is that it?"

"Yes. I know Carson pushed you to hire me. And you're right. I'm just not comfortable with that."

"Honestly, Tessa. You're clearly very talented. You impressed us. I really do feel you would make a great addition to our team."

"Well, thank you, Jason."

"So…how do I change your mind?"

"You don't. But I will definitely tell Carson how terrific you've been. I'll make it very clear to him that you, and everyone at IMI, have been helpful and welcoming. I'll let him know that the offer is excellent, but that it just doesn't work for me right now."

"You mean that." It wasn't a question.

"Yes. I do."

"What else can I say?"

"Nothing. Thank you again."

Jason let it go then. He wished her well and said goodbye.

After she hung up, she wondered if maybe she'd lost her mind to turn down a second chance at the big time. But it didn't really feel like she'd blown it. It felt more like the right choice, one that worked for her.

She should call Carson. She'd promised him that she would call as soon as she heard from IMI.

However, she had something a lot more important than a job offer to tell him about. And she couldn't make herself call him until she'd figured out what to say. And as for that, she had nothing.

Another day went by. Thursday she had an idea: maybe a letter. At the very least it might help to write down her thoughts, to plan out what to say to him.

She wrote the letter—or rather, an email. In it she told him she was pregnant and she was keeping the baby and she was sorry, but that was just how it was.

It was awful, that email. Whiny and wimpy. She

trashed it and tried again. That time, she opened with "I love you."

Ugh. Opening with "I love you" and moving right on to, "And I'm having your baby."

That somehow didn't work, either.

She tried writing it out on actual paper, the way she had the letter to Della. *Nope.* Putting it on paper didn't make it even one tiny bit better.

About then she had the blinding realization that telling a man you're having his baby was something you ought to have guts enough to do straight to his face.

So, okay. She needed to return to LA and speak with him in person. Probably the best plan was just to book a flight and go to him.

But that seemed all wrong. The poor man deserved at least a little warning. He didn't need her showing up on his doorstep out of the blue, babbling about love and babies.

Finally, on Friday, she made herself call him.

At least he picked up on the first ring. "Tessa. What a surprise." And not a happy one, judging by the ice-cold tone of his voice. "How are you?" Before she could decide how to answer that, he added, "I understand you turned down the job with IMI."

She winced and stifled a groan. "You, um, talked to Jason, then?"

"I did. And he talked to you…when was it?"

She let out a slow, careful breath. "Wednesday. And, yes, I promised I would call you. I'm sorry I didn't."

"You're sorry. Now, that really helps, Tessa. That makes me feel all warm and fuzzy inside."

"You're mad." She stated the obvious because she didn't know what else to say. "You're really, really mad."

"Figured that out, did you?"

She had so messed this up. Better, she decided, to cut to the point. "Look. I called because I…want to see you."

"Excellent," he muttered, ladling on the sarcasm. "I've got a few things I have to deal with here. Then I'll fly up there on Wednesday."

Her stomach lurched. "Did you just say you're coming back to Rust Creek Falls?" Hope bloomed within her. Bright, beautiful, ridiculous hope.

Hope for what, she wasn't sure.

But maybe he wasn't as finished with her as she'd thought.

"Yeah. Wednesday." He still sounded as cold as the dark side of the moon.

"Carson, are you sure? I'm happy to come there."

"Happy. Interesting word choice. No, I'll come to you."

She got the message. "You don't believe I'll actually show up, do you?"

"And what, I wonder, could possibly cause me to doubt that you'll do what you say you'll do?"

She was very close to yelling a few bad words into the phone and hanging up on him—because she knew he had a right to be mad at her and she didn't know what to do to make it better. She really, truly sucked at relationships. Women like her should not only *not* be allowed to get pregnant; they should never fall in love. People only got hurt when women like her fell in love.

"All right," she said at last. "See you Wednesday, then."

"Dinner," he growled at her. "I'll pick you up at seven. We'll go to that Italian place in Kalispell."

"Okay. That's good," she said. "I—I'm looking forward to seeing you and…" About then she realized she was talking to dead air.

He'd already hung up.

Chapter Eleven

Carson's plane landed in Kalispell at a few minutes past noon on Wednesday. He rented a car and headed for Rust Creek Falls, planning to go straight to the boardinghouse. So what if he was several hours early? He would surprise her. Maybe he'd catch her at a weak moment and she'd say something honest for a change.

He was still very angry at her. And he would probably say things to her that he'd regret later.

Well, too bad. There was no way he could wait until seven to see her. He'd already waited twelve never-ending damn days since she left him in Malibu. Because if she wanted to talk to him, she could damn well pick up the phone and call.

But she hadn't called. Until Friday.

And as of now, today, this moment, it was enough.

He was finding her immediately, and they were having it out. If it was over, he would damn well know sooner than later.

At the south end of town, he turned onto Main Street, headed north. He crossed the Main Street Bridge and saw a whole lot of red, white and blue up ahead. Coming even with the cluster of public buildings between the bridge and Cedar Street, he rolled by the library, all decked out in patriotic bunting. The town hall façade was the same—and the Community Center on the other side of the street, too.

Monday had been the Fourth of July. They must have left the decorations up.

Damn. He'd missed the parade. No doubt there had been babies involved, lots of flag-waving and veterans in uniform, chest candy glinting in the midday sun. True, he had no interest in small-town parades. Still, he felt strangely regretful that he'd missed the Rust Creek Falls version of the Fourth.

Did they have a barbecue in the park after the parade? Had Tessa been there?

He was so busy feeling left out and kicking himself mentally for even caring, that he was not the least prepared when Homer Gilmore suddenly materialized in the middle of the street waving his arms wildly, shouting, "Stop!"

Carson wasn't going very fast, but Homer had appeared out of nowhere. Carson hit the brakes, hard. Rubber squealed and burned as he slid to a stop a hair's breadth from mowing the old fool down.

"What the hell, Homer?" Carson yelled out his open driver's side window. "I could have killed you. Have you completely lost your mind?"

Homer didn't answer. And he didn't even look bothered that he'd almost become roadkill. Instead, he pointed a scrawny finger heavenward, as if to say, *Hold on a minute.*

Carson leaned on the horn.

Homer moved then—and fast, too. He darted around to the passenger door and tapped on the window.

Reluctantly, Carson rolled it down. “What?”

Homer stuck his head in. “We need to talk.”

“No, we don’t. It didn’t go well with the moonshine that night.”

“What’s that mean, exactly?”

“It means that Drake Distilleries is having nothing to do with that stuff of yours. End of discussion.”

Instead of replying, or pulling his head out of the window so that Carson could move on, Homer reached in and popped open the door.

“Homer, don’t—” But Carson was too late.

The old miscreant had already hopped in. “Take me to the Ace in the Hole. I need a burger. And we still need to talk.”

Someone honked. Carson checked the rearview mirror to see that a quad cab pulling a horse trailer had stopped behind him. The driver honked again.

“Let’s go.” Homer made a shooing motion with his left hand as he hooked the seat belt with his right. “You can’t just park yourself in the middle of Main Street, blocking other people’s way.”

At the Ace in the Hole, Homer insisted on a quiet booth in the back. “So’s we can talk business private-like.” He ordered a double-decker cheeseburger with fries and a beer.

Carson hadn’t eaten since before he’d left the house in Malibu that morning, so he went ahead and ordered the same. “Now what?” he asked the old man once their waitress had brought them their beers.

Homer took a pull off his longneck and set it down hard. He burped good and loud. "I needed that."

Carson tried again, speaking slowly, as one would to a child. Or an idiot. "Did you hear what I said back there on Main Street, Homer? I'm not interested in your moonshine formula anymore."

Narrowing his reddened eyes and bunching up his grizzled eyebrows, Homer leaned across the table. "You tellin' me you didn't have the best night of your life that night?"

Carson scoffed. "I'm not telling you anything of the sort. I can't even remember what happened that night. That moonshine of yours causes blackouts, Homer. I had one. And so did Tessa. That is dangerous stuff. You're lucky no one's sued you yet—not to mention, had you arrested."

"Arrested? For what?"

"I don't know. Running a moonshine still without a distilled spirits permit? Or maybe just plain drugging people?"

Homer drew his scrawny shoulders back and announced with a sniff, "Everybody who drinks my 'shine does so of his or her own free will."

Now Carson was the one leaning across the scratched table between them. "Don't give me that. I've heard the stories. You spiked the wedding punch a year ago, on the Fourth. The people who drank it then had no idea what they were in for."

Homer took another swallow of his beer. He set the bottle down more gently that time. "I just wanted 'em to loosen up, you know? Make connections, have some fun."

Carson opened his mouth with a comeback. But what was the point? He might as well argue with the wall. "Whatever excuses you want to make for yourself, at least get clear on the fact that I'm *not* buying your moonshine formula."

Homer's eyes lit up as he stared past Carson's shoulder. "Oh, look. Here come our burgers."

The waitress served them. When she left, Homer dug in. Carson ate, too, his mind on Tessa, on what she might be doing right now. He hoped she would be at the boardinghouse when he finally ditched Homer and got over there.

The old man demolished his meal in no time flat, finishing up the first beer and ordering a second one. Finally, he wiped his mouth with his napkin and pushed his plate away. "Nothin' like a burger and a beer, I always say."

"Homer, are we clear, then? I'm not buying your moonshine. There will be no deal."

Homer only grinned wide, showing off those yellowed teeth that had never made the acquaintance of a competent orthodontist. "I do like your style, Carson Drake. And I just need a few more weeks to decide for sure if I can work with you."

About then, Carson realized that trying to get on the same page with Homer Gilmore was an exercise in futility. The old guy lived in his own world on his own terms. "Whatever you say, Homer." He put his concentration where it would do some good: on eating his burger and enjoying his fries.

And then Homer asked in a very serious tone, "So, what do you think about the situation with Tessa?"

The old guy was more than a little creepy. At that moment, Carson almost felt that Homer could see into his brain. Carson answered warily, "I…like Tessa. Very much."

Homer waved a bony hand. "I didn't ask if you *liked*

her. I asked how you're doing with her having your baby and when are the two of you steppin' up and makin' it legal? That's what I asked."

What the...?

Carson choked down a last bite of burger and pushed his own plate away. "Who told you that Tessa is pregnant?"

Homer thought that was funny, apparently. He chortled. "Nobody told me. Nobody *had* to tell me. You both had my moonshine, didn't you? And everybody knows what happens when a man and a woman drink my moonshine together."

The sudden knot in Carson's stomach untied itself. Tessa wasn't pregnant. Homer was just being Homer. The old coot had probably been sampling his own product.

"Well?" Homer demanded.

Carson leaned forward again and pinned Homer with a cold glare. "You don't know what you're talking about, old man. And you should know better than to go spreading stories you made up in your head."

Homer gave a slow and weirdly satisfied nod. "You're protective of that sweet girl. That's a good thing. A man should be protective of his woman." He leaned in, too, until his road map of a face was only inches from Carson's. "And I don't carry no tales," he muttered on a beery breath. "This here conversation, it's just between us. Strictly man-to-man. You can walk out of here dead certain that I will never share your private business with another living soul. Now, if you'll excuse me, I need to see a man about a horse."

Homer got up and followed the signs to the men's room. Carson paid the bill and finished his beer, his impatience growing as the minutes ticked by and the old man failed to reappear. The guy was not only a menace to society with his dangerous moonshine and his tendency to pop up out of bushes and materialize out of nowhere in the middle of the street; he was downright rude. Carson should just get up and go. It wasn't as if he'd even wanted this impromptu meeting with the old reprobate.

Finally, he decided he could use a trip to the men's room himself. He got up and went in there.

Empty. *Of course.*

He took care of business. On the way out, he asked the waitress if she'd seen where Homer went.

She shook her head. "Sorry. I never saw him leave your booth."

Five minutes later, Carson parked on the street in front of Strickland's Boarding House and marched up to the front door.

Old Gene answered his knock. "Hey." Gene wore a wide smile. Whatever might be going on with Tessa and whatever Old Gene knew about it, he seemed to have no issue with Carson. "How you doin', son?"

The tension between Carson's shoulder blades eased a little. "Great, thanks."

"Lookin' for Tessa?" Old Gene ushered him in. "She's down in the basement on laundry duty."

And just like that, Carson was heading down the back stairs. He found her at the folding table busy with a tall pile of towels. Both of the dryers and the two washers were going, making enough noise that she hadn't heard him coming. She just went on folding, her back to him, completely unaware of his presence.

His footsteps slowed at the sight of her. He paused at the base of the stairs, his heart roaring in his chest, his belly tight, burning with a potent mix of frustration and yearning. She wore Chuck Taylors, torn, faded jeans that clung to her fine butt and a striped tank with a neck so wide, it had fallen down her arm one side to reveal the soft curve of her shoulder. Her hair was piled in a sloppy bun at the top of her head, wild curls escaping in little corkscrews along the back of her neck.

His heart rate slowed to a steady, hungry rhythm and the burning in his gut became something closer to arousal than anger. It was the best he'd felt in days.

"Tessa."

Her slim shoulders stiffened. She dropped the hand towel she'd just grabbed and whirled to face him, those dark eyes taking him in, that wide mouth not quite knowing whether to smile or to scowl. "Carson."

The sound of his name on her lips broke the spell that held him rooted in place. Yeah, they really needed to talk. But more than that, he had to have his hands on her.

In five long strides, he eliminated the distance between them, reaching for her as she grabbed for him. He lifted her, and she jumped right up into his waiting arms, wrapping those slim legs good and tight around his waist, plastering her sweet self against the front of him.

She was on him like a barnacle, her hands in his hair, those lips he needed so badly to taste hovering just out of reach. "You're early," she whispered, wonderfully breathless with what just might be a longing equal to his own. *God.* She smelled so good, sweet and fresh, like rain and flowers and fabric softener.

"We have to talk." He growled the words at her.

She cradled his face between her two small hands. "I know. Yes. I know we do."

He couldn't wait a minute longer to have her mouth on his. She must have felt the same. Because her soft lips came crashing down, closing on his with a whimper of need.

So good. Incomparable. Tessa's hot little mouth moving on his, her sweet tongue spearing in, warring with his, her arms closing tighter, her body pressing closer.

When she tried to lift her mouth away, he reached up a hand, his fingers spread wide to cup the back of her head. He guided her back to him, taking her mouth again.

The second kiss tasted even better than the first. He held her firmly in place and plundered her mouth for all he was worth, lowering her to the folding table as he kissed her, laying her out onto the warm pile of towels.

Finally, when she pushed a little at his shoulders and wiggled in his hold with growing resistance, he lifted up enough to look at her, at her mouth all swollen from his kisses, her hair tumbling down, coming loose from that topknot, her eyes dazed and dreamy. "I need an hour," she said breathlessly, "to finish up the laundry."

He stroked a hand down her arm, along the gorgeous curve of her hip. Holding her gaze, he demanded, "Then we talk."

"Yes."

"No blowing me off this time."

She shook her head. "I swear." She reached up, pressed her cool, smooth hand to his cheek. Damn, he had missed her—those gold-flecked, coffee-brown eyes, the sweet and husky sound of her voice, the gentle touch of her hand. Everything. All of her. "One hour," she vowed. "And we'll talk."

He helped her fold the towels and sheets. They worked together silently, all the things that needed saying hanging in the humid basement air between them. He had about a thousand questions—most of them beginning with the word *why*.

For now, though, he didn't ask even one of them. No

point in getting into it until they could be alone, with no chance of interruption.

Between loads, they went upstairs together and visited with Melba and Claire in the kitchen. Melba asked him how long he would be in town this time.

He cut a quick glance at Tessa. Their gazes caught and locked. He knew she was waiting for his answer—an answer he couldn't give right then. "Not sure. It depends."

"Will you be needing a room?" Melba asked next.

He'd already reserved his former suite at the Manor. But he might want a room at the boardinghouse, too, depending on what happened when he and Tessa were alone. "Still got the room next to Tessa's?"

Melba set down her coffee cup and rose from the table. "Been saving it for you."

Tessa's eyes widened at her grandmother's words, but she didn't comment.

Melba led him to the office, where he took that room for the rest of the month. If things went badly with Tessa, he might never set foot in it. But if he wanted it, he would have it. Never hurt to keep his options open.

It was after four when he helped Tessa fold the last sheet.

Then she said, "Come upstairs to my room."

"Not here," he replied. The boardinghouse was a second home to her. Her sister or one of her grandparents might come tapping on the door at any time. No. He wanted her on his turf. "Let's go to the Manor. We can talk in the suite. No one will bother us there."

She regarded him so seriously. He had no idea what might be going on behind those fine brown eyes. "Okay. I'll just grab my purse."

At Maverick Manor, in the sitting room of his suite, she took the sofa. He started to sit beside her, but she put up a hand. "Would you sit across from me? I want to be…face-to-face."

Was that a bad sign?

Lately, with her, he just didn't know.

His gut knotting up again, the muscles between his shoulder blades drawing tight, he took the club chair across the coffee table from her. "All right. We're face-to-face." *Now, what the hell is going on with you?*

"I…" She gripped the sofa cushions on either side of her, as though to ground herself. "I'm sorry I didn't call you when I turned down the job with IMI. I should have."

He did want to talk about what had happened with IMI. Still, he had the strangest feeling that she'd just detoured from the main subject. Whatever that subject might actually be. But fine. He had plenty to say with regard to the job at IMI. "You said you would call."

"Yeah, I know. And I apologize."

"But why didn't you?" He kept his tone as soft and even as he could manage. "Am I that hard to talk to?"

"No," she said instantly. And then, "Yes." And then, "I think I mentioned before how it's all happening so fast with us. And I, well, I've been feeling kind of overwhelmed. I told you I'm no good at this, at trying to make a relationship work." Now she seemed flustered, and she rushed to add, "I mean, if a relationship is what we have, though I suppose it's too early to get real specific as to what exactly to call this thing with us, and I…" She was clutching the cushions again. "Oh, God. I'm making no sense, none at all."

He almost laughed. "On second thought, forget about why."

Her eyes softened. And so did that mouth he was longing to kiss. "You mean that?"

"Yeah. It's all right. You're sorry you didn't call, and

I accept your apology. Let's leave it there." He really wanted to touch her, to hold her. But she was over there, and he was over here. He needed to rectify that problem, and soon.

And then, miracle of miracles, she held out her hand. "I know I asked you to sit over there. But would you come here? Please?"

He wrapped his fingers around hers, got up and scooted around the table to join her on the couch. With a sigh, she swayed against him. He gathered her close, pressed his lips against her hair. "I still have questions."

A small sigh escaped her. "Go ahead."

"Did Jason or his team give you a hard time about how your job with the Storm woman ended?"

She stiffened and drew away. "Absolutely not. They really did plan to hire me and Jason was… I like him. He called me personally to tell me I had the job. It was a good offer. And when I turned it down, he made a real effort to change my mind. We did speak of it, of course, of Della, but she wasn't the issue. I promise you."

"So then, what was the issue?" He suspected that LA was the problem, that having to live there was a complete deal-breaker for her.

If so, where did that leave them? He would do a lot to be with her, but he needed to be in LA much of the year to run the Drake companies effectively. Relocating to the wilds of Montana wasn't going to cut it for him—even if he had grown strangely fond of Rust Creek Falls.

"The truth is, Carson…" She faltered again, scooting farther away from him and grabbing for the sofa cushions. "I really don't want a job that I get because you want me to have it. I don't want a job I get on your say-so because my new boss wants to keep you happy."

So, then, in spite of what she'd said a minute ago, Jason

and crew *did* mess it up. If so, heads would roll. Carson asked in a carefully neutral tone, "What you're saying is they made it clear to you that they were only hiring you because *I* wanted you hired."

Her dark eyes flashed. She tapped one of her Chuck Taylors impatiently. "Of course not. I've told you. They were gracious and perfectly reasonable and they never said any such thing. Still, we all knew exactly what was going on."

"Which was?"

"Seriously, Carson. How many ways do I have to explain this?"

"What I'm saying is, even given that I instigated the process, they *wanted* to hire you. I just don't get it. Where is the problem?"

"I told you the problem. I want to find my own damn job."

"And you did."

She shot him a narrow-eyed glance, then instantly looked away. "I have no idea what you're talking about."

"Look at this logically. You just said that IMI made you a bona fide offer, that they wanted to hire you. So you did it. You found a great job. All I did was get the ball rolling. Because face it—even *I* couldn't get you hired if you weren't going to be able to do the job."

"Please. You so could. And I don't want that. I don't want you to get me a job. I want to get my *own* job. Yes, I'm stumbling around in the dark about this, having a hard time finding my way. But still, I need to do this my way, for myself."

"I think you're being naive."

Her sweet mouth thinned to a hard line. "Thank you so much for your input."

He tried to make light of it. "Ouch. The sarcasm is killing me."

Hectic spots of color flamed high on her cheeks. "Let's make a deal. You stop treating me like a silly little woman and I'll control my sarcasm."

"I was not—"

"Yes, Carson. You were." She was looking right at him now. It wasn't a happy look. For a long count of five, she glared at him and he tried to figure out what to say next that wouldn't have her bouncing to her feet and heading for the door.

Because she mattered to him. A whole lot.

It was of paramount importance to him that somehow they work this out. That she not give up on him.

On them.

All he'd wanted for years was his freedom, to taste every delight life had to offer. He worked hard and played hard. It had been great.

But now there was Tessa with her dark gypsy eyes and her wide mouth made for kissing, with her sharp mind and guarded heart. Now freedom didn't look all that wonderful, frankly. Freedom just felt like loneliness.

Now he really needed to figure out how to keep her from walking away.

Finally, she spoke. "I'm going to say all this one more time, and you'd better be listening. Jason and the team at IMI treated me well, with courtesy and professional respect. It's not their fault that I'm not going to work for them. I said no to their offer, and I'm glad that I did. It was the right choice for me. I regret that I didn't keep my word and call you about it. That's on me, and I'll do better next time."

He took her hand. When she didn't instantly jerk away, he considered that a good sign. "Okay."

She swallowed hard. "Okay, what?"

He rubbed the back of her hand with his thumb, loving the feel of her, skin to skin, wanting to kiss her, wondering how long he would have to wait before she let him. Was he totally whipped? It kind of appeared so. "Okay, the job wasn't right for you and you need to run your own career without interference from me."

"That's it, yes. If I want your help, I'll ask for it—and then you can decide if you even want to help me." At least she said that kind of tenderly.

"Of course I'll help you any way I can." The words came out raw sounding, rough with emotion. He made his confession. "I'm a complete fool for you, Tessa."

The sweetest, softest sigh escaped her. "You are not in any way a fool."

"Oh, yeah, I am. For you, I am. It's been crap in LA without you. You're what I think about. You're what I want." He reeled her in.

And she let him, thank heaven.

Damn, he was starved for the taste of her. He wrapped his arms around her and lowered his mouth to hers.

The kiss was long and deep and thorough, and Tessa reveled in it.

When he eased his hand up under her shirt, she didn't stop him. Far from it. She moaned in invitation and pushed her breast into his palm.

When he took her shirt away and unhooked her bra, she loved it. When he unzipped her old jeans and guided her to her feet so he could slide them down to a pool of tattered denim around her ankles, she loved that, too.

He went to his knees on the rug. She stared down at his dark head as he untied her shoes. At his command, she stepped out of them.

Next he took down her satin boy shorts with the lace inserts on the sides. And then he pressed his mouth to the hot, feminine core of her and did things to her that probably ought to be illegal.

She combed her fingers through his hair, clutching him to her, whispering his name, knowing herself for a dishonest coward—and crying out in pure joy anyway as she came.

Later. The word whispered through her mind as she pulled him to his feet and stripped off his shirt, so eager to get to his bare skin that buttons went flying.

Later, I'll tell him. We'll go to dinner. I'll tell him then, just as I planned.

But now…

Well, now she was the one going down to her knees. She took him in her mouth, loving the salty taste of him, taking him so deep, sliding her tongue along the thick vein that ran the length of him, until he moaned her name and fisted his hands in her hair.

When he pulled her up, threw her over his shoulder and headed for the bedroom, she laughed and kicked her feet and pretended to protest. And then he put her down so carefully on the bed, as though she were precious, fragile. Breakable.

She didn't let herself even think that she should tell him the truth about the baby first and take her pleasure later. When he rolled on a condom, she didn't say a word about how they no longer needed one—well, at least not for contraception.

She just opened for him and pulled him into her yearning arms and let the wonder roll through her, let his slow, hot, skilled caresses obliterate her until she was only a conduit for each thrilling sensation. Twice more, she came. It was magnificent.

And when she finally felt him pulsing within her, she gloried in it.

Later, she thought, when she held him close afterward. *I'll tell him at dinner, just as I planned.*

At the Italian place in Kalispell, they got the same booth they'd had the time before—in a quiet little corner where they could talk without being disturbed. She joked with him that it was so nice be back at "their" Italian place.

He agreed. "We need to come here often."

She wondered how they would do that, with him living in LA. But then, maybe *she* would move to LA, too, and they would find a favorite Italian place there.

Maybe it would actually work out between them. She could find freelance work much more easily in LA. They would live together and raise their baby together, and maybe find a little getaway place of their own in Rust Creek Falls. They could visit a few times a year.

Maybe.

Or maybe not.

Maybe that was all just a crazy fantasy.

Who could say?

The first step was to tell him.

And she hadn't even gotten there yet.

But she didn't let all those maybes show in her expression. She only laughed and said, "Yes. We should come here to 'our' Italian place at least once a week."

She ordered veal, and he had the chicken Parmesan. When he poured her a glass of Chianti, she didn't stop him, though that would have been a good lead-in to breaking the news she should have shared hours ago. She let him pour the wine, and she never touched the glass.

If he noticed, he didn't let on.

He talked about Drake Distilleries, about the terrific ad campaign IMI had developed for an all new product line of flavored liqueurs. And Drake Hospitality would soon be opening a new club in San Diego. He said he wanted to take her to the big first-night party at the end of August. She said she would love that, though August seemed a million years away and she thought to herself that anything could happen by then.

He didn't even *want* children.

How could this possibly end well?

Panic jittered through her.

She quelled it and reported that she'd picked up more work through her website and, yes, there had been a parade along Main Street on the Fourth of July. "It was strangely similar to the one on Memorial Day."

"I'll bet. Barbecue in the park afterward?"

"How did you guess?"

He gave a low, sexy chuckle. "What's Independence Day in Rust Creek Falls without a parade and a barbecue after?"

"It was fun," she said. And then confessed, "I wished you were here."

He set down his wineglass. "Me, too." He said it quietly. And his dark eyes seemed to say she was the only other person in the world right then.

Just the two of them, together. It could work. She knew it could.

Except that it *wasn't* just the two of them.

Because baby made three.

He smiled at her, a musing kind of smile.

She asked, "What?"

And he said, "I think I'm starting to like it in Rust Creek Falls. Ryan said it would happen. I hate when he's right."

The waitress served the main course.

Carson dug into his chicken parm and started telling her about how he'd run into Homer before he came looking for her at the boardinghouse. "I'm serious," he insisted. "Literally, I *ran* into Homer—or almost, anyway. He popped up out of nowhere in the middle of Main Street. I barely hit the brakes in time to keep from plowing him down. He wanted a burger and to talk about his moonshine. So I took him to the Ace in the Hole and tried to tell him that the moonshine deal was off. He refused to hear me, just kept saying he needed another few weeks to make up his mind. It only got weirder."

"Knowing Homer, I can't say I'm surprised." She twirled up a bite of linguini.

"He asked me how the 'situation' was with you."

"That's a strange way to put it."

"I thought so, too. And then he said he knew you were pregnant and what was I going to do about that?"

She froze with her forkful of linguini halfway to her mouth. Her face must have said it all.

Because Carson was suddenly watching her way too closely, eyes sharp and assessing.

Her hand was shaking. Slowly, she lowered her fork to her plate.

He suggested, way too gently, "Right now would be a great time to reassure me that it's not true."

Chapter Twelve

Carson waited for her to laugh and tell him that he really shouldn't jump to conclusions.

But she didn't laugh. She just went on staring at him through wide, haunted eyes, her linguine-wrapped fork abandoned on her plate.

Finally, in a voice that came out sounding way more freaked than he meant it to, he demanded, "It's true, then?"

Those thick dark lashes lowered. He watched her draw a careful breath and then let it out with agonizing slowness. Finally, she looked at him again. "Yes. It's true." She said the words flatly. Quietly.

Still, they echoed in his head like a shout. "But I don't..." He had no idea what he was trying to say. He took another crack at it. "So it was the night of the moonshine? You're saying Homer had it right?" He still couldn't believe it.

"Yes."

How was this even possible? He struggled to process. "But…the condoms, the morning-after pill…"

One slim shoulder lifted in a sad little half shrug. And then she craned across the booth toward him and insisted in a hot, angry whisper, "I did take that pill. I swear I did."

"Whoa. Hold on."

"What do you mean, hold on?" She was still whispering, but each word came out sharp and furiously clear. "I didn't ask for this, Carson. I did everything in my power to prevent it—well, except *not* to drink Homer's moonshine. I really should have thought twice before I did that."

"Stop. Listen. I'm not blaming you for getting pregnant. I believe you took that pill."

"Then why did you say—"

He cut her off with a wave of his hand. "Look. It's kind of a shock, okay?"

She sagged back into the red pleather seat. "Well, all right. I hear that." She picked up her fork—and then put it back down again. It clattered against her plate. "Suddenly I don't feel much like eating."

Neither did he. And he had a question he had to get an answer to. "Were you ever planning to tell me?"

"Of course."

He was far from convinced. "When?"

She winced—and made her answer into another question. "Over dessert?"

"Dessert," he echoed, remembering all the days she hadn't called him, recalling the day just past, when she'd kissed him and held him and they'd had it out over the job at IMI. So many chances she'd had to tell him.

And she hadn't.

"Carson, I…" She started to reach out. He stiffened,

not ready for her touch, not willing to be soothed by her. She saw him flinch and dropped her hand. "I promise you, I was getting to it. I really was."

"Getting to it how?"

"I'm not really sure. But I was working up to it. I *was*."

He drank some more Chianti, noticing for the first time that her glass was still full. And come to think of it, what about that champagne she wouldn't drink in LA the evening after the interview with IMI? And what about the way she just stopped talking to him then, no matter how hard he knocked himself out to convince her to let him in? "You've known since LA," he accused.

"I—"

"Don't you lie to me, Tessa. Don't you dare."

"Fine. All right, I suspected something then. My period was late. But I didn't take a test until I got home."

He just shook his head. "I thought we'd really made progress. I thought you were finally opening up to me today when we talked about that damn job you wouldn't take with IMI. I thought we were getting down to the crap that really matters. And then I took you to bed." He couldn't get over that. "We went to bed—and still you didn't tell me."

"Carson, I—"

"Do you trust me at all?"

"I'm trying."

"Uh-uh. Wait a minute." He jabbed an index finger in her direction. "This is it, isn't it? This is the real reason you didn't call me when you turned down the IMI job. This is the real reason you finally did call. You're holding all the information, and I'm in the dark, sitting here thinking how we've gotten past a rough patch and now I'm feeling so close to you…"

"I didn't blow you off. I was just waiting for the right time, that's all."

"From my side of the table, Tessa, I can see a long series of right times, none of which you took. On the contrary, you waited. You saved it up to tell me in a restaurant, in public, instead of earlier when at least we were alone and didn't have to have this out in whispers."

Her soft mouth trembled. She drew herself up. "All right. Yes, I should have gotten to it sooner. I made it seem like my issue was only about the job with IMI, just like you said. I made you think we'd worked through the problem when I hadn't even told you the real problem. And then, well, you kissed me and I kissed you and all I wanted was to be with you, to make love with you and forget about the future and how to tell you that there was a baby—about how and when and where to go from here. Okay, maybe getting to it here at the restaurant was a bad choice. But I wouldn't have let the night go by without telling you. It's why I called you and said we needed to talk. It's huge and I know it and I…well, now it's all blown up in my face. But you really do need to know everything."

He jerked up straight, every nerve at attention. "What the hell. There's *more*?"

"Stop looking at me like that. I just mean you should also know I'm keeping this baby. I want this baby no matter how bad a mother I'm going to turn out to be and—" She made a soft little sound, something midway between a moan and whimper. "God. I don't know. What else is there to say right now? I'm pregnant and I'm keeping it and that's about the size of it."

He could not sit there for one second longer. Not without picking up his plate and throwing his half-finished chicken Parmesan at the empty booth across the way. He slapped his napkin onto the table and slid from the booth. "Do not move. I'll be right back."

"Carson, please try to—"

"I need a minute."

"Carson—"

He didn't want to hear it, refused to hang around and listen to her next excuse. He turned his back on her and headed for the men's room.

There was nobody in there. *Thank God for small favors.* He splashed water on his face and stared at himself in the mirror over the sinks.

"A father..." He blinked at himself in disbelief and then scoffed at his dripping face. "You. A dad." He swore low, a string of harsh words, as he whipped a few paper towels from the dispenser and wiped the water off.

He'd never planned to be a dad.

But then, he hadn't planned on Tessa, either. He was one of those guys who'd thought he'd learned his lesson when his marriage failed. He'd spent years purposely never getting all that deeply involved.

Until Tessa.

One look at her and not getting involved went right out the window. Insta-love, insta-lust. Whatever it was, he'd known at the first sight of her that she was a game changer.

But a kid?

He hadn't bargained on a kid. He tossed the towels in the trash bin and stared at himself in the mirror some more as the shock of it faded.

Yeah, he was still seriously pissed at her for the way she'd handled this.

Which was *not* to handle it at all.

But he was also starting to get that itchy feeling at

the back of his neck, the one that told him he'd behaved badly.

Worse than badly.

Like a complete ass.

He'd let his anger get the better of him. She hadn't trusted him on so many levels, had been living with this secret for at least a couple of weeks now. He'd known there was a problem, had done everything but beg her to confide in him.

Still, she'd kept it from him. And that really got to him. For the first time in years, he wanted more than a good time from a woman. He wanted her to talk to him, to trust in him. But she hadn't.

And that made him want to break something big and heavy—something that would make a lot of noise as it shattered.

It really wasn't like him, to lose it like this. He ran a string of successful companies. He knew how to keep himself in check.

Except, apparently, when it came to Tessa.

Tessa and their baby.

Our baby.

My God.

He bent over the sink again and splashed more cold water on his face, dried off for the second time and raked his hair in place with his fingers. Then he retucked his shirt and straightened his jacket.

Ready as he'd ever be—which was to say, not ready at all.

But he had to get back to her. He wouldn't put it past her to get up and walk out. Because she'd screwed up by not telling him, by lying about it and insisting that nothing was wrong. And he'd been a jerk when the truth finally came out. Who knew what she thought of him right at this moment?

Parents. They were going to be parents. God help the poor kid.

He hadn't realized he'd been holding his breath until he came out of the hallway from the men's room and saw that she was still in the booth. *Good.* He got over there fast and slid in across from her.

But his moment of relief didn't last. The first words out of her mouth were, "I've had enough for tonight, Carson. Please take me back to the boardinghouse now."

He quelled the urge to argue. She looked tired, worn-out. And he needed some time to process all this, time to figure out how to work through this with her. He might be shocked all to hell to learn he was going to be a father, but she'd been carrying the burden of that truth for weeks now. *She* was the pregnant one, the one who needed a little tender care and understanding—neither of which he'd provided so far.

"Tessa, I—"

She didn't let him finish. "Please. No more tonight. I just can't take it right now."

Carson spent that night alone in his suite at Maverick Manor. He never went to bed. He watched bad late-night television without paying attention.

And he thought about Tessa and the baby and what he would do.

By morning, everything was clear. He got online and chose a ring, then called his assistant at home. She promised to get the ring from Cartier and get it to him overnight. The size would probably be wrong, but he could have it fixed in a matter of a day or two. If he was taking a knee, it seemed important that there *be* a ring, and a gorgeous one, even if it didn't quite fit.

Once the ring was handled, he called Tessa. She answered, which he decided to take as a good sign.

"Hi." Her voice was soft, a little sleepy. Something inside him ached in a way that was both painful and sweet. "You're up early."

"I didn't sleep. I've been thinking."

"Yeah." She made a soft sound—a sigh, a stifled yawn? "It's a lot to take in—I know."

"I want to see you. I promise not to be an ass."

Another sound that might have been a husky little chuckle. God, he hoped so. "Good to know. And yeah. We still need to talk."

"How about breakfast? If you come here, there's room service." He braced to be more convincing when she said no.

But then she said, "Half an hour, I'll be there."

"I'll order ahead. What do you want?"

"Poached eggs and toast and maybe some fresh fruit?"

"You got it."

She smiled when he opened the door, a weary little smile. He wanted to pull her close for a kiss, stroke her hair, rub her back. But that seemed wrong, somehow, after all that had gone down the night before. They needed to make up officially, before there could be kissing.

Didn't they?

The food arrived a couple of minutes after she did. The living area of the suite had a table with four chairs. They sat there. He spooned eggs Benedict into his mouth, hardly tasting it, not knowing how to begin.

This was hard. Wanting her so much, knowing from

the first that she was someone special. And yeah, okay, they both had issues, but didn't everybody? He'd set his sights on working through them. And then it had all gone wrong so suddenly when she stopped talking to him during her visit to LA. Yesterday, he'd just started to let himself think they were getting somewhere.

And then he found out about the baby.

Everything felt backward. They should have had more time to find their way as a couple before something like this happened. Neither of them had been thinking about having kids.

In fact, as he recalled, they'd both agreed that they were hopeless with babies—which was just fine because neither of them planned to have any.

Damn Homer Gilmore and his magic moonshine. Damn him to hell and back.

She spooned up berries from her fruit bowl—and then dropped them back in the bowl again. "Carson, I feel so terrible about all of this."

"Don't," he said, taking care, as he hadn't the night before, to speak gently, to use an affectionate tone. "Don't feel terrible. Just eat. Then we'll talk." He braced for her comeback.

But there wasn't one. She stuck her spoon back in the berries and got to work finishing her meal.

Twenty minutes later, they moved to the seating area. She took the sofa. He got the club chair.

Just like yesterday.

Today it was his turn to open with an apology. "I really was a jerk last night. I'm sorry."

She gave him a gentle smile and proceeded to be a lot more gracious than he'd been. "It's all right. It was a shocker, and I made a mess of telling you—or *not* telling you I guess is more accurate. But it's done now. You know about the baby. We can move on. And I, well, honestly, Carson. You don't have to worry."

He frowned at her. "I should be worried?"

"Well, I mean, I wouldn't blame you for wondering if I'm after your money."

He let out a sharp bark of laughter. "Come on. You wouldn't even let me find you a great job. You're the most independent woman I know. Not to mention you've got an excess of foolish pride."

"I'm only saying that I don't expect anything of you—I promise."

I don't expect anything. He didn't like the sound of that. "That's garbage. You damn well should expect things of me. You should expect *everything* of me." He said it a little more forcefully than he meant to.

She fiddled with the collar of the silky blue shirt she wore. "Well, fine. You seem pretty sure of all this. What *should* I expect of you? What does 'everything' mean?"

He reminded himself to speak quietly, reasonably. "I can tell you what *I* expect."

"Thank you. Please do."

"I want to take care of you. I want us to be together. That's what *I* expect, and you damn well should, too."

She looked at him sideways. "Together as in…?"

He'd jumped ahead. He knew he had. He shouldn't be saying this today. He needed to wait for the ring, at least. And a better understanding between them probably wouldn't hurt, either. Right now, they were just supposed to be healing the wounds they'd dealt each other yesterday and the two weeks before that. "Okay, I'm rushing things."

She hugged her arms around herself. "Carson, I'm not following."

He hated the damn coffee table. Twice now it had

stood between them. He rose. "Come over here." When she only gazed up at him, bewildered, he reached across and captured her wrist. She allowed him to take it, though somewhat reluctantly. "Over here." He tugged her up off the cushions and led her to the center of the room where no furniture was in the way. As soon as he had the space for it, he dropped to one knee.

By then, she knew what was coming. "Oh, Carson." Her mouth twisted as she stared down at him.

He should knock this off. Now. But it just wasn't in him to back down at this point. He had to take a crack at getting a yes out of her up front, at cutting through all the yada yada and sealing the deal. Once he got her commitment, they could work through all the rest. "Marry me, Tessa. You're all I think about. You're all I want. I'm crazy for you—and yeah. I know it's fast. I know it's scary. I know if I said that I loved you right now, you probably wouldn't believe me. So I won't say it, okay? I won't say it yet. But won't you just take a chance on me? If you'll only say yes, we can make it work. I know we can."

For a moment, he actually thought he'd done it. He knew she would say yes.

But then she dropped to *her* knees in front of him, which put her as close to eye to eye with him as possible, given his extra height. Now they knelt together in the center of the room.

"Tessa?" he asked, as she took his face between her hands. He didn't think he liked where this was going somehow. But it did feel good, her soft palms against his skin. Her cheeks had gone bright pink, and her eyes gleamed with what might have been tears.

Or, just possibly, laughter.

"You haven't mentioned the baby," she whispered downright tenderly.

"The baby." It came out gruff. "Of course, the baby. That's why we need to get this going, get it together. We need to be married so we can deal with all our crap and be ready to be actual parents when the baby comes."

She feathered her fingers along the hair at his temples. That felt terrific. What she said next? Not so much. "You've mentioned more than once that you never wanted children."

He turned his face into her hand and pressed a kiss to the heart of her palm. "And you've said the same to me."

"Not my point."

He was starting to get irritated. "There's a point?"

"Yes, Carson. The baby is the point. I don't really think you're ready for this…to marry me when you've barely known me a month because we're having a baby when you don't even *want* a baby."

"How about you let *me* be the judge of what I'm ready for? I want to marry you. We can work it all out."

"I just don't think it's that simple. As things stand now, I'm ready for you to be however involved you want to be. You didn't sign up for this, and I understand that. I can totally accept your not really being there for our child."

"What are you talking about? I *want* to be there."

"I'm saying that if we were married, I'd have higher expectations of you, and our child would, too."

"Fine. Good. I already told you. You should have expectations. So should the kid. Bring them the hell on."

"If we were married," she kept on way too patiently, "I would expect you to be a hands-on father, to be involved with our child."

"Involved. Fine. I can do that."

She let her caressing hands fall to her sides with a tired

sigh. "Carson, you don't even like children." She got up and stood gazing down at him until he began to feel like a complete idiot, still kneeling there on the floor.

He rose, too, and reminded himself that he wasn't going to grab her, wasn't going to try to kiss some sense into her. "This is just not going the way I pictured it."

She took his hand. He tried to find some comfort from that, from the fact that she'd touched him, that she looked up at him with soft eyes and a gentle smile. "We don't have to rush into anything." She brought his fingers to her lips and she kissed the backs of his knuckles, one by one.

"Tessa." Her name came out rough with all the emotions he wasn't all that good at dealing with. "We can make it work. Give us a chance."

"I am, Carson." Her voice sounded a little rusty, too. "Definitely."

"I gave up a perfectly wonderful wife for you." Where had that come from? He had no clue.

But she didn't take it badly. On the contrary, she chuckled. "I think you gave up your wife so that you could be free to enjoy all the world has to offer you—including a whole bunch of gorgeous women, serially and probably in groups."

"Very funny." He scowled down at her. "And also wrong. I gave up my marriage for *you*. I just didn't realize it at the time. Everything was and is for you. I wanted to be ready when I finally found you."

"That was kind of twisted—but also just beautiful." She went on tiptoe, offering that mouth he somehow never got enough of kissing. He should have resisted. She'd really pissed him off.

But he couldn't. He lowered his head and kissed her, just a quick one, because he couldn't *not* kiss her. "Marry me," he commanded.

She rose up and kissed him again. Her breath smelled of berries and cinnamon. "I can't. Please try to understand."

He caught her shoulders, fingers digging in—until she winced and he loosened his grip. But he didn't let her go. "What do you need?"

"Need?"

"What do I have to do to get you to say yes?"

Her dark eyes searched his face. "Passion fades, Carson."

"Not mine for you."

"It's too early to know that."

"Not for me. What about for you?" He ran the back of his finger up the silky skin on the side of her neck. She shivered a little. He drank in that unwilling response. "Are you afraid you're going to get tired of me?"

Her gaze never wavered. "No. I'm not. You are…more than I ever bargained for. And in the best of all possible ways."

"Good answer. So then, if you trusted me, if you were sure you could count on me and that I would treat our baby right, *then* would you say yes?"

She didn't even have to think it over. "Yes. I would."

"All right, then. Prepare to learn to trust me."

"Only you could make that sound like a threat."

He caught a curl of her hair and wrapped it slowly around his finger. "I'm going to have to fly back to LA today."

Her eyes went stormy. "But you just got here. And weren't we just talking about working things out? How can we do that if you're in LA?"

"Come with me."

"No, Carson. Right now I need to be here. I can't just run away to your world. Not right now."

He pulled his finger free of that shining coil of coffee-colored hair. "I knew you would say that."

"They why ask?"

"Never hurts to try. I won't be gone long. I need to clear my calendar, take care of a few things that can't wait."

"How long is not long?"

"A couple of days, three at the most."

Tessa kissed him goodbye a few minutes later. It was a very long, deep kiss, and it took all the willpower she possessed not to let that one kiss melt into another.

And another after that.

Not to grab his hand and pull him to the bedroom and have her way with him. Preferably more than once.

But that didn't seem right, somehow. Why it didn't, she wasn't exactly sure. Maybe because he was leaving again so quickly. She could get whiplash; he was here and gone so fast.

Of course, she could have flown back with him. He'd asked her to come.

But that didn't seem right, either.

Nothing seemed right.

As she drove back to the boardinghouse, she kept remembering him dropping to his knees in front of her, replaying all the beautiful things he'd said to her. He'd melted her heart with his words—melted her heart and almost her panties.

But she needed to be careful. She lifted a hand from the steering wheel, pressed it to her flat belly and reminded herself that she had more than just her own heart to consider now. Beautiful words were one thing—and hadn't she heard them all before? Hadn't Miles sworn he would love her forever?

For some men, forever didn't last very long. Carson swore he wasn't like that—or at least not anymore, not when it came to her.

But he had been like that once, with Marianne, hadn't he? Yes, everybody made mistakes and what had happened with Marianne had been several years ago. Some relationships just didn't work out.

Still, she just needed to be careful and not allow Carson to do what he did so very well—sweep her right off her feet and into his waiting arms.

In her room at the boardinghouse, she dug into a couple of small projects she had in the works. When she checked her email, she found one from Jason Velasco. He asked how she was doing—and mentioned that "her" job was still available if by any chance she'd changed her mind. He wrote, *I still have that sketchbook of yours. Do you want it back? Excellent work, by the way.*

At first, she felt a little annoyed. Carson had probably put him up to it.

But then, really, so what if Carson had been behind Jason making contact again?

Tessa realized she could get to like Jason. And professionally, it never hurt to cultivate good contacts. She composed a friendly reply and sent it off before going downstairs.

At lunchtime, she helped out in the kitchen and then moved on to laundry duty. When she came back upstairs, her grandmother called her into the kitchen. Melba plied her with iced tea and lemon bars and asked how "things" were going with her and Carson. Tessa looked into her grandma's loving eyes and almost told her about the baby.

But she was only five weeks pregnant. Who could say what the future might bring? Telling her family about the baby could wait awhile.

"He had to return to LA for a few days."

"But he's coming back?"

"That is the plan, yes."

"Will he be staying here?"

"I don't know. I think he's keeping his suite at Maverick Manor, too."

"I hope he stays here. I like your young man. He's very charming and yet direct. And he's helpful, too. Pitches right in. And it's obvious he's in love with you."

"Oh, Grandma…"

"Not that his being in love with you surprises me. Any man with sense would fall in love with you."

She reached across the table and squeezed Melba's arm. "Love you."

"You be sure to tell him we miss him and he should stay here."

"Of course, I'll tell him you miss him. But as for staying here, I think I'll let him decide that for himself."

"Fine, then. Don't tell him. I'll do it myself."

As it turned out, Melba didn't have to tell him.

That night, he texted Tessa: Back with you Sunday. Staying at the boardinghouse. Because I miss you and I need to be close to you.

Can't wait, she texted back.

So you miss me, too. I knew you would.

My grandmother adores you. I have no idea why.

Give her my love.

Give it to her yourself when you get here on Sunday. How long are you staying?

If no disasters arise here, until the end of the month—or until you agree to come back to Malibu with me.

What to say to that? All possible answers seemed dangerous.

Before she could decide on a response, another text popped up from him.

What are you wearing?

She burst into a loud laugh lying there on her bed before texting back. I did not have sex with you this morning and I am not sexting with you tonight.

Come on, just a hint. I really liked those little satin panties with the peekaboo lace on the sides that you were wearing yesterday.

Perv. They're called boy shorts.

And I like them.

She giggled. And then, out of nowhere, her eyes misted over. She stared at his words on the screen, her throat clutching and her heart filled with longing.

Because she loved him. She really did. Even though it was way too soon, even though she feared it couldn't last and she had the baby to think of, too. The baby needed a mom who made good choices, a mom who didn't just rush into marriage because the father offered—well, okay. Carson had more than offered. He really did seem to want to marry her.

And, well, she wanted to marry him, too.

She loved him. And she desperately wanted everything to work out.

Which was why they needed to take it slow.

Tessa? Where'd you go?

I'm right here.

Everything okay?

I miss you, Carson. You've only been gone since this morning and I miss you so much.

Two more days. I'm there.

She whipped a tissue from the box on the nightstand, dabbed at her eyes and then texted, I'm glad. And I should go.

Wait.

The phone vibrated in her hand with his incoming call. She put it to her ear. "What?"

"I need to say good-night to the baby."

Her poor heart melted all over again. She swiped at her eyes some more. "She doesn't understand words yet."

"Put him on, anyway."

"Hold on a sec. You think it's a boy?"

He answered, "I do," in an intimate tone that set her nerves humming.

"Well, *I* think it's a girl."

He chuckled. "Just put him on."

"Fine. Here you go." She pressed her cell to her stomach and heard Carson say something, though she had no idea what. She put it back to her ear. "Done?"

"For now." His voice was rough and tender. "Good night, Tessa."

She disconnected the call before she could end up bawling on the phone to him, crying out her love, promising him anything he wanted, all of her, forever.

If only he would love her back and never leave her.

And never, ever break her heart.

Chapter Thirteen

Carson boarded the plane for Montana at eight Sunday morning. He picked up a Cadillac SUV in Kalispell and headed for Rust Creek Falls, stopping off at Maverick Manor on the way into town to drop off some things he didn't need right away. At a quarter of noon, he pulled into the boardinghouse parking lot. He grabbed his suitcase and briefcase and went in through the back door, which Melba left unlocked during daylight hours.

The back hall was empty, but he could hear voices from the dining room and knew that Claire and Melba would be in the kitchen preparing lunch, with maybe little Bekka there, too. And since it was Sunday, probably Levi as well. And Tessa would most likely be with them, pitching in. Rather than drag his stuff to the kitchen with him, he raced up the backstairs to leave it in his room.

Tessa's door opened as he strode along the upper hall. She emerged, in old jeans and a wrinkled Drive-By

Truckers T-shirt, her hair piled up in the usual messy knot at the top of her head.

She froze at the sight of him, those eyes that tipped up just right at the corners going wide with surprise. "Hey." Breathless. Eyes shining. The moment was unbelievably sweet.

"Hey." His suitcase and briefcase hit the floor with a matched pair of thuds.

She ran for him. He reached out and caught her as she jumped into his arms, wrapping herself around him the way she liked to do. He buried his face in the crook of her neck, sucked in the wonderful scent of her skin. She whispered, "I missed you."

And then she fisted a hand in his hair, pulled his face up to hers and kissed him.

At that moment, as her mouth crashed into his, he was absolutely certain she would say yes, and soon.

Three days later, he wasn't so sure. She kept saying she wasn't ready yet. She kept telling him she needed more time.

Lots more time.

He didn't have lots more time. And they needed to be together from now on, needed to learn *how* to be together, to build on the chemistry and commonality they already shared. A long-distance relationship wasn't going to cut it.

But he couldn't stay in Rust Creek Falls indefinitely. And she wouldn't come to LA with him. Not, she insisted, until she was sure they were going to be together "in a permanent way." He was all for permanent. And he told her so.

And then she would cycle right back around to how

he couldn't know that. Maybe it wouldn't work out. And where would they be then? Where would their baby be?

He reminded himself he still had time. Till the end of the month, before he had to be back in LA to get serious about the brandy liqueur product launch and handle preparations for the new club opening in San Diego. He told himself that no matter what happened, no matter how long she stalled him, he wasn't giving up. He'd find a way to make it work long-distance, if that was all she would give him. He would stick with her, prove himself true to her.

And somehow, they would end up together.

But he hated that bastard Miles, who had messed her over. That loser had made it way too hard for her to trust again. She doubted her own judgment, and she was scared to death to follow her heart. And that left both of them hanging.

Carson needed to break the damn stalemate they seemed to be caught in. Somehow, he needed to find new ways to convince her that he meant what he promised her: that forever could be theirs—hers, his and the baby's—if only she would reach out and claim it.

On Thursday, he went to the Manor to catch up on some business. While he was there, he called Ryan.

"Heard you were in town again." The lawyer sounded way too pleased with himself. "Can't stay away from a certain hot brunette, can you?"

Carson cut to the chase. "I'm in love with Tessa, and I want to marry her, but she won't say yes."

There was dead silence on the other end of the line. Then, finally, Ryan said, "Didn't I tell you this would happen? It's Rust Creek Falls—am I right? Maybe there's something in the water or—"

"Don't push it, Ryan."

"Aw, come on. Let me gloat at least a little."

"No way." Carson tapped the seal of the bottle that sat on the coffee table in front of him. "However, you do get a bottle of really good Scotch."

Ryan chuckled. "You brought me the Drake Imperial?" At Carson's grunt of affirmation, he crowed, "Now I know you're grateful."

"Yes, I am, as a matter of fact. And didn't you also predict that I would move to Rust Creek Falls?"

"Yes, I did."

"I would move here tomorrow if I could. But I can't."

"I'm speechless."

"You're never speechless. And I need your help again."

"Man, whatever you need, it's yours. I'll do what I can."

"Good. Say I had a reputation for not loving children…"

"Well, given that you've told me any number of times that you're never having children, I would probably have to say that your reputation is richly deserved."

"So, then, how do I change that?"

"You're saying Tessa wants children?"

Carson debated his options: tell Ryan the whole story—or not? He decided to hold back. As of now, the baby was nobody's business but Tessa's and his. "Yeah, Tessa wants children—or at least, she doesn't want to marry a man who doesn't want children."

Ryan made a low, thoughtful sound. "Just so we're clear, you *have* changed your mind about kids, then? You really are willing to be a dad one of these days?"

"That's right, I am." *And a lot sooner than you might think.*

"Love." Ryan's tone was downright reverent. "It's amazing."

"When you're through being awestruck, I'm open to ideas."

"Right. Well, I do have suggestions. Two of them. Number one, buy a place here in Rust Creek Falls. Promise Tessa you'll come here as often as possible, at least a few times a year—and mean it. That should help to reassure her she won't be leaving behind the town she loves."

"That's good. I like it."

"I'll text you the number of a good local Realtor."

"Terrific. But what about how to convince Tessa that I do want children?"

"Well, I think you have to spend some time with children as a way to help you prove to yourself and to her that you really do enjoy them."

Enjoy children. That was asking a lot. He did want the baby, but as for kids in general, well, he mostly wanted nothing to do with them until they were old enough to hold a job and appreciate a good cigar.

He asked, "How exactly am I going to spend a lot of time with kids?"

"Easy. Rust Creek Falls is crawling with babies right now. You know about Jamie Stockton?"

"Who?"

"Jamie Stockton. Recently, his wife gave birth to triplets. She didn't make it."

"You mean his wife died having those babies?"

"Soon after. There were complications, and she didn't pull through."

Carson felt vaguely sick. What if that happened to Tessa?

But it wouldn't. *No freaking way.* He wouldn't allow it.

Ryan asked gingerly, "Carson, you okay?"

"I'm fine, I... My God, the poor guy."

"Yeah. Very tough. And Jamie's a rancher. The man's

not only lost his wife—he's on his own running his ranch with three babies to take care of. With all the babies born lately, Country Kids day care is full."

"But isn't Walker Jones opening a Just Us Kids center here any day now?"

"Just Us Kids opened last Monday. But there's another problem. The cost of professional day care for three infants is through the roof. So several women in town have established a baby chain for the triplets."

"A baby what?"

"Chain. People volunteer to give a hand with the little ones so that Jamie can put in a full day's work on the ranch."

"Wait. Hold on. Are you suggesting I should babysit *triplets*?"

"Carson, you have to start somewhere. Might as well jump right in. Let me call Fallon O'Reilly. From what I've heard, she's the one running the baby chain."

After he hung up with Ryan, Carson called the Realtor his friend had recommended. He told her what he was looking for, and she promised to show him some houses the following afternoon.

The next morning, when Carson should have been at the Manor dealing with any number of minor business emergencies that kept cropping up in his absence from Drake headquarters, Carson drove out to Jamie Stockton's ranch instead.

A pretty redhead answered the door. "Carson, right? Ryan said you'd be coming. I'm Fallon O'Reilly, a friend of the Stockton family. I'm pretty much in charge of the baby chain." She held out her hand. Carson took it and gave it a shake. "Come on in."

He stepped over the threshold and followed her down a hallway.

She chattered back at him as she went. "Jamie's out mending fence. But he said to tell you thank you."

"Happy to help." He tried to sound confident. But a baby was crying at the end of the hall. He longed to spin on his heel, race back out the front door and burn rubber getting out of there.

Three hours later, he'd not only changed two loaded diapers; he'd rocked all three blue-eyed Stockton babies, whose names were Jared, Henry and Kate. One by one, they wailed when he held them, their little faces going beet red, tiny noses and rosebud mouths twisting, miniature fists flailing. Even worse, when the one he held started crying, one or both of the other two would get going, as well. Poor Fallon would have to settle them all down.

At least the redhead had sense enough not to leave him alone with the children during the ordeal. She told him not to take all the howling personally. "They'll get used to you. You'll see."

The first couple of hours crawled by. All he wanted was out of there. But at the end, Fallon made him hold the smallest baby, Kate, again. He fed Kate a bottle. She started out bawling, same as before. He rocked her gently and kept his body loose, his face calm. Eventually she seemed to settle a little. Finally, with a heavy sigh, she latched on to the nipple, shut her eyes and got to work on that bottle. He wouldn't go so far as to call her happy to have him holding her, but at least she seemed willing to relax and let it happen.

Carson felt pretty damn good by then. Who said he didn't like babies? He did, damn it. He liked babies—and they could learn to like him.

He could do this. *Piece of cake.*

Before he left, Fallon put him on the schedule. He had nine to noon, Tuesday and Thursday, for the next two weeks. Fallon said that most of the time, he would have another babysitter to help him. With three babies to look after, it worked best to have two sets of ready hands. There would definitely be another sitter working with him next time, on Tuesday. After that, well, they would see.

Carson returned to the Manor for an online meeting and to make a few calls. He ordered a sandwich from room service and ended up working until about two.

When he got back to the boardinghouse, Melba met him in thc hallway. "I thought I heard you come in. Claire's baking cookies."

"Chocolate chip?" he asked with enthusiasm, though he already knew. The mouthwatering smells of warm sugar, vanilla and melted chocolate had greeted him when he walked in the back door.

"Come with me." Tessa's grandmother led him to the kitchen, where Claire was just taking another batch from the oven.

Melba put three cookies on a plate and filled a glass with milk for him. "There you go." She patted his back and took the seat next to him.

He bit into a warm cookie. "These are perfect, Claire."

Tessa's sister sent him a smile from her spot at the stove just as Tessa herself appeared in the open doorway. She looked amazing, as always, in shorts and a Save the Whales T-shirt, her hair loose on her shoulders, all wild and curly, her unforgettable face scrubbed clean of makeup.

There was that moment again. Their eyes met and—bam. He'd never met a woman like her. She did something to him, rearranged every molecule in his body with nothing more than a look.

They were going to make it. They would be a family. It was all going to work out.

He wouldn't have it any other way.

She grabbed a plate and chose two cookies for herself, then dropped into the seat next to him. A little groan escaped her as she took that first bite. He did love a woman who ate like she meant it. "Best ever, Claire," she said, then slid him a glance. "How's everything over at Maverick Manor?"

"Fine. I took a long meeting with a group of distributors, made some calls, handled email."

"Sounds productive."

He laid it on her. "And before that I spent three hours at Jamie Stockton's ranch helping Fallon O'Reilly look after Jamie's triplets."

Slowly, Tessa set down the remains of her cookie. Claire and Melba shared a look, and Melba patted him fondly on the back again. Oh, he was getting in good with Melba. And that pleased him no end.

A man needed to get in good with his future wife's grandmother.

Tessa finally forced a laugh. "You're not serious."

"Oh, but I am." He ate another delicious bite of warm cookie. "It was touch and go at first. But I'm getting the hang of it. I joined the baby chain for Tuesday and Thursday morning next week and the week after that."

"Baby chain. By that you mean you're babysitting Jamie Stockton's triplets?" Her tone, hitting midway between stunned and disbelieving, was not especially flattering.

"Yes, I am." He reached for his last cookie.

Tessa stood up and offered her hand. "Come with me."

"As though I could ever refuse you anything." He turned to the others. "Melba, Claire. Thanks for the cookies." The women gave him nods and smiles as he rose and followed Tessa out.

At the base of the back stairs, she turned to him. "What are you up to?" The words made demands, but her tone was sweet. Tender. Maybe even pleased.

He swallowed the last bite of his cookie and brushed the crumbs from his hands. Then he touched her. Because he wanted to. Because she always felt so right. Because he couldn't imagine the rest of his life without her in it. He traced his finger down her soft cheek, guided a wild curl away from her eye. "Finding out if maybe I could like babies."

"And?"

He bent close and brushed a kiss across her lips. "I'm thinking it's doable."

"Carson..." She said it on a cookie-scented sigh, those dark eyes shining up at him.

"I have an idea. I'm thinking we could do it together, take care of Jamie Stockton's triplets. I'll call Fallon and tell her I have another victim—I mean, babysitter."

She smiled at his silly joke, but then she caught her lower lip between her teeth and worried it a little. "Babies always cry when I hold them."

"I understand. Believe me. They do the same with me. Today was two and a half hours of nonstop wailing. I couldn't wait for it to be over. But I stuck with it. And then near the end, the baby girl, Kate, gave in and let me hold her. I fed her a bottle. I have to say, once you get a fresh diaper on them and they finally stop yowling, they're kind of cute."

She gazed up at him so steadily. "Tuesday and Thursday, you said?"

He nodded. "Nine to noon."

"Well, all right. You call Fallon. Tell her I'll be coming with you to help out."

"Excellent. And about this afternoon. You free?"

She went on tiptoe and kissed him. "I am."

"Good. I've got three houses to look at and I want you to come see them with me."

"Houses? Why?"

"Don't ask so many questions. Just be patient. Everything will become crystal clear in the end."

It was after five when they finished touring the last house. A two-story tan clapboard with black shutters, the place was a fixer-upper on five acres just a mile southwest of town, not far from the Crawford ranch, the Shooting Star.

The Realtor shook their hands and said she would call Carson in the morning to talk about the properties they'd seen and to offer a few more houses he might want to look at. He and Tessa stood on the front step and watched her get in her car and drive away.

"Sit with me." He pulled Tessa down beside him on the top step. "So, what do you think?"

"I think you haven't explained to me what is going on."

He entwined his fingers with hers. "I can't move here year-round."

"I know."

"However, I'm actually to the point where I would do it, for you—and also because I somehow feel more at home here than I ever have anywhere else."

She squeezed his fingers. "You feel at home here? Really?"

He met her eyes and never wanted to look away.

"Maybe it's Claire's cooking. Or the way your grandmother treats me like one of the family."

"She's a card-carrying member of the Carson Drake fan club, and that is no lie."

He teased, "You don't have to sound so perplexed about it."

"I'm not. We all know your charms are legendary."

"You noticed. Excellent. Now, where was I? Oh, yeah. I would move here, but I can't run my businesses effectively unless I'm in LA most of the year."

"You really..." Her soft voice broke and the words got lost. But she found them again. "You really mean that? You would do that? Move to Rust Creek Falls?"

"I would if I could, for you. For the baby."

She leaned her head on his shoulder. "It's so crazy. I think I believe you."

He switched hands, taking hers with his right hand, wrapping his left arm around her shoulders. "Maybe someday, when our son is all grown up and ready to take over the Drake companies—"

"Carson," she chided. But he heard the smile in her voice. "She's not even born yet."

"You're right. And I don't want to make his choices for him, anyway. But right now, what I *can* do is buy a house here. I figure I can get away a few times a year, stay a few weeks each visit." She didn't reply, but she did hold his hand a little tighter. He said, "I want you to help me choose the house."

She tipped her head back. Her eyes were stormy, full of longing. And doubt. "I need more time, Carson. Please try to understand. You're being so completely wonderful. I *want* to go for it, marry you, move to LA and be with you. But then I start thinking that I've only known you for a matter of weeks. Yes, we made a baby. And, yes, we need to deal with that. But I don't want to rush into anything. It's too soon. And I refuse to make the same big mistakes all over again."

Don't compare me to that douche bag. Somehow he managed not to say that. He kept his breathing even, held the angry words inside. Instead, he asked her gently, "Did I say the M word just then?"

"No, but—"

"Did I ask you again to move to LA with me?"

"No, you didn't."

"All I said is I'm buying a house here, and it's important to me that you like the house I choose."

Another silence from her. But at least she didn't let go of his hand. Finally, she offered, "Well, if you want my opinion…"

"Please."

"Something on Falls Mountain, maybe? With lots of windows and great views."

He thought of Collin and Willa Traub's house, tucked among the big trees, with the world spread out below them. "I like that idea, though it could be hard to get to in the winter."

"Collin and Willa seem to manage. And as you said, you'll only be here a few times a year. You could easily skip our Montana winters. They can be pretty rough."

He tried not to be annoyed that she assumed he couldn't take the winters, that she spoke so easily of him in the singular, without her. Instead, he drew satisfaction from the knowledge that they'd both been thinking of the Traubs and their gorgeous rustic house. "I have a feeling Christmas in Montana is something I won't want to miss. Christmas on Falls Mountain. I like it. I want that."

She chuckled then. The sound wrapped around his heart. "Well then, you'd better get that Realtor on it—don't you think?"

The next morning, Saturday, when the Realtor called, he told her he wanted property on Falls Mountain. She said she'd check around a little and call him back in an hour.

Fifty minutes later, she called again. "I have one house available. It's just a cabin, really. Six hundred square feet. On the northwest slope."

"Too small."

"Yes. You'd be buying it for the land, and then you would have to build."

"I'd like to see it—and now you've got me wondering. How about any other nice pieces of property on the mountain? Just the land, I mean. I could build my own place. Anything available?"

"You've read my mind, Carson. I have two parcels you can look at. One is halfway up, not far from the falls. The other's nearer the summit."

He told her he wanted to see all three—the cabin and the two parcels. She said she could show them to him that day, and he agreed to meet her at the cabin at one o'clock.

When he hung up, he tapped on Tessa's door. A moment later, it swung open. She had a pencil stuck behind her ear and a curl falling over her eye. She blew the curl aside.

He resisted the need to get his hands on her. Bracing an arm on the door frame, he asked, "Working?"

"Catching up on a few things, yeah."

"How about a ride up Falls Mountain?"

Her slow smile lit a fire down in the core of him.

"The Realtor found some possibilities?" At his nod, she asked, "When?"

"We should leave in the next twenty minutes or so."

"I'm in."

He couldn't bear not touching her, after all. So he reached out and guided that misbehaving curl away from her eye and behind the ear without the pencil in it. Her skin was cool satin. "Can you swim at the falls?"

"Yes, though it's really cold. There's a pool at the base."

"Do I need a suit?" Skinny-dipping held definite appeal.

"Sorry, but yeah. On a pretty Saturday in July, the odds are high we won't be alone."

"Board shorts, it is. And let's take a picnic. After we're done seeing properties, we can visit the falls. Swim. Have some lunch."

"Twenty minutes. I'll meet you in the kitchen, and I'll have our lunch ready." Before he could steal a kiss, she shut the door on him.

They saw the cabin property first. It was deep in the woods, on the north side of the mountain where the sunlight was sparse, with no views to speak of.

Tessa shook her head. "This isn't the one."

He agreed with her.

Next they drove to the land near the summit.

"This is more like it," he said as they stood on a point overlooking the rolling valley below. He would build the house back toward the hillside, with lots of wide windows facing the view, and he'd get with Collin, make a plan to pave the road that turned to dirt on the second half of the ride up here.

Because he *would* be coming to Rust Creek Falls every

Christmas. And Tessa and their baby would be coming with him.

Tessa said, “I’m guessing this is it.” She gave him a look—full of excitement and pleasure.

It took all the will he had not to drop to his knees in the dirt right then and there, in front of God and the Realtor and all those tall trees, not to beg her all over again to wear his ring. Somehow he kept hold of himself.

They got in the vehicles and drove down to the land near the falls. It was a nice piece of property, but it didn’t compare with the one higher up.

He told the Realtor that he would meet her Sunday afternoon at her office to make an offer on the property near the summit. She said she would call the owner’s Realtor and let him know the offer was on the way. Then, with a last wave, she got in her mini-SUV and headed down the mountain.

It wasn’t far to the falls. They found a parking spot by the road and took a little trail that wound among the bracken toward the roar of the falling water.

In no time, the trail opened up to a flat section of bank and the falls high above. It was a gorgeous sight, the wall of water spinning and foaming as it fell, droplets gleaming like diamonds in the shafts of sunlight that found their way through the trees as the water tumbled into the pool below.

Best of all, they were alone. No one else had decided to visit the falls that afternoon—at least not so far.

He spread a blanket on the bank, and she set down the picnic basket and their towels. They stripped off boots and socks, jeans and shirts. He got down to board shorts. And just the sight of her standing there in a red-and-white polka-dot bikini reminded him forcefully of how much he wanted her.

"Last one in's a city girl!" he taunted and ran for the pool.

"Cheater!" she shouted and took off after him.

He got there first and ran right in, with her close on his heels.

"It's freezing!" He dunked himself, fast, just to get it over with.

"Told you so." She laughed and started splashing him.

"Now you're going to get it." He jumped on her and dunked her. She shot out of the water a moment later, droplets flying every which way as she shook her head from side to side.

"You drive me crazy." He grabbed for her, needing to pull her close and steal a long, hot kiss in the icy, churning water.

But she shoved him away with a teasing laugh and swam for the falls. He chased after her. She swam fast, vanishing under the falling water, with him close on her heels.

It was eerie and gorgeous behind the falls, the echo of the tumbling water a constant, slightly muted roar, rough gray rock rising up around them on three sides. She swam to the curve of the cliff face and held out a hand for him.

He took it. She pulled him toward her.

As soon as he found his balance on the rock, he reeled her in. Laughing, she let him hold her.

He kissed her then, finally. Her lips were cold, her body covered in chill bumps.

"I could kiss you forever," he said, when they finally came up for air. "Tessa. I love you." *There.* He had said it outright. The world seemed to stop on its axis as they stared at each other. "I swear to you. You're the only woman for me."

She gazed up at him, her lips slightly parted. And then she whispered so sweetly, "And I love you."

It was a great moment. He wanted to wrap it in tissue paper, tie it with a satin bow, save it in his heart and soul for all time. *Marry me*, he almost demanded.

But she must have known what he would say, must have seen it in his eyes. She touched her cold fingers to his mouth. "Don't..."

And he let her stop him. He pressed his lips together over the words, held back the demands that tried to push from his throat. He knew in his head that it hadn't been all that long since the Memorial Day Baby Bonanza Parade, when he first caught sight of her in that silly stork costume and knew he had to meet her. A matter of weeks, that was all. A month and a half.

But he also knew what he wanted. And she'd just said she loved him. They needed to get started on their life together. It hurt him, killed him a little, every time she told him no.

"Carson," she coaxed, her voice warm and tender, though the icy water pebbled her skin and she shivered in his hold. She curled her cold little hand around the nape of his neck and pulled him down for another kiss. "I love you," she whispered.

He drank those words from her parted lips, wrapping her tighter, kissing her endlessly.

Finally, she pulled away and admitted, "My teeth are chattering. Let's go back to the blanket and dry off before I freeze to death."

Reluctantly, he released her and followed her back through the veil of tumbling water. They swam to the bank, climbed out and ran for the blanket. She was still shivering, so he pulled her between his legs, grabbed her towel and rubbed her hair and then her shoulders.

He couldn't resist kissing her. Something about her just drove him wild. He pressed his lips to her still-wet hair, licked the water off her cold cheek, kissed his way downward to the crook of her neck, where he nipped her with his teeth.

She laughed, twisting in his hold to face him as she teasingly batted him away. "Stop that. Don't you—" She stiffened in his arms, her eyes locked on something over his left shoulder.

He searched her suddenly pale face. "What?"

"Look." She said it way too softly, staring wide-eyed at whatever it was behind him.

Stark alarm hollowing his gut, he turned his head and looked.

Slowly, crouching low, a full-grown mountain lion emerged from the rim of trees that surrounded the pool. Its black eyes pinned them. The laid-back ears and long, twitching tail said it all. The cat had identified them as prey.

For Carson, time stalled.

The roar of the falls receded beneath the roaring of his own blood in his ears. His heart pounded hard and deep, every nerve rising to high alert, each muscle drawing tight.

He knew total fear. It was invigorating. Everything came crystal clear.

An image of his late father flashed in his head. Beyond how to use a rifle and track big game, Declan Drake had taught Carson the habits of all the larger predators.

As a rule, mountain lions were solitary creatures, shy of man. But if they got really hungry or were ill or injured, all bets were off.

This cat had blood on its flank. It had been wounded

and now all its instincts pushed it to retaliate, to attack. Somehow, Carson was going to have to take it down.

"Go," he said softly to the woman in his arms. Keeping his eyes locked on the lion, he took her shoulders and pushed her up and away. "Don't run. They try to latch on at the back of your neck, so turn and face him. Back away slowly."

He felt her leave him, felt the lack of her as she scrambled up and stumbled back. *Good girl.*

In slow motion, or so it seemed to him, while still on the ground, he turned his body so he fully faced the threat. His mind went blank as adrenaline spurted, and his body reacted automatically, even with his brain on hold. When the world came clear again, he was standing fully upright.

The cat kept coming in absolute silence, moving faster now.

Carson planted his feet wide and spread his arms, trying to look larger, more threatening, trying to change the cat's mind about defining him as prey. He let out a deep, loud bellow of rage for good measure.

Didn't work. The cat never hesitated. It came on faster still.

Carson bellowed again and braced for the fight.

With a feral cry, the lion pounced. Powerful rear legs launching, deadly claws reaching out, it flew straight at him.

Carson punched his right arm forward, ready for the catch.

Chapter Fourteen

Tessa swallowed a scream as the big cat pounced.

She needed a weapon. She needed to help. Sheer terror coursed through her, every nerve on red alert. Instinct ordered her to flee. But her heart was having none of that.

A weapon, damn it! She glanced around frantically.

A big rock, maybe. She didn't see one. *And where is a nice, sturdy stick when you need it?*

Close to hand, she had only a pile of their clothing. She could throw a shoe at the animal, but that wouldn't do much. There was the picnic basket…

Okay, then. She dipped to her knees and scooped it up by the handle.

When she looked again at Carson and the cat, she couldn't believe her eyes. He had the animal by the throat—his long, powerful right arm outstretched. The cat danced on its hind legs, lurching as it struggled. It had its paws wrapped around his arm, sharp claws digging in.

Carson was strangling it. And there was blood. *Carson's blood.* Flowing down his arm, the side of his neck, his shoulder…

"Tessa, get out of here!" he shouted at her.

Her mind went dead blank. What was the matter with her? She needed to stay focused.

And, no, she was not leaving. Forget about that. And the basket? What good was the basket? If she beat the cat with it, maybe. But the goal was to help Carson. She mustn't do anything that would dislodge the stranglehold he had on the animal. Clubbing the cat might jar Carson's grip.

And then she remembered the cheese and salami she'd brought for their lunch. And the knife to cut them with. It wasn't much. But if she could get in close, maybe…

The cat made weird growling, shrieking sounds, gurgling as it struggled. Carson held on. But for how long?

She upended the basket. Cheese and salami, baggies full of summer fruit, and rolls of crackers fell out—and there! *The knife!*

She pounced on it, grabbed it and moved in on the man and the cat.

"No!" Carson shouted. "Tessa, get away! Don't!"

She ignored him, sidling closer, thinking that she had to do something. She raised the knife high.

And in the split second before she brought the knife down, a loud crack sounded.

The cat made the strangest sighing noise—and went limp in Carson's grip.

Tessa let her hand fall. The knife tumbled, forgotten, to the ground. Carson stood so very still, his grip remaining firm around the throat of the cat. Slowly, he lowered the animal to the dirt and gently laid it down.

She ran to him, dropping to a crouch at his side. “Carson…”

“I’m okay.”

But he didn’t look okay. There was way too much blood. More than one of the gouges on his arm would need stitches.

They both heard the footsteps at the same time and looked up from the still body of the cat to the rim of tall trees. Collin Traub, Nate Crawford, Sheriff Gage Christensen and three other local men emerged into the sunlight. Each carried a rifle.

“Damn good shooting,” Carson said in a flat voice.

Sheriff Christensen patted one of the other men on the shoulder. “Tim here’s the best there is.” He turned his gaze to the cat. “It attacked old Mrs. Calloway’s dog up on Eagle Ridge. She shot it. We’ve been tracking the poor thing to finish it.”

Tessa didn’t care about any of that. Not right now. “Help me get Carson in the SUV and down to the clinic. He needs a doctor *now*.”

Carson walked to the SUV on his own steam. Tessa sent a little prayer of thanks to God that it wasn’t that far. Collin offered to drive. It was a steep road with lots of switchbacks, a road that Collin knew well.

Tessa surrendered the wheel and sat in back with Carson, who had her T-shirt and his wrapped around the worst of his injuries. The adrenaline rush was wearing off by then. He was starting to feel the pain, lines etching in his forehead, a rim of white around his beautiful mouth.

He leaned his head on her shoulder. She eased an arm around him and willed Collin to drive faster.

At the clinic, Emmet went right to work. There were shots to numb the pain, a thorough cleaning of each wound—and a lot of stitching. Carson was up-to-date on his tetanus shots. Though the cat had shown no signs of being rabid, Emmet followed protocol and gave Carson the first in a series of rabies shots and also a shot of rabies immune globulin.

Tessa stood by Carson's side, holding his left hand—that arm was uninjured—as he endured Emmet's care. Carson seemed pretty stoic about it, though she didn't see how he could stay so calm. With every prick of the needle, every swipe of sterilized gauze as Emmet cleaned him up, every last stitch as Emmet sewed the wounds shut, Tessa had to keep an iron grip on herself or she would have screamed terrible things at poor Emmet, would have demanded he go easier, be gentler, even though her own eyes told her he was careful, skilled and kind.

She just couldn't bear it, seeing Carson hurt. She tried to take comfort from the fact that he didn't need to be airlifted to the hospital in Kalispell, that he was conscious through all of it and he didn't even require a transfusion. He had saved them, plain and simple, and he was going to be all right. All that was good, she reminded herself. Much better than it might have been.

Carson would have scars from this. Emmet teased that scars were sexy. Carson actually chuckled at that and shook his head.

The best part was that she got to take him home to the boardinghouse as soon as Emmet was through stitching him up.

As they were leaving, Emmet thanked her for the ads she'd placed back in June. More medical help was on the way. And Rust Creek Falls needed it. In the past week, there had been a sudden spike in pediatric illnesses. With all the new babies in town, the clinic was really having trouble providing needed services.

Tessa gave Emmet a quick hug and whispered, "Thank *you*, for taking such good care of Carson."

Someone must have called her grandmother because Melba and Gene were waiting in the boardinghouse parking lot when they drove in. Melba hustled them inside and said she had a bed ready in a downstairs room if Carson couldn't manage the stairs.

He put his good arm around her. "It's okay, Melba, really. I can make it up to my room."

Her grandmother stared up at him with tears in her eyes. "It was such a brave thing you did."

He glanced at Tessa. She felt that quick look as a physical caress. "In a situation like that, a man just does what he has to do."

Melba said, "I praise the Lord you're going to be okay."

He kissed her on the forehead. "I am fine—I promise."

"No, you're not," she argued tartly. "But you will be. And that's what matters."

"Come on, son," said Old Gene. "Let's get you upstairs."

In his room, Melba fussed over him terribly. Tessa shooed her grandmother and grandfather out to the hallway and helped him into a pair of sweats and a clean T-shirt.

When Melba bustled back in, Tessa ducked into her own room to get out of her still-damp bikini and into dry clothes.

When she went back to the room next door, Melba was getting him comfortable, arranging his pillows just so. He admitted that, yes, he was hungry, so Claire brought up lunch for him and served him right there in bed. Levi brought Bekka in, to see for herself that "Car-Car," as Bekka called him, was going to be all right.

Finally, almost an hour after they pulled into the parking lot, Tessa's family left them alone.

Carson patted the bed on his good side. Tessa couldn't get there fast enough. She crawled in beside him and cuddled close, pressing a kiss to the side of his throat that didn't have a bandage on it.

"I love you," she whispered in his ear. She had a whole bunch more to say—so much. Everything that mattered.

But he only gathered her closer, pressed his lips to her hair and let out a slow sigh.

When she tipped her head back to look at him, his eyes were shut. She watched as his breathing evened out and he slept.

Tessa drifted off, too.

When she woke a couple of hours later, he was lying on his good side, watching her.

She hid a yawn. "Do you need one of those pain pills Emmet gave you?"

He shook his head. "I was just trying to figure a few things out, trying to work out how to tell you…"

"What?"

"First, what you did was dangerous, stepping in with that knife when I told you to get away."

She almost laughed but somehow held it in. "Are you going to lecture me for not running off and leaving you there?"

"Yeah." His voice was rough with emotion. "You could have been hurt, and you put yourself in danger. And I can't stand to think that maybe—"

"So don't think it. And spare us both the lecture. It's not going to do any good. You needed help, and I was bound to give it. That's what people do when there's trouble—especially when there's trouble for someone they love."

"If something had happened to you—"

She stopped him with a kiss. "It didn't. Let it go."

A little grunt of pain escaped him as he shifted. "I did have it handled."

"I saw that. But it was taking too long, and you were hurt. And I just…needed to speed things up."

"With your trusty cheese knife."

They stared at each other. And then they both started laughing. It felt so good, to lie there with him, sharing silly and slightly hysterical laughter, safe and cozy together in her grandmother's house.

Finally, he said, "I'm definitely going to need an extra arm to take care of Jamie Stockton's triplets on Tuesday."

"Use mine."

Dark eyes gleamed. "I was hoping you'd say that. Thank you. I will. Here's a question for you. How am I going to bear it in a couple of weeks when I have to leave you?"

She gazed at him steadily, sure in her heart, in every part of herself, at last. "You're not."

He reached out with his bad arm, wincing as he moved it. And he traced her eyebrows, one and then the other, his touch featherlight. "How so?"

She put it right out there. "Because you're going to take me with you."

His eyes widened, warmed, even misted over a little. "Damn. Do you really mean that?"

With a laugh of pure joy, she slid back off the bed.

"Hey!" He tried to reach for her, but his injuries slowed him down a bit. "Get back up here." She shook her head as she went over the edge to the floor. "Tessa, what are you doing?"

She came up on her knees and stretched out her hand

to him. He took it with his right hand, grunting in pain as he moved his bad arm. "Oops. Sorry." She tried to let go.

But he held on. "Too late. I've got you now. What's going on?"

And she did it. She said it. It was all so very simple. "Carson, I love you. I want to spend my life with you. I want to be there, if you're ever in danger, if you're ever alone and need someone to lean on. I've been so worried that I couldn't count on you. But now I see that I couldn't bear it if you needed me and I wasn't there for *you* to count on. I have to be there for you, Carson. I need to be at your side. I just...well, I guess there's something about a life-and-death situation that brings everything so very clear."

He stared at her intently, as though he would never look away. "I noticed that, yes."

"I'm not afraid anymore, Carson. You're nothing like any man I've ever known before. What happened in the past, the bad choices and stupid mistakes that I made—I own them. I learned from them. I'm ready to move on. Ready for *you*, Carson. Because with you, it's so different. With you, it's so good. I love you and I trust you and I want to be with you. I want to marry you and move to California with you. I want to build a house with you up on Falls Mountain where we can come when we want to get away. I want you with me when our baby is born. I want us to raise her together. I want us, you and me, to be together in the deepest way, as husband and wife. I want it all with you, Carson. Please make me the happiest woman in the world. Please say that you'll marry me and be my husband for all of our lives."

"Yes." His voice rumbled up, thick with love and hope and longing. "Dear God, how I love you." He tugged on her hand. "Damn it, Tessa. Why are you on the floor?"

"I'm on my knees. You know, like people do when they propose?"

"Get up here."

She didn't have to be told twice. She surged up.

And then he said, "Wait." She just stood there by the bed, feeling slightly bewildered. "The bureau. Top left-hand drawer. Front right corner." She blinked at him, confused.

He chuckled. "Go. Open the drawer. Look."

So she went over there, opened the drawer, pushed his T-shirts aside and found the red leather ring box trimmed in gold. "Oh, Carson..."

"Your grandmother told me your size." His voice was as ragged and rough as her own. "I hope it's okay."

She flipped the top back, saw the giant diamond and the matching platinum band. "Oh, Carson, it's beautiful."

"You're sure? Because if you want, we can—"

"It's perfect." She took out the engagement ring and put the box with the wedding band still in it back in the drawer. Then she gave the diamond to him and held down her hand. He slipped it on her finger. It glittered so brightly. Tears filled her eyes. "Just exactly right."

"Come here," he commanded.

She didn't have to be told twice. She joined him on the bed, and he pulled her into the shelter of his good arm.

When his lips met hers, it was a promise. *Their* promise. For now and forever.

For the rest of their lives.

Epilogue

They were married two weeks later, out in the national forest, in a high meadow with the Rocky Mountains all around them.

Tessa wore a strapless white dress with a poufy white skirt and a vivid red satin sash. Her bouquet was all roses—red, white and blue. She wanted a patriotic wedding and she got one. In honor of Memorial Day, the day that they met.

After the ceremony, they went down into town for a red, white and blue reception in Rust Creek Falls Park. There was barbecue and wedding punch. The guests took turns guarding the punch bowl to keep Homer Gilmore from getting up to his old tricks.

Homer did put in an appearance to wish the bride and groom a lifetime of happiness—and to offer Carson one more chance at the magic moonshine. Carson thanked him for the good wishes, told him again that the deal was off and warned him to stay away from the punch bowl.

The cake was five layers, decked out in Old Glory colors, flags flying over the bride-and-groom topper. And after dark, as Tessa and Carson danced beneath the moon, Melba, Gene, Tessa's mom and dad and her two sisters passed out wedding sparklers. Willa Traub, Callie Crawford, Kristen and Ryan Roarke and several other friends hurried to get them all lit. Tessa whirled in her new husband's arms as the sparklers flashed and glittered all around them, bright and golden, lighting up the night.

Ten months after their wedding, on Memorial Day, Tessa woke in their new vacation house on Falls Mountain to the sound of a baby crying. Another cry joined the first.

The twins, Declan and Charlotte, were awake.

Tessa cuddled closer to Carson, wrapping her leg across his lean waist, pressing her lips to the hard curve of his shoulder.

He kissed the top of her head and grumbled, "I know. It's my turn." He sat up and swung his legs off the far side of the bed.

She stretched and yawned. "I'll get the coffee going for you."

Not much later, he brought the babies into the great room. Tessa sat in the big rocker, and he helped her get settled to nurse them in tandem.

It was a challenge, taking care of twins. But Tessa had found she loved every minute of being Charlotte and Declan's mom. As it turned out, once she put her mind and heart into it, she wasn't such a disaster with babies, after all.

And about that job with IMI? She'd changed her mind and taken it. A month after the wedding, she'd gone to work for Jason Velasco. IMI was a progressive company.

They gave her a flexible schedule with a lot of time working from home. Plus, she'd chosen an excellent, loving nanny, so the babies were happy when she and Carson had to work. True, pumping milk for twins at her desk was getting old fast. But so far, she was managing.

Charlotte finished breakfast first. Carson took her off to change her diaper. Once Declan was done, Tessa changed him, too, and then carried him back to the great room. She laid him down beside his sister on the play mat in front of the big window that looked out over the Rust Creek Valley, green and glorious far below in the light of the rising sun. She set the mobiles spinning, and the babies seemed happy enough for that moment to lie there and watch them.

Carson held down a hand to her. She took it, and he pulled her up into his waiting arms. He kissed her long and slow. "It's our anniversary, remember?"

"How could I ever forget?"

"A year to the day since I first saw you at the Memorial Day Baby Bonanza Parade."

"With my dorky yellow beak and my big orange feet."

He laughed, and then he kissed her again. When he lifted his head, he tipped her chin up with a finger. "You changed my life. I thought I was doing just fine before you came along. I thought I was happy. I didn't know what happiness was."

"I love you." Her voice was husky with emotion. "Always." She rested her hand on his right arm, traced the ridges of scar tissue under her fingers, loving the feel of them. They were a keepsake, a reminder of all they had together, of all they held precious. Of what they could have lost. "So?" she asked. "Breakfast?"

He nodded. "And then we'll take the twins down into town for the parade."

"And to the barbecue in the park after that."

"And then to the boardinghouse to say hi to Great-Grandma Melba."

She beamed up at him. "It's going to be a beautiful day."

* * * * *

ONE
Summer
AT THE ISLAND

ONE
Summer
AT THE CASTLE
MATHER
JORDAN
BENNETT

2 free books!
ONE
Summer
AT THE LAKE

ONE
Summer
AT THE VILLA

ONE
Summer
AT THE RANCH

ONE
Summer
AT THE BEACH